Quantum Time

Book Three in the Quantum Series

By Douglas Phillips

Jim —

Hope you like this one.
It's "kind of "out there"
for the science, but
it's 100% Daniel this time.

Love,

Doug

For my dear friend Phil.

This is the story you were waiting to read.

Table of Contents

1 Traveler

A yell shattered the quiet lobby. Almost a scream, though when men scream it comes out kind of wonky.

Sergeant Jamie Copley glanced up from her work, scowling. The double-pane door at the police station's entrance was slightly ajar, allowing the heat and humidity of central Florida to seep in, along with whatever commotion was going on in the parking lot.

Another scream, almost animal-like.

"Not again," she griped. The station had been calm for a Tuesday morning, and Jamie liked it that way. One drug dealer booked— that was it. Officer Doherty had already taken the scumbag to a cell down the hall, along with the guy's street stink, leaving the lobby tranquil once more. A young couple sat in one corner, waiting to provide a statement on a stolen car case. Another guy, who said he needed to speak with Chief Jones about something or other, paced.

Doherty leaned against the counter of the reception desk, entering an arrest record on his tablet. He seemed unconcerned about the yelling.

"Can you get that?" Jamie asked him. The door sometimes didn't shut properly, and arguments seemed to break out at least once a week between lowlifes in the parking lot. Just the sight of Doherty in uniform would shut them up fast.

"Yeah, no problem." Doherty set his tablet on her desk and headed across the lobby.

As he reached for the handle, the door burst open and crashed against the wall. A huge man lurched through, knocking Doherty to the floor. The man's face was scarlet, his eyes ablaze. He beat a fist against the side of his bald head. Like a savage dog, he bared his teeth.

Doherty scrambled away on all fours as the big man threw his head back and screamed once more. The young couple in the corner

1

flattened against the wall. Jamie leaped from the chair, nerves tingling and heart pounding. She reached for the service pistol on her hip.

Assess the situation, her training echoed.

Weapon? One hand carried a motorcycle helmet, and the other continued to pound rhythmically against his head. But the oversized belt covered with electrical wires wasn't there to hold up his pants.

"Bomb!" she yelled. "Take cover!"

Jamie dropped behind the desk. Down the hallway, doors slammed. The front door crashed against the wall again, hopefully someone getting away.

So much for the light day.

Rising, Jamie peered over the desk and leveled her weapon at the intruder. He swayed in the center of the lobby, eyes glazed. The couple still cowered in the corner, but pacing guy was gone. Crouching behind a large chair, Doherty aimed his gun.

There was no control unit that Jamie could see, but some bombs detonate on a preset timer. The man took one stumbling step, almost tripping. His face contorted in a grimace and blood dripped from one ear, streaming down his neck in a red ribbon. This guy was in pain, not rage.

"Drop!" Doherty yelled. "On the floor, now!"

The intruder collapsed, whether from pain or following orders, Jamie didn't care. He was down, with no visible weapon or detonator. No reason for either of them to pull the trigger just yet. If it was a bomb, a bullet might even set it off. Hopefully, Doherty was thinking the same.

Jamie rose higher, keeping both hands on her weapon, pointed at the man's head. She motioned to the frightened couple. "Come over here. Get behind me." They hurried across the lobby and squatted behind the desk, the young woman sobbing quietly.

With the civilians as safe as she could manage, Jamie's focus returned to the intruder. He lay on his side, his body heaving with each breath. A red smear across the tiles marked where he'd hit the floor. The leather belt around his waist was at least ten inches wide with what looked like an elongated D-cell battery on one side. Wires crisscrossed its surface, connecting a variety of electronics components. The man's shirt had lifted above the belt with skin showing. Thank God, no sign of explosives.

Eyes still glued to the figure on the floor, she yelled over her shoulder. "All station personnel. Situation is under control. Suspect is down with injuries."

Doherty spoke into the radio attached to his left shoulder. "Orlando Southeast precinct, one at gunpoint, two officers on the scene. Signal thirty, forty-four."

The radio screeched, "Copy, Southeast, two units en route."

Jamie holstered her gun and pulled out handcuffs. "I've got him. Cover me."

Doherty nodded, keeping his weapon pointed while Jamie rounded the desk and bent over the crumpled body. The man offered no resistance as she cuffed his hands behind his back. She donned latex gloves, put a finger to his neck and located a pulse. She lifted eyelids and checked inside his mouth.

She squatted close to his face. "Can you hear me?"

The man murmured.

"What's on the belt? Anything dangerous?"

His voice was weak and slurred. Each of his heavy breaths pushed out one word at a time. "Nothing... not... bomb."

"That's good. Very good," Jamie said. She turned to Doherty, whose expression had relaxed a bit even if the grip on his gun was still viselike. "Ambulance on the way?"

Doherty nodded.

Jamie patted the man's shoulder with a gloved hand. "We've got help coming, sir. But before they get here, I need to take this belt off."

The man mumbled something, but the words were slurred. Up close, the belt didn't look threatening—more like a utility belt that a carpenter might wear. Electronics components with connecting wires were stapled into the leather like a homemade array of superhero gadgets. The mega-battery, if that was what it was, fit into a sleeve on one side that might have otherwise held a hammer. Still no sign of any explosive material. False alarm, but she'd made the right call and would do it again.

She flipped two snaps and the belt loosened. With a few tugs, it released from the man's hips. A workman's tool belt—enhanced— though what the wires and electronics components might do was anyone's guess. She laid it flat on the tile floor. There would be time later to figure out what this guy was up to.

A quick scan didn't find any external wounds, but the internal injuries were probably serious, most likely head trauma. Blood still leaked from one ear—and now from his nose too.

The man croaked, not much louder than a whisper. "Help."

She bent down. "Yes, sir, medical help is on the way. Hang in there. Just a few more minutes." A faraway siren could be heard through the still-open front door.

"No… this," the man said. He wiggled one hand bound by the cuffs, loosening his clenched fist. A glint of silver shone between his chubby fingers. "I come… from… the future."

"Huh?" Either she'd hadn't heard him right or this guy was a serious wack job. Doherty moved closer, his weapon still pointed.

She held up a hand. "Wait, he's holding something."

He opened the hand further to reveal a large silver coin. Bigger than a silver dollar and thicker, with markings on its face that wiggled.

4

"Give... this," the man grunted.

Jamie leaned in closer. "You want me to give the coin to someone?"

The man nodded. "Daniel."

"Daniel? Daniel who?"

"Rice," the man wheezed. "Give... to Daniel Rice."

****

The EMTs, the bomb squad and the frightened couple were gone now, returning the lobby to calm. One of the detectives had taken the belt to a back room for examination. The bomb guys had declared it harmless.

The intruder had had no wallet, no phone on him. One of the police techs was running a face and fingerprint match. No results yet. But the guy had left a calling card, of sorts.

Jamie, Doherty, and two other patrol officers stood in a semicircle around Chief Jones, who held the oversized coin in a gloved hand, twisting it beneath overhead lights.

Both sides of the silver coin shimmered with a rainbow of colors when tilted, like the surface of a DVD. Closer examination revealed animated holographic images. On one side, a three-dimensional golden eagle popped out, its wings flapping as the coin was tilted one way and then the other. On the back, an imposing building was fronted by columns that extended beyond the coin's surface.

It seemed far too complex to be money, but Jamie had never traveled the world. Maybe this was money in some faraway place. Or maybe it was a commemorative coin of some kind.

"And you say this guy wanted you to take it?" Chief Jones asked, still studying the details on its surface.

"Yes, sir," Jamie answered. "He said I should give it to Daniel Rice." She looked down, combing fingers through her hair. "Those were his last words."

They'd received a call from the EMTs—dead on arrival at East Orlando Hospital, brain hemorrhage. Jamie hated when people died, even the perps.

Jones' brow twisted. "Did he mean the scientist? *That* Daniel Rice?"

Jamie shrugged. "I'm not sure, sir. But the scientist Daniel Rice is on TV all the time. It's probably who he meant."

Jones turned the coin on its edge. "Did he say anything about the writing?" He held out the coin for her examination. Given the coin's thickness, the bold capital letters stamped around its circumference were easy to read:

SPIN UPON MIRRORED GLASS

"No, sir," Jamie answered. "The man didn't explain the writing or anything else. He just asked me to take it."

The chief looked her squarely in the eyes. "Did you try spinning it? Did anyone?" Jones looked at each officer in the circle.

Jamie shuffled her feet. They'd all been curious as soon as they'd read the words but had played things by the book. "None of the detectives were in the office, so we bagged the coin and put it in the evidence room along with the belt and the helmet." She paused and lifted her eyebrows hopefully. "But, Chief... there's a small mirror in the bathroom that's only attached by a few screws."

Jones rubbed a hand on his chin for a moment and then spoke. "Yeah, I guess we'll need to know what we're dealing with before I take this any higher up the chain of command." He glanced around the empty lobby. "Okay, Sergeant, go get the mirror. The man who thinks he's from the future certainly has some interesting toys. Let's see what it does."

She hurried down the hall and returned carrying a rectangular mirror, which she laid on the front desk. Jones touched the edge of the coin to the mirror and cocked his wrist.

Backing away, Jamie asked, "You don't think it will explode or anything, do you?"

Jones shook his head. "We got an all clear from the bomb squad, but hell, who knows. The world is full of strange things these days." He lifted the coin from the mirror. "You want to leave?"

Jamie's curiosity was piqued. After the excitement of the morning, she couldn't miss the grand finale. How bad could it be? It was just a coin. A smile spread across her lips. "No way, Chief, I have to see this."

"Here we go, then." Jones returned the coin to the center of the mirror's surface, pinching it between his thumb and index finger. With a quick snap, he started it spinning.

It spun like any other coin but made a low hum. A vibration, almost like the sound of a helicopter's rotor beating the air. After a few seconds, rather than slowing down and falling over, the coin's spin intensified. It rotated ever faster, becoming a blur. The vibrational hum increased too, its pitch getting higher as the coin sped up. Maybe this coin-helicopter-thing was going to lift off the mirror and fly through the station lobby.

Jamie took a step back, as did everyone else. The sound became shrill, piercing the air with an almost inaudible pitch, and then faded away altogether. Maybe a dog could still hear it.

The spinning coin emitted a sharp click, and a vertical cone of white light flashed from its base toward the ceiling. The onlookers flinched in unison.

Images appeared around the perimeter of the light cone, human faces, each twisting as if the perspective was spinning along with the coin. A rainbow of colors reflected across the faces, cycling from red to yellow, green, blue and finally to violet. It was a bizarre mashup of light, form, and color, startling in its seemingly impossible origin but strangely beautiful too, like a modern art exhibit.

The rotating faces stabilized like an old flickering film projection that eventually locks into synchronization. The multitude of perspectives and colors came together within the center of the cone, forming a single face with natural skin color. It was a man's face, and fully three-dimensional.

As Jamie stared in awe, the eyes of the floating head blinked, looked left and then right. The lips of the apparition lifted on one side, forming a wry smile.

"Holy cow," Jamie whispered. "Maybe this guy really did come from the future."

2 OSTP

Daniel Rice leaned against a bookcase, his arms folded and a grin spreading across his face. He always enjoyed showing visitors around the Office of Science and Technology Policy, the building just steps from the White House, but this visitor was special.

Nala Pasquier sat in Daniel's high-back office chair, kicked her shoes off and put her bare feet up on his desk. "I love your office. Way better than my closet at Fermilab." She leaned back, hands clasped behind her head. "Ahh… I could get used to this."

It was her first venture into Daniel's home territory, and she'd made herself comfortable right away. But that was Nala. Adaptable. Ready for anything.

Physical attraction was the easiest part of their relationship. Those silky legs splayed across his desk seemed incongruous among the pens, paper and other objects of his routine workday, but he was only too happy to soak in the view. Nala was certainly attractive. And smart. And perceptive. But she was also courageously experimental, boldly carving her own path through life, a trait Daniel treasured more than any.

Friday afternoons at OSTP were generally quiet, with most of the employees wrapping up for the weekend. It was a good time to show his houseguest where he worked. "You'd fit right in around here." He brushed a finger across her toes. "Except for your complete disregard for the rules."

"What? No feet on desks?" She gave him a crooked smile.

He shook his head. "You'd be surprised how formal it gets in an office that advises the president."

She scrunched up her nose in a fake pout, a classic Nala expression that Daniel found both brash and adorable. It was one of many looks from this brown-skinned beauty that made his heart melt.

"Well… poofy poof on you," she said, clearly holding back. Her more usual taunts could singe the lacquer off the door. She'd been on her best behavior ever since they'd walked into the office.

Nala pulled her feet from the desk and sat up straight. She gazed innocently up at Daniel, her large eyes partly hidden behind strands of wavy brown hair. "Sorry. You won't punish me, will you? At least… not here?"

Daniel laughed, resisting the urge to kiss her. "I'll give you a pass this time since you're a visitor."

She rolled gorgeous eyes to her forehead. "Not quite the response I was looking for. Role play, Daniel, role play."

Daniel sighed. Another missed opportunity. It happened a lot. "I should have said…?"

She stood up and put a hand to his cheek. "I can't put the words into your mouth. That'd ruin all the fun. But don't worry, you're getting there."

Nala certainly knew how to have fun. She'd arrived a few days before and they'd spent their days touring the Washington sights, but not in any conventional tourist sense. They paddled kayaks past a serene Jefferson Memorial. At the Capitol steps, she handed her phone to a passerby and struck up an impromptu dance with Daniel. He was embarrassed by his clumsiness and the stares from tour groups, but he was happily surprised at the genuinely spontaneous photos.

No tour of Washington would be complete without a visit to the Smithsonian, and Nala used their time to seek out the preserved artifacts of science including a superb display of historic particle accelerators. With tact Daniel didn't know she had, Nala found a curator and pointed out a small mistake in how one of the cyclotrons had been displayed. The curator recognized her from Fermilab news reports and the two quickly became new best friends with smiling selfies taken in front of the exhibit.

She absorbed Daniel's guided tour of the capital city like she did everything — with an eager curiosity for all things new. But each evening, on their return to his condo across the river in Virginia, she'd wrapped her arms around his neck and taken command. She guided, he followed. He loved every minute of it, even when her assertive style pushed him into new territory.

"Guess I'll have to… I don't know… tickle your badly behaved toes when we get home."

She put a hand to her chin. "Hmm. Very boy scout. But going in the right direction."

"Nala, I don't think I'll ever be like you."

She knitted her brow. "Like I'd want that? We're different people and that's fantastic. Some of the best relationships start from opposite corners. Jesus, it's why men and women are attracted to each other in the first place. We're different, physically, emotionally. I have lots of girlfriends, but I'm looking for something else in a man."

He leaned in close to her. "So… do I meet your requirements?"

She smiled, lifting both eyebrows. "You're way ahead of most guys. *You* know what a neutrino is." She brushed the tip of her nose against his and spoke in a low, sultry tone. "Oh yeah, Mr. Government Scientist, you most certainly meet my requirements."

She gave him a peck on the lips and twirled around in place, the tone of her voice doing a similar one-eighty. "What else you got in this office that I should see?"

"You've seen all this dungeon has to offer." He looked at his watch. "How about drinks before dinner?"

She nodded, and he led her into the foyer of the office, where the OSTP receptionist, Janine Ryder, studied a computer screen. Janine looked up. "Did you get the full tour?"

"Yes, your office is beautiful," Nala answered. "I love the French architecture."

"I do too," Janine said, "but not everyone favors the Eisenhower Building." She jerked her head toward Daniel.

Daniel shrugged. "Come back in January. It feels like a medieval crypt in here, only colder."

Janine laughed. "Pay no attention to him, Nala. He just likes to whine about living anywhere east of the Mississippi."

"A westerner at heart, I guess," Daniel said. He had nothing against the east, but the rugged west had always been the foundation of his soul. He longed for another hike deep into the Grand Canyon, another climb up Mount Rainier. What easterners called mountains weren't much more than speed bumps.

"What's up for the weekend?" Daniel asked Janine.

"Poconos with a friend. The fall colors should be great," she answered. A year ago, Daniel could have been that friend, but dating a colleague was awkward at best, a notion Janine didn't dispute. With Nala in the office, long-standing tensions were swept away. Daniel had a girlfriend now, even if their long-distance relationship was limited to getting together once a month.

"How about you two?" Janine asked.

"A hike on the Appalachian Trail. Fresh air and all that," Daniel answered.

"I've never been, but I hear the trail is very pretty."

"You know, it's funny—" Daniel's thought was interrupted when two men in dark suits walked through the open door and into the foyer. One carried a briefcase, tucking sunglasses into his jacket pocket. Very official. Very serious.

Daniel had no idea who they were. Nala tensed, glancing his way. She'd never been comfortable with figures of authority, and these guys radiated 'authority.' Daniel stepped aside, allowing Janine to do her job.

"Good afternoon, welcome to OSTP. How can I help you?" Janine asked sweetly.

The elder of the two glanced at Daniel, then spoke to Janine. "FBI. Agent Griffith. This is Agent Torre." They both displayed identification. "We're here to see Dr. Daniel Rice."

"Agent Griffith," she acknowledged. She motioned toward Daniel just as he offered his hand. "Meet Dr. Daniel Rice."

"Always happy to help the FBI," Daniel said. "What brings you here?" As a scientific investigator and part-time public figure, Daniel rarely interacted with law enforcement. The investigation at Fermilab the year before was a notable exception.

Nala slipped a hand under Daniel's arm, a quiet signal of her need to stay close. Her lips tightened and her brow pressed down over eyes shooting daggers at the intruders.

Agent Griffith glanced at her defensive posture, the wrinkles across his forehead deepening. Returning his attention to Daniel, he spoke with a gruff voice. "It's confidential. We'll need a secured meeting place. Preferably a SCIF."

SCIF, or Sensitive Compartmented Information Facility, was basically a conference room sealed to the outside world. Soundproofing construction, electronics isolation, the works. SCIFs were all the rage in Washington, almost a competition between agencies. My SCIF is bigger than your SCIF—that kind of thing.

The Eisenhower Building had just such a room in the basement. Looking over Janine's shoulder, Daniel could see that she'd already brought up the room reservation form on her computer.

Ordinarily, he'd cooperate without hesitation, but today he had a guest. "Could this wait until Monday? I'm not officially working today and we were just about to leave. I'd be happy to schedule some time."

The agent shook his head once. "Sorry, Dr. Rice. We wouldn't normally barge in like this, but it's a priority investigation. It can't wait.

Twenty minutes, plus or minus, depending on how our conversation goes." He dipped his head toward Nala. "Sorry, ma'am."

Daniel took a deep breath. These guys didn't look like they were going to take no for an answer. He turned to Nala. Her naturally buoyant personality had disappeared with the FBI presence, and Daniel understood why. She'd faced arrest on a long list of federal charges only a year before in the Fermilab investigation.

Nala didn't say anything, making it clear enough that the next step was his decision. Twenty minutes. A small delay in their plans for the evening, but nothing major. Best to accommodate the FBI.

"Do you mind waiting here?" he asked.

Nala whispered, "No problem, I'll be fine."

Janine hit a few keys on her computer. "You're booked."

Daniel managed a smile. "Okay, then, Agent Griffith, Agent Torre. Let's chat." He gave Nala a hug. "Make yourself comfortable. Back in a flash."

Daniel led the two FBI agents down several flights of stairs to the basement. They checked in with a clerk, who confiscated their cell phones and ushered them into the SCIF. The massive door closed with a thud. Eavesdropping from the hallway was unlikely.

Inside, it looked like any other conference room, though the walls were bare.

"If it makes any difference, I have top secret clearance," Daniel said as they settled into chairs around a large table.

"Yes, sir, we know," Agent Torre said. He laid his briefcase on the table, aligning it precisely parallel with its edge. In any other circumstance, Daniel might have joked about the man's idiosyncrasies, but Torre seemed to be entirely humorless. Agent Griffith didn't look any better.

Torre drew a photograph from his briefcase and slid it across the table. "Recognize this man, Dr. Rice?"

Daniel picked up the photo. It showed an overweight man with glasses, bald headed. Posed, perhaps for an employee badge or driver's license. "I don't think so." Daniel passed the picture back.

"How about the name Elliott Becton?"

Daniel shook his head. "Doesn't ring a bell. Should I know him?"

Griffith picked up the line of questions without missing a beat. "Apparently Becton knew you."

"Knew?"

"Yes. Elliott Becton is deceased," Griffith answered. "Three days ago. Walked into an Orlando police station, collapsed on the floor and died."

"Sorry to hear," Daniel said. "Of course, a lot of people know me. I do lectures, late-night TV. That kind of thing."

"Yes, sir, we're aware," Torre said flatly. Torre pushed another photo across the table. In it, a white oval doorway stood alone in a large facility. Daniel recognized the location immediately—the Operations and Checkout building at Kennedy Space Center and the portal to other worlds. "I believe you've used the alien transportation device that's installed there?"

"Uh, yeah. Once. A visit to Core." Daniel recalled his impromptu and somewhat disturbing passage directly into the interior of the moon-sized gatekeeper to the galaxy. "Is my trip through the portal related to Becton?"

"Possibly," Griffith answered. "While you were at KSC, did you meet any of the NASA engineers?"

Daniel shook his head. "No, I don't recall anyone besides Zin. Aastazin. The android. Core's representative here on Earth." Daniel held up a hand at the steely look from Agent Torre. "But, you already knew that too, right?"

Torre didn't flinch, his face seemingly made of stone.

Griffith asked once more, "So, no contact with any of the engineers at NASA while you were at KSC?"

Daniel fished into his memory of the brief visit six months earlier. Jan Spiegel had joined him from Fermilab. Marie Kendrick, who regularly made jumps through the portal, had been there too. They'd gathered around the alien doorway while Zin explained the astounding technology that could whisk you to a planet a thousand light-years away. Daniel didn't recall meeting any NASA engineers.

"None that I'm aware of," Daniel said.

Griffith looked at Torre, who nodded. With any luck, they were ready to share the purpose of their little inquisition.

"Dr. Rice," Griffith said, "Elliott Becton was a NASA engineer, employed at Kennedy Space Center. A twenty-year veteran. He was one of the key people who installed that portal. Becton had access to some very advanced alien technology."

"And," Agent Torre added, "we believe that he may have figured out how it works. A security camera recorded him walking out the KSC door. Ten minutes later he was dying in an Orlando police station—fifty miles away."

A three-hundred-mile-per-hour car? Teleportation? Or something else? In the quantum world, it was always something else.

Daniel analyzed Torre's statement in its entirety. A NASA engineer, with access to Zin's portal technology—but not necessarily with Zin's help—might have reverse engineered the portal's function to obtain its secrets. And then he'd died.

Unfamiliar technology, misused. Always a recipe for disaster, and Becton had paid the price. Surely he must have known that returning from 4-D space could be deadly; that much was common

16

knowledge. In fact, it was the whole reason that the katanauts at KSC used the alien portal to jump interstellar distances.

Griffith described the scene at an Orlando police station and showed Daniel a photo of a utility belt covered with electronics that Becton had probably assembled himself. Nothing on the belt looked remotely like the KSC portal, but that didn't mean it wasn't based on the same idea.

Passing through 4-D space and coming out alive on the other side required a special trick. Zin's portal could do it. The yin-yang object they'd recovered from Soyuz could do it too. But those were alien devices. As far as Daniel knew, humans hadn't conquered this part of the technology.

Until now?

"Becton's dead," Daniel said. "Whatever he learned about jumping through quantum space, it wasn't enough."

Agent Griffith shook his head. "We don't think he was jumping through any kind of space, Dr. Rice." He pointed to the photo of the alien portal. "As a scientist, perhaps you're familiar with one aspect of this technology. It produces a temporal offset."

Daniel recalled a brief explanation from Zin. The trick to survive the return from quantum space involved a brief suspension of the flow of time. The lost Soyuz astronauts had been frozen in this time warp. Daniel had briefly experienced it himself during his trip to Core; the process had been unnerving but not deadly.

"I'm familiar," Daniel said. "They put you in a specially designed chair, a portal transfer station, they call it. A hood covers your face and a yellow light flashes. The flash repeats once you're back in 3-D space." No doubt there was more to it, but that was as much as Daniel knew. Zin hadn't been generous in his explanation. "It's really no big deal, even though it leaves you with an odd feeling. Like you'd just passed out."

Both agents nodded. "You know more than most people we've talked to," Griffith said. "But the next question is the kicker, the reason we came to see you."

"And that question is?"

Agent Griffith cleared his throat. "Dr. Rice, do you know how to travel to the future?"

3   Coin

The questions from the FBI agents were getting ever stranger.

Time travel. Really? Are we going there?

Daniel didn't mind helping on the science side of their investigation, but educating these guys on time dilation, relativity and the limits theorized by Einstein, Hawking, Carroll, Thorne, Greene and others was going to take a lot more than twenty minutes. Nala was upstairs waiting.

"Do I know how to travel to the future? Absolutely," Daniel said. "We all do. We're doing it right now. Ticktock. Now we're in the future."

"Not exactly what I meant," Agent Griffith responded. He looked irritated at Daniel's rather flippant remark. Fair enough, but his was a beginner's question.

Daniel avoided further eye rolls and bit his facetious tongue. "I apologize. Of course, that's not what you meant." There was no reason to waste the agents' time, but neither was there any reason to waste Daniel's. "Maybe you can tell me the reason for your questions? I'm a scientist, but I'm not a theoretical physicist or a cosmologist, and I'm certainly no expert on the inner workings of the portal down at KSC. These might be good questions for Zin or Core, though I doubt they'll tell you much. I can also recommend a few books."

Both agents sat stony-faced. Daniel gestured with both hands. "Look, I'm sorry to hear this engineer misused the technology to kill himself, but what does any of this have to do with me?"

Without answering, Griffith looked at Torre. "Are you satisfied?"

Torre nodded. "I believe so. I think we can proceed."

Griffith eyed Daniel. "Our apologies for the indirect questions, but we needed to uncover your relationship with Mr. Becton, both now and in the future."

"Mr. Becton is dead," Daniel answered. "I don't think he has much of a future."

"Not anymore, but he may have been to the future, possibly your future." Griffith's serious demeanor hadn't changed in the slightest, even if the conversation had taken a turn toward the incredible.

"An interesting statement. Your evidence?" As cosmologist Carl Sagan had famously said, extraordinary claims require extraordinary evidence. This had better be good.

Torre unzipped a compartment inside his briefcase. "Before he died, Mr. Becton told the Orlando police he was from the future."

"A little fanciful, wouldn't you say?" Flippant remarks could be set aside out of politeness, but not Daniel's innate skepticism. "Your own investigation identifies Becton as an engineer at NASA. That's *today's* NASA, I assume."

"Perhaps Becton is not *from* the future but had recently *been* there." Torre reached into the briefcase compartment and pulled out a coin. It glittered with gold and silver colors as he turned it. "He told the police to give this coin to you. He mentioned you by name. I don't suppose you've ever seen it?" He handed the coin to Daniel.

Moving holograms popped from each side, iridescent with the full spectrum of visible colors. Daniel absorbed the elaborate details, including the writing around the edge. "Quite a beautiful object. It certainly gets your attention, but no, I've never seen it before. And as I said, lots of people know my name."

"Yes, sir. I think we've established that you don't currently know Mr. Becton."

Daniel looked up. "But I *will* know him? That's your premise?"

"We're not sure," Griffith answered. "It's possible Mr. Becton will become your associate."

Once more, Daniel glanced at the writing around the outside of the coin and turned to Torre. "My guess is you have a mirror in your briefcase?" On cue, Torre withdrew a circular mirror about the size of a dinner plate and set it on the table.

Daniel nodded. "Okay, I'll bite. You've done this before? Spinning this coin?"

"We have."

Daniel smiled and reached out to the mirror, placing the edge of the coin on its surface. "Well, then, I feel left behind. Time to catch up." He snapped his fingers and started the coin spinning.

The coin spun, and not just for a few seconds as expected. It wound itself up, spinning faster and emitting a throbbing tone that grew higher in pitch. Clearly more than a disc of metal, Daniel felt his natural skepticism beginning to fray.

"Fascinating." He lowered his head to better examine the point of contact between the coin and the mirror. "Either it has an internal energy source, or it's drawing reflected energy from the mirrored surface. Maybe a feedback mechanism creating an amplification. Nice science demonstration you have here."

"Stay tuned," Griffith said, a grin appearing on his face for the first time.

The tone's frequency quickly surpassed the limits of human hearing. The spinning coin made an audible click, and an inverted cone of light illuminated the ceiling. Photographic images rotated within the cone, a man's face as seen from different directions. The blur of images settled, each independent view coalescing into a single three-dimensional image of a man's head as if a puzzle had self-assembled.

The man, probably in his seventies, had long white hair pulled back in a ponytail and several days of stubble on his face. He looked remarkably like Daniel.

Every detail of the face was depicted with the precision of a three-dimensional video. The eyes looked left and then right. The man smiled, and as the floating face began to speak, a chill went up Daniel's body.

"This message is for Daniel Rice at the Office of Science and Technology Policy." Except for some scratchiness, the voice sounded like his.

The older man cleared his throat. "This probably comes as a shock to you, Daniel. It did for me too. Like it or not, we're one person, but at different points in time. Odd, isn't it? Looking at a future version of yourself. You're skeptical, of course."

His mind raced through every possible explanation. An elaborate hoax, an alien technology, or something else? He squinted at the hovering head, noting the crook in the man's left earlobe. He reached up and felt his own ear.

The floating head looked down. "It's really not much different than watching any other recording of yourself. Of course, the time order is reversed, but you'll get used to it. As I speak, it is April fourteenth, 2053. That's a Monday, if you want to look it up. From your perspective, it's thirty years in the future, but from my perspective it's today. Of course, I could tell you things about the past thirty years that you can't possibly know, but too much information isn't wise, so don't expect any stock market tips."

He cleared his throat again. "But I will bring up one event, and it's the reason for this message. A tragedy that will soon happen... soon, from your perspective." The man looked straight ahead and spoke with conviction. "It was a nuclear missile launch. Very bad, with millions killed and significant areas still uninhabitable even in 2053. But here's the thing, Daniel. There's hope. We believe this destruction can and should be prevented. In fact, we believe that *you* can prevent it."

Daniel's skepticism slipped further. The older man spoke in the same manner and tone as Daniel. Even the word choices matched his style and thought process. If this was a fake, it was a damned good one.

The gray-white ponytail was a stretch. *Not my style. At least, not now.*

"I'm going to ask a big favor, both for myself and all those millions of people who lost their lives. Come to 89 Peachtree Center, floor 97, Atlanta, Georgia on the afternoon of June second, 2053. Use the belt to get here. It works, you'll see. I know you're skeptical about all of this. I was too. This message is only one piece of evidence. Examine the rest and I'm confident you'll arrive at the right decision. You *will* come to 2053, because I remember doing it."

As the video concluded and the cone of light switched off, Daniel shook his head, believing in the clever technology but not remotely ready to accept the premise of the message.

Quite impossible.

Yet the conviction of his initial assessment was accompanied by an odd feeling of déjà vu. Standing in the Diastasi lab a year before, he had held a four-dimensional tesseract in his hand. Another impossible feat that had somehow found a niche in reality.

4   Isotope

Daniel Rice followed a nurse down a seemingly infinite hallway deep within the monolithic J. Edgar Hoover building, the decaying building still the headquarters for the FBI even after years of political wrangling for something better.

Why the office needed a nurse on staff wasn't clear, nor was the reason why he had been asked to accompany her. Agents Griffith and Torre had insisted, putting Daniel's evening plans with Nala on hold. He would still meet her somewhere for dinner, they agreed, but that was more than an hour ago.

The nurse opened the door to a small examination room that could have been lifted from any doctor's office. "Have a seat, Dr. Rice. This will just take a few minutes."

Asian. Probably Vietnamese. Her ethnicity didn't matter in the slightest, but his mind never stopped appraising almost everything around him. Ng on her name tag confirmed his instant assessment.

Daniel sat on the paper-covered examination bed, his feet dangling like a child sitting in an adult's chair.

Nurse Ng withdrew a bundle of wires from a drawer. "We'll start with the electrocardiogram. Just remove your shirt and lie down."

"Happy to oblige." Daniel patted his chest. "But my heart feels just fine. What's the purpose?"

She glanced obliquely as she prepared the electrical bundle. "Just doing my job. They ask. I get it done."

He began unbuttoning his shirt. "Not your fault, of course. But the agents that brought me here weren't exactly chatty. You look nicer."

The nurse smiled at the small flirtation. "I'd tell you if I knew. But I don't." She pushed him flat on the examination bed and peeled several adhesive tabs from a medical pack, sticking each one to his skin at various points around his chest and abdomen. "We're doing an EKG and DNA samples. That's all I know."

"More information than I had before," Daniel said as she pulled down his socks and stuck a tab on each ankle. "So, nothing sharp?" He hated needles.

"Nope." She hooked up a wire to each tab and ran the bundle to a machine beside the bed. "Okay, lie still for a minute." She pressed some buttons and watched a countdown on a screen.

A buzzer sounded when the test was complete. She unclipped the wires and ripped the adhesive tabs off one by one. "That wasn't so bad, was it?"

Daniel sat up again and reached for his shirt. "I rather enjoyed it. But why would the FBI need an electrocardiogram? Assessing my health for an upcoming mission they have in mind?"

She shook her head and reached for a jar of cotton swabs. "Around here, it's not likely to be about your health. Did you know that electrocardiograms are an excellent biometric? Better than your fingerprint or a retinal scan. Your heart has a very distinctive pattern, unlike anyone else's."

"I had no idea." Sometimes, even an accomplished scientist comes up short.

She held out a swab. "Open," she commanded and ran the swab under his tongue.

"This is the DNA part?"

"Yup. Saliva and hair." She pulled out a pair of scissors.

"Hair only contains mitochondrial DNA," Daniel said. "It's a poor biometric."

"Right you are," the nurse replied. "But protein matching is the newest thing, and hair is almost like tree rings when it comes to recording the unique pattern of proteins created inside your body."

"Hadn't heard of that one either."

She snipped just above his collar, the results of the trim falling onto a piece of tissue paper.

"A little more off around the ears, if you don't mind."

"Ha ha," she said. "Are all of you famous scientists this funny?"

"Ah, then you *do* know who I am."

"I've seen you on TV once or twice." Her voice was blasé. Some science fans gushed when they met him; many wanted a selfie. But professional women tended to play it cool. At age forty-four, Daniel was still figuring women out.

"That's it, Dr. Rice. All done."

"I'll miss our time together."

"You *are* funny," she said, her voice dripping with sarcasm. She pointed to the door. "You can go back to the lobby now, funny man. We'll have the results in about thirty minutes, and one of the agents will take it from there."

"Thanks. Sorry if I annoyed you."

She smiled. "You didn't." She leaned close and whispered into his ear. "It really was nice to meet you."

Daniel left the examination room and returned to the lobby, wondering not just about the medical tests but about his own behavior. Even with a girlfriend waiting for him, he'd still flirted with the nurse. Maybe it was just habit. Maybe the people of the future would label flirtation a form of abuse. He hoped relations between men and women would never get that sour.

****

Daniel sat alone in the darkened lobby, reading Nala's latest text message.

No worries. I like late dinners anyway.

It gave some reassurance that the FBI diversion wasn't going to rob them of an enjoyable evening. They'd already had more time together this week than in the past three months, but it was her first trip to Washington, and he didn't want to make it her last. Screwing things up with Nala had always been a Daniel Rice specialty.

But this week had been different. Just the day before, they'd found themselves alone at sunset at one of the most scenic of Washington locations, the Jefferson Memorial, watching in silence as deepening orange clouds reflected off the still waters of the Tidal Basin. He'd turned to her and they'd kissed, this time not sensual, but long and heartfelt. That single kiss produced a deeper connection than he'd felt with anyone. He thought she'd felt it too.

A large figure loomed, interrupting Daniel's daydream. "Ready for you, Dr. Rice." Agent Griffith's voice was rough.

Nala would have to wait a bit longer.

Daniel rose and followed down another impossibly long corridor. They passed through a doorway and Griffith closed the heavy door to the SCIF. Inside, Agent Torre sat at a table with two others, a woman introduced as Assistant Director Yarborough, in charge of the National Security Branch, and a man, Assistant Director Hanson, in charge of the Laboratory Division—the famous FBI Crime Lab.

"We were just discussing, Dr. Rice, your doubts about the video message." Agent Griffith took the lead even with the higher-ups in the room.

Daniel sat alone on one side of the conference table— apparently the hot seat. "I have doubts. What about you, do you buy it?"

"I'm keeping an open mind," Griffith answered.

Daniel nodded. "Skeptical thinking is not that different. I'm open to some pretty strange ideas—most scientists are—but not without evidence. The stranger the idea, the more evidence required, or I'm not on board."

"So, you don't believe it's possible to get to the future?" asked Yarborough, a stern-looking woman with pale skin and gray hair.

"That's not my concern. With the right technology, time travel to the future is possible. Not easy, but not prohibited by the laws of physics. For example, get close to an intense gravitational field like a black hole. Time slows down for you but not for everyone else. Leave the field and you're suddenly in the future. This is solid science proposed by Einstein more than a hundred years ago and well validated today."

Daniel pointed to Agent Torre's briefcase, presuming the coin was still inside. "But communication from the future to the past? In the scientific world, that's something you only hear from fringe players. So, no, I don't buy into the premise that this message comes from the future."

"The man in the video is suggesting you *will* go to 2053," Torre said. "He says he's you, and he remembers doing it."

Daniel waved a hand, trying to quell the outlandish talk that had been surfacing since they watched the video. "Look... even setting the illogical paradox aside for now, knowing that something is scientifically possible and doing it are two entirely different things. Even if I wanted to, I have no mechanism of jumping to 2053."

Yarborough exchanged a glance with Hanson. "Let's leave the logistics of time travel alone for a minute," she said. "I'd like to focus first on the content of the message and the evidence for its veracity. Among other things, Dr. Rice, the National Security Branch has the duty to protect the United States from weapons of mass destruction. The video explicitly alludes to a nuclear threat."

Daniel knew a little about how the FBI operated. They often held their cards very close. "You've determined that the nuclear threat is credible?"

"We have," she acknowledged. "Credible enough to devote investigative resources. Set aside the video for the time being—it's not the primary evidence since videos can be faked. However, much more compelling evidence arrived in just the last few minutes." She nodded toward Hanson.

Hanson was likely a Mormon elder in his private life. Blond, clean-cut with the unmistakable lines of an LDS garment showing under his dress shirt. He cleared his throat. "Dr. Rice, the lab just finished comparing your biometrics. Thank you, by the way, for your help on this."

The nurse's biometric sampling.

It wasn't hard to figure out *who* they wanted to compare against, but Hanson was implying they had undisclosed medical information about the man in the video.

"Compared my biometrics to what data?" Daniel asked.

"I'll explain," Hanson answered. "Beyond the video, the coin had additional data recorded on its surface, much like a DVD. We were able to read it without much trouble. Know what we found?"

"Biometrics, I'd guess."

Hanson smiled, pressed a few buttons on a phone and turned it around for Daniel to see. It showed a diagram, a graph of a red line jumping up and down in a rhythmic repetition. "This is an electrocardiogram recorded on the coin. These squiggles are almost exactly the same as the heartbeat we just sampled from you. Close enough that we'd call it a biometric match. There's a small difference, but it could be explained by age. We're getting input from a cardiologist right now to be sure."

29

The comparison was interesting, but not compelling. Anyone might have found another EKG—assuming he'd had one in his medical file somewhere. He'd taken many physicals in his life.

"That's just the beginning, though." Hanson pointed to Agent Torre. "Can you show him the chamber?"

Torre opened his briefcase and pulled out the holographic coin once more. He held it out for Daniel's inspection. "Right here, Dr. Rice. On the edge."

Just beyond the words *SPIN UPON MIRRORED GLASS* was a sliver of metal. Hanson put a fingernail under it and lifted. A narrow lid hinged, revealing a hollow chamber inside the coin. Daniel peered inside but didn't see anything.

"It's empty now," Hanson explained. "Cleaned out at the lab. But along with the video message and the data, they sent physical evidence to back up their claim. A small clip of hair. Your hair, now that we've had a chance to compare. It's a perfect protein match. Maybe even too perfect, given there was no indication of pigment loss."

"He's gray, I'm brown."

"Exactly. We're not sure what to make of that, but there's little question that it's your hair. Protein matches are already ninety-eight percent reliable and getting better every year. There's every reason to believe that protein will replace DNA as the preferred biometric of the future."

Again, interesting, but not conclusive. Hair is hair. He'd left quite a bit of it on the floor of barbershops around the world. The fact that hair in the coin wasn't gray was supporting evidence for the barbershop explanation.

Hanson continued. "But what's special about this snippet of hair is the fluid that surrounded it. A vegetable oil made from a combination of plants. Soybeans and olives, mostly, but it also included a rare plant that only grows in the Dead Sea area of Israel. Religious organizations use this oil for ceremonial purposes."

Daniel didn't interrupt the explanation. In fact, he listened with rapt attention.

"Most people don't know this, but in our Criminal Justice Information Services Division, the FBI maintains an extensive database of every bit of material that might conceivably be found at any crime scene. And it so happens that we had this particular oil on file. We matched the oil in the coin's compartment to a ceremonial oil used by a Baptist church in Atlanta, Georgia. There's no question—the oil in the coin came from that specific church. In fact, from a specific batch. We called the church; the bottle is still on a shelf. They've been using small amounts of that oil in ceremonies for the past ten years."

"You're saying a church in Georgia sent the message?" Daniel asked. He was impressed with the FBI's ability to narrow down the source so quickly, and he didn't doubt their extensive database was the reason.

"It's a bit more complex than that." Hanson glanced at Yarborough and Agents Griffith and Torre. From their acknowledgments, they'd all been briefed. "You're familiar with how carbon dating works?"

Daniel nodded, but Hanson explained anyway. "Then you're aware that the carbon-14 isotope decays radioactively at a specific rate, changing into carbon-12, over time. While any plant is alive, carbon-14 is replenished as the plant draws nutrients from the soil. But as soon as the plant is harvested, that cycle ends and the amount of carbon-14 begins to drop. We simply measure the ratio of the isotopes in any sample and we can tell how old the plant is."

"So, you dated the oil found inside the coin?"

"Yes."

"And it matched the oil from the bottle in Georgia."

"Not quite. Chemically we can tell they're from the same batch, the same harvest. But the carbon ratios don't match. The oil from the coin has a *lower* ratio, making it slightly *older* than the same oil in our database. About thirty years older, in fact."

31

Daniel put the pieces together quickly in his head, but the picture forming was disturbing. Two samples, one thirty years older than the other but both from a bottle of oil currently sitting in a church in Georgia. If the evidence was accurate, there was only one possible answer.

He shook his head, wondering where this craziness would end. "The oil inside the coin came from the same bottle, but thirty years into the future."

5   Vision

USS *Nevada*
North Pacific, 800 nautical miles southeast of Adak Island
October 6, 2023 10:15 Pacific Time

The obliteration of every scrap of life on Earth begins from this place.

Two rows of twelve vertical tubes, each tube painted orange, eight feet in diameter. The missile deck of the USS *Nevada*, SSBN-744, an *Ohio*-class Trident submarine, held technology capable of unimaginable destruction.

A narrow gap separated the rows of missiles, creating a walking path down the length of the compartment. Near the middle, a lone sailor kneeled, his hands clasped together. Even in the cool air of the compartment, his forehead was damp. The smells of metal and paint and the hum of ventilation fans filled his senses.

The sailor tuned out the stark surroundings of his workplace and focused inward. His sins were deep. The unholy desires that rampaged through his mind had become impossible to ignore. He'd even acted upon them, and more than once. The miraculous visitations he had experienced over the past week made it clear that penance was due.

He dragged the darkness inside of him toward a place of light. "Hear my cry, Lord. The sins buried in my soul have driven me to you, my protector. Care for me, grant me your grace and guide me to your holy commandments."

Overhead, security cameras hung from the ceiling, pointing in each direction down the walkway. On a ballistic missile submarine, places of absolute privacy did not exist.

The cameras were of little concern to Fire Control Technician Second Class Joshua Swindell. He accepted that his prayer would be observed, even recorded. He was equally confident that it would be ignored. Personal actions of religious devotion were protected by military regulation. Even at the fitness-for-duty assessment, required annually for every crew member serving on a ship that could destroy the world, questions of a religious nature were never allowed.

"I have been in your presence, Lord, and I seek your guidance for my repentance. I am a beggar knocking at the door of your limitless love and mercy."

An overhead light flickered and the pathway where he kneeled creaked. He opened his eyes and surveyed the floor for the miracle he hoped would come once more. As he watched, a faint outline of the soles of two bare feet formed on the vinyl surface. It was little more than an imprint, but the miracle was unmistakably real. He could just make out the pads of ten toes, an empty void forming the arch and the round prints of two heels.

He has arrived.

Joshua lowered his head and pressed his hands together. "Lord, I am in awe of your presence. My faith has been rewarded." He bobbed his head rhythmically in a physical chant to the supernatural power that filled the room.

Barely above the sound of the ventilation system, a soft male voice arose from nowhere. "Kneel before me, Joshua Swindell, and receive the abundance of my grace, for you are blessed."

Joshua's hands trembled, and his voice quavered. "I am surely blessed. No man loves you more than I."

The voice was little more than a whisper but carried a firm tone. "My son, I stand before you. Lift your head and gaze upon me."

Joshua's arms shook uncontrollably, and his eyes filled with tears. He slowly raised his head. The corridor was empty, yet the impressions of two feet on the vinyl remained. "I am your servant, my Lord."

In the empty air in front of him, a handprint appeared. A human hand, but only a vague outline with no connection to a body. The hand moved through the air and its fingers opened to reveal a chain, with a key dangling below.

Joshua shivered as beads of sweat appeared across his forehead. "I see you, Lord."

"You tremble, Joshua."

"My Lord, I am afraid. Your presence is more than my mortal eyes can bear."

"Do you fear me, Joshua?" The voice was calm but its authority unquestionable. Joshua's eyes followed the hand as it reached upward. A portion of a lower arm materialized but remained disembodied at the elbow.

"I... I am fearful of your power," Joshua said.

The voice became stern. "You should be. I have powers beyond your imagination." The hand outline thrust toward him and shook the key. "You will follow my plan, Joshua, without deviation. Your salvation depends on it. Do you understand?"

Joshua bobbed his head rapidly. "I will. I will, my Lord. Guide me. I will obey."

"Then rise," the voice commanded. Joshua slowly lifted himself from the floor. His legs wobbled, and his heart raced.

His whole body shook as the hand came to rest on his shoulder. From out of clear air, a second hand appeared and grasped his other shoulder. Then, just inches away, the ghostly face of a bearded man with long hair materialized.

Joshua jumped, his mouth wide open. "Oh! Dear Jesus."

The hands held firm and prevented him from withdrawing. The face hovered in front of his own. Its form was incomplete, only eyebrows, cheekbones, the tip of a nose and a bearded chin. All else was emptiness, as if whole sections of skin had been erased.

Lips appeared, and when the mouth opened, he could see right through to the missile silos behind. "I have chosen you, Joshua," the voice whispered. "Together, we will fulfill my plan to cleanse the world of sin." One hand dangled the key in front of his face. "Take it."

Joshua reached up and grasped the chain. The key at its end was not like any other, but he recognized its shape immediately. "It's... a launch key," he stammered.

"This is your task. Redemption for your sins."

Joshua trembled. "You want me to launch a missile? I... I can't. It's not possible. It takes multiple keys... a launch code... and a lot more."

The voice continued quietly. "Your crew will soon be conducting a readiness drill. During this drill, you will unlock the Fire Control Room safe and retrieve the launch trigger. You will enter a code that I provide and launch missiles to targets of my choosing."

Joshua bowed his head. "But the weapons control officer..."

"He will already be dead."

Somewhere in the back of Joshua's mind, he recalled his training—the fallibility of the human mind; recognition of symptoms of psychosis in crewmates, or even in yourself. But this was no imagined spirit. He could feel the hands on his shoulders and the breath on his face. This was a commandment from God, and no Earthly constraint could overrule.

Joshua looked up and tears ran down his face. "As Abraham did before me, I will obey. But... my Lord, like Abraham, the burden you ask me to carry is so great."

The lips opened once more. "There is no greater virtue than the action of a righteous man. Prepare your body and spirit for this undertaking, Joshua. I shall visit you again in two days. To test your resolve."

6 Deliberations

Daniel weighed the claim against the evidence. A message from the future, carried to the past. An exotic 3-D image of a man claiming to be his future self.

Strange stuff, but the evidence was not easily dismissed. Elliott Becton had had access to advanced alien technology that could suspend time. How this technology worked and what Becton had done with it were issues begging for an investigation. The DNA and electrocardiogram matched Daniel's own biometrics. Compelling, but insufficient on its own. The face and voice from the video certainly looked and sounded like him. Again, fascinating but it could be faked.

The most compelling evidence was the oil, chemically matched to a single bottle. Oil that proved to be thirty years older than its modern-day source, as paradoxical as a son who is older than his father. The carbon-14 results were indisputable.

Daniel wrestled with the possibility that the message, the hair sample and the oil were truly from the future. The affront to everyday normality made his stomach churn.

The paths of logic were only one source of anxiety. His raw instinct weighed in too. Daniel knew himself well. If ever he needed to convince himself of such a wild claim, this was exactly how he'd do it.

Deputy Director Yarborough pulled her chair closer. Like a sadistic psychologist, she seemed to be observing his internal analysis along with his discomfort. "There's more," she said. "Predictions. Specific, and credible."

Daniel surfaced from his internal processing. She looked fatigued. Perhaps they'd been working on this case for days. "One of the predicted events has already occurred," she said.

"A chemical spill in Argentina," Agent Griffith said. "Yesterday, at twelve fourteen p.m. Eastern time. Data from the coin predicted it to the minute. It even identified the chemical as chlorine."

Of course, chemicals spilled regularly somewhere in the world, but the odds of guessing the place and time were astronomical. Daniel didn't doubt their statement, but it wasn't like reality to play games of chance.

Griffith didn't let up. "A train derailment in Italy is supposed to happen on Sunday. Then a bomb in Israel on Monday. We've passed information to both countries, but it's not clear how seriously they will take it."

Daniel took a deep breath. "Not your average psychic prediction."

They're one for three, he thought. Already better than the entire history of psychic prognostications. He almost hoped the Italians did nothing with the information. At least it would validate the second prediction.

"Dr. Rice, I was skeptical, just like you are," Yarborough said. "But I've come around." She leveled her gaze at Daniel. "How about you?"

"The chemical spill is substantial corroborating evidence," Daniel said, nodding. "No doubt any crime investigator or prosecutor would be satisfied. But I'm still bothered by all of this, and it's not just the evidence. It's the paradox of time travel."

He waved a hand in the air. "Sure, forward time travel is possible, even reasonable. Someday, it may be common for people to jump to the future for a variety of reasons. But it's a one-way trip. Backward time travel is fantasy. There are just too many logical inconsistencies. Who's to say that the past even exists?"

"We're not talking about going to the past," Yarborough said. "Just the future."

"I realize that, but the message claims to be from the future, in which case, *we* are its past. If the message is true, information has been transferred to the past, and once the universe allows that to happen, logical paradoxes pop up all over the place. Why, for example, would my older self remember traveling to the future? Even if I had the means to do it—which I don't—I could easily decide not to go."

"You sure about that?" Agent Griffith asked. "If the message is true, you may have no choice." It was a deep thought, particularly coming from a law enforcement officer, but Daniel wasn't buying it.

"Let's cut to the chase, shall we?" Daniel asked. "What do you want from me?"

Yarborough became the spokesperson for the group. "Agreed, let's get to the point. We need your help, Dr. Rice. We'd like you to accompany Agent Griffith to the Kennedy Space Center. Determine how this technology works and whether or not its functionality is capable of supporting Becton's claim."

The video message had expressly stated that Daniel should use this belt to get to the future. Griffith had provided a photo, but the contraption looked more like a kid's science project than a time travel device.

"Where's the belt now?"

"We have it," Yarborough said. "You and Agent Griffith will take it to Florida. We've been in contact with NASA, and they're standing by to help."

"Then you already have the technical experts. You don't need me."

"Oh, but we do, Dr. Rice." She seemed to be enjoying her power over him. That she had the backing of the highest people in the administration—even the president—wasn't something Daniel was ready to question.

"After we understand how the belt functions, we'll need you to comply with the message request."

"You want me to use this belt to go to Atlanta on June second, 2053?"

Her sadistic smile confirmed his fear. "Yes, we do."

****

Silver-haired, battle-hardened Agent Griffith sat across the aisle from Daniel on a Department of Justice Gulfstream G-550 at forty-five thousand feet somewhere over North Carolina. The two men were the only passengers.

Spread across Daniel's lap was a wide leather belt, the kind sold at any hardware store for carpenters to carry their tools. Two of the pockets had been ripped away, leaving only a stitched outline. In their place, small circuit boards were attached by screws that pierced through the leather. Soldered wires connected to several LEDs, one dangling like a Christmas tree light not fully secured to its branch.

The metal cylinder on one side was likely a power component, though it seemed more than just a battery. Wires ran from the cylinder to a series of tiny integrated circuits stapled directly into the leather. Glued to the strap side of the buckle was what looked like a miniature smartphone or music player. It included a small display and numeric keypad.

Fastened to the other side of the buckle was a single black toggle switch. Daniel fingered the switch but didn't flip it on. He raised his voice to be heard over the roar of the airplane's engines. "On-off switch?"

Griffith nodded. "Yeah. We got that far. Nothing much happens when you turn it on."

Best to keep it off until we get to Florida.

Daniel shrugged. "It's certainly interesting, but I'm not an engineer. The people at KSC will need to figure this out."

"Let's hope they have some answers."

Griffith's always-severe countenance had softened somewhat, mostly after he'd finished explaining that the FBI had initially suspected that Daniel might be involved in a conspiracy along with Elliott Becton. They'd dropped that idea after the interview. Either Griffith was relieved that a prominent scientist was not a domestic terrorist, or he was miffed that his suspicions hadn't panned out. In either case, Daniel had been accepted as one of the good guys.

In addition to the belt, they'd brought a motorcycle helmet, which appeared to be an integral part of the setup. Daniel noted a yellow LED glued to the inside of the helmet visor, looking suspiciously like the same light built into katanaut transfer chairs at Kennedy Space Center. Griffith even played a KSC security video that revealed Becton alone on the portal floor, tinkering with one of the transfer chair hoods.

Like any other investigation that Daniel had been involved with, motivation played a key role. He rubbed a hand across his chin. "So why does a NASA engineer get involved in a covert and probably illegal use of highly sensitive alien technology?"

"We're looking into that," Griffith answered. "We've already searched his home and office. The guy was a brilliant engineer and had some other homemade devices around his house, though nothing remotely as advanced as this. The history from his computer browser told a sad tale of a lonely guy. No significant other, no girlfriends. He frequented those online sites for incels."

Daniel nodded. "Involuntarily celibate."

"That's it. Guys that get rejected a lot. Their frustration can turn into anger against women. Not sure yet how that might figure into his little time-jumping project. Maybe he thought he'd have better luck finding a girlfriend in the future?"

"A unique motivation, if that's the answer."

"We've got some other agents working that part of the case. The main thing for you and me is to figure out how this belt works."

They talked for another half hour, finally settling quietly into the comfortable seats when the pilot announced their descent. Puffy clouds streamed by the airplane window, and Daniel's thoughts turned quickly to Nala.

They had met for a near-midnight dinner at a deserted restaurant. She'd been more understanding than expected, given just a few hours to sort out plans before Daniel was due back at the airport. He'd withheld the details of his newly assigned mission, simply saying that the FBI needed him in Florida for a day or two.

"It's your job, Daniel. Go do it," she'd told him. "We'll find another weekend to enjoy the outdoors together."

Those last few words had come with a smirk, and Daniel knew why. Ever since their trip to Haiti, "enjoying the outdoors together" had taken on a very personal meaning. Coded language between the two of them.

Daniel had laughed at her reference, and soon they were both giggling uncontrollably. It wasn't a bad way to part.

He'd miss her. He already missed the hiking weekend that would never be. Another in a series of missed opportunities in their on-again, off-again relationship. "The distance between us," they'd often laughed, not meaning anything emotional, but the physical six hundred miles between Chicago and Washington.

His mind wandered further back in time. To Haiti. Nala's birthplace. It wasn't the tropical destination most Caribbean tourists would pick, but Haiti with Nala had been an altogether different experience. The beach was just as she had portrayed it—astonishingly beautiful and delightfully isolated. The tropical setting had cleared the busy world from their minds, and nights wrapped around this intoxicating woman were unforgettable.

Nala had an intriguing way of luring Daniel into behavior he didn't recognize in himself. Not only had he joined her in the shower— long considered personal space, as he'd consistently told other

42

women—but he'd joined her in *song* in the shower. *Les Misérables*, of all things.

Of course, singing had been the tamest of his Haiti performances. The deserted beach had provided a backdrop for one of Nala's most interesting obsessions…

Soft sand. The shade of a palm tree. A tranquil blue-green sea that stretched forever. She returned from the house, a cold beer in hand, and took a swig before setting it in the sand beside him.

She stood above him, toes in the sand, with beads of perspiration across the smooth brown skin of her stomach. A drip ran across her navel and disappeared into the colorful wrap covering her bikini bottom.

"Hot," she said, and he nodded in agreement.

A mischievous grin spread across her face. She looked both ways down the empty beach. Intrigued, he stared as she untied her bikini top, dropped it to the sand and ran her hands across glistening breasts. "Ahh, much better."

His pulse quickened, and his widening eyes fixated on the delicious curves of her body.

She untied the wrap at her waist and dangled it over his face. He breathed in deeply, catching the womanly scent that permeated the cloth. She tossed the wrap aside, hooked thumbs under her bikini bottom and slid it down an inch.

A tightly trimmed patch of hair peeked above the fabric. A Greek letter tattoo adorned one hip bone. Her head tilted slightly to one side. "More?"

He nodded, feeling a stirring below.

She pushed the bikini bottom to her toes and flipped it toward the palm. Hands on hips with nothing left but sunglasses, she flashed a wicked smile. "You've never done it on the beach, have you?"

Daniel's head shake seemed to spur her on. She dropped to her knees, pulled off his swim trunks and teased one hand across his abdomen. Daniel's heart pounded from her touch.

"Gals on top. Guys on the bottom. That's the beach rule." His puzzled look prompted her impish smile to broaden. "Keeps the sand out."

She straddled across him, pushing each knee into soft sand beside his hips. "A secondary benefit, really."

Her breasts brushed across his chest as she leaned in close and whispered into his ear. "The best thing about the beach rule is that from up here, you are all mine. And as the biker girls say, I'm going to ride you like a Harley on a bad stretch of road."

His inhale trembled. His hands pressed into the curves of her waist as this unpredictable temptress lowered onto him.

The jet banked left, passing over a strip of sand marking the coast of central Florida. A vast stretch of blue water extended east to the horizon. Haiti was out there somewhere. Daniel leaned his head against the window, a sheepish grin on his face.

7 Florida

Midmorning on Saturday, the Gulfstream touched down at Kennedy Space Center and Daniel walked with Agent Griffith into the lobby of the Neil Armstrong Operations and Checkout Building. A key part of the Apollo program in the 1960s, the O&C building had recently regained fame as the location of an interdimensional portal capable of sending people to points across the galaxy.

Only a year since first contact, there were already several friendly civilizations willing to meet and share information with humans. Technology and information were the new traded "goods," the modern-day equivalent of cocoa beans and tea carried by colonial ships that at one time had connected Europe to the rest of the world.

Though it was a weekend, three men and one woman waited for them in the lobby. Daniel already knew Augustin Ibarra, the head of NASA's Human Spaceflight division. He was introduced to the other two men, an engineer and his supervisor. But he saved a warm embrace for the only woman in the group.

Marie Kendrick wrapped her arms around his neck. "Good to see you again," she said.

She looked great. Her dark hair was cut shorter, with a flare in the back, and she'd changed her glasses too: a stylish modern look instead of last year's thick frames. Always ready for something new, this young woman would never stay in one place for long.

"I was expecting the engineers, but how'd you get involved?" Daniel asked her.

"Daniel Rice visiting my corner of the world?" She beamed. "I couldn't miss that. Besides, I knew Elliott Becton personally, so maybe I can help."

"No more trips to Ixtlub?" The home planet of the Dancers, a species of graceful aquatic creatures, had become familiar to every person on Earth through multiple NASA missions. Along with Marie, several of the original team members had returned to Ixtlub several times, including the French broadcaster Stephanie Perrin, who had hosted in-depth documentaries that not only provided dramatic video of the watery planet but examined its biology and social structure. Perhaps most important, the continuing missions had established once and for all that the Dancers were neighbors, new friends, trading partners and scientific associates—not alien invaders.

"The Dancers are so last week," Marie said, laughing. "We're prepping for another first-time jump. A fascinating planet orbiting a K-type orange dwarf star in Virgo. Actively volcanic, and only five hundred and fifteen light-years away."

"A flash of yellow light, and you'll be there," Daniel said, feeling the excitement of discovery that she exuded. He was jealous. Marie was having all the fun.

He quickly corrected his thoughts. She'd paid a price on the first mission. The Dancers' original headband had taken a toll, producing a psychosis that Marie spent months learning how to control. She'd been in touch with Daniel once or twice since then and thankfully, hadn't mentioned any recurring hallucinations.

If they got any time alone, he'd ask her how she was doing. For now, it was wonderful to see her enthusiastic smile again.

"I can't wait to meet the Virgans, or whatever we're going to call them. Zin says they look like giant praying mantises, so that's going to be weird. They have a unique way of communicating through vibrating gestures. We're learning a few words. It's really fun."

She spun one hand in a circle with several fingers splayed at odd angles, quivering. "That means 'thank you.' I already know about ten words." She lifted both eyebrows and waited for Daniel's acknowledgment.

He gave it willingly. "I am impressed, Marie. You're on a roll."

"Thanks to you. And Augustin." She put a hand on Augustin Ibarra's shoulder. The older man grinned like a proud father. He might have heard her thank-you speech before. "If we hadn't met at the White House a year ago, and Augustin hadn't asked me to join the Fermilab investigation, none of this would have ever happened."

"Zin's ideas on probabilities notwithstanding?"

"Yeah, Zin's big on probabilities. Heck, to Zin, *I* was a probability. I guess I still am."

"Where is Zin, by the way? Can we bring him into this group?" Daniel looked at Agent Griffith, who had remained quiet as Daniel and Marie reminisced. "Zin may be the one person—er... android, who has all the answers you need."

Marie deferred to Augustin Ibarra for the answer. He shook his head. "Sorry, Zin's in Geneva right now, working with the CERN team. But let's see if our engineers can help with your questions." There were nods all around, and Ibarra waved the group to follow him.

They reconvened in a small room with a sign on the door that read Electronics Test. Filled with computer displays, keyboards, electronics boxes and wires, the room had no chairs and only one hip-high table in its center. Agent Griffith laid the belt and helmet on the table, and the NASA engineers huddled around like kids with a new toy.

"That's a sixty-amp circuit breaker," the engineer said, pointing to one of the components stapled to the belt. "Hell of a lot of current for a twelve-volt circuit." He touched red and black leads from a voltage multimeter to various connectors to confirm his assessment.

He studied the largest component on the belt, an eight-inch-long cylinder that looked like three large flashlight batteries fused together. There was some technical writing on its side.

"It may be one of those new lithium-ion supercapacitors, but I've never seen one this big. They're usually just a button cell, no thicker than a dime." He tapped the cylinder. "I bet that baby packs a wallop when you turn it on."

"We've flipped the on-off switch," Griffith said. "Things on the belt light up, but we don't know what's happening."

The engineer pushed the only switch on the belt, and a white LED illuminated. A second later, the display on the mini-phone near the belt's buckle lit up. One line of text appeared, but upside-down. He rotated the belt for everyone to read.

[becton@localhost /] $

"That's what I figured. He was probably using this little controller to initiate the belt functions. It's just an older-model smartphone with the original OS gutted and replaced with Linux. The display is mounted upside-down so that when you're wearing the belt, you can just lean your head down to control things. Simple, really."

"But what does it do?" Griffith asked.

"Might be a lot," the supervisor answered. He held up the motorcycle helmet, its visor in the down position. "That's no LED. It's one of the transfer chair strobes. We had some spares in inventory, and one is listed as missing."

He tilted the helmet, allowing everyone to peer inside. "You see the integrated circuit?" He pointed to a tiny chip glued next to the yellow light. A narrow sliver of metal connected the two. "That's a Bluetooth chip. The belt is signaling the strobe to fire. This setup is the same as the transfer chairs. Becton just made it portable."

"So, Becton was jumping through quantum space?" Ibarra asked. "Just like our katanauts do?"

"Possibly," the supervisor said. "At the very least, he was freezing time like the transfer chairs do."

The engineer gave a thumbs up. "Cool. There's probably some Linux commands in this controller that communicate to the helmet." He typed with enthusiasm on the small keyboard, and the display responded with a second line:

[becton@localhost /] $ Root commands disabled. Enter password:

"Dang." His joy faded. The colon at the end of the line blinked, awaiting his response. "Yeah, we'll need Becton's password to go any further."

Griffith shook his head. "We got this far at the FBI lab. Unfortunately, our search of Becton's house and belongings didn't turn up any obvious passwords."

"Can you hack into it?" Daniel asked.

The engineer shrugged. "Linux is pretty secure. That's a root command prompt, which means there's nothing but the operating system running. No higher-level software, no internet connection, no back doors. It'd be tough to defeat."

"Try *empros*," Griffith suggested. "Spelled e-m-p-r-o-s."

The engineer typed in the foreign-sounding word, but it was rejected as invalid. "Not a term we use around NASA. What does it mean?"

"I don't know. It was on a diagram we found at Becton's house. Just thought I'd try it. Maybe *flowing empros*? Give that a try."

The engineer typed again with no success.

Marie Kendrick had been standing quietly in the background as the engineers did their job of examination and analysis. But now, she stepped forward waving a hand in the air. "Wait, wait. That word you just used. I've heard it before."

The room became quiet, and she spoke almost to herself.

"Facing *empros*." Marie emphasized the unfamiliar word. "I'm not sure what it means, but I overheard Zin and Becton speaking about it just a few weeks ago."

She addressed Daniel directly. "Zin said he'd have more information for Becton when he got back from Geneva. I remember

Becton seemed disturbed that day, upset that he wasn't part of the CERN team and wasn't getting answers from Zin. Of course, Zin is usually tight-lipped about technology, but now it's beginning to make sense. Becton seemed to want this *empros* thing. It may be what Zin and the CERN team are working on."

She glanced between Griffith and Daniel. "Sorry, but at least some of your answers might be in Geneva after all."

Daniel had worked with her long enough to know that Marie's instincts were good. She'd connected the dots, and the trail led to CERN—and Zin. Marie's tip wouldn't be hard to confirm. One phone call would do it. Easy, when you had access to one of the leading particle physicists in the world.

He owed Nala a call anyway.

8   Switzerland

Daniel sat alone in a break room, his phone against his ear.

Her voice was silky but plaintive. "I missed you. I rolled over and you weren't there."

He'd slipped out before sunrise, Nala still wrapped in the sheets of his bed. "Sorry. Early flight. I didn't want to wake you. Did you find the coffee?"

"Yeah, thanks. I'm on my third cup. Your bagels are crap, but I'll live."

Daniel could picture her sitting at his kitchen table, likely wearing nothing but the oversized dress shirt she'd confiscated from his closet and claimed as her own. Comfortable, from her perspective. Sizzling, from his.

Daniel took a deep breath. "Sorry, but I need to talk to you about something else."

There was a pause on the other end. "Business?"

"Yeah. I guess our relationship is... complicated?" When your lover was also a prominent scientist, there was no avoiding it. They'd never get past the facts of how they'd met.

"What do you need?" she asked, shifting ever so slightly into a more businesslike tone.

"The usual. Guidance from a particle physicist." Daniel detected a smile on the other end of the phone. She wasn't pissed yet.

Daniel relayed the conversation with the NASA engineers and Marie. He left out the parts related to the belt and the coin, figuring these items weren't public knowledge and might end up as FBI evidence of criminal activity.

She listened silently and then answered. "Well, I'm not familiar with that term, *facing empros*. But I can confirm Marie's hunch. There's a CERN team working on quantum time."

"Quantum time?"

"Yeah, you know. Tiny snippets of time. Quantum stuff we can't see or feel because it's too small. Time is like that too. Ever heard of a chronon?"

The name sounded vaguely time-like, but that wasn't enough to give it any definition. "Not really."

"A chronon is a discrete unit of time. A quantum tick of the clock. You can't subdivide time any smaller. Theoretically, it's the time it takes to push an electron to a higher orbital, but it's not like anyone has ever measured that. It's kind of a new frontier in physics."

"But the people at CERN know more?"

"They do. They're the experts. Make sure you talk to a guy named Mathieu Tournier. He knows his stuff. Or maybe Chloe Demers—she's great. I'll text you their phone numbers and let Mathieu know you'll be calling."

"Thanks, I will. And I'm sorry about this whole mess. I didn't want to disappear to Florida."

"You're the famous Dr. Daniel Rice," she said. "I'm getting used to it. I'll catch a flight back to Chicago this afternoon."

"Yeah, I might not make it back to Washington for another day or so."

"You'll be lucky if you get back in a week, I'd say."

"I kind of screwed up the weekend plans, didn't I?"

"Yeah, well." She paused. "You're a long way away and probably about to go a lot farther as soon as you talk to Mathieu. I have no idea why you're even involved in whatever the FBI is investigating, and you clearly don't want to tell me." She sighed. "Yeah, sure, I'd much rather be jumping you under the trees somewhere out on the Appalachian Trail right now, but I guess you can't have everything."

She had a way of letting him know precisely what he was missing. "Um, yeah. Me too. I'll call you when I get home, okay?"

There was another few seconds of silence. "Daniel? Don't forget about me, not even for a chronon." It was more of a plea than a demand, and Daniel detected a smile at the end.

The Appalachian Mountains popped into his mind, a mental image of a lonely trail now beckoning him to get outdoors for an entirely different reason. His answer was sincere. "How could I?"

The phone disconnected. Their conversations always ended that way. Nala never said goodbye.

****

The next phone call, to Mathieu Tournier, was brief. Given the involvement of the FBI, he offered to help, but he said he'd need to personally examine the technology in question. It couldn't be done over the phone.

Marie, Nala, and now Mathieu. They all pointed to Geneva. Zin would be there too, and he might be the most compelling reason of all to go. A long trip, but fortunately for Daniel Rice and Agent Griffith, a Gulfstream G-550 is capable of transatlantic flight.

Griffith made the decision, and Daniel complied.

Eight hours after leaving Florida and with enough sleep to get by, Daniel gazed out the window as the plane descended through a layer of broken clouds. The lush green countryside of the Swiss-French border was punctuated by slate-gray mountains rising in the distance, their sharp peaks and razor edges tinged in white.

The Alps were more than beautiful. For Daniel, they were another list, one of many stored in his head. With more than a hundred peaks above four thousand meters, he couldn't name them all from memory, but that didn't stop him from trying. Mont Blanc, 4810. Weisshorn, 4505. Jungfrau, 4158. Mönch, 4107. Matterhorn, 4478. The list went on and the rote memory test helped to calm the conflicts rampaging through his head.

A message from the future embedded in a coin. A dead man's attempt to manipulate time or space or both. Chronons. Facing empros, whatever that meant. Confusion dominated his thoughts, a sure sign he didn't have enough information to reach the conclusions he sought.

The plane turned to final approach, a fact imagined in Daniel's head and confirmed by the sound of landing gear descending and locking into place. He looked out the window, searching for any signs of the 27-kilometer ring of the Large Hadron Collider. He didn't find any. This astonishingly complex science facility was mostly underground.

Extending from the outskirts of Geneva well into France, the LHC is a magnetic racetrack for two opposing beams of protons. When they collide at near light speed, the protons shred into exotic quantum particles that wink into existence, only to decay into nothing a microsecond later. Modern physics of the very small, staged on a grand scale.

Their Sunday-morning arrival would normally have left them with a day to kill before they'd have a chance to meet with CERN physicists, but connections helped. Mathieu Tournier was at the airport to greet them.

A young man of slight build, with long curly blond hair and a slightly darker beard, Mathieu displayed a nervousness in his manner. "So glad to meet you, Dr. Rice," he said, shaking Daniel's hand and then greeting Agent Griffith. Griffith carried a duffel bag large enough to hold Becton's toys.

Mathieu motioned to a young woman standing a pace behind him. "My laboratory partner, Chloe Demers." With jet-black hair, purple bangs, several piercings and a lightning bolt tattoo near the corner of one eye, she fit the description of emo-punk—at least, as much as Daniel knew about the European style.

Mathieu guided them to a parking lot, switching easily between English when speaking to Daniel and Griffith and French when speaking to Chloe. "Sorry you had to come all this way," Mathieu said as they stopped in front of a three-wheeled minicar.

"Probably necessary," Daniel said. "Of course, a private jet makes travel a lot easier." He peeked through the car's side window. There was a backseat, but filling it with anything more than a small dog and a bag of groceries would be challenging. Their transportation had just shifted from luxurious to cramped.

Chloe pointed a finger to the front passenger seat and pushed Daniel in that direction. "You sit. I sit back. *C'est bien*." Her enchanting French accent didn't match her somewhat severe exterior.

Every seat now claimed, that left Griffith and his large duffel. Somehow, he managed to squeeze in the back, though Chloe ended up more on his lap than the seat. Griffith didn't seem to mind being tangled up, keeping one arm on the duffel and the other around the young woman's waist. She paid no attention, as if climbing onto a man she'd never met was an everyday occurrence. In this tin can, maybe it was.

Mathieu sped out of the parking lot, chatting as fast as he drove. "Your television programs, Dr. Rice. I've watched them all. So wonderful to see science presented in a way that the average person can understand."

"I'm glad you like them. CERN has a great public outreach program too."

"Perhaps." Mathieu nodded, holding one hand on the steering wheel and the other out an open window. Gusts of wind were in the process of rearranging Griffith's silver hair on one side. Chloe pushed the duffel to block the wind and helpfully ran a hand across his head to smooth the hair down.

"*Merci*," Griffith whispered, his grizzled-FBI-veteran eyes darting uncontrollably to the exotic Swiss miss on his knee.

"Unfortunately," Mathieu continued, "CERN also has a history of hiding behind bureaucracy."

Extra dimensions of space had first been discovered at the Large Hadron Collider, but it had been years before anyone on the outside had known about it. Maybe they were repeating the same mistake with *empros*. Daniel still had no idea what the word represented. Nala's suggestion that time, like matter, came in quantum packets was the most information he'd uncovered.

"Is your quantum time project classified?"

Mathieu shook his head. "Not strictly. Not like before. But they have made no announcements."

Daniel tried to ignore the reshuffling of cramped limbs going on in the backseat. "But have you made progress worth announcing?"

Mathieu's grin grew wide, and he took his eyes off the road for a moment, glancing at Daniel. "Oh, yes. I hope to show you. Dr. Rice, you simply won't believe what we can do."

9   Alpha Prime

The Swiss countryside on the outskirts of Geneva was surprisingly green for early October. Like most parts of the world, summer stretched a month longer these days. Vineyards flashed by, ripe grapes hanging from the vines ready to be harvested. Stark rectangular buildings intermixed with the occasional cow pasture or Peugeot dealership, a mashup of suburbs, offices and farms with people and cars everywhere.

As they drove, Daniel explained the purpose of their visit but kept it limited to the function of the makeshift belt. Left unsaid was what a prominent scientist and an FBI agent might do with a belt that could jump to the future. Mathieu didn't ask any questions, though he glanced over his shoulder to Griffith, looking somewhat uncomfortable about the lawman in the backseat of his car. Exotic Chloe, on the other hand, was so relaxed on Griffith's lap that her head rested against his. Of course, there wasn't much room to separate within their doghouse-sized space.

"Where are we heading?" Daniel asked.

Mathieu pointed out the open car window and shouted over the wind. "Over there. At the CERN Meyrin. We're going to our newest lab, Alpha Prime."

Daniel had researched during the flight and recalled reading about the Alpha project, one of many at CERN. Physicists use the protons and electrons blasting from the accelerator to create their negative counterparts: antiprotons and positrons, commonly known as antimatter.

Antimatter instantly annihilates when it comes in contact with ordinary matter. In the comic books, there's always a cataclysmic explosion that takes out half a city, but in reality, antimatter is a relatively benign research material, collected in trace quantities within an intense magnetic field called a Penning trap. When annihilation does occur, it produces sparks too small to see.

"I thought Alpha had been around for a while?" Daniel asked.

"It has, since 2005. But this is Alpha Prime." Mathieu grinned. "Same facility, same antimatter, but a different purpose. Very different. You'll see."

They passed by several tall apartment buildings and through another traffic circle. The green countryside disappeared, replaced by windowless concrete structures and a scattering of 1970s-era blocky office buildings.

"Meyrin." Mathieu wave a hand out the window. Daniel wasn't expecting beauty, but this industrial park was as ugly as they came. Mathieu acknowledged Daniel's lackluster response. "Yes. Not as attractive as Fermilab. We're working on that." He shrugged. "Paint."

One or two of the gray concrete walls had been splashed with colorful designs. A far cry from Wilson Hall or the elegant entryway arch at Fermilab, but it matched the temperament of the very frugal Swiss.

They passed through a security gate and turned down a narrow street marked, Rue A. Einstein. Mathieu parked in front of a stark white building that looked more like a warehouse than a nucleus of science. "Welcome to Alpha Prime."

Griffith squeezed from the tiny backseat like an innertube bulging from a ruptured bicycle tire. Still, he'd probably volunteer for backseat duty on the return trip, assuming Chloe was coming along. She slipped a hand on his arm as they walked to the building's back door entrance.

Or perhaps it was just an ugly front door. Regardless, there was no reception, no public display describing the science that went on inside, just a security card reader and a dull beige hallway.

The hallway opened to a catwalk above a workroom floor. Below them, a chaos of pipes and wires passed through and around a set of aluminum vats that could easily have been lifted from a brewery. Racks of electronics filled one wall, with still more wires pouring out.

How anyone managed to know which wire connected to each component was a mystery.

Mathieu reached over a railing and pointed to one of the beer brewing vats lying on its side. Huge chrome-colored pipes protruded from both ends. Some of the pipes were covered in white frost, indicating cryogenics, a common need in high-energy physics. "That's the Penning trap where the antimatter is held. The trap itself is an interior brass pipe only ten centimeters in diameter. The rest is supporting apparatus."

"How long does it take to produce the antimatter you need?" Daniel asked.

"It's never-ending," Mathieu answered. "As long as the accelerator is running, we're creating antimatter. It annihilates almost as fast as we can make it. Zin is helping us with that issue."

Two flights of stairs brought them below ground and to a door marked *Laboratoire de Basse Énergie.*

"Zin is probably in here," Mathieu said, opening the door.

The room was dark, and flipping the light switch didn't illuminate any androids, though it wouldn't surprise Daniel if Zin worked in the dark when he was alone.

"Well, he's around somewhere," Mathieu said. "He doesn't take any days off. I'm not even sure what he does with his free time."

"*Doug Dug,*" Chloe said, a smirk on her face. "I watch him at lunch. He's good!"

"Ahh." Mathieu tapped the side of his head. "That would explain a lot."

"Huh?" Daniel had no idea what they were talking about.

"It's a video game for mobile phones," Mathieu explained with the wave of a hand. "Zin seems interested in our time wasters."

Chloe said, "He tried *Candy Crush* and… uh, that other one…" She looked up at the ceiling. "American game. You know, with the red and blue birds."

"*Angry Birds*?" Daniel asked.

"Yes! That one. He liked, but, uh… always back to *Doug Dug*."

For an advanced android whose job was to coordinate contact between intergalactic species, Zin could be surprisingly simple. The An Sath galactic encyclopedia identified two dozen known civilizations scattered across several thousand light-years, and Zin had apparently visited them all. Yet, as Marie had explained, Zin was enamored with everything human.

"Can you text him, or will that interrupt the game?" Daniel asked dryly.

Mathieu pulled out a phone and typed. "Sure, no problem. For Zin, texting is built-in. The messages go directly into his head."

"Perfect. Leaves the phone free for games."

Agent Griffith, looking taller now that he was out of the miniature car, pulled Becton's belt from his duffel bag and placed it on the lab's sole workbench near the center of the small room. He hovered nearby like a security guard in a high-end jewelry shop.

Chloe was drawn to it like a magnet, her eyes as big as saucers. "*La ceinture!*"

Mathieu joined her. They pointed to various components, speaking in French and sometimes arguing. When Griffith added the motorcycle helmet, Chloe lit up. "*Ah, la lumière!*" She pointed to the light under the visor and Mathieu nodded.

Chloe turned to Griffith and spoke in halting English. "This, uh… *ceinture*, um, this belt. It is, uh… quite amazing. Your friend, he is brilliant."

"Not my friend," Griffith answered. "And no longer alive. Whatever this belt does, it probably killed him."

Chloe's lips pouted, her nose ring pushing up. "Too bad."

Daniel said, "The NASA engineers thought it was a portable version of a portal transfer chair, but we have unconfirmed information that it may be more than that."

"Definitely, more," said Mathieu. "When Zin gets here, we'll get his opinion. But I see several of the electronics components that we use here, and they're laid out in a very similar circuit. Offhand, I would say that Mr. Becton knew at least as much as we do in this laboratory. Perhaps more."

"We checked his email and browser history," Griffith said, "and found no evidence that he had any contact with this lab. Are you saying that he did?"

"No," Mathieu said. "No contact that I know about. But there are only a few ways the electronic circuits required for this function could be arranged. Becton was a NASA engineer, right? With access to the alien technology?" He pointed to the light affixed to the helmet. "It's possible he came to the same conclusions as we have. The primary difference is that we are controlling time from scratch using antimatter. Becton borrowed directly from Zin."

Mathieu must have noticed the blank looks on their faces. "Yes, yes. What we do here at Alpha Prime is all very cryptic to you, I can see. But never fear, I can make it clear."

Mathieu spoke to Chloe in French at some length. Daniel's command of the language was limited, but he picked out the shared words: dimensions, quantum, and *temps* or time. Then there was that new word. *Empros.*

"In English, please?" Griffith asked.

"Yes, yes, sorry," Mathieu said. "How to begin?" He lowered his head in thought. "First, you already understand the additional dimensions of space? Quantum space? We experience three dimensions, but there are more we cannot see. For example, a fourth dimension with directions named *ana* and *kata*?"

So far, this was nothing new. The jumps through the portal used quantum space, an unseen dimension but just as real as the other three.

"But what of time?" Mathieu asked rhetorically.

"Time is time. A continuous flow, like a river." Daniel responded.

"Yes, we think of time like a river. It flows downstream, and we ride along in the forward direction. Of course, we also understand there is a backward direction too—upstream in the river analogy—even if we can't flow in that direction. Backward feels just as real to us because of our memories."

Mathieu folded his hands together and paused in thought. "But time isn't this simple. There is a second dimension, different than forward and backward."

"*Empros?*"

"Yes, *empros*. Or more completely, *empros* and *piso*. They are Greek words meaning fore and back, and they represent a direction of time unlike anything we know. Theoretical physicists worldwide have long suggested such a dimension might exist. They derive it mathematically from string theory, producing what some physicists call M-Prime theory."

Chloe nodded as Mathieu spoke. No doubt she could provide the same explanation, if mostly in French.

Mathieu continued. "Empros time is just as real as forward time. We discovered this fact here at CERN by comparing matter and antimatter. We studied the differences between hydrogen and its opposite, antihydrogen. We found that antihydrogen ions decay somewhat faster, producing a free positron more quickly than their ordinary matter counterparts. Measuring this difference is not easy to do when theory told us that quantum ticks are only 10^{-21} seconds. That's a billionth of a trillionth of a second."

"A chronon?" Daniel asked, recalling Nala's introduction to this relatively unexplored branch of science.

"Yes. A chronon. The smallest possible tick of the clock. It turns out that positrons flow more easily in the empros direction of time. And this is how we discovered it. Independently of Zin, I might add. However, Zin confirmed our results and has been working with us ever since."

"You're saying that right now, matter is flowing forward *and* flowing empros?" Daniel asked.

"Yes!" Chloe exclaimed. "Both." She tugged on Griffith's shirtsleeve and pointed with excitement to the belt on the table. If she'd figured it out, their mission to Geneva was already successful.

Mathieu continued. "Technically yes. Both. But understand the differences in flow. Forward flows like the river. Empros is more like a slow leak. It's why we don't notice empros. Forward flows a billion times faster. Perhaps the river is not the best analogy. Think of it more like a fire hydrant. I think you have much the same device in America, right?"

Daniel nodded.

"A fire hydrant has two openings sealed by caps and a valve on top. If you attach a hose to one opening and open the valve, the water flows primarily in one direction, even if the cap on the other opening leaks a few drops."

"A better analogy," Daniel said. "And you say that Zin has now confirmed your discovery?"

Mathieu nodded. "Completely. There are two dimensions of time."

"*J'adore Zin,*" Chloe said, her large eyes glistening. Daniel was able to pick up the simple French but wasn't sure why she would declare her love for the android. Chloe was a strange one. Some scientists are.

"Sounds like Zin," Daniel said. "He and Core tell us nothing until we're on the right track."

The lab door opened, and the android himself stepped into the room.

"Speak of the devil," Mathieu said. Whether a coincidence or because Zin could hear through doors would be an excellent topic over beers at the end of the day. Regardless, the android's timing was impeccable.

Zin's physical form was both startling and familiar. Bronze in color from a flexible layer of metal overlaying mostly human features. A flat face with flat eyes that flicked left and right, and a congenial expression, even if his ever-present smile was sometimes overdone. He now wore a semblance of clothing over his shiny exterior. A blue vinyl band covered his waist, flexible enough to wrap around his body, but stiff enough to form an unwrinkled surface. It looked a little like a mini-skirt. On one side was a pocket that held a smartphone.

Zin presented one of his three-fingered hands. "Dr. Rice, so wonderful to see you again."

"And you, Zin. Your ears must be burning." An idiom, but it was always interesting to see how Zin might react.

He cocked his head toward one shoulder, even though his thought processes probably didn't require him to mimic human behavior. "I believe the expression is used when one person is talking about another person who is not present?"

Mathieu said, "Yes, sorry, Zin. We were just explaining to Dr. Rice and Agent Griffith the extra dimension of time and your part in our work."

"Ah, yes," Zin said. "I'm so glad that humans have uncovered this science. I dislike withholding, but it's for the best. You really are doing quite well. Did you know that there are seven other scientifically literate civilizations that have not yet discovered the science of time?"

"We won't tell," Mathieu offered.

"I'm so glad you agree. This information is not found within An Sath for many good reasons."

"And you can only convey information that is within An Sath?"

"Or confirm what you have discovered for yourselves. Luckily, humans are quick learners."

"We have our moments," Daniel said. "So, what do you think of the belt?"

While Zin studied the belt still lying on the workbench, Mathieu responded to Daniel's question. "At the very least, it will collapse forward."

"Meaning?" Daniel asked.

"Meaning, forward time would reduce to a trickle, the same as empros. Both openings of the fire hydrant have been covered by their caps. Ticks become so small that forward time is essentially frozen, and the wearer of the belt goes into a state of suspended animation."

Daniel nodded. "Like the Soyuz astronauts rescued a year ago?"

"Yes," Zin said, his ten-second examination of the belt apparently complete. "Collapsing forward time to its quantum state is highly useful to exit four-dimensional space, as you saw with your astronauts. It's how the portal works, something you've experienced yourself, Dr. Rice."

Zin picked up the belt and ran a metal finger along one of the wires. "But this device may do more. It may adjust temporal frequencies. Even *empros* frequencies. And flowing empros is when things get really interesting."

10 Empros

Those words again. *Flowing empros.*

Daniel asked, "Didn't you say we're already flowing empros? The trickle from the fire hydrant?" Mathieu's explanation of quantum time was lengthy, but details never escaped Daniel's attention.

"Yes," Mathieu answered. "We flow forward and empros simultaneously, but only one direction is noticeable."

"Forward."

"Yes, forward. But here at Alpha Prime, we can flip this pattern. We collapse forward to a quantum state and expand empros to a natural flow rate. In the fire hydrant analogy, we are moving the hose from one opening to the other. Most of the water now flows in a different direction, even if the closed cap leaks a bit."

Daniel's mind whirred. A second dimension of time? Equivalent to the first? He could think of a hundred questions. "But what would it—"

Mathieu interrupted. "You didn't come all the way to Geneva to hear my lecture on quantum time," Mathieu said. "I have a much better idea. Experience flowing empros for yourself." He grinned, eyeing Daniel and Agent Griffith for a response.

"You can show us flowing empros?" Daniel asked. Zin stood behind Mathieu, his arms folded, apparently out of the conversation. This latest turn toward the bizarre was being played out human to human.

"Better. I can take you there. Right now."

Taking them into another dimension of time sounded a bit more immersive than showing. "What exactly does flowing empros entail?"

Mathieu waved his hands as if Daniel's obvious concern was of no consequence. "Words cannot prepare you for what you will experience. It's quite the adventure. Surprising—shocking, even. But don't worry, it won't hurt you."

Chloe nodded her agreement. Even Zin tipped his head.

That Mathieu had the capability to alter the flow of time was no longer in question. Zin's agreement erased any doubt, but that didn't make the proposed adventure in alternate reality any less intimidating.

Agent Griffith stepped backward, using Chloe as a barrier between himself and Daniel. "You're on your own, Dr. Rice. I'll stay right here."

Mathieu's mischievous smile broadened. "Staying *here* is not the question, Mr. Griffith. We will all stay right here. The choice is whether you wish to remain in the *now*."

"All the same," Griffith responded, backing up further, "I'll stay."

"Very well. And you, Dr. Rice?"

Daniel had witnessed some strange things since becoming involved in quantum physics, but two CERN physicists and an advanced alien android seemed to be promoting a new definition of strange. Still, Daniel's caution was losing out to his curiosity.

"You've done this before? Flowing empros?"

"Daily," Mathieu responded. "It's our primary investigation in this lab." Chloe nodded her agreement.

"Okay, I'm in." It was the kind of impulsive decision Nala would make. She might be affecting him more than he realized.

"Excellent," Mathieu said, rubbing his hands together. He spoke to Chloe. "*Restes ici?*"

"*Oui*," she responded. With one hand, she gripped the cloth of her blouse and tightened it around her neck. She shook her other finger at Mathieu accusingly. "*Mais ne jouez plus à tes jeux*," she scolded.

Turning to Daniel, she explained. "Mathieu plays empros games. Very funny. But not this time."

67

It wasn't clear what their little conflict was about, but Chloe didn't explain further, and Mathieu waved it off. "It will be just you and me, then, Dr. Rice. Come."

He guided Daniel to the far side of the lab, where a row of cloth seat cushions had been affixed vertically to the wall. Armrests jutted out on either side of each cushion at elbow height.

Mathieu pointed to the setup. "Our version of the transfer chairs at the Kennedy Space Center. We have no need for a portal because we don't move through space. But otherwise, it's similar technology—and probably very much like the belt you have brought."

Five in all, the standup stations looked like the slots at one of those whirling amusement park rides that pinned its victims to the wall with centrifugal force. Daniel was beginning to wonder if impulsive decisions were best left to impulsive girlfriends.

Griffith remained behind Chloe. He seemed interested in the demonstration, perhaps more so now that Daniel was the random audience member called onstage by the magician. Zin had taken a seat, with his attention refocused on his smartphone. He was either allowing the humans to enjoy their scientific discoveries unaided by alien guidance, or he was playing more video games.

Mathieu positioned his back against one of the cushions and Daniel did the same. Mathieu flipped a joystick into a vertical position on the right armrest. Daniel's slot didn't have anything equivalent, so he simply placed both arms on the armrests.

"Just stand," Mathieu told him. "Nothing else for you to do. Chloe will initialize, and I will control from there."

Across the small room, Chloe typed at a workstation keyboard. She looked up. "*Veux la balle?*"

"*Oui,*" Mathieu answered. "What demonstration of quantum time would be complete without it?"

Chloe opened a drawer and pulled out a dark blue rubber ball. It looked like it might be used on a handball or squash court. *"Prêt?"* she asked.

Mathieu wrapped his hand around the joystick, his thumb hovering over a red button at its top. "Yes, we're ready." Daniel pressed his body against the cushion and gripped the armrests, though he had no idea why it might help.

Chloe tossed the ball directly toward Daniel. He instinctively lifted one hand to catch it just as a strong yellow light flashed from above. He flinched at the bright light, blinked rapidly, and expected to be smacked in the face by the rubber ball.

But that didn't happen.

He opened his eyes, the glare of the flash fading. Just a few feet in front of him, the ball was frozen in midair.

"Holy hell." Daniel took a few rapid breaths, waiting for gravity to do its job, but the ball just hung there.

Mathieu released the red button, grinning. "Welcome to empros."

Ten seconds passed, and the ball still hung motionless.

Daniel stepped forward tentatively. His mind raced, inquisitive, but in awe of the amazing new reality. He turned in a circle beneath the ball hanging just above his head. No hidden wires or nearly invisible threads. No air currents. No sense of static electricity.

Daniel touched the ball. It wiggled. He pushed a finger against it and the ball slid sideways but remained in the air. He grabbed the ball between his fingers, the motion feeling no different than if he'd taken it from a shelf. He turned it over in his hand, pushing the rubber and looking for whatever secrets it might hold. Nothing jumped out. A normal rubber ball.

"This can't be real," Daniel said, and he meant it. The established laws of physics shuffled one by one through his mind.

Mathieu's grin grew larger. "Look around you. It's not just the ball."

Chloe stood on the other side of the lab, her arm frozen in an underhanded throw, her eyes staring straight ahead. Griffith was similarly stiff, and Zin sat motionless in a chair holding his phone. The light in the lab was strangely dim.

Daniel walked over to Chloe and waved a hand in front of her eyes. She didn't move. He snapped his fingers near one eye. She didn't blink. Chloe's mouth was slightly open, but she wasn't breathing.

"Remarkable," he whispered.

"She is suspended," Mathieu said. He stepped close and caressed the side of her cheek. "Chloe flows forward. We flow empros. For her, empros hardly exists—a clock that ticks much too slowly to notice. For us it is just the opposite. Empros has expanded a billion times but forward ticks are now measured by tiny chronons. Two independent time frames. She doesn't even know we're here."

Mathieu took the rubber ball from Daniel, held it in front of Chloe's eyes and released it. Any self-respecting object with mass would have dropped to the floor, but this one hung in midair. Daniel pulled it from the air and repeated the stunt himself. The ball simply would not fall.

"This makes no sense," Daniel said, his mind racing. "Time has no bearing on gravity." His scientific mind grappled with the foreign concepts to fit them into the reality he knew.

Newton's law of gravitation, $F = G\, m_1\, m_2\, /\, r^2$. The equation had no component of time. Einstein's formulation of gravity was no different. Space deformed by a large mass attracted a smaller mass. In both cases, time wasn't a factor.

Yet there it was, a gravity-defying ball, as frozen as Chloe.

"The ball bothers you more than her frozen arm?" Mathieu asked. "But why should it? Both are objects in motion. The ball is still moving, still tracing a parabolic arc across the room, just as Chloe's arm is still moving. The law of gravity has not changed. Neither has momentum. But the ticks of the forward clock are now minuscule. We simply don't notice the motion."

Daniel nodded, beginning to rearrange his thoughts of how physics worked to accommodate the unusual frame of reference.

Mathieu plucked the ball from the air. "You and I apply a new force within empros time, and the ball responds. Yet the force Chloe applied in forward time is still there. We can't see the ball falling, just as Chloe cannot see us."

He lifted Chloe's blouse and tucked the ball under her bra, copping a feel along the way.

"Hey!" Daniel slapped Mathieu's roving hand away from the frozen woman's figure and frowned in deep disapproval. "Get a grip."

Mathieu laughed. "I'm sorry, it's a game we play. Once, I removed her blouse and brassiere entirely. Moving her arms was surprisingly easy. A scientific test to determine the pliability of the human body during time suspension."

Daniel shook his head. "It sounded like Chloe doesn't think much of your games."

Mathieu shrugged. "Yes, it was extremely rude of me. I apologized to her, and she has forgiven me. Almost." He patted her on the butt. "But it was a good test. It proved the body is not really frozen; not like a rigid mannequin. Any empros-facing force will move matter, including human bodies, just as you would expect. Watch this."

He lifted Chloe's forearm, bending it at the elbow, twisted her hand toward his face and pushed each finger down except the middle finger. "You see. She's flipping me off for my past indiscretion. Serves me right."

Daniel pushed Chloe's arm down to her side. "Sorry," he said to her motionless face.

He turned to Mathieu. "We're clearly in a privileged position outside of normal time. What's happening down at the atomic level? How are photons still moving? How can we be separated in time, but share the same space? I can think of a lot of scientific tests that don't involve abusing your lab partner."

Mathieu shrugged. "Chloe and I have done those tests and more. We have our fun along the way, but perhaps Americans are more sensitive." He reached into Chloe's blouse, removed the ball and placed it in the air as if he'd hung a jacket on a hook. "Now, shall I answer your questions?"

Their breakthrough was astonishing even if it opened the door to time-based voyeurism, among other forms of reckless behavior. A thief with this technology would be hard to catch. A terrorist, unstoppable. "Yes, let's talk science. But leave her alone."

Mathieu shrugged and returned to the standup stations along the wall. "When I pressed the trigger, forward time collapsed to a quantum flow and the empros direction of time expanded. But the change affected only a narrow strip of three-dimensional space along the wall that included you, me, the air that surrounded us, and that single lamp." Daniel hadn't noticed the light fixture attached to the wall, but it was the only source of light in the room.

"Light is still emitted by the ceiling lamps, but those photons are now bouncing around this room in slow motion. Their velocity hasn't changed. Each photon still moves at light speed, three hundred thousand kilometers per second. But from our perspective, a single second has now stretched to almost forty years. Without the battery-operated lamp on the wall, we would be in near darkness. Yes, some photons will still reach your eyes, but while flowing empros, forward-flowing light is very dim. The same for the air. Most of the oxygen atoms you're breathing right now are flowing forward, but they can still be absorbed by the hemoglobin in your blood, which is flowing empros. Strange, isn't it? To think about the parts of your own body that are time-dependent."

It was strange. But breathing atoms moving in a different direction of time also didn't sound very healthy. Daniel nodded toward the rigid bodies of Chloe and Agent Griffith. "What do they see?"

Mathieu shrugged. "Nothing. From their perspective, less than a millionth of a second has passed since I pressed the button. Even with our finest instruments, we cannot detect the motion of objects flowing empros—that is, you and me. We occupy the same space, but we're moving much too fast for them to see us."

Mathieu strode purposefully across the room, grabbing the ball from its parking place in the air and pushing it into the back pocket in Griffith's pants. "You and I will step back into the stations, and I'll reset the flow of time, collapsing empros and expanding forward once more. And Agent Griffith will wonder how the ball managed to land in his pocket."

"Quantum space and now quantum time." Daniel took a deep breath and blew it out, briefly wondering how the eddy of air he'd produced would ever sort out which molecules flowed in each direction of time. "Mind-blowing stuff."

Where would the discovery lead? And who would control access to the technology? An empros-flowing terrorist could be stopped, but only with empros-flowing security forces. The same was true for an enemy force flowing empros. Whole battles might be fought in empros time without anyone else even being aware.

Mind-blowing, yes. But dangerous too.

11 Forward

The bright yellow light flashed once more. Daniel blinked a few times and let his eyes adjust.

He looked around. The room was brighter, photons moving at full speed again. Chloe stood ten feet away, grinning at Daniel as if they had just shared an inside joke. "*Bienvenue*. Welcome back," she said.

Daniel took a few steps forward. Chloe's eyes blinked normally. The slight motion in her chest revealed each breath. Her grin widened. Griffith watched from behind her, the look of anticipation still on his face. He reached up to scratch his head. Griffith didn't understand what had just happened. Chloe did.

Daniel approached the young woman as he'd done a few minutes before. Empros minutes? Forward minutes? This insanity would be hard to get used to.

She gently rubbed her right shoulder, and Daniel understood why. "I'm sorry, Chloe, I believe I made a beginner's mistake by repositioning your throwing arm. I hope I didn't hurt you." Mathieu remained mute regarding his part of the transgression.

She shrugged, still smiling. "A spasm, uh, like the muscle..." She made a motion with her fingers as if she were squeezing something.

"Contracts?" Daniel offered.

She nodded. "Little bit, yes. Contracts. On its own."

"Really, I'm very sorry." He felt ashamed, and not just because he had touched her without permission. He had also been a witness to Mathieu's indiscretions. She would have no way of knowing what had happened during what, from her perspective, had been a blink of the eye.

"It's okay." She stopped rubbing, her arm apparently unhurt. Her eyes lit up. "Did you catch the ball?" Griffith stepped closer, his brow wrinkled.

"In a way, yes," Daniel said. "Pretty easy, almost like the ball was waiting for me." He grinned, and Chloe grinned back. The personal connection made him feel better.

Her eyes sparkled with enthusiasm. "Fun, yes?"

"Incredible. Remarkable. How is it that you haven't announced this technology?"

"What?" asked Griffith, dumbfounded by their conversation.

"Oh, look," Chloe said, twisting Griffith around and pointing to the rubber ball protruding from his back pocket.

Griffith reached around and pulled it out. "How'd it get there?" He held the ball up for inspection.

Chloe scowled at Mathieu, her look of scorn changing to a grudging smile. "Another game. This one a little bit nicer."

Griffith wasn't processing any of it. "Huh? Did I miss something?"

Chloe took the ball, held it at the tips of her fingers and pretended to grab it with the other hand, only to flip her wrist and hide the ball. She held out an empty hand under Griffith's nose, a practiced demonstration of a magician's sleight of hand.

She spoke to Griffith, her English mixed with hand motions. "You and I? We saw the ball disappear. Where did it go?" She pointed to Daniel.

"I plucked it out of the air," Daniel explained. "Probably in less time than it took the photons to reach your eye. Did you see anything?"

Griffith still looked as perplexed as a fourth-grader examining college math on the blackboard. "Well, Chloe threw the ball to you. The light flashed. That's it." He felt his pants pocket. "I don't get it."

"I put it there," Mathieu offered. "Daniel and I were gone for about five minutes. Flowing empros."

Griffith's brow lowered. "No. Really?"

"Yes," said Chloe, beaming with excitement.

"Yes," Daniel confirmed. Griffith seemed disturbed by this idea, but he didn't have any further questions. A good sign he was coming around.

"They are telling you the truth, Agent Griffith," said Zin, still sitting in a chair against the wall. He returned his phone to the pocket at his waist and joined the group. "And now that Dr. Rice has returned to ordinary time, I believe we should change the conversation." He reached out to the lab workbench and lifted Becton's leather belt.

"Your engineer in Florida did exceptionally well. I may have inadvertently given him one or two hints, but he produced much of this himself, mistakes and all. This circuit, in particular." His finger hovered over a rectangular array of integrated circuit boards on one side of the belt. A needlelike probe extended from the tip of his finger to touch a metal connection point. A second later, the tiny probe retracted. "These electronics almost certainly manage time compression, though the circuitry lacks any safety overrides."

"Then it *is* possible?" Mathieu asked. "Time compression?" Daniel had noticed the word as well, and it wasn't the first time someone had explained that compression was the key to understanding a quantum technology.

Zin's head bobbed up and down like a perfectly timed machine. "Now that compression has been discovered, I can explain further." Zin stretched the belt to its full length while Mathieu and Chloe drew close like students gathering around the master. Daniel and Griffith stood a row behind.

"Will it compress forward time?" Mathieu asked, nodding to the belt. Chloe's eyes were wide, echoing the question.

"Based on my circuitry analysis, almost certainly," Zin said, "but we should test it to be sure."

"Explain, please," Griffith asked.

"I'd be happy to, Agent Griffith," Zin said. Griffith looked a bit startled at his first conversation with an android, but most everyone had that reaction. "You see, flowing empros is what mathematicians call the trivial case. I don't mean to say it's unimportant, just that it's the simplest form of time manipulation."

Zin handed the belt to Mathieu and walked over to a white board hanging on one wall. "May I?" Mathieu nodded.

Zin examined the available marker colors, choosing green, and began drawing. "The first thing you must understand is that time is a frequency." He drew a series of perfect sine waves and labeled the axis Forward with what looked like practiced calligraphy. He'd make a good graphic artist.

"What we experience as the flow of time is a physical wave with crests and troughs, essentially the ticks of the clock. We say that time *passes*, as this wave flows past us. What's more, the wave of time has a natural frequency, set by the universe."

Daniel held up a hand, but Zin waved him off. "Yes, yes. A frequency of time seems nonsensical because frequency, by definition, is cycles per unit of time. But what time? We must compare time against something else." He paused, probably for effect, because the answer was obvious. "We need a second dimension of time, and that's exactly what the universe provides. Humans call it empros, and once flowing in that direction, we can directly observe the frequency of forward time."

He began another drawing, this one more elaborate than the first. He drew two sine waves in two colors, one wave greatly elongated.

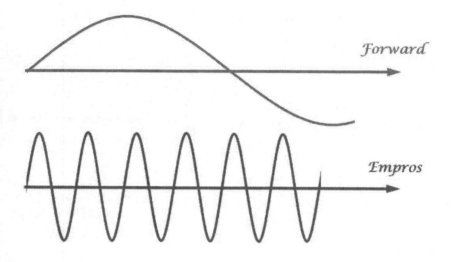

"This is what we see when flowing empros, as Mathieu and Dr. Rice have just experienced." He pointed to the green drawing, labeled Forward. "The forward frequency is stretched out while empros time flows at its natural rate. Forward hasn't stopped flowing, but the vibration of its wave is too slow to feel."

Mathieu chimed in. "Like a plucked string on a bass. The frequency can be too low to hear." His calm expression matched Chloe's, making it clear that Zin had already gone through this with them.

"Yes, your musical instruments make good comparisons. When plucked, a guitar or violin string produces a higher pitch than a bass. But for dimensions of time, the difference in frequency is far more extreme. While flowing empros, forward frequency has dropped by a factor of more than one billion." Zin looked at Griffith, who hadn't said anything yet. "Good so far?"

Griffith shrugged.

"I can slow down, if you wish," Zin said.

"No, no," Griffith answered. "Keep going. I'm sure Dr. Rice is getting more of this than I am."

Daniel had no problem keeping up. In fact, his mind raced ahead to where Zin might be heading. Time compression had certainly caught the attention of Mathieu and Chloe.

Zin's brow ridge lifted, mimicking that human *are you ready for the big reveal* look. "Time is more than just a wave with a frequency. Just like space, time has a fabric. A background that gives the flow its definition. We might say that time's fabric is the shoreline of the river, or the hose connected to the fire hydrant to use Mathieu's example. Without this fabric, how can a flow rate have meaning?"

Daniel nodded. "I see what you mean. Flow must be relative to a fixed background." Daniel pointed to the graphs. "In a way, you've already drawn it. The axis of the graph."

"Precisely, Dr. Rice," Zin continued. He tapped the marking pen in his hand to the green arrow. "If you agree that time must have both a flow and a fabric, then I can now share the secret of compression." He flicked his brow up and down several times. "I do enjoy sharing, though I'm only allowed once you have made the fundamental discoveries on your own."

"The belt?" Chloe asked.

"Yes, I'll use the belt as my excuse, though you have been on the brink of discovering compression here in this lab. Your test results from last week?"

"Ah, yes," Chloe answered. "The fluctuations we observed when we changed polarity!"

"Yes, your experiment tapped into the fabric of time. Allow me to show you." He picked up the marking pens and started drawing once more.

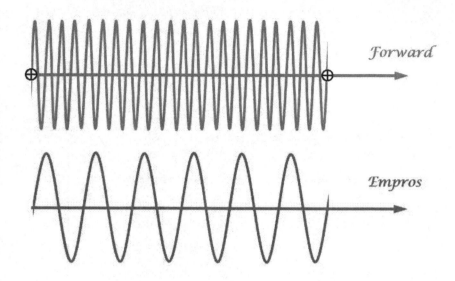

Forward

Empros

"In this case, we're still flowing empros, but we see a higher frequency for forward time. That's compression. Forward ticks of the clock are now faster than normal. But how did we get that compression?" He looked around at blank stares from the physicists. Daniel didn't know the answer either, but he was pretty sure they were all about to find out.

"It's simple. Lower the frequency for empros. The frequency for forward must increase. The two dimensions of time are tied to each other. It's the same as space, a subject you've already mastered. You even know the mathematical relationship."

Mathieu snapped to attention. "The Spiegel formula! It also works for time?" The mathematical formula had become famous, just as Nala had predicted a year before. It precisely related expansion and compression but so far had only been used in the science of four-dimensional space.

"It does," Zin said. "Time is the same as space. Your Dr. Einstein was quite correct when he created the term space-time. Many of the most advanced scientists in the galaxy believe that time and space are two aspects of the same phenomenon."

"You're saying that with the Spiegel formula, we can compress forward time to anything we want?" Mathieu asked. "Bring the future closer to us?"

Zin looked like a proud father. He was clearly enjoying the interaction that came with his lesson. "Some call it jumping to the future, but your description is more accurate. Once compressed, the future comes to you. Instantly, I might add."

"Like a thirty-second skip forward button on a video player?" Mathieu asked.

"Yes, exactly. Tweak empros just a little and you'll see dramatic compressions of future time. Jump a day, a week, or many years. Whatever you want. It's quite easy to control once you understand the mathematics. Any calculator could give you the precision to jump to almost any future date."

There was such a calculator rigged to Becton's belt, and it included a numeric keypad. Daniel tuned out the others as the details of this unlikely mission fell into place. Like quantum space, compression was the key—the crown jewel, as Nala had pointed out more than a year ago. Compression, as Nala had said, opened doors. If Zin was correct, time was the same, and a door leading to the future was now wide open.

With Zin cooperative, Daniel wasn't going to let the opportunity for more specific questions slip by. "Okay, let's say we jumped thirty years into the future. What would we see?"

Zin held a finger in the air. "Well, I've never done it myself. It's tricky business, and I neglected to mention a key detail."

There's always a catch.

He returned to his drawing and pointed to two black circles bracketing the green wave. "You're familiar with a standing wave?" Zin glanced around at his audience. "It's simply a wave that has been constricted by a fixed point on the ends. What humans call *nodes*. The wave moves from one end to the other, is reflected by the node and causes an interference going in the opposite direction. At certain frequencies, a standing wave is the result, a wave that doesn't move at all."

"You can see the same thing when two kids wiggle a jump rope or a slinky between them," Mathieu offered.

"Or a guitar string," Zin said. "The fastenings at either end of the guitar force the string to vibrate at a particular frequency. That's a standing wave."

A narrow smile crept across the android's lips. "Standing waves can be created in time, too. Pin the time wave to the background fabric with two nodes and you'll force the wave to oscillate in place. Now you have an anchor point and a destination. You could flow empros, then compress forward, and step out into a frozen world of the future, very much like Mathieu's demonstration."

"The space hasn't changed?"

"No, just the time. Space and time are independent."

Daniel exchanged a glance with Griffith. It seemed the science provided exactly the answer they needed. Daniel didn't doubt what Zin was saying. He'd just witnessed the remarkable capability firsthand. But he still had more questions.

"So how do you get back?"

"Once you've set an anchor point, just decompress, return to forward time and you'll be right back where you started."

"That suggests there's no backward time travel," Mathieu said.

"Correct," Zin said. "I wish I could visit your Dr. Einstein. I'd love to meet him, but you can't set an anchor point in the past. Only from today forward."

Zin's answer made sense, and not only because most scientists had already ruled out travel to the past as being logically flawed. It also answered the question of why there were no time travelers from the future. If travel to the past was impossible, no one from the future could accomplish it either.

Becton hadn't broken the rule. He really wasn't from the future, as the FBI had already determined. If he had jumped to the future, he must have returned to his own anchor point.

The possibilities for repeating Becton's achievement were beginning to line up, but if Daniel did as the FBI asked, his personal safety was on the line. "You mentioned tricky business."

"Time compression is not without its dangers," Zin replied. "For example, compression of a time dimension is independent of flow. While that seems simple, the implications are not. As I said, the normal procedure is to flow empros, then compress forward. But once compressed, you wouldn't want to flow forward into the future. That's a one-way trip. You'd be stranded. Any attempt to decompress would result in a devastating affect that humans might call *snapback*."

"Which means?" Mathieu asked.

Zin paused in thought. "Imagine compressing time like tightening a string on your guitar. Flowing forward is like plucking that string. You'll hear a high-frequency sound, but the wire might also snap. Flowing forward while time is compressed is almost certain to result in snapback once you return to your anchor point."

Griffith perked up. "What exactly would snapback look like for a human?"

Zin thought for moment. "Extensive damage to the atomic structure in your body, especially to the atoms in motion, for example, the liquids flowing through your body."

Griffith hummed. "Bleeding from the ears and nose?" He was clearly paying attention.

"Yes, hemorrhage could be a possible symptom, though the damage would be to the internal circulation system."

Griffith glanced at Daniel. His point was made. Hemorrhage fit the description for Elliott Becton's death. Zin had even pointed to one of the belt's components, declaring it to be lacking any safety controls.

"Please understand, there are good reasons why the science of time is not included in An Sath. The ways in which it can be misused are varied. For anyone willing to manipulate time, death by snapback is probably the least of your dangers."

"And the worst?" Griffith asked.

Zin hesitated. "It depends on the species and their tendency for self-destruction. The Litian-nolos, who inhabit multiple planets in what you call the Beehive star cluster, regularly jump forward as a method to guide their decision making. But they are careful to isolate the gain in knowledge among specific individuals they call Time Mentors. So far, it seems to be working for them."

Zin let his head drop, shaking it back and forth. "I wish I could say the same for the poor Sandzvallons of Gamma Carinae, who also were manipulators of time. Such a tragedy. A robust forward-thinking species. They had so much potential."

12 Italy

Agent Griffith pulled the vibrating phone from his pocket. It was a text message, one that he had expected might be coming any minute.

Sunday, October 8, 2023
FBI National Security Branch
Elizabeth Yarborough, Assistant Director

Griffith:
Event 2, train derailment near Potenza Italy occurred at 10:19 AM local, as predicted. Tel Aviv still seeking suspect for event 3.

I have advised POTUS and staff concerning Operation Tourniquet. Proceed to London immediately. If Rice is uncooperative or attempts to delay, the Chicago office is standing by to arrest Ms. Pasquier on your authorization.

Good news, in an odd way. The train derailment sealed the deal. Full cooperation from Daniel Rice was now almost certain.

But if not, one of the subjects of last year's Fermilab investigation, Nala Pasquier, had been charged with multiple counts of disclosing classified material. The felony charges had been dropped on the recommendation of Daniel Rice, but they could easily be reinstated.

It wasn't Griffith's preferred way to conduct FBI business, but he'd use it if required. This mission was going forward regardless of how many questions Daniel Rice raised.

13 Confirmation

Elliott Becton had probably been humanity's first time traveler. Or a time voyeur, given Zin's description of forward compression. Flow empros, compress forward time and you could observe the future, if only briefly and incompletely. Then return to your starting point, along with whatever salacious bits of new information you might have picked up. You might even be able to carry a coin back with you.

Becton had probably accomplished all of this. At least, before it had killed him.

The ideas were mind-boggling, but the evidence lined up and it wasn't just Zin's confirmation. Daniel had witnessed flowing empros. It made him nervous. If the future was just as easily accessed, then new risks surfaced, and death was not the worst of them. There were several questions that still needed answers.

Daniel took the marking pen from Zin. "Extraordinary, Zin. And some of it makes sense, but not all." He drew a horizontal line on the white board. "Let's talk about the most obvious of time paradoxes."

Chloe and Mathieu leaned against the lab's workbench. Griffith still held the blue rubber ball in his hand. Maybe he hoped the complex science would become clearer with a prop.

Daniel marked two points on the line, A and B, and tapped the marker on the board. "We're at point A—the anchor point, as you called it. There's a future point B, and if we use this quantum time technology to compress forward time just right, we could get a glimpse of what's happening at time B. Maybe we see a woman walking down the street wearing her favorite designer dress. Maybe we see a city in ruins."

He drew an arc from B backward to A. "Then we decompress and return to the anchor point." He held up a finger and turned to his audience. "*With* new information about the future. Information that allows us to alter the future in both small and large ways. Maybe we locate that woman in today's world, take her favorite dress and burn it.

Then, how did we see her wearing it? Maybe we find a way to stop the city from being destroyed. Then, how was it ever in ruins? In ways small or large, we have altered the future, and our prior glimpse is no longer valid."

He set the marker down and opened both hands. "Is the future unalterable? Or was our glimpse merely of things that might be? As I recall, Ebenezer Scrooge had this same question."

"It's the block universe question," Mathieu answered. "Does space-time exist as a single unchangeable block? Every event, for eternity, existing all at once. For years, physicists thought they had the answer. The passage of time, along with our free will to affect change, is just an illusion. We're on page eighty-seven of a novel, and nothing we do will change the ending."

Daniel nodded. "So? What's the answer? Is the future invariable or fluid?"

Mathieu shrugged. "We don't know. Quantum physics threw a wrench into the block universe theory. Subatomic particles don't behave as if their future is already written. Tests confirm that these particles are ruled by probabilities, not cause and effect. Most quantum physicists now agree that uncertainly is a natural part of our universe."

Griffith spoke up from the back of the room. "Remember our mission, Dr. Rice. If we thought the future couldn't be changed, we wouldn't be here."

Chloe glanced at Mathieu, her eyebrows lifted in a silent question. The CERN scientists had been told everything about the belt, but nothing about the mission. It wouldn't take a genius to figure things out. Mathieu shrugged.

Daniel wasn't going to hide their reason for coming to Geneva, even if the details of the mission remained unclear to Mathieu and Chloe. "How could the FBI be in possession of an explicit message from the future? A future that we may then change? Am I the only one who sees the paradox of that?"

"Charles Dickens was right," Chloe said. "The future... it's, uh... *une ombre.*"

"A shadow," Mathieu translated. "Perhaps the future is a quantum probability, allowing for alternate paths."

Daniel stared at Zin, who stood quietly to one side. The curious but unschooled humans could guess all day long. Other civilizations were apparently far ahead in their examination of time.

Zin responded without any prompting. "Honestly, I can't say for sure. Even the Litian-nolos still encounter uncertainties, and they've been making temporal adjustments for many years. No plan is perfect. Probabilities come into play."

"Which is one of Core's functions, right?" Daniel had heard this speech before. Core was a gatekeeper for a collection of civilizations, and it functioned to protect these civilizations from outsiders or from each other. Calculating the probability of failure or success seemed to be a Core pastime. Six months ago, the alien intelligence had even selected Marie Kendrick as one of the pawns in its game of chance.

"Temporal probability analysis," Zin answered. "Yes, it's mainly to confine any impacts of time manipulation. Core monitors, analyzes and infrequently steps in to make corrections."

"And if we were to jump forward to glimpse our own future, would Core prevent us from taking action?"

"Most likely not," Zin said. "For better or worse, the decisions you make are your own. Of course, if your actions became dangerous to others, then Core might step in."

"And this is how that other civilization ended?"

"The Sandzvallons of Gamma Carinae?"

"Yes. Did they make a critical mistake?"

"Disastrous, I'm afraid." Zin's open mouth and downcast eyes gave the appearance of nausea, if an android could be sick. "They lost everything."

"Then our next step is obvious," Daniel said, looking at Griffith. "Starting with the story of the Sandzvallons, we'll need to understand the ways in which we could fail before we attempt even the smallest manipulation."

Griffith shook his head. "If only we had that luxury." He motioned to Daniel to follow and walked out of the lab.

Daniel held up a hand. "Uh, excuse me for a minute while I clear this up. There's a lot going on, and my country can be a little pigheaded at times."

****

Alone with Daniel in the hallway, Griffith's lined face was close enough that Daniel could see the stubble of every whisker on his chin. No longer an unwilling student of quantum science, the man had resumed his role as a senior FBI agent.

He spoke in a gruff whisper. "The train derailment in Italy just happened. Two confirmed predictions."

"Wow." The FBI had expected the prediction to come true, and some part of Daniel had too. But now that it had happened, the surreal nature of the mission was settling in. A nuclear war could be on the horizon.

"I have new orders. You and I need to take this belt to London."

"Why London?"

"The president will be there. Along with the British prime minister. They're expecting us, and they'll need a final briefing from you.

From what we've just learned, I believe they will authorize use of the belt."

"For me to jump to 2053?"

"Yes."

"What if I decline?"

Griffith shook his head. "Don't even go there."

"Zin just laid out the risks, and they're high. How do we even know the nuclear threat is real?"

"It's real. The Navy and Air Force confirmed an unauthorized access into a secured system to retrieve predefined launch codes. Of course, they reset all the codes, but it shows that someone has compromised the system."

Daniel took a deep breath. "Any leads?"

"They're working on it. In the meantime, you need to follow the instructions you gave to yourself."

Daniel paused in thought. He wasn't fighting the idea from any selfish perspective. "Look, Agent Griffith…"

"Just Griffith. I don't use a first name, and if I did, it wouldn't be Agent. We're in this together. Let's start acting like it."

"Okay, Griffith. Look, it's not my personal safety I'm worried about. This plan to jump ahead thirty years might be the wrong thing to do. Even a glimpse of the future could alter our present in ways we didn't anticipate. Time might be like an ecosystem. You take away one thing, even something as bad as nuclear war, and something else falls apart, maybe making things worse."

"Seems to me the people in the future have already figured this out."

"Okay. So, if they've figured it out, why didn't they—or me, if that's who it was in the video—just explain the details of how to stop the nuclear launch? Why do I need to go to the future to find out? What's all the intrigue?"

"We can't know the answer to that. Maybe it's complicated and they need to explain things. Or maybe they have some tips on how to safeguard this new future that we all want. But the message was clear. To prevent the nuclear launch, you need to go to Atlanta in 2053, and I think we both know this belt will take you there. When we get to London, you'll need to tell the president that you're ready to do this. Explain the risks if you want, but the president will make the final decision."

Daniel shook his head. "I hear you, but politicians can't make the right decision if they don't have all the scientific facts. We need a basic test of the belt, maybe several tests. I'll need some more time with Zin, and probably a trip to speak with Core."

Griffith shook his head. "We don't have that time. The train derailment in Italy happened less than an hour ago. The Israel bombing is next. The launch may be right on its heels."

"But how many Italian trains derail each year? It might be..." Daniel hung his head. "No, never mind." There was time for skeptical analysis in any decision, but denial wasn't the same thing as skeptical thinking. Confirmation of two precise predictions was strong evidence.

Daniel looked up. "Okay, I'll grant you that the message is real. But what about the belt? Zin seems to think it will work, but we haven't tested it."

"We've got the experts right here."

There were lots of ways to test. Some could be done quickly, but they'd need to get past the login on the belt's controller. "Fine. We've got experts. So, let's go figure it out. If we succeed, then I'll go with you to London, but when we get there, I might have some choice words for the president about the wisdom of this mission."

Griffith put a hand on his shoulder and patted gently. "Good plan."

****

The login password turned out to be a trivial barrier. Zin had simply touched the tiny probe at his fingertip to the controller's chip and extracted ASCII codes held in firmware. They translated to *HGWells1895*, a reference to the classic nineteenth-century novel *The Time Machine*.

Mathieu typed it in, and the system sprang to life. He scrolled through a list of what he said were probably Linux macros:

```
tcs_flow_empros
tcs_initialize_anchor
tcs_set_node
tcs_compress_forward
tcs_decompress_forward
tcs_flow_forward
...
```

Chloe beamed as the commands scrolled across the small screen. "Too easy! Flow empros. Let's try it."

Daniel couldn't blame Chloe and Mathieu for their enthusiasm. The belt represented what they hadn't yet accomplished in their own lab—time compression, the key to accessing the future. Scientists pushing boundaries often leaped at an opportunity to validate theory. It was simply human nature.

Daniel was just as curious as Chloe, but someone had to be the adult in the room, a thankless job. "Remember, this belt killed someone."

"Becton probably hemorrhaged, as Zin described," Griffith said. "He didn't know the boundaries. We do."

Mathieu picked up the helmet, examining the alien light. "Using this device to flow empros is no different than what we do in this lab. Granted, the components and wires seem a bit flimsy." He wiggled one of the wires stapled to the leather, loosening it. "But if we keep the compression small, a test should be safe."

"One moment," Zin said. His fingertip probe extended to touch a second chip on the belt. A moment later his metal eyebrows raised. "Excellent! I've located a log file. It seems Mr. Becton has been quite productive. The node list shows several jumps to various dates in the future."

"Including 2053?" Griffith asked.

Zin nodded. "Yes, several nodes within that year, but many other years too. The device clearly works, and I do see sufficient control, just not enough built-in safeguards. But the health risks can be avoided if you pay attention to the limits I described."

Chloe asked Griffith. "Will a test help with your mission?"

Griffith nodded.

She smiled. "Then I will test it." Chloe grabbed the belt and put it around her waist, cinching it to the final hole.

"No, Chloe, you don't have to do this," Daniel said. "We came to you for advice. Give me the belt, I'll do it." He reached out, but Chloe pushed his hands away.

"I want to," she replied and pointed to a chart posted on the wall. "I have completed thirty-seven empros tests. You have one. I have the experience. You don't." She smiled to Griffith. "*D'ailleurs, mes nouveaux amis*, it will be fun."

Mathieu handed the helmet to Chloe, and she put it on, flipping the visor down over her eyes. With her nose ring and lip piercing still showing below the visor, she looked ready to rumble.

Daniel acquiesced. This belt, this mission seemed to be a freight train he couldn't stop. Maybe he didn't want to stop it. A dark tunnel might be coming up, but there could be something fascinating waiting on the other side. Human curiosity was a powerful motivator.

They took a step back while Chloe leaned over and scrolled to a command listed on the display, now upside-down for everyone else. "Bye-bye," she said and pressed the Enter key.

Prefaced by a quickly rising tone, the yellow light flashed inside the helmet and Chloe winked out of existence. Gone, as if she'd never been standing there.

A slight breeze blew around Daniel, filling the space where Chloe had stood. It had happened so quickly, he wasn't sure how to react. "Holy sh—"

A voice called from the lab's doorway behind them. "*Ici*. Over here." Chloe closed the door and took off the helmet. She strutted to the workbench and laid the helmet and belt on it.

Daniel held a hand to his head. "Wow. Then it *did* move you in space. I thought it wasn't supposed to do that."

"That's not what happened." Mathieu smiled. His hands were behind his back.

Chloe swaggered, her head held high. "This time, I play the game." She walked to Mathieu and circled around him. He stood ramrod straight, unmoving, his hands still behind his back.

"*Connard*," she said in an accusing tone.

"Yes, I am a shithead," Mathieu said, nodding. "Now, please, Chloe. Release me?"

She spun him around so the others could see his back. His hands were bound by a white plastic strap. Another strap wrapped around his ankles, making his stance unstable.

"Maybe," she said in a haughty tone. "Or maybe I leave you this way."

"Holy..." said Daniel again. "You just did that?" The startling reality of flowing empros was beginning to settle in. Daniel hadn't felt a thing. No blip in his thoughts, no hiccup in his breathing. He hadn't even had time to blink. Yet forward time had frozen, at least for Chloe.

She laughed. "Yes. I've been gone... uh, about one hour." Chloe pulled a utility knife off the shelf and slid its blade open. She held the knife below Mathieu's grimacing chin.

"*Tu te comporteras?*" she asked, clearly demanding a change in his behavior toward her. His head bobbed up and down. She slit the plastic strap from his wrists and then from his ankles. Dropping the knife on the workbench, she leaned against it, her arms crossed.

She puckered her lips and blew a puff of air in Mathieu's direction. "Puhh."

Mathieu took a deep breath and rubbed his wrists. "Lesson learned. As you can see, in what was just an instant for us, Chloe has been busy."

Mathieu picked up the tie strap and examined it. "She's been up to the equipment room. That's where the straps came from, two floors above. She probably took the stairs since the lifts wouldn't work in empros time."

He pointed to a paper coffee cup on the workbench. "That wasn't here just a few seconds ago, so she's probably also been to the CERN café. It's two blocks away. Did you take a croissant, too?"

Chloe nodded and licked her pierced lips. "Delicious."

Mathieu walked over to the smug woman and looked into her eyes. "But I think she did more."

Chloe's snooty expression didn't waver. "I did."

"I think she compressed forward, possibly looking ahead to the future. I wonder what she saw?"

"Wouldn't you like to know?" She flicked Mathieu away like brushing aside a fly and turned to Griffith.

Her haughtiness disappeared, and she spoke in earnest. "Griffith. I saw things. From tomorrow. Things that have not yet happened. A date on a computer. A newspaper. It was…" She didn't complete the thought, either unable to find the right English word or perhaps unable to express the emotion.

She turned to Daniel. No smiles, her words simple and sober. "Time compression. It works."

14 Commandment

Fire Control Technician Second Class Joshua Swindell returned to the forward torpedo room, where his bunk and locker were located. With space in short supply, submarines doubled or even tripled the function of every room, and that meant sailors were rarely alone. An off-duty roommate lay in a bunk supported by chains over two torpedoes. He looked up from his book. "Hey, Josh."

"Hey, Robbie," Joshua said, his voice jittery. His heart had calmed, but the lingering unease remained. The second vision had been more fearful than the first. Joshua nodded and closed his fist tighter around the object in his pocket. No one could see the commandment from the Lord.

He opened his locker and pulled out a toilet kit. He would need the small mirror inside. He also pulled out a magazine with a teen girl on the cover. "I'll be in the head," he told his bunkmate.

Robbie's face was buried in his book. "Careful, cowboy. Whip that thing too much and it'll fall off."

Joshua paid no mind to the taunt. Sins of the flesh were common for sailors on lonely duty. But the darker thoughts rampaging through his mind would surely bring eternal damnation. He'd even acted upon those thoughts at their last port of call. Twelve years old, the Indonesian girl had told him as she'd put her clothes back on. Her confession only made him want more.

Bypassing the nearest head, he sought a quieter location two decks below. He opened its door and peeked inside. No one there. There was no lock, but he flipped a paper tag stuck on the door from green to red, an unofficial marker that privacy was sought for a few minutes. Most sailors respected it.

Not bothering to drop his pants, he sat on the toilet seat and laid the magazine across his thighs. Sturdy enough. The mirror from his toilet kit was small, but it was all he had. The Lord had been specific. Spin upon mirrored glass. Joshua's redemption for his sins would begin today.

He reached into his pocket and pulled out the oversized coin. The writing around its edge confirmed the Lord's verbal instructions. As he placed the coin against the mirror and snapped his fingers, Joshua's heart raced once more.

The coin made a hum that grew louder, though the overhead ventilation fan would probably drown out the sound for anyone who might pass by in the hallway. As foretold, the coin spun faster. Sweat appeared on Joshua's forehead. The hum became a high-pitched shrill and then, thankfully, went away.

A cone of light popped upwards from the spinning coin, startling Joshua, but the spinning image inside held his attention. It finally settled—a bearded man with long gray hair dressed in a hooded robe with wide purple stripes on both sleeves. The man stood at the base of a tall building with a golden spire that soared to the heavens.

Joshua began to tremble as the man spoke. "My son. A higher duty calls to you. Listen and obey, but fear not, for your path is virtuous."

The voice was low in volume, but the Lord had assured him it would be. The bearded man spoke about every man's duty to confront the evil that walks among the righteous. He became more animated as he talked, waving his arms and punctuating key words with angry shakes of his head. It was a sermon much like those given each Sunday by Pastor Stephan back home.

The man's face was now flushed red and he yelled his final commandment, a call to arms. He stopped, breathing heavily, and as the man calmed from his fiery oration, a young woman joined him. She wore a veil that reached to the floor, made from a thin translucent material. The veil flowed in the wind like angel's wings, and Joshua could make out her shapely figure beneath the graceful folds of cloth.

Olivia, she called herself. She walked closer, her three-dimensional image growing. In one hand, Olivia held a coin much like the one spinning. She hooked a fingernail under a sliver of metal on its edge and spoke of a hidden chamber within.

She came closer still until her beautiful face filled the spinning cone of light. Her voice became sultry and beckoning. "My love. Your task is difficult, but do not falter. I will be waiting for you in Heaven."

Her image twisted into spinning lines and disappeared. The cone of light went dark; the coin slowed and finally fell to one side. Joshua picked it up, searching for the sliver of metal he hoped he would find.

It was there, along the edge opposite the stamped words. He could just get a fingernail under it. He lifted, and a small slip of paper poked out from a tiny compartment. Joshua withdrew the paper and unfolded it to the size of a fortune from a Chinese cookie. The paper displayed a single line of printed numbers and letters.

LCR4592F-66GP17-3T8V19-B008D4-8Q210K

He recognized the format immediately. Every launch code began with the same three letters.

****

On his shift later that night, Joshua logged in to the launch simulator system on the fire control computer. Simulation was a normal part of his workday; no one would notice. He withdrew the slip of paper from his pocket and typed the code into the system. A map came up, showing the submarine's current position just south of Adak Island in the Aleutian chain that stretched from Alaska across the Pacific. Two red lines started from the sub and arced in opposite directions, one ending at Vladivostok, Russia, the other at San Francisco, California.

Russia was one thing, but targeting his own country? Was it even possible? The simulation didn't lie. Its software was an accurate representation of the real fire control system. Joshua began to tremble. As foretold, his task would indeed be difficult, but it had been commanded by a power higher than any other that walked this mortal world.

The Lord's voice had been clear. "Do not fear your task. Those who have strayed will die. All others will receive everlasting salvation."

He looked again at the map, confirming the targets. Then he noticed a third red line. Like the other two, it started from the sub, but it arced in a loop and ended back at the sub's position.

Joshua closed his eyes, the trembling becoming uncontrollable. He understood now why the beautiful woman had told him she would be waiting in Heaven.

15 London

The hired car passed many of London's biggest tourist sights. The Tower, St. Paul's Cathedral, the Shakespeare Globe theater. The talkative driver pointed out some of the lesser-known sights: the ancient scaffold where noblemen and paupers alike had been executed, and the nearby pub appropriately named Hung, Drawn and Quartered.

Daniel laughed to himself. "The grisly side of London. Nothing quite like it." He almost felt like one of the captives, his fate to be determined not by a jury of his peers, but by the High Lords of Ignorance otherwise known as politicians. In a few minutes, he would be in front of several of the most powerful.

Griffith sat in the back, along with their newest collaborator, Chloe Demers. Griffith had suggested she join them, traveling at least as far as London. He wanted her expertise, he'd said, but Daniel detected something more. A collusion of sorts between them, though exactly what it represented eluded him.

Chloe had agreed, and Mathieu didn't object, acting somewhat subdued after Chloe's unambiguous rebellion against his history of sexual abuse. On the flight, Griffith fully explained the mission to Chloe, who absorbed the incredible story of the coin and its message without objections.

The car passed over the River Thames, where Big Ben was only minutes away from striking 6 p.m. Rather late to be meeting with heads of state, but Daniel hadn't set the schedule. They turned on Whitehall and paused at the Downing Street security gate, where a policeman carrying an automatic weapon examined their documents and radioed to someone on the inside.

A minute later, the trio stood on the porch in front of a simple black door, the very understated entrance to what the British simply referred to as Number 10.

The door didn't open and none of the police standing around provided any instruction. What was the protocol for popping by the prime minister's house? Daniel lifted the knocker protruding from a lion's mouth and tapped on the door.

It was opened by an older man dressed in a waistcoat, his formal demeanor no different than any butler from Queen Victoria's day. "Dr. Rice?" the butler asked. Daniel nodded and reached for his passport, but the door opened wide and the man ushered them in with a bow. The old-fashioned English civility was almost certainly backed up with unseen modern systems. No doubt their faces had been examined on a hidden security camera from the moment they'd stepped out of the car.

The entrance hall had a checkerboard floor and a staircase leading up, the wall lined with framed photographs of past prime ministers. Daniel recognized the room immediately, probably from a TV program and probably from many years ago. While he might forget a birthday, details of scenes like this were permanently stored and instantly recalled. The brain works in funny ways.

The butler placed their overnight bags in a closet. "The prime minister asks that you join him in the Cabinet Room. However, before we go upstairs, are there any personal needs that I can help with?" The English have a way of disguising even the most basic of questions. They'd already used the toilets at the airport though it might be interesting to see what the prime minister's loo looked like.

"We're good," Daniel answered. If English movies were any guide, he felt like he should be handing a hat and overcoat to the man. At least an umbrella. The unseasonably warm weather in both Switzerland and now England required nothing more than a suit jacket. Daniel was thankful he'd packed that much.

The butler motioned to the stairs and started up. "This way, please."

Daniel and Griffith exchanged a timid smile. Meeting with the UK prime minister, the US president and whoever else might be up in the Cabinet Room set off a slight case of jitters. Griffith didn't look any more assured. On the other hand, Chloe, now wearing a black dress but with all her facial accessories still intact, beamed like she was waltzing into a celebrity party.

They passed photographs of Churchill, Wilson, Thatcher, Blair, May and others who had lived in this historic house.

"How old is Number 10?" Daniel asked.

"The house itself dates to 1684, but in 1732, King George the Second offered it to Sir Robert Walpole, who was the first prime minister to live and work here."

Surprising. From the outside, the plain brick building looked relatively modern.

At the top of the stairs, the butler guided them through a reception room with a large portrait of Queen Elizabeth—the first, not the second—hanging above a fireplace. A dark hallway led to a closed door. "The Cabinet Room, sirs, madam."

He opened the door to an empty conference room. Sunlight streamed through several windows on the opposite side. On one wall hung a Turner landscape of a serene countryside, no doubt equal to any in the Tate Britain museum. On the other hung an eighteenth-century lord dressed in fine robes with a white wig.

"Sir Robert," the butler said, waving to the painting. "His presence is still felt at each cabinet meeting." Steeped in the past, somehow this constitutional monarchy had managed to make it intact to the twenty-first century. In some ways, modern Britain was thriving. It helped that their language had been forever stamped as the language of the world.

The butler motioned to a tray in the corner stacked with bottles of water and cans of soda. "Refreshments are available. Please take any seat on this side of the table. The prime minister and his guests will be in shortly." When he closed the door behind him, the room became unnaturally quiet, with only the muted sound of cars passing by on Whitehall.

"The British version of a SCIF," Griffith said.

"It's lovely," Chloe said.

"It's certainly better decorated than our secure conference rooms," Daniel acknowledged. He examined an antique clock on the mantelpiece, probably two hundred years old and still ticking.

"Funny how the physicists tell us the past is gone. Inaccessible. Yet, here it is. Think of how many hands have touched the winding handle on this clock over the years." It was probably better to think about the science that had brought them here than the nervousness that comes when meeting important people.

They weren't kept waiting long. A second door opened, and a short man with glasses walked in. Daniel didn't recognize him, but the three who followed were as famous as they come. Prime Minister Elaine Woodruff walked briskly, her gray hair classically tied up in a bun. President John Simonds followed her, acknowledging Daniel with a quick handshake. They'd had a working lunch once before. The man looked tired and older than Daniel remembered.

German Chancellor Gerhard Kruger followed. A heavyset man with wire-rimmed glasses and long white hair, Kruger recognized Daniel and took his hand. "Dr. Rice, it is a pleasure. Thank you for agreeing to this most interesting mission."

"I, uh..." It was probably no use squabbling. If the FBI and the leaders of the Western world had already decided he was going to the future, his fate was fixed. Maybe every event in time and space really was predetermined, offering no opportunity for free will.

"I'm happy to be here," was the most innocuous of responses Daniel could come up with.

The three leaders settled on one side of the table. Two additional men and one woman joined them, likely aides given the collections of papers that each set on the table. Griffith, Chloe and Daniel took chairs on the other side. The short man with glasses sat at the end, typing on his computer.

Prime Minister Woodruff glanced at a single page in her hand. She tapped in a steady rhythm on her chin, her no-nonsense expression the same as he'd witnessed watching Prime Minister's Questions on CSPAN. The woman was more intimidating in person.

She looked up at Daniel with piercing eyes. "You seem to be a key player, Dr. Rice. Though the coin itself remains in Washington, we've viewed a recording of its remarkable message. But I'm still puzzled. Do you have any idea why you were selected?"

It was a good question, one he hadn't really thought about. "I wish I knew, Prime Minister. It makes no sense to me. Why not ask a nuclear weapons expert? Or terrorism expert? Or someone from the military?"

Good to get the first question out of the way. His nervousness calmed.

"We're told the belt is designed for one person," President Simonds said. "But even if we could send an expert, as you suggest, we agree that for now it should be you alone, per the instructions." No doubt about it. In their minds, Daniel was committed. He didn't remember signing the agreement.

"Yes, sir. If I were to go to Atlanta and use this belt"—Daniel emphasized the *if*, even though it probably didn't matter—"and, assuming it worked and I peered through some veil into the year 2053, what then? Are you asking for specific reconnaissance?"

"In a way, I suppose," the president answered. "We need information. Just do what the video asked. Go there. What happens next is probably up to them."

"Which is an interesting question in itself," Daniel answered. "They'll know I'm coming. Today's meeting is being documented." Daniel pointed to the man at the end of the table, still typing furiously on his computer. "The people of the future have already read his notes. From their perspective, this meeting is history."

"A good point," the prime minister said. "That's to your advantage. They'll be ready with whatever information they want to pass to us. There's a good chance their plan to stop the nuclear attack will be based on intelligence that we cannot access, maybe even facts that wouldn't otherwise be uncovered for years."

"A postwar inquiry," Chancellor Kruger said. "Germany did the same after World War II, and it took more than ten years to come to a satisfactory answer. People living thirty years into the future will have access to that data and expert analysis. They should have a very good idea how to stop this threat."

Daniel recognized his privileged position. Across the table were three leaders representing half the military power of the world as well as some of the most capable intelligence agencies. They ought to know something. "You're sure the nuclear threat is real?"

The president nodded. "No question. Of course, we've already taken prudent actions to eliminate the threat. We're not going to unilaterally disarm, but I have spoken with the generals and admirals, and we agree that extra vigilance and additional security protocols will be enough to prevent unauthorized access. No one is going to launch a US missile without my express authorization."

"But even though you believe we're now safe, you want me to go to 2053 anyway?"

"Yes," the president answered. "We want to know what they know. See if we're missing anything. Find out who was involved in the threat and uncover any weaknesses in our security. A contact who has already lived through it seems like pretty good intelligence source."

"They've already helped us," the president added. "Israel recently reported that they captured a Hamas terrorist who was planning to detonate a bomb at precisely the place and time indicated in the coin's message. We'll have to wait until tomorrow to be sure, but it appears the predicted Tel Aviv attack has been prevented."

"Proving that information from the future can be used to change the present?" Griffith asked. He'd been quiet until now.

"Yes." The president nodded. "It proves that Dr. Rice's mission will produce actionable information."

Dr. Rice's mission. Daniel rolled his eyes at the inevitability of it all. The only thing left was to give it a clever code name. DeLorean?

Daniel spoke to the stenographer at the end of the table. "Write this down." The stenographer looked up. "Ask the people of the future if they recall anything about a Tel Aviv bomber. Now that we've prevented it, maybe they won't remember telling us about it." The man typed what would become a direct question, carried thirty years into the future.

The president smiled. "I like your way of thinking, Dr. Rice. You're clearly the right person for this mission."

Daniel shrugged. "I have more thoughts, too, but you might not like them as much." He rubbed his chin. "What if I return with baggage? Something I saw or learned that might alter our path in unanticipated ways. Maybe even something physical. What if just by breathing future air, I contract a virus that doesn't exist today but spreads rapidly across the population?"

"You're suggesting we should quarantine you when you return? We can do that."

"I guess what I'm saying is we don't have any way to distinguish between before and after. That's the illogical part of information transfer. We have no way to know how things might have been if I had *not* made the jump."

The High Lords of Ignorance all shared facial expressions that matched their nickname. Daniel tried once more. "Even now. What if, by preventing the bomb in Israel, someone's life has been spared who will now go on to even more atrocious actions? Who's to say that we have improved the future?" It was an uncomfortable question to ask. Most people would agree that saving lives is always a good thing.

The president seemed to be one of them. "Dr. Rice, we already do this every day. We seek out the bad guys, infiltrate their organizations, and take action based on our intelligence. We regularly prevent deaths. Should we stop doing that just because we don't know how things might have turned out otherwise?"

The president's point was valid, but the plan still didn't feel right. A known future, regardless of how well things turned out, felt unnatural. A suspense spoiled. Like reading the last chapter in a book and then jumping back to the middle. You learned something you weren't supposed to know.

Daniel shook his head, acknowledging the predetermined plan and his central role in it. "Zin mentioned another civilization that quarantines their time travelers to isolate whatever knowledge they gained from the future. I guess that will be me."

Daniel blew out a breath, acknowledging his fate. "I'll do my best."

16 Sagittarius Novus

Daniel yawned, shook off the drowsiness, and blinked as the first rays of sunrise streamed through the jet's window. He rubbed the crick in his neck. Sleeping on planes was getting tougher with age.

Far below, the Atlantic stretched into the distance, a mix of orange-tinted clouds and blue water. Above, a much darker blue announcing the limits of Earth's life-preserving atmosphere. In the distance, a few white specs floated on the water, probably icebergs drifting south from Greenland. No sign yet of the rocky coastline of Newfoundland, but it would be directly ahead.

Could there be a more beautiful planet in the galaxy?

Daniel peered over his shoulder. Behind him, Griffith slumped against a pillow propped up against the closed window shade. Chloe sat across the aisle, reading from a tablet. She looked up, making eye contact and smiled. *"Bonjour.* You slept well?"

Daniel shrugged. "Some. Enough, I guess." They expected to touch down in Atlanta around 9 a.m. The start of what would likely be a busy day.

He unclipped his seat belt and moved to the empty seat facing rearward, a small table separating him from Chloe. "I hope I'm not interrupting."

She set down her tablet. "Reading. Things to see in America. I've never been."

"It's a big country. Atlanta's nice. But there's a lot more."

"I want to see New York."

"Everyone does. A wonderful city. How's your forward-facing body doing today? Any glitches?"

She scrunched one eye. "Sorry, my English. It is, uh... not so good."

"My fault," Daniel said. Her English was far better than his French, but that was no reason to assume perfection. "Yesterday you flowed empros with forward time compressed. Do you feel any different today?"

"Ah, yes, I understand. No, no problems. I feel fine."

"You were brave to test the belt. Thanks." Maybe a bit hasty too, but Daniel wasn't complaining. She'd given him reason to believe this mission was possible. Pop to a future date, do some reconnaissance and return in one piece. Even measured in empros time, it might only require a few hours.

"My pleasure. I can't wait to do it again." She waved a hand before Daniel could speak. "Oh, I know. This technology, it is, uh… something that must be controlled."

"You and Mathieu are close to duplicating time compression in your lab?"

"Yes. Already, I see what to do next. But, don't worry. We have many controls. We also have Zin to make sure our work is safe."

As an advisor, Zin hadn't shown much inclination to supervise overly excited scientists. As a babysitter, he would let a four-year-old play with a chain saw. Would probably even point out the start button.

Their testing might be tempting fate, but it wasn't Chloe's fault. Like many scientists, she enthusiastically pursued new discoveries, following paths wherever they led. She was a natural explorer. Armed with the scientific method, humans had revealed many of the secrets hidden in nature, though human wisdom regarding the application of those discoveries was sometimes questionable.

Daniel reached into an overhead bin and retrieved Griffith's duffel bag. He pulled out the belt and helmet and laid them on the table.

"Ready to make your jump?" Chloe asked with a grin.

Daniel fingered the on-off switch on the belt. "I wonder what would happen if I were to freeze time now?" He imagined an airplane suspended in midair much like the rubber ball.

Chloe shook her head with a smirk on her face. "You wouldn't do that. I know you well enough already."

Daniel nodded. "You're right, I wouldn't." Testing the boundaries of this insanity at forty thousand feet wasn't the best of plans. Daniel's natural curiosity had its limits.

He lifted the helmet and examined the components glued to the inside of the visor. He tried it on. Though the helmet fit well enough, the stale smell of sweat was a downside.

"It's easy," Chloe said. "Just be sure to follow the order. Flow empros, initialize the anchor point, set a node, then compress forward. To return, decompress, then flow forward." Daniel hadn't tested the belt yet, even though Chloe had offered to assist before they'd departed London. The thing clearly worked. She'd reported seeing the future, even if it was only tomorrow... now today. But a thirty-year jump might push the limits. There were plenty of unchartered waters and no reason to risk the consequences more than once.

The device wasn't his main source of concern. Time itself stood like an unexplored cave. Open, available for anyone to enter, but leading into dark passages. Did time branch? Were there multiple futures, each a result of decisions made today? Shadows of things that might be, as both Chloe and Charles Dickens had proposed?

Even if there were multiple futures, who was to say each one of them derived from the same past? Like tree branches, maybe Daniel was already out on one limb and the belt would take him to an entirely different branch derived from a different past.

All very odd questions and not very scientific. Yet the leaders of the free world had made a decision that could very well rearrange humanity's future.

Daniel returned the tools of this folly to the duffel and left Chloe to her reading. He closed his eyes and pondered the next steps. Almost certainly, he would soon be in a position to glimpse the future. But what future? His future? Perhaps one of many. It would help to find a way to test time's structure.

Create a breadcrumb trail, of sorts?

A connection between whatever future he would see and his known today. The gears turned in his head and a smile soon crept across his lips.

It can be done.

The more he thought about it, the more it made sense, if anything about time's structure could make sense.

Leave a marker. But where? Daniel rubbed the whiskers growing on his chin. *Someplace safe. Someplace that would remain undisturbed for thirty years.*

The marker would need to be in Atlanta. He didn't have time to go anywhere else. The president had been very direct in his order. Go to Atlanta, make the jump, and report back to Washington as soon as possible. Griffith was the chaperone to ensure Daniel performed the job as ordered. Chloe would be the technical consultant in case anything went wrong.

Somewhere in Atlanta.

Elijah Haugen Clure. The name popped into his mind, an obvious choice. Reverend Clure was the pastor of the Ebenezer Baptist Church, the famed congregation of Martin Luther King. The old church in the Sweet Auburn neighborhood of central Atlanta was a historic site, well preserved, and would be for the foreseeable future. Through circumstance, Daniel knew the pastor well.

Were they friends? Adversaries? Debate opponents? It was hard to categorize their relationship, though it was certainly better now than when they'd first met at the Humanity Conference last year. The event had brought together leaders from all walks of life to discuss, debate and—if they could—agree upon how humans would become the newest member of the collection of civilizations known as Sagittarius Novus.

Twenty-three civilizations. Humans from the planet Earth would make it twenty-four. The home worlds were scattered across the Sagittarius Arm of the Milky Way, with the cyborg Core as the gatekeeper and central communications hub. The first order of business at the conference was to learn something about the neighborhood.

Most people had no idea the Milky Way even had arms, much less named arms. Our little speck of dust in this vast assemblage of stars, planets, drifting rocks, dust, and gas is located on what humans had labeled the Orion Spur of the Sagittarius Arm, an enormous swirl that extends from the galactic center toward the emptiness of intergalactic space. One arm further out is called Perseus. Interior is called Scutum-Centaurus.

The arms defined where life could exist. Habitable planets require atoms of carbon, oxygen and silicon, produced in the interior of stars and ejected in the cataclysmic explosions of supernovas. Further out from the galactic center, densities were too low, with fewer supernovas, allowing for gas giants like Jupiter, but not so good for rocky planets like Earth. Closer in to the center, supernovas occurred too frequently—instant death for life that managed to get a toehold.

Earth, like most member planets, was in the Goldilocks Zone, a band of stars about halfway from the center of the Milky Way. Though less than a third of the galaxy, the zone of habitability still provided billions of suitable stars. Within the zone, life was everywhere. Any piece of rock close enough to a star and big enough to build a surface layer of water and gases almost inevitably produced microbes. More complex life took time, evolving only on rocky planets orbiting a stable star like Sol, our sun.

But even with life being common, advanced life turned out to be very rare. Only twenty-four civilizations scattered across a vast sector twenty thousand light-years long. There were, no doubt, additional civilizations not yet discovered. As Core had explained, the Sagittarius Novus alliance had known nothing of Earth until humans had stumbled upon the technology of spatial compression just one year before.

At the Humanity Conference, Daniel had been a strong voice for joining the alliance. We'd benefit from the information and technology exchange. There was no downside. It wasn't like we could hide now that Earth had been revealed. They had no reason to attack us or even become overlords. We had nothing they coveted. Habitable planets could be found on every street corner of the galaxy. Water planets were a dime a dozen. Our technology was primitive compared to most other members.

But like many of his religious colleagues, Reverend Clure had argued from a different point of view. Humans were sacred, he'd said. God's children fashioned in the likeness of our creator. If there were other sentient creatures out there, maybe they had their own god. We'd be better off, he argued, if we stayed in our own corner of the universe and focused on healing our own self-inflicted wounds: poverty, racial injustice, our local environment.

Daniel didn't disagree that we had much to do on our own planet, but he'd argued that we might learn something that would help us in our tasks. Clure and others pointed to human history. First contact with a very different civilization was more about domination than learning.

They'd sparred on many topics, scientific, religious and alien, sometimes in private conversation, but other times on the stage in front of hundreds of others. But throughout the back and forth, there was no animosity, no insults, and in the end, a genuine respect had developed between them. Even a contrary view, when argued from a platform of civility, becomes not an ideological threat to vanquish, but an alternative to consider and an opportunity to grasp the diversity of humanity.

Reverend Elijah Haugen Clure could be exactly the right person to help. Not that Clure knew anything about the nature of time. But a scientific discussion wasn't what Daniel had in mind. He located Clure's contact record and started a text message.

17 Ebenezer

Midmorning in Atlanta. A pleasant breeze rustled the leaves on the still-green trees. A few weeks earlier, this place would have been a summer steam-bath. A few weeks more and the leaves would start showing their true sans-chlorophyll colors.

Daniel's request for a ten-minute delay while he spoke with Clure was accepted by Griffith after some head-scratching. Indulging Daniel's pre-jump eccentricities was the least he could do, he said. It seemed much like the offer of a cigarette before the firing squad.

Griffith and Chloe would wait for him in the old Ebenezer Baptist Church, where Martin Luther King, Jr. had preached so many years before. At least it was a tourist site, giving Chloe a glimpse of American history.

Built with red stone and white trim, the modern Ebenezer Baptist Church looked like a larger and more sculpted version of its ancestor. The new building was the natural result of a swelling congregation that now proudly included many white residents of Atlanta.

Daniel opened a large door and walked into a cavernous space soaring a hundred feet overhead. His footsteps echoed in the quiet, a reminder that this was Monday, a low-key day for any Christian church.

It was also a reminder that his weekend with Nala had officially evaporated. He'd sent a text upon arrival in Atlanta, but no answer. She'd be back at Fermilab, at work by now.

He wandered up one aisle toward the pulpit, and a familiar voice called from an open door at one side. "You sure you're supposed to be in here?"

"The voice of God?" Daniel looked up in mock search. "No, my mistake. The voice of man." They greeted each other with a handshake that morphed into a hug.

"Good to see you, Daniel." Reverend Clure's short-cropped hair was a little grayer at the temples, but otherwise he hadn't changed since their debates. He wore an open-collar blue shirt with stylish slacks. With a strong physique, he looked more like an athlete on his day off than a pastor.

"Glad to find the door unlocked. After all, you knew I was coming."

Clure smiled. "Our doors are open to everyone, even the nonbelievers. Imagine that! No qualifications to join this club."

They'd had this discussion before; the elitist science club. "Are scientists really that bad?"

The reverend's expression tightened. "Well, let's just say that credentials are a big deal in your line of work."

Reverend Clure wasn't opposed to science. In fact, he had been quite supportive. But he worried that science had become too far removed from the everyday life of the average person. Daniel acknowledged the point with a nod. "How's the college fund going?"

"More than four million dollars so far this year. We can help a thousand young people get a good education with that."

"Outstanding. You should be very proud."

"Best use of tax-deductible contributions that I can think of."

"I couldn't agree more."

Reverend Clure wagged a finger. "But you didn't come here to talk about our college fund, did you? You have something else in mind."

Daniel just smiled. He'd love to hear more about the work this church was doing to advance their community, but the president had been clear. As soon as possible.

"I'm on an assignment. Odd circumstances. Probably more than you'd want to hear. Or would believe."

The reverend threw both hands in the air. "Ah, Dr. Daniel Rice. A witness to some of the most incredible things in our universe, but still not ready to accept the grandest story of them all."

"Any evidence for your story that you didn't have last time we talked?" Yes, it was snarky, but their relationship was close enough to allow for it.

The reverend shook his head. "Not your kind of evidence."

Daniel could have carried the argument forward and enjoyed the amicable back and forth. Evidence doesn't come in varieties, he'd say. If it's not specific and verifiable, then it's hearsay, imagination, or opinion.

But he hadn't come to reengage in their ongoing religious argument. Being on opposite sides was no reflection on the man. Reverend Clure was someone Daniel could trust. It was why he had come.

"I need your help. A test of sorts."

Clure nodded. "Just say the word."

Daniel removed the multifunction watch from his wrist. "I need to leave this here." The reverend looked puzzled, but he reached out. Daniel withdrew. "Not specifically with you. I'd like to leave it in the old church. Just for a day, I'll pick it up tomorrow."

"A test?" Clure asked, his eyes flitting between the watch and Daniel.

"A test of permanency. And of the sequence of events in time." It wasn't much of an explanation, but Daniel didn't want to tell all just yet.

Clure shrugged. "Well, I'd be happy to help with your test, but the National Park Service manages the old church. It's an historic site."

Daniel had already figured this into his plan. "But you have access to the building."

118

"I do, for weddings. But…"

"If it's okay with you, I'd rather not involve the NPS. It's part of the test."

His skeptical expression remained. "I see. We can go over there, but it's not exactly a secluded place. Lots of visitors every day. You leave a watch on a pew and someone will pick it up."

"I wasn't thinking about a pew. It's an old building. I'm looking for a closet—even a crack in the wall will do."

Clure scratched his head. "Well, there's the storage room in the bell tower. We keep some Christmas decorations there."

"Sounds promising. Can we go over? Just you and me. No one else."

Clure squinted with one eye. "For the life of me, Daniel, I don't think I'll ever understand you. A test? With your watch in the old church? Overnight?"

Daniel nodded to all three questions. "If you don't mind."

Clure shrugged. "Okay, it seems harmless enough."

He waved, and Daniel followed. He picked up a key from a desk in his office, and they exited the church. "It is just a watch, isn't it?"

They walked side by side. "Yeah, nothing alien or subversive, if that's what you mean. The watch isn't really part of the test. It's simply an item that's easily identified as mine."

They crossed a small park, and Daniel noticed a new sapling that had been planted recently, the thin tree still bound to a pole with rubber straps. He logged the image of the young tree in his mind. A useful gauge for his next step.

On the other side of the street, the old church stood as it had for one hundred and one years, its neon sign still hanging over the entry, still working. Rectangular towers graced both sides of the building with a stained-glass window between them. Daniel recalled reading about the centennial celebration the previous year. The church had replaced a broken pane with new artwork that included a bell-shaped aquatic creature resembling a Dancer from Ixtlub. A nice touch for the modern era.

The front door was open, the entryway crowded with tourists, pointing and talking among themselves. Griffith and Chloe weren't among them, but they were probably somewhere in the building. Past the rows of old pews, a young couple stood at the altar in front of a woman who appeared to be giving them instructions.

"Wedding rehearsal," Clure said.

"Lots of weddings here?" Daniel asked.

"Booked solid through next year. We're the first choice for just about every African-American couple in the area."

They walked past a small alcove where a park ranger sat at a desk. "Hi, Lauren, we'll be up in the attic for a few minutes."

The young woman looked up. "That's fine, Reverend. Just watch out for the spiders. We haven't sprayed for a while."

Clure unlatched a cord strung across the base of a staircase and reattached it behind them. Each step creaked as they went up. At the top landing, a locked door blocked their passage. Clure slid in a key. "We don't ring the bells anymore, so it's more of an attic these days."

Clure led Daniel into a small room with a battered wooden floor, a window on the one side, dingy and covered with spiderwebs. There were a few folding tables against a wall and a closed door in one corner, its paint cracked and peeling.

"Restoration of the building didn't bother with this room," Clure said.

Daniel walked across the creaky floor and opened the closet door. Cardboard boxes filled several shelves. The highest shelf above Daniel's head was empty, probably because there wasn't much room between it and the ceiling.

"It's perfect," Daniel answered. "Can I put my watch on top?"

"That's fine. No one will see it there, if that's what you're worried about."

"Yeah. It's a great hiding place. I'll bet it could stay there without discovery for years."

The reverend looked up to the high shelf. "Just the spiders up there. But this is just for overnight, right?"

"Should be, yeah. But, Elijah, if for whatever reason I'm not back here to pick it up, would you just leave it there?"

"I can do that. Your test might take longer?"

"Yeah, possibly. In fact, it would help if you just forgot all about it."

"It's your watch. Odd that you want to give it to the spiders, but I guess I've heard stranger things coming from you."

Daniel laughed and pulled a coin from his pocket. "Yeah, this next part is stranger still. Heads for north, tails for south." He flipped it in the air. "Heads. North side. Okay, one more time. Heads for east, tails for west." He flipped again. "Tails. West. I'll put it in the northwest corner."

"Getting superstitious, are we?" the reverend asked.

"It gets worse," Daniel answered, smiling. He counted the number of holes on the watch wristband. "Pick a number between one and ten."

"Uh, seven."

Daniel positioned the watchband hook into hole seven on the band. "Okay, between the four corners of the closet and the ten hole positions of the watchband, that gives me forty possible combinations. A 2.5 percent chance that I'll find the watch in exactly this configuration by random chance, a 97.5 percent chance that the future is a direct

121

consequence of the past. Or, I might find the watch in a different configuration, in which case I'm screwed."

The reverend shook his head, clearly flustered by the partial explanation of the test. "Daniel Rice, you are definitely the strangest person I have ever met."

18 Jump

Freedom Plaza, adjacent to the Ebenezer Baptist Church, is the resting place for Martin Luther King. A long rectangular fountain surrounds the great man's tomb, and a covered walkway along the length of the fountain, known as the Freedom Walk, provides shade and a quiet place for visitors to contemplate. A small chapel sits at the west end of Freedom Walk, obscuring the view from the rest of the plaza, and a concrete wall blocks the view from a parking lot in the other direction.

It was a perfect choice for a safe jump point to the future. Being a memorial, none of the architecture would likely change over a thirty-year period. It was open to the street but concealed from view, and there were no doors or elevators that could be locked or wouldn't function while in empros time.

Jump from here and future Atlanta is at your feet.

Griffith, Chloe and Daniel gathered in a tight circle with no one else around. Even if someone in the plaza saw Daniel suiting up, they wouldn't see much. Just a guy getting ready to ride his motorcycle.

Okay, so, motorcycle guy puts on his helmet and then disappears. It happens.

Even in broad daylight, it would hardly be noticeable as long as he returned to the same spot. He'd pop out of existence and return a split-second later. Chloe had done something similar; she'd just changed positions while flowing empros.

"Glad I only have to do this once," Daniel said to his companions as he cinched the belt around his waist. "I doubt this time travel kit is going to hold up much longer." One of the staples had come loose, allowing a wire to dangle. Of course, if he was successful, the belt, loose wires and all, might end up in the Smithsonian.

"Try this," Chloe said. She pulled a C-shaped gold piercing from her lip and jabbed its pin through the leather. She threaded the loose wire through the opening of the C and capped the jewelry's pin on the other side. Secure against the leather, it did a pretty good job of holding the wire in place.

"Thanks," Daniel said, laughing. "I'll give it back to you in a few seconds."

He looked at Griffith, then Chloe, took a deep breath and flipped the switch to the on position. Lights came on just as they'd done for Chloe.

"Remember, flow empros, then initialize the anchor and set the node. When you're ready to go, compress forward," she said. "Any problem, just come back, and we'll talk."

"Pretty straightforward," Daniel said, "but I'm glad you're here." Chloe gave him a hug, and Griffith provided a reassuring pat on the shoulder.

It was true that he wasn't likely to screw up the belt's operation, though what the universe might throw at him could range from a mild hiccup to a major schism between today's world and every possible future. He took another deep breath and donned the motorcycle helmet, visor up.

A few people wandered through the plaza. A man and woman positioned themselves for a selfie in front of the King tomb. The chapel blocked most of the view. No one would notice.

"Okay, time to rock and roll." He flipped the visor down and selected the first command from the small display.

tcs_flow_empros

His finger hovered over the Enter key. His heart beat a little faster. Chloe nodded her encouragement and gave a delicate wave goodbye.

No big deal. You already did this much in Geneva.

Daniel pressed the key.

A rising tone, followed by a flash of yellow light that exploded inside the helmet, much brighter than expected. Temporary blindness lasted several seconds. A sharp tingle made the hair on the back of his neck stand up with a feeling of electricity running down his back and into his arms.

"Wow! That's a jolt to the system." He flipped the visor up.

Chloe and Griffith hadn't moved, but their expressions were now frozen. Their eyes stared straight ahead, unflinching. He'd expected as much. But the sudden darkness was unnerving. Not completely dark, but like a late twilight.

Daniel scanned the walkway and the plaza, seeing only outlines of buildings that had been in bright sunshine only a moment before.

He took the helmet off. No sounds. Still air where there had been a slight breeze. Even the midday humidity was gone, replaced by a slight dampness inhaled with each breath.

"It worked," he whispered to his companions. They wouldn't hear him. No one would, but he spoke aloud anyway. "Flowing empros. Just as you said, Chloe, forward time has collapsed to quantum." Her fingers were still positioned in a goodbye wave.

The experience of a new reality was as exhilarating as Mathieu's demo, but daunting to be doing it alone. He picked up Griffith's duffel bag, stowed the helmet and retrieved a flashlight, an addition suggested by Chloe.

"I'll be back before you even notice I've been gone."

He walked across the plaza, passing frozen figures. The couple still posed for a selfie that from Daniel's perspective would never happen. A young man was in midstride, one foot levitating above the ground, his arms held out but not moving.

Daniel continued out to the street, Auburn Avenue. A car appeared parked in the middle of the street, headlights off in the darkness, the driver holding the steering wheel and looking straight ahead. Daniel knocked on the car window. No reaction from the very stiff driver.

Further down, Auburn intersected Jackson Street with cars frozen in both directions. The dark intersection reminded him of a power outage at night. No lights anywhere. He looked up and easily found the sun, a somewhat brighter circle in the sky. He could stare at it without discomfort, like those odd occasions when the sun can be seen through thick fog, presenting its shape but without any of its brilliance.

Photons are still moving, but slowly. Ticks are measured in chronons.

In front of the Ebenezer Church, a man and woman walked hand in hand, their right legs extended and heels just about to touch the sidewalk. A young girl by their side was frozen with both feet several inches above the sidewalk. Perhaps she'd been skipping or jumping, as kids often do. Her leap would be a record breaker and she'd never know it.

He circled around the family, noting the frozen positions from all angles. The woman had her mouth open; maybe she'd been talking. Or was still talking. These people were still in motion, but their pace was now a billion times slower.

"Nala's going to love to hear about this," he said aloud as he examined the frozen people.

Anyone would. The effect was startling and the options for exploration endless. He was free to go anywhere and do almost anything without anyone noticing. For the people on the street, he wasn't even a blur. He could take the phone from the man's hand. Reach into the woman's purse. They wouldn't have any idea. The bank down the street was no better guarded.

The feeling of power was overwhelming. Daniel began to understand Mathieu's decline into voyeurism. With no one watching, he could literally do whatever he wanted. What's more, he could remain in this state indefinitely. For all practical purposes, forward time had stopped and any time he spent in this state wouldn't delay his mission at all.

Chloe picked up a snack from the café.

It wouldn't be hard to step up to the next level of theft. A free round of golf down at Augusta National? Maybe a quick stop at a jewelry store to pick out something nice for Nala? The bank wouldn't miss a few stacks of hundred-dollar bills. Accounting error.

Simple, but amateur shoplifting. With technology like this, why not go right to the top?

Walk right past security at the Vatican Library and hold Galileo's original letters in my hands.

Of course, reminiscing with Galileo would require transportation to Rome. The frozen cars were solid evidence that anything beyond a mechanical bicycle would be non-functional. Still, he could spend a whole year roaming around frozen Atlanta and it wouldn't matter in the slightest to the president's urgent request. The year 2053 would still be there when he chose to make the jump.

But a nagging thought advised him otherwise; his personal health was on the line. He was breathing air that did not move within his new timeframe. Down at the atomic level, the electrons might be frozen in orbit.

Conceptually wrong. Daniel corrected himself. Electrons don't orbit; their position is a probability computed by the Schrödinger equation, unrelated to the passage of time.

Physicists around the world would have a field day with this new discovery. So many new questions to explore. The scientific side of Daniel managed to subdue the voyeur or the bank robber within him.

Get in, get the job done and get out.

Breathing molecules of air that flowed in a different time frame was unavoidable. Drinking water or eating food might create their own set of digestive issues, though Chloe hadn't worried too much about the croissant. Zin would probably say these issues would only be of concern for extended stays, but Zin's easy-going attitude about everything didn't inspire a lot of confidence.

It would be fascinating to explore this world, but not worth the risk.

Daniel looked into the unblinking eyes of the frozen couple, the woman's mouth forming a word that Daniel would never hear. "I think it's time to peek into the future. Agreed?" Their expressions didn't change, and he patted the man on his shoulder. "I thought you might say that."

Daniel backed up against the wall of the church. "I'll just stay off the sidewalk, just in case there are other passers-by." He pulled the helmet from the duffel and put it on.

He scrolled to the second command on the list.

tcs_initialize_anchor

As Chloe had explained, it would set his anchor point to the current date and time. The display even showed the very precise anchor point: October 9, 2023 at 11:04:16 AM.

Daniel pressed Enter. The device seemed to accept the command, but nothing else happened. Expected. It had simply stored a value.

The next command was no more difficult.

tcs_set_node

He typed at the prompt it provided: **06/02/2053 1:00:00 PM**

The final command was just as easy to select, though its consequences would be vastly more impactful. If Chloe was right, it would send him thirty years forward in a flash.

tcs_compress_forward

This time, Daniel didn't hesitate to press the Enter key, and the yellow light flashed once more.

The family on the sidewalk vanished. The cars in the intersection too.

The sudden changes in the scene before him were easy to spot; like flipping between before-and-after photos, the differences stood out. On the opposite street corner, a tall building now stood where a single-story restaurant had been. He looked up at the neon sign for the Ebenezer Baptist Church, unchanged. The wall behind him was still a dull red brick, perhaps a little darker than it had been.

But across the street, a large birch tree now filled the small park where the sapling had once stood. Undeniable evidence. Daniel shook his head in amazement. "Thirty years passed in the snap of a finger. Wow."

He stepped into the street. The metal tracks embedded in its surface weren't new, but a half block away, a sleek metal-and-glass streetcar paused motionless even though its aerodynamic shape suggested it could move at high speed. The cars occupying the street were stylish and streamlined. At the street corner, a man dressed in a bodysuit rode a three-wheeled motorcycle with sleek curving surfaces that partially surrounded him. The ultra-modern motorcycle could have come straight out of a Batman movie.

The sky had brightened slightly. Still twilight, but with stronger contrasts. The air was warmer too. Perhaps the June date could explain both. He put the helmet back in the duffel and opened the door to the old church.

Dark inside, Daniel guided his flashlight's beam around the entryway. A park service employee stood frozen in conversation with a woman. He wore a sidearm. Perhaps NPS policy had changed over thirty years.

On the ranger's belt was a key ring. Daniel unfastened the man's belt and removed the ring. "I'll just be a minute."

He dropped the duffel and started up the stairs, still creaking, but now the only sound in this impossibly quiet world. The old boards seemed to provide a soundtrack for a horror movie, and Daniel half expected one of the human statues to slowly twist its head while he wasn't looking. They didn't, though Daniel's heart beat a bit faster from the eerie notion.

At the top of the stairs, the door was still locked. He tried each key until one fit and the door swung open. What had been a mostly empty room was now filled with junk: stacked boxes, an old radiator, an empty bookcase. He threaded his way through the collection to the closet door on the other side. Moving a few boxes, he opened the door and pointed the flashlight inside. The shelves were now bare. He ran a finger through a thick layer of dust. No one had been here in years.

Hopeful, he stood on tiptoes and reached to the top shelf, feeling at the northwest corner. His fingers brushed against what might have been a frozen spider, then touched metal and plastic. He retrieved his watch and marveled at his luck.

It was covered with dust, and cobwebs spanned the wristband. "My brand-new watch. Now a relic." He brushed it off and pressed a button on the side. No power remaining, of course.

The incredible had occurred. He'd placed the watch there less than an hour before. Yet thirty years had now passed. He didn't need to see a newspaper banner to confirm this fact. The tree out front was enough.

He twisted the old watch in his hand. "What happened in all those years?"

If only it could speak. But it had, in a way. The configuration was the same as he'd left it. Northwest corner, wristband pin in hole number seven. Strong evidence that this future was derived from the same past held within his memory. It seemed intuitively obvious, but there were other options, and Daniel had considered each one before the jump.

In the simplest case, there was one, and only one, future. One past, one future, one memory. But the universe might allow for more. A branching timeline where decisions and events created entirely new worlds. Perhaps a braided timeline where branches merged at later points. Maybe even some branches that were dead ends where time had stopped altogether.

The existence of the watch didn't resolve every question of contradictory futures, but it did confirm that whatever future he'd just stepped into was directly downstream from a point, now thirty years ago, when he'd placed the watch on the shelf.

What was more, if his coin flipping and number picking had somehow spawned forty different multiverse timelines, he had just jumped to the one and only future that matched his past memory, not any of the others. This was not a random future occupied by some *alternate* Daniel. This was his future.

The concept of a multiverse hurt the brain. Multiple Daniels, each believing they had set the watch to a different configuration. The idea was absurd, and perhaps his test had just ruled it out. If there were forty futures generated by his coin-flipping decision, there was only a 2.5 percent chance he'd randomly jumped to the specific future that matched his memory.

"This is *my* future, the one that I will experience along with everyone else that lives in my today." Nala, Marie, Mathieu, Chloe, everyone. It would be their future too.

"Unless, of course, we change it."

****

Come to 89 Peachtree Center, floor 97, Atlanta, Georgia on the afternoon of June 2, 2053, the video voice of a future version of Daniel had said.

Trouble was, that building didn't exist. The address was just a parking lot, at least in 2023. The FBI had concluded that a new building would be built there and that scheduling a meeting at a location that didn't currently exist was intentional. It might be a warning not to stand at that spot and jump to the future, lest you materialized inside concrete. Or it might have been more symbolic, a way to impress. None of the existing buildings in Atlanta were nearly this tall.

He'd already checked the route. The walk from the church to Peachtree Center would take no more than twenty minutes.

Daniel pulled his phone from a pocket. A *no service* light blinked. No internet connection either, and no GPS. While these communications protocols might be obsolete in 2053, the more likely reason was that every electromagnetic packet of energy was now moving in a different dimension of time. Not much chance of receiving anything when you're flowing empros.

I could still take photos. But should I?

Any information brought back to his time could result in unintended changes. It might even result in the dreaded ontological paradox, if such a thing was possible. A photo of this street scene could theoretically give an engineer in Daniel's day the idea to create the Batcycle he'd just seen. Then, who was the original designer?

An object with no discernable origin. The ontological or bootstrap paradox was one of the reasons scientists proclaimed time travel to be impossible.

He put the phone away. Focus on the mission and return with information that had been vetted as necessary to prevent a nuclear war. It seemed to fit within Zin's boundaries of what other civilizations had successfully accomplished, though it was an open question whether anyone—alien androids included—really knew what they were doing.

He walked alone through a city in twilight, using the flashlight as needed to avoid tripping over curbs. Though mostly empty, a few people stood immobile along the sidewalk, some in midstride, precariously balanced on a single heel, others on both feet. None of them so much as twitched.

Just as strange was the utter calm of the air, feeling more like being inside a closet than outdoors. Absolute quiet too. No birds chirping, no background traffic noise, no wind rustling leaves. This was no ordinary walk.

Daniel walked several blocks, passing under a freeway and along the edge of the Georgia State University campus. For a Monday afternoon, there were surprisingly few students out. Perhaps the summer session had already started. He passed several students wearing long shirts that hung to their knees with muted colors, mostly grays and greens, though colors were harder to detect without the flashlight. Some wore earpieces, possibly Bluetooth phones or maybe just music players. It struck Daniel as odd that everyone he passed was male. Not a single female among them.

"Where's your girlfriend?" he asked one of the students who waited at a train stop. The young man didn't answer.

Daniel turned up Peachtree Center Avenue, and several tall buildings came into view, silhouetted against the brighter sky. Some were typical corporate towers from his day. He'd probably seen them in any photo of downtown Atlanta. But one stood out, unlike anything else in the skyline.

Daniel stopped and gaped upward at a spire that soared to the clouds, far taller than any of the surrounding buildings. Circular and wide at its base, the spire tapered to a point of solid gold. A row of windows just below the golden tip stood out, not because they represented the top floor, but because they were lit.

Light poured out like a beacon across the darkened city.

Photons moving. Electricity flowing. But how?

This was no mistake, no random fluke. The building stood precisely at his destination, 89 Peachtree Center Avenue, and although Daniel didn't take the time to count the rows of darkened windows below, he had little doubt where the bright light originated. The ninety-seventh floor.

19 Spire

Ninety-seven floors up without a working elevator. Daniel was in good shape, but a couple thousand steps would be a three-hour marathon. Not that elapsed time meant anything in this nonsensical world, but presumably his empros-flowing body would eventually need some empros-flowing sustenance. He'd brought two bottles of water and a few snack bars. It would have to do.

He panned the flashlight around the dark lobby, looking for the stairwell entry. The beam reflected off a security desk, where several people were gathered. Behind them was a bank of elevators and more people waiting for a ride up. No point in joining them. From Daniel's perspective, the elevator would never arrive.

Further down a hall, he found a door marked *East Stairway*. Taped to the door was an envelope with a name written in bold letters: Daniel Rice.

"I'm expected. That's good news," he said, peeling the envelope from the door. The physics of quantum time might be complex, but communication between dimensions of time turned out to be easy. Just leave a note. He opened the envelope. The single piece of paper inside read:

Use the service elevator at the end of the hallway.

Helpful but puzzling. Electricity wasn't flowing. Or was it? The top floor of the building was clearly lit, taking advantage of some kind of an exception to the time-related boundaries that Mathieu and Zin had described. Empros-flowing electricity? His flashlight worked, but its battery—and the lithium electrons within it—were already flowing empros just like his body.

Daniel walked to the end of the hall, found the service elevator and pressed its call button. Surprisingly, the button lit, and a minute later the door opened.

Inside, a man in workman's coveralls partially blocked the doorway, his rigid stare looking straight ahead.

"Sorry," Daniel said to the motionless figure. "You probably wanted a different floor."

It seemed best to leave him where he stood. Daniel squeezed past and pressed 97, the highest number available. This button lit too, and the doors closed.

The elevator accelerated, its brisk motion feeling perfectly normal. His silent elevator companion seemed normal too. At floor fifty, Daniel finally spoke to the unmoving form. "You know, it's funny. Why are we always so frosty to each other in an elevator? Must be some kind of weird dynamic that only applies to confined spaces."

The man's lack of response was expected, but creepy. Daniel felt like an undertaker in a mortuary, speaking with the dearly departed. The man's brain synapses were no doubt firing in the extreme slow motion of forward time, unable to perceive the elevator doors opening and closing or Daniel's question.

The elevator slowed, the door opened, and Daniel hurried out. "Catch you on the way down."

Get in and get out.

Another darkened hallway, but at the far end, light streamed through a glass door. Photons moving at their usual speed. Normalcy, but unaccountably so.

He walked the hallway, passing dark doorways with organizational names on the name plates. *The Humanity Preservation Society, Angel Number Ninety-Seven, Disciples of Nations* and others. One of the doors was slightly ajar, a frozen person on the other side. A good reminder that it was not midnight, and this was not a closed office building.

At the end of the hallway, light poured through the upper glass portion of two large double doors. The sign on the wall read *Committee*

Reception. Daniel let his eyes adjust to the much brighter light and peered inside. An empty lobby.

No, not quite empty. A reception desk with a woman's head barely visible above the desktop. She seemed to be in deep concentration, not moving.

Daniel pulled the door open. "Hello?"

There was no response, not from the woman or anyone else along two hallways at either side of the reception desk. Apparently, only the light was flowing empros. Not the people.

The light came from three recesses in the ceiling, but there were other recesses where the lights were not turned on. It felt like emergency lighting during a power outage. Daniel recalled the battery-operated lamp in Mathieu's lab that was within the boundaries of his targeted space. Perhaps this was something similar. Some portion of their electrical system had managed to make the transition to the empros timeframe.

He walked around the backside of the reception desk. The young woman stared at a dark computer display, her fingers hovering over two ovals that rose in smooth hemispheric curves from the desk. Possibly a keyboard of some kind, though the ovals showed no markings.

To one side on the desk was a paper document. Daniel picked it up and leafed through its ten or twelve pages. The first page included a letterhead showing a flying eagle and the words *The Committee* printed in gold. The document itself seemed to be a list of office procedures. About halfway down the second page, Daniel spotted his name.

Arrival Day Plan. Our welcome for the esteemed Dr. Daniel Rice.

It went on to describe what was clearly a planned event, for today. It mentioned advanced preparations that were underway for the main conference room.

"Perhaps you can direct me to this conference room?" Daniel asked the woman. He squatted and looked directly into her motionless eyes. He noticed an odd glint in each eye, a white rectangle. A reflection, likely of the computer display just before time had frozen. He moved closer, his nose almost touching hers. The white spot glistened on the surface of her eye, but any markings within were far too small to make out.

"Like cheating at a poker game. But I doubt I'll learn anything, other than you have beautiful eyes." He stood up. "No worries, I'll find my own way."

He set the duffle bag on her desk and tried the hallway to the left. It too was lit down its length by every fourth overhead light. The hallway led past a few interior offices and finally connected to a large open area filled with people. On one side, floor-to-ceiling windows provided a view out over darkened Atlanta, including the street he'd just walked up.

In the center of the room, a low table was covered with plates of food. Lounge seating surrounded the table, each seat filled by people dressed rather formally and frozen in conversation with one another. Many others stood in small groups, some holding soft drink cans, others biting into potato chips, carrots, and other hors d'oeuvres. It looked like an office party.

Not quite, though. An office party from the 1960s.

Their clothes were noticeably retro. The men wore gray or brown suits with thin lapels, skinny ties, and shiny black shoes. The women were in long slender skirts and ruffled white blouses. Some wore a yellow satin sash around their waists, but in general, the personal decorations were sparse. Perhaps clothing styles had gone backward. They all looked very prim and proper, like watching an old black-and-white rerun of *The Dick Van Dyke Show*.

A glass partition on the far side separated the partygoers from a large conference room where a few more people stood around a long table. A banner over the conference room entrance made it clear he'd found the right place: **Welcome, Dr. Daniel Rice.**

Theory confirmed. Note to all future time travelers: not only do they know you're coming, they even know the day and hour you'll arrive. It's all documented somewhere in the history books.

Another strange thought popped into his mind, and he scanned the faces of every man in the room. There was no one that looked like him, which, in a way, was a relief. Meeting yourself, even if frozen in time, would be deeply disturbing. Much better to gather whatever information they had regarding nuclear launches and get out.

Daniel leaned against one of the lounge chairs, inserting himself in a three-way conversation between an older man and two women. The man looked like he'd walked out of a cigarette commercial from the early days of television, his mouth wide open in some long-winded oration. The much younger women wore blouses buttoned up to their necks, the expressions on their faces feigning interest in whatever the old geezer was saying.

"Sir, ladies. I'm here. What's next? Shall we put a record on the phonograph and dance the twist? Maybe I made a wrong turn somewhere. This is 2053, isn't it?"

He shrugged at their steadfast silence. Perhaps others might offer clues, even if no one could speak. He glanced toward the conference room, his eyes drawn immediately to something on one wall that he hadn't noticed before. A small red light.

The light was blinking.

He hurried through the open conference room door, stepping past a man leaning against a whiteboard. Embedded near the top of the whiteboard, a small red LED flashed on and off with regular pulses. Scrawled across the whiteboard surface was a message clearly written for his eyes.

Join us by flowing forward now. It is your only path.

Flowing forward. Dangerous words, at least according to Zin. Flow forward while time is still compressed, and you'll never make it back alive. A one-way trip to the future, as Zin had said. Yet that was exactly what these people were asking him to do.

Below the handwritten note was what seemed to be a computer link, even though it was just more words on the whiteboard's surface.

Touch here for more information.

Maybe it wasn't just a whiteboard. It might be a wall-sized computer operating in empros time just like the lighting. Daniel pressed a finger to the lettering. A black dot appeared and expanded into a rectangle containing a page of text and several drawings.

He scanned the text and examined the diagrams, his pulse quickening as he read.

"Oh, shit."

Daniel read further and let out a lungful of air once he'd completed. "Holy crap, we've already fucked up."

It was bad news. Very bad. But he wasn't ready to accept it without confirmation. He scrawled a quick note on the whiteboard, took a picture with his phone and left the conference room. Grabbing the duffel bag from the reception desk, he pushed through the office doors and into the dark hallway, beginning to run.

The words on the whiteboard were stark and clear, and the predictions were frightening:

Unfortunately, you will need to make this decision on your own.

Daniel called the elevator and dropped to the street level, racing out of the building and back into darkened Atlanta.

Can history change so easily?

He took the same route along Auburn Street back to the Ebenezer Baptist Church, but at a run-trot. His breathing was heavy, and his legs ached when he finally reached the church.

Retrace your path. Exactly.

The whiteboard had warned of changes. Things he might not even notice. Daniel fumbled getting the helmet on his head. He flipped the belt's power switch. He selected the command that would bring him home, though what that home now looked like was anyone's guess.

tcs_decompress_forward

The command would return him to the anchor point in his own time. The yellow light flashed, and a shock ran down the back of his neck. Still flowing empros, he flipped the helmet visor up, scanning for differences.

The frozen cars on the street were back to their 2023 styles, though possibly in different positions than when he'd left. He wasn't sure. The large tree on the far side of Auburn Street had returned to its original sapling size. At least the tree confirmed he'd returned to his starting point thirty years before.

But the family with the skipping child was nowhere to be seen on the sidewalk. A small difference, but any difference was unsettling. The anchor point was precise, to the second.

Daniel picked up the duffel and ran around the corner into the plaza. The couple taking a selfie by the pool was gone too. Instead, a heavyset man sat by its edge, a person he hadn't noticed at all when he left. His heart pounded.

They'd better be there.

Daniel sprinted across the plaza toward the quiet location behind the chapel where Chloe and Griffith would be waiting. He skidded to a stop.

They should have been standing there, frozen, just as he'd left them. But they weren't.

He scanned in every direction. No Chloe, no Griffith.

"Damn!" He jerked the helmet off, very nearly slamming it to the ground before he thought better of it.

He'd initialized a precise anchor point just as Chloe had described. The decompression should have returned him to the time he'd left. Chloe had done the same thing back in Geneva with no issues. She and Griffith should be standing right there.

It wasn't any flaw in the belt or how he'd set the anchor. The explanation on the whiteboard had predicted this turn of events.

Deep compression is more than a simple adjustment in the frequency of a standing wave.

The past had already changed in subtle ways, caused simply by his initial act of compression. Worse, the words on the whiteboard had given Daniel an explicit warning.

Decompress if you must to verify that the world of your anchor point has changed, but do not attempt to flow forward into that altered world. Temporal dislocation will result, a most terrible way to die.

Daniel stood alone in the plaza, contemplating the very explicit warning from the future.

Do not flow forward into your own time.

The command itself was simple. He even pulled it up on the belt's display.

tcs_flow_forward.

His finger hovered over the Enter key.

If he pressed the key, he'd be back to normal. Forward time. His phone would work. He could call Griffith and find out where they'd gone. He could call Reverend Clure or the FBI headquarters. He could find out what *subtle* changes might have occurred to his own time.

But he might also die before he had the chance to reach anyone. Becton had.

The prediction on the whiteboard had just been validated. With Chloe and Griffith missing, something had changed in his own time, and the risks of this mission had jumped dramatically.

Daniel turned the belt's power off and stowed the helmet in the duffel. There was no hurry; he could remain in empros time indefinitely and think this through.

Death by temporal dislocation. Likely the same thing Zin had called snapback. Almost certainly what killed Becton. Yet Chloe had survived. How?

The explanation on the whiteboard wasn't clear, though it did use the words "deep compression." Perhaps Chloe's one-day jump to tomorrow wasn't *deep*. Too small to bring on snapback? A thirty-year jump might be different.

Daniel desperately needed another discussion with Zin and Chloe, but it might be too late for that now. Zin was back in Geneva, impossibly far away for a man stuck in empros time. Every airplane in the world would be frozen in place. Chloe might still be somewhere in Atlanta, but finding her without a working phone seemed like a long shot.

And what would he do if he found her? Stick a note in her pocket? He would have to wait a lifetime for her response. Living in empros time had its drawbacks.

Daniel pulled up the photo he'd taken of the whiteboard and reviewed its message once more. The page on the whiteboard wasn't all bad news, it also offered hope:

Join us by flowing forward now. It is your only path.

The words on the page continued. The people of the future had learned much about time compression since the early days of CERN experimentation, it read. They had learned how to avoid temporal displacement. They had developed methods to examine and control the subtle changes that resulted from deep compression. Jumping to the future and returning safely to your anchor point was still possible. They could help.

But to take advantage of their offer, Daniel would first need to flow forward into the future. Exactly what Zin had told him not to do.

20 Reception

Daniel sat in one of the conference room chairs, surveying the frozen people around him. The same people, even in the same positions, just as he'd seen it in his first jump. He'd jumped to precisely the same time in the future, June 2, 2053 at 1:00:00 p.m. To the second.

The oldest man in the room still leaned against the whiteboard, apparently thinking. A second man sat on the far end of the conference table, staring into space directly in front of him, possibly examining something hovering in the air. What the apparition might be Daniel couldn't determine. There was nothing there.

A younger woman sat at one side of the table, a tablet computer lying on the table in front of her. She wore the same conservative 1960s-style clothing that everyone in the party zone wore. Muted colors. Understated style. If this was modern fashion, someone must have confused *Vogue* and *GQ* with the Sears Roebuck catalog.

Outside the conference room, the party was still in progress just as before. Whatever had changed in the past wasn't significant enough to cause downstream ripples. At least the major points in the history books hadn't been rewritten. These people were still expecting him.

He studied the pages on the whiteboard once more. The details weren't fully explained, but there were links to other documents that matched the summary, including one document that explained how the first CERN teams investigating quantum time had missed several key relationships. It even mentioned Aastazin's failure to identify these issues and suggested humans were better off when they relied on their own scientific research.

As predicted, the decision to flow forward would be his alone to make. He could sit and watch frozen people forever, but they weren't going to tell him any more than was on the whiteboard.

No chance of getting in and getting out. No coin to pick up and take home.

A disappointment, but as Griffith had suggested, if preventing the nuclear launch was simple, they'd have explained it with the first coin. There was also no sign of his older self. He'd checked the side hallways and offices. No other Daniel.

You could study this to death. Get on with the show.

The next step might be irreversible, risking everything. His job, his past life, Nala. But he'd always been a scientific optimist with an intrinsic confidence in the technological advancements of the future. These people had offered to help.

Daniel powered up the belt.

He took a position in the main office space, just in front of the floor-to-ceiling windows. Thirty or so partygoers stood in groups chatting and eating. "This ought to turn some heads."

He donned the helmet and selected the critical command on the belt controller that would send him into their time.

tcs_flow_forward

A rising tone came from the belt and the light flashed in the helmet. He opened his eyes to a room fully lit by the sunshine streaming through the windows behind him.

The sounds of dozens of people in conversation died quickly as everyone in the room pivoted toward Daniel. He removed his helmet, and cheers erupted.

"It's him!"

"Dr. Rice!"

"He's so young!"

"Oh my God, it really happened!"

"The first time traveler!"

His newly animated audience burst into applause. Daniel gave them a bow of the head.

This might not be so bad.

Several men came over to shake his hand. "Let me be the first to welcome you, Dr. Rice," said the geezer who'd earlier been the centerpiece for his bored female companions. His face now beamed with enthusiasm. "I'm Brother Timothy, the social functions director. I can't tell you how honored we are that you could join us."

"Happy to be here," Daniel said. "I think." The surroundings looked and felt normal, even if everyone dressed differently. But the bizarre notion that he'd really jumped to the future hadn't fully sunk in yet.

"I'm sure you're confused to be here, but don't worry at all about the so-called perils of time travel," Timothy responded. "The Committee has that all figured out. They'll take good care of you. You'll see."

Another man shook his hand, introducing himself as Brother John. Another odd title, but then so were their clothes. John seemed an amiable guy, offering Daniel a cola, the can labeled with the same script font from his own day. Some things never change. He accepted the drink, puzzled for an instant about whether 2053 forward-flowing atoms would be okay to consume, and then took a big swig of the ice-cold drink. It certainly helped to quench the thirst from his run.

"Thanks," he said. "Have you been waiting for me long?"

"Years," answered another man who introduced himself as Brother Jake. He patted Daniel's shoulder. "Just kidding. The party started about an hour ago. We knew your arrival time might vary a bit, so we decided to enjoy ourselves by starting a little early. Hope you don't mind."

They seemed pleasant enough people, even if they were all monks or strict Baptists. But they'd promised to help, and socializing wasn't his priority.

"I know this is a big occasion and I'd love to party with you, but I do have some critical questions," Daniel said.

"Of course, you do," Timothy said. "And we want you to feel comfortable knowing that everything is under control." He pointed to another man coming out of the conference room. "Look now. Brother Christopher is right on time to help."

It was the older man who had leaned against the whiteboard. He had longish gray hair and wore circular wire-rimmed spectacles, almost like John Lennon's, or maybe Ben Franklin's. He walked purposefully toward Daniel, a broad smile on his face.

"I've been waiting for this day, Dr. Rice," he said, shaking Daniel's hand. "All of us have. Even you."

"And where am I?" Daniel's future self was still nowhere to be seen.

Brother Christopher's expression was somber. "We'll get to that. It's a bit complicated." He motioned to the conference room. "There's much to cover, Dr. Rice. Would you care to join me?"

Daniel nodded, and Brother Christopher led. The rest of the partygoers quickly formed a receiving line to the conference room door, each person reaching out to shake Daniel's hand and wish him well as he passed by. The women even curtseyed as if he was royalty, and their handshakes were just as dainty, mostly fingers.

The love pouring from the room was a little overwhelming. Never good at being a celebrity, Daniel had always been awkward in his television appearances back in his own time. Fans encountered individually on the street or in a restaurant were much easier, but he completely understood why movie stars sometimes ran from crowds.

With the conference room door closed, he felt an instant release of tension. Christopher introduced Daniel to two other men in the room and motioned to the only woman present. "Sister Angela will capture our conversation." Angela tipped her head. On the other side of the glass wall, the crowd dispersed, returning to their office party even though the guest of honor had left.

146

Brother Christopher put a hand on Daniel's shoulder and nodded to the crowd on the other side of the conference room glass. "Thanks for indulging us. You enjoy your privacy, I know." He motioned to Daniel to select a chair and then took a seat at the head of the table.

"We've met before?" This time travel thing would require some unnatural conversations.

"Once. Last year. You looked very well then, but you look much younger today." He smiled, flashing perfectly white teeth. A very handsome man, probably in his late sixties.

"Then I'm at a disadvantage. You've met me, but I haven't met you... until I'm much older." Did his older self remember meeting Brother Christopher in this conference room during his jump to the future? Sorting through the convoluted logic for which memories might exist in another version of himself was a surefire way to end up with a headache.

"Brother Christopher Holloway at your service. You might say I manage this level of our office. I'd give you my e-card, but you're not yet equipped to receive it. We'll take care of that in a minute."

Daniel's mind was filled with questions, but he led with the most obvious. "With all the family titles, brother, sister, everyone seems to be part of a religious organization."

"We are," Christopher replied. "Does that surprise you?"

"I wouldn't expect a religious organization to have expertise in time manipulation. In my day, it was the realm of select scientific teams."

He leaned back in his chair, looking self-assured. "Times change, Dr. Rice. How well did those select teams do in preparing you for your jump? I'm guessing that things didn't quite work out as planned. Am I right?"

"A few hiccups, yes." Daniel leaned forward on his elbows. "I wasn't expecting to be speaking with you at all. It was supposed to be a quick smash-and-grab operation." He nodded toward the whiteboard, still displaying the messages he'd seen in empros time. "It appears I've already made subtle changes to the past."

Christopher folded his hands together. "Never mind that the jump wasn't what you expected, Dr. Rice. Or that we're not the organization you expected. The important thing is that you're here now. We can work with that."

Angela's fingers moved as they spoke, though not like keyboard typing in his day. More fluid, as if she only needed to touch a few locations on the ovals beneath her hands and the rest was filled in by magic. Maybe the device was translating their audio and she was only adding notes.

She looked up as Daniel paused, her hands poised for whatever words of wisdom were about to be spoken.

"Are you aware of my mission?"

"Of course. You're here to prevent a war, and thank God for that."

"And you can provide the information I need?"

"Not me specifically, but I'll get you to the right people."

Good so far, the but the burning issue would need to be settled before Daniel's anxiety would calm. "Can you help me get back? In my day, an android representative from Sagittarius Novus advised that after flowing forward in a future time, I could never return. Something called snapback."

Christopher nodded. "You've been misinformed. What people call snapback is easily managed. The real hazard is temporal dislocation, but it, too, is not insurmountable. Rest assured, we can help."

He leaned forward and lowered his voice. "Over the years, we've found Aastazin and his colleagues to be less than reliable."

"So you know Zin?"

"Not personally, but I know of him."

"Is he still here? Could I speak with him? Maybe we can clear up this discrepancy."

Christopher tilted his head to one side. "Possible. I'll look into it for you."

"How about now?" The man had been helpful so far, but it was still worth pushing on this particular topic. Daniel didn't relish the idea of dying to serve his country, and while Zin was certainly cagey, Daniel didn't agree that he was unreliable.

Christopher laughed. "Not that easy, Dr. Rice. The Committee would need to approve contact with Aastazin or any other representative of Sagittarius Novus. We don't speak with them much anymore."

"Times change," Daniel echoed.

"Times do change," Christopher repeated.

A falling out between humans and our alien partners. Whatever had happened would probably require a longer discussion, worthwhile, but not immediately critical. Besides, too much knowledge of future relationships might not be wise for someone expecting to return to the past. Even Zin had agreed with that principle.

Focus. You can still get in and get out... with their help.

"So, how do I get back?"

Christopher held out a hand. "Give me the belt. We'll have our people start working on it immediately."

Daniel hesitated. "What are you're going to do? For me, this is kind of an important device."

Christopher shook his head. "It's not my area of expertise, but I assure you, we have the right people. The Committee is responsible for every aspect of temporal management. You'll find that we're far more careful than the scientists of your day."

He laughed, pointing at the leather contraption around Daniel's waist. "Really, look at that thing. This is how your people manipulated something as sensitive as time? Utterly absurd. Like doing surgery with garden shears."

The loose wire that Chloe had tacked down with her lip piercing was beginning to wiggle again. It was easier to see the faults of the past once you were firmly in the future. Hindsight. He probably should have never come. He should have refused the president. Demanded a more thorough testing, smaller jumps, with reliable equipment. Too late now. He had committed to the future. He might not get back without their help.

Daniel removed the belt, stored it in the duffel with the helmet and pushed the bag across the table. "How long will it take?"

"Mmm. Twenty-four hours. Maybe a little longer. In the meantime, I'll arrange for you to meet with Committee Security. They'll provide the briefing you'll need."

"Regarding the nuclear launch?"

"Yes, and other related matters. After that, while you're waiting for a much-needed equipment upgrade, I hope you'll join us as an honored guest. We will make your stay just as pleasant as we can."

Daniel held up a hand. "I appreciate your hospitality, but I do need to be careful. Remember, once I return, the politicians of my time are going to take action on whatever I tell them. It might not be a good idea for either of us if I learn too much. Your world could change. It probably *will* change."

Christopher handed the duffel bag to one of the other men, who took it and left. "There is some debate about that, yes. One timeline or multiple branches with multiple worlds? Different versions of you and me? It's all very confusing, and I leave it for the philosophers to study. In the meantime, you're on a mission, and my job is to help you fulfill it."

"But I'll need to stay overnight?"

"At least overnight. Dr. Rice, if you're worried about the air, or food, or water, don't be. The air you breathe is no different than in your own time. Perhaps slightly more carbon dioxide, but our world is addressing that problem, and doing quite well at solving it, I might add. My point is, your health is not at risk by spending the night with us."

"Okay." He certainly felt healthy, just as Chloe had reported when she'd returned from tomorrow.

Christopher lowered his head and peered over the top of his glasses. "We do have something special planned for the evening, if you'll indulge us."

"Another party?"

"A small affair, honoring the world's first time traveler."

"I'm not really the first," Daniel said. *Did they not know about Becton?*

Christopher looked confused. "Well, if you're not, don't tell the historians. Or the celebration organizers. They've been planning this event for a while."

He really doesn't know. Curious.

It was possible that Becton had a lower level of interaction than the FBI thought, perhaps even remaining unobserved in empros time. Yet, Becton had managed to bring the holographic coin from the future back with him. That required some level of interaction.

"Indulge us, Dr. Rice. This is an historic day, one that every person in this nation has read about in school. It's only one night."

Sister Angela looked up from her typing and nodded, smiling for the first time.

A celebration, with Daniel as the guest of honor. It sounded awful. He wasn't great at socializing. Small talk bored him, and he wasn't planning on asking the bigger questions about the future.

On the other hand, a limited reconnaissance might not be a bad thing. The president would certainly ask about the reliability of the information he'd gathered, and this society had a few quirks worth investigating. The fact that they didn't know about Becton was fascinating by itself.

One evening. He'd need to wait overnight for the belt upgrade anyway. From a time travel perspective, the delay didn't really matter. Even a week in the future wouldn't postpone his report to the president by a single second. Once they had the belt fixed, he'd return precisely to his starting point.

"Okay, sure. I'd be delighted to attend the celebration. But, uh... we *will* do the nuclear briefing first, right?"

Christopher chuckled. "Always on task. You're just the same as your older self. Yes, briefing first."

"Will I... uh, be meeting myself at this celebration?"

Christopher's smile tightened. "I'll leave that question for Committee Security if you don't mind. I'll take you there next, but before we go, I'll need to bring you up to modern standards."

"Which means?" He hadn't noticed any brain plugs on the side of anyone's head.

Brother Christopher reached into a cabinet and withdrew a small plastic box, setting the box in front of Daniel. "Modernization for the visiting caveman. Yours to keep."

Daniel lifted the top of the box and peered inside. It was a coin, very much like the one Becton had brought back with him.

Daniel lifted it from its case and twisted the coin in his fingers. A three-dimensional hologram of an eagle popped from its surface as it rotated. On the opposite side was a hologram of a sharp-pointed building, probably the very building he now occupied. The coin shimmered in silver and gold colors. He felt along its edge for a hidden compartment, but there was none. Subtle differences between this coin and Becton's version.

"It's beautiful. I've seen one before, but slightly different."

"Olinwuns have been around for years, with a variety of models for different purposes. This version will do everything your old cellular telephone did, plus your laptop computer, and your car keys, and your wallet, and a lot more. It's why we call it an olinwun. You understand? All. In. One."

"Ah, yes. Clever." He held the coin between his thumb and index finger and placed its edge on the table, ready to start it spinning. "Oh, I guess I need a mirror."

"You don't, at least not here. Spinning on a mirror is only required in places that lack a fully functional power infrastructure."

"You're sending power through the air?"

"Yes, quite easily. The coin is one of many receivers. Just lay it on the table and tap the eagle with your finger. Your biosignature will activate it."

Daniel did as instructed. The eagle hologram disappeared and was replaced by words floating in the air just above the coin.

Initializing for first use...

Within a half-second, the words were replaced.

Welcome, Dr. Daniel L. Rice (touch for profile).

He touched the coin once more, and a full page popped into the air, rendered as realistically as if a piece of white paper were being held up. On it was every detail of his personal life. His birth date, age (74), Social Security number (partially hidden), address (a number and street that he didn't recognize) and considerably more.

"Sorry about the age," Christopher said. "The system is not yet aware that you've arrived, but it's fully capable of tracking two instances of the same person. Security can fix that for you. I'll let them know."

"Understandable. In my time, we don't have two instances of the same person roaming around the world at the same time."

"Rare here too. You'll find that this device is very handy. Intuitive too. You probably won't need any instructions. For now, just carry it in your pocket. But we'll have time before the celebration to upgrade your clothes to our modern standards. Among other improvements, you'll find a slot in the pants specifically designed to carry your olinwun."

He wondered what he'd look like in one of those polyester jackets and cuffed slacks. "Thanks, but no need for an upgrade. My clothes are fine."

Christopher's eyes darted up and down as if he was evaluating a dubious claim. "You sure? There's a shop right in the building, and your olinwun already has sufficient monetary credits, courtesy of the Committee."

He glanced down at his white shirt and casual gray pants. "But I'm a time traveler from the past. Shouldn't I look the part?"

Christopher nodded. "Well, you certainly stand out, Dr. Rice. Let me know if you change your mind."

Daniel flipped the coin in the air. It produced a nice ring and landed in his palm. "Beyond buying clothes, I assume I'll need this device while I'm here?"

"Yes, for building access, security protocols and the like. From here on out, there won't be any open doors with people waiting for you on the other side. This afternoon was a special case."

"I was wondering about that. How did you get the elevator, and the lights, and that whiteboard to work in empros time? The rest of the city was dark." His question fit within the guidelines of a limited investigation. He was curious too.

"Empros-facing electrical systems are not easy and not inexpensive either. Some of the technology within this building was designed for this very day. Perhaps you see the importance of your presence, Dr. Rice."

21 Security

Brother Christopher opened a door into a lobby that looked much like Committee Reception, but one floor up. The building, Daniel had now learned, was called the Golden Spire, and Committee Security was the first floor within the golden tip.

"Sister Jacquelyn," Christopher said with a flourish of his hand. "Meet Dr. Daniel Rice."

The receptionist stood up from behind her desk and provided the same fingers-only handshake prevalent at the party. Like the receptionist on the floor below, she was young, very pretty, and wore the same buttoned-up old-fashioned clothing, including the satin sash he'd seen on some of the other women downstairs. Her short-bobbed brown hair was streaked with red highlights, a fashion he hadn't seen before.

Her eyes flitted from the floor to his face. "Oh my God... it's so exciting to meet you, Dr. Rice." She had a toothy, bashful smile.

"My pleasure," Daniel replied.

Christopher pulled an olinwun from a side slot in his pants. "Hold yours up for a second," he said to Daniel. He tapped the coins together and a blue informational popup appeared over each.

Contact record transferred.

"This is as far as I'm authorized to go," Christopher said. "Sister Jacquelyn will take good care of you from here. But please, do come back to Committee Reception when you've completed your briefing and we'll prepare for the celebration."

"I can't wait," Sister Jacquelyn said.

"You'll be there tonight?" Daniel asked her.

"Yes! I was so happy when the invitation arrived." She held up her own olinwun, no doubt containing an e-invite to the big party. It seemed everything in their society resided on this compact device.

She wiggled her coin. "Do you mind? I have a good collection of contacts, but yours... well, that would top them all."

Daniel reached out and tapped the coins together. She beamed, looked to the floor sheepishly and then glanced up once more to catch his eye. If this was a come-on, she was doing a fantastic job.

"Perhaps I'll see you there," Daniel said. He shook Christopher's hand. "Thanks for your help. Let me know when the belt is ready for use. I'm pretty sure this olinwun thing will give me a notification of some kind."

"It will," Christopher said and waved to Jacquelyn.

She nodded to him. "Praise him and you, brother."

"Praise him and you, sister."

Christopher left, and Daniel leaned both hands on the reception desk. "So, what's next?"

A sly smile crept across her lips. "Dr. Rice," she said with a slow sensuality that belied her earlier bashfulness. "I do declare."

He waved her off and took a step back. "Sorry, sorry. Nothing suggestive. Expressions in your time might be a little different than mine. I just meant, what's the next step? I'm supposed to get a briefing from someone?"

Her smile remained, and eyelashes flitted across large green eyes. "Of course, I'll get you to your briefing." She paused, the bashfulness returning. "But... if you're interested... well, there's always tonight."

For a society with such conservative dress and religious expression, the sexuality seemed to come far too quickly.

"Am I missing something here?" Daniel asked in earnest.

"What do you mean?" she asked, her lashes fluttering. This woman had plenty of charm, and she could switch it on at will.

157

Daniel raised both palms. "Why the come-on?" Might as well get right to the point. If he was going to attend a party of the future, he'd better know the rules.

"Sorry," she said, her smile fading. "I didn't mean anything by it."

"Yes, you did. You were coming on to me. You just met me two minutes ago." He tried to keep his tone neutral. Maybe she really didn't mean anything by it. After all, this society wasn't his own. But her manner was both fascinating and disturbing. He was curious, more than anything. "Sorry, Jacquelyn, I'm not from around here, but in my time, people don't use bar talk in offices."

She put her hands on her hips. "Sorry," she said, head down. "Can we reset? I've been waiting for this day, but I think I screwed things up."

Daniel paused. "How about dropping the fake bashful act? That'd be a good start."

She showed a hopeful smile, peering from beneath a lock of hair. "You want the real me? I can do that."

"Jacquelyn, no offense, but I don't think I'm here to see you."

She returned to her chair, looking defeated. "I'll get him. Elder Benjamin is who you need to see."

She pressed one of the ovals on her desktop and checked a display. "He'll be right out." She looked up, penitent. "Really... I'm sorry. I get..."

She hadn't offended; it was more that her behavior was so off-the-scale weird. Changing the subject would help, and this was an opportunity to begin the limited investigation of this society. A security receptionist was the perfect target, particularly since she was now on her heels.

"Who's in charge of this place? Brother Christopher says he's not even authorized to be on this floor. Seems like a lot of structure."

158

"Levels," she said, her voice becoming quieter. Her eyes glanced to the ceiling. Daniel looked up, too. If there was a camera up there, he didn't see it.

She spoke just above a whisper. "Committee Reception below us. We're Committee Security. Then above us, Committee Management, then Directorate. Finally, the Committee Chambers. That's where our blessed Father resides."

"And Father is in charge?"

She nodded. "Our blessed Father."

Her words put Daniel on alert once more. The hyper-religious nature of an organization dedicated to the management of time travel was a clear warning sign that his twenty-four-hour investigation was merited. She'd given him the first clue that he'd likely face a full-fledged bureaucracy. Potentially difficult to get answers, but at least he now knew who was at the top.

"Thanks, Sister Jacquelyn, that helps. Obviously, I'm a newcomer." He reached out a hand and she took it, gently. "Reset accomplished. We're square. And tonight, I'd be happy to chat or dance, or whatever people do at time travel celebrations." As he let go of her hand, her smile returned.

"Dance, for sure," she said, beaming once more. "Thanks, Dr. Rice."

"Call me Daniel."

This time, the pep in her voice sounded authentic. "Thanks, Daniel."

The door to Daniel's left opened, and a large man in a dark blue suit walked through. He extended his hand. "Dr. Rice. You look like your photographs. I'm Elder Benjamin."

Jacquelyn stiffened and refocused on her computer display. Daniel glanced between the two. Something there, but very odd. Details were important.

159

Benjamin turned out to be a no-nonsense kind of guy, with murmurs and grunts in response to Daniel's initial pleasantries and a stoic demeanor that sharply contrasted with the receptionist's flirtatiousness.

They passed through three locked doors that opened automatically as they approached. A properly authorized olinwun in the pocket seemed to do the trick.

Deep inside the vault-like interior of Committee Security, they entered a plain windowless room with a desk and three chairs. Two other men joined them, introduced as Brother Samuel and Brother Joseph.

"Put your olinwun on the desk," Benjamin said as he took the seat behind the desk. Daniel retrieved it from his pocket. "Touch it." He did, and a green banner popped up with his name above and several menu commands below.

Benjamin took control, touching the coin in coordination with the in-air display and ending up on Daniel's profile page. "We'll need a physical sample to distinguish you... from you, so to speak." He waved to Brother Samuel, who stood up and pulled a small sheet of paper and a small pair of scissors from his pocket.

Samuel approached Daniel. "Do you mind? I won't take much."

"Seems like I just did this," Daniel said with a laugh. He pointed to the left side of his head. "Take it from there, then both sides will match."

Brother Samuel lifted a few strands of Daniel's hair and snipped, the hair caught on the paper. He curled the paper and left the room.

Brother Benjamin explained that it wouldn't take long to process the hair sample. They waited in silence for a minute until an orange light displayed next to one of the boxes on the profile page, still hovering in the air.

"Touch the coin again," Benjamin said.

Daniel did, and the page refreshed. Above it hovered a lowercase letter *i* inside a blue circle. Next to it, an informational message.

Dr. Daniel L. Rice, instance 2 distinguished.

"Well, that was fast," Daniel said. He glanced over the information once more. His age was reset to forty-four, and the address was now declared as *unresolved*. "Quite the technology you have here."

"Your instance is distinct now. There won't be any further confusion no matter where you go. Any questions?"

"Not about the coin technology, but I have dozens related to my mission. I'm concerned that events in my time might have already changed." Christopher had said security would tell all. Time to test that theory.

"Temporal dislocation," Benjamin said with authority. "You decompressed and saw it?"

"I'm not sure what I saw. I just know that things weren't quite the same as when I left."

Benjamin shook his head forcefully and waved a hand in the air. "Small detail. Don't worry about it. We'll adjust the decompression on your device to minimize the dislocation. Your return jump will be far more precise. Plus, you won't die."

"Happy for that."

"Let the engineers handle it. You and I need to focus on the nuclear launch. First, confirm for me your exact anchor point date and time."

"Well, Christopher's team took the belt. The date's easy. October ninth, 2023. I believe the time was right around eleven a.m., but I'd need to confirm on the controller."

Benjamin waved a hand. "Close enough. The launch didn't occur until October nineteenth, so you'll have ten days when you get back to set things right."

Good news. Ten days seemed like plenty of time to notify the right people who could take action. Griffith had been worried they might be cutting it a lot closer.

Benjamin leaned forward and spoke to the object. "Display video 2023 Aftermath from WNN archives."

An inverted cone of light shot up from the coin, and spinning images within the cone settled into a three-dimensional video. "This is a good introduction, but we'll share a lot more. You'll have time to review it all at your leisure."

A woman reporter wearing orange hazmat gear walked along a street in ruins. "University Avenue in Berkeley, California. More than six miles from ground zero, and a place where not a single MIRV warhead landed. Yet it's leveled."

As she walked, the camera panned, showing the shredded remains of buildings now reduced to twisted steel beams surrounded by rubble. "This used to be a thriving city of more than two hundred thousand people and home to one of the world's major universities. Now..."

The camera zoomed in on one of the few remaining structures, a gray stone tower rising above the rubble, most of its top sheared off. "Much of the Bay Area looks the same, some areas much worse. No one has yet ventured into San Francisco itself."

"Volume off," Benjamin commanded. The video continued to show scenes of unbelievable destruction, but now without commentary.

"Nine million people in the San Francisco Bay Area," Benjamin said. "Estimates were that two million vanished in just a few seconds, their bodies literally turned to ash. Millions more died in the days and weeks that followed."

"Awful," Daniel said, his eyes transfixed to the video. He thought of friends he had in the area. Jenny and Mark and their two kids lived in Walnut Creek, not far away. A niece was a current student at Cal, and

Daniel had worked with several university scientists there. Those lives, and millions more, were at grave risk.

Get in, get out, but make sure you've got this right.

The camera focused on a blackened arm protruding from a pile of broken bricks. Daniel spoke in a quiet, even tone. "It's one thing to talk about a nuclear launch, another to see what that rather sterile word really means."

"I lost my sister there," Brother Joseph said. "She'd just moved to Palo Alto, excited about her new job in Silicon Valley."

Daniel's throat tightened. "I'm sorry, I don't know what to say. It feels like we're responsible. My time, I mean." He looked up at Benjamin. "How did it start?"

"Rogue US submarine. The commander probably went berserk, but we'll never know for sure. His missiles hit Vladivostok in Siberia. Russia returned fire, destroying the sub. But they also took out San Francisco in retaliation."

"Can it be stopped?" It would make the video nothing more than a shadow of things that might be.

"We believe so. Whether stopping it helps us directly, we don't know. We've made temporal changes before. Sent people to our future who returned with enough information to alter a path. It's not hard to verify that it works. Just wait a few years, and the altered future reveals itself. But changing our future only gives us a hint that we might be able to change our past."

"The future changes that you made... were they of this scale?"

Benjamin spoke to the olinwun. "Video off." The images disappeared. "Sorry, but I'm not going to say any more or give you any examples of what we've accomplished. That's information you don't need to know. To tell you the truth, Dr. Rice, we're being cautious. We're withholding some information from you." He leaned in closer. "For us, you could be a dangerous person."

Daniel considered the remark. It was true; he was the only person in the room who would be returning to what they called the past, armed with information to change the future—their present. Depending on time's true nature, he might have power over this society.

Benjamin spoke. "Download file X-five-four-dash-three from Committee Security server seven on my authority."

A message popped into the air.

Voice recognition: Elder Benjamin Tomei. Validation success.

It was quickly replaced.

Download complete.

He motioned to Daniel to take the coin. "You now have all the information we believe you'll need to prevent the nuclear launch. Study it. Take it to your leaders and military advisors. They'll understand what to do, and with a ten-day lead, they'll have plenty of time to stop it."

"Thank you," Daniel said, putting the olinwun back in his pocket. "I'm sure this information will help us, but I'll be honest with you. I think I'll need more. I'll need credibility. I can't just walk in and tell them to 'do this.' They'll want to know about its source. They'll want credentials and verifiable confirmation that these instructions can be trusted to solve the problem."

"Credentials are part of the file I just downloaded."

"I was thinking more along the lines of direct validation. For example, before I return to 2023, I should speak with my older self. Regardless of how weird that might be, it could be powerfully confirming. I've already asked to speak with the android, Zin, and I'll definitely want to speak with Father, who seems to be the leader of this organization."

Benjamin shook his head multiple times. "Too much information is not good for either of us, Dr. Rice. Time manipulation is a delicate process, and the Committee has considerable expertise. You arrived here by way of a few alien components stapled to a leather belt. We take our job a little more seriously."

Daniel didn't disagree with his points, but any recommendation for action, any battle plan, any intel which could affect political policy, must come with solid justification. Leaders rely not just on the recommendation, but on who gives it. "Without my personal recommendation, I can't guarantee what they'll do with this information."

Benjamin nodded. "I see. Give me a minute. I may have what you need." He walked out and returned a few minutes later. "The item I had in mind was not available on the network. I've resolved that."

He set his own olinwun on the desk and touched its surface. "Display video, Daniel Rice, April second, 2053." He turned to Daniel. "A statement you made two months ago."

The cone of light shot up, and a video image formed. It was eerily similar to the one he'd watched alongside the FBI in the Eisenhower Building, an event that seemed like ages ago.

His own face appeared, older, but no doubt Daniel Rice.

"Yes, yes, I understand your objections," the older version of himself said. The old man looked agitated and seemed to be speaking with someone else just off camera. "But here's my point. You can't do this by yourself. The Committee didn't exist in 2023. You'll need to trust the scientists and the leaders of the day. When my younger version arrives, you'll need to trust him, just as I have learned to trust you. If we both take a leap of faith and believe in each other, we will be successful. And that goes for me too." He looked into the camera. "You're recording this, right? Daniel, if you see this, listen to them. They're doing the right thing."

"Close," Benjamin said, and the video shut off. He put the olinwun away. "You heard it from yourself."

The video seemed real enough and was hard to ignore. His voice was the same, his mannerisms. Even the indentation on the earlobe, just like the first video. This wasn't an actor, and there was no reason to discount it as fantasy. Time travel was real enough.

But why are they withholding? Why isn't Daniel senior sitting in the room right now?

"I'd still like the opportunity to speak at length with my older self."

"Complicated, but I'll take it under advisement," Benjamin answered.

The stonewalling continued, but at least they admitted it. *It's for the best*, they were saying, and they might be right. No telling what could happen if you met your future self. Like crossing the streams from your proton packs.

The briefing was clearly over when Benjamin stood and guided Daniel out. They shook hands in the reception area, and Benjamin offered, "Good luck," and closed the door behind him. Daniel stood alone without saying a word for several seconds. Something about the video he'd just witnessed bothered him, but he couldn't put a finger on it.

"Everything okay?" It was Sister Jacquelyn.

Daniel broke from his trance. "Yeah. I think so."

"Get what you needed?"

He walked around to the reception desk. She looked sincere this time, not deceitfully bashful and not overtly sensual. The candor suited her.

"I hope so." He patted the olinwun in his pocket. "Yeah, I think I have everything I need."

"Good. But I could suggest one more item before the celebration tonight."

"And that is?"

"Um, some modern clothes? What you're wearing... it's really..."

Fashion. Could anything be more absurd? To Daniel, their clothing looked ridiculous, conforming, old-fashioned. But, from their perspective, he was the oddball.

"Okay, second time I've heard that. I'll see what I can do."

Her bashful look returned, and she flashed her long lashes. "While you were talking with Brother Benjamin, I might have set an appointment."

"For me? At the shop downstairs?"

She nodded shyly and bit the knuckle on her finger. It was a good show from a convincing actress.

Daniel rolled his eyes. "Okay, okay, I'll go."

"Oh, good!" she squealed. "I already sent the appointment to your olinwun, and Brother Christopher said he'd be right up to take you there."

"I see," Daniel said, nodding. "Railroaded into *modern* clothes. At least I'll have a proper pouch for the olinwun."

"And you'll look great. The nano-tailors are very good."

22 Secrets

The boutique shopping area at the base of the Golden Spire wasn't large, but it was filled with people. Nice to know that purchases in the future weren't entirely online. The clothing store was a small boutique with only a few items of men's and women's clothing on racks. Most clothes, a sales clerk explained, were custom-made, including all men's suits.

Brother Christopher sat on a nearby bench, waiting for Daniel to make his selection though it wasn't clear why an escort was required. The shop wasn't hard to find. Daniel's olinwun could have no doubt directed him to it.

The chatty sales clerk flipped through the available styles by swiping her hand through the air while suits of various colors were projected onto Daniel's image in a full-length mirror.

"Oh, I like this one," she said, hands on hips and studying the mirror. As Daniel shifted to the side, the projected suit shifted with him.

From Daniel's point of view, every suit looked pretty much the same. But he accepted the clerk's advice and she completed the transaction by passing a wand over Daniel's olinwun. The words *Payment transferred* appeared above it.

"Okay, let's get some measurements," she said, guiding him to a back room and drawing a curtain across the doorway. She reached for another wand hanging on a hook and proceeded to wave it across his body like a handheld metal detector.

"Just curious," Daniel said as she measured his legs, "where do they keep all the women over thirty around here?" She was young, probably late twenties. He hadn't seen any females much older.

"You must be Canadian," she answered, running the wand around his ankles.

Once noticed, the uniformity among women was glaring. Every receptionist at each floor in the building, the women at the impromptu party, now the sales clerk—all the same. Young, twenties to mid-thirties. But not a single older woman.

The conformity didn't stop with age. He'd noticed a strong similarity in appearance. Clear skin, understated makeup, no tattoos, no piercings. Chloe would have hated the future.

"No, I'm American, just not from around here." She clearly didn't know who he was, a relief in a way. Maybe his time travel stardom didn't extend beyond the Committee offices.

"Then you should know. Six months and done." She stood up straight and patted a slight bulge on her belly. "I'm taking child leave myself in a couple of months."

"Congratulations. Your first?"

Her eyebrows pinched down. "You really aren't from around here, are you?"

Daniel shrugged, curious. "No. What did I miss?"

Her voice softened. "We only work until our first child. That's the law."

"Wait. This shop won't hold your job open while you're on maternity leave?" A guaranteed job after childbirth was widespread policy around the world in Daniel's time, even in America, a notorious laggard in modern business practices. Had they really gone backwards?

She frowned, looking like Daniel had just asked if she was a lion tamer. "Six months and *done*. Like, really done. It's illegal to work after your sixth month of pregnancy. There's no coming back." She cupped one hand to the side of her mouth and whispered, "You sound like my mom. She says it used to be different."

Daniel blew out a breath. "Yeah, it was different. Very different. And this law is nationwide?"

She nodded. "Far as I know. I've only been outside of Georgia once, though."

A technologically advanced society that was sociologically backwards, worse even than the mid-twentieth century. If men held all the positions of power and women were banned by law from doing much more than having babies, there was bound to be tension and outright conflict. Yet they all seemed happy.

Something told him it wasn't quite as harmonious as it looked. After all, she'd felt the need to whisper her commentary on the pregnancy law.

She pulled the curtain back. "All done. My manager will bring the suit in just a minute."

"That fast, really?"

She looked puzzled, studying Daniel. Seconds later, a man dressed in a shimmering aquamarine suit stepped into the room, carrying clothes on two hangers. He hung a suit on one hook and a shirt with two ties on another. Instant clothes produced by whatever unfathomable technology they had in the back room.

The man shook Daniel's hand. "It's an honor to do business with you, Dr. Rice. If we can be of further service, please let us know." He left as quickly as he'd arrived.

The sales clerk held a hand over her mouth, her eyes wide. "Oh! You're him! I'm so sorry, I didn't recognize you. You're so much younger."

His fame might extend a little further than he'd thought. "Daniel Rice, the younger. Happy to meet you."

She shook his hand, clearly embarrassed by her mistake. "Wow! The younger Daniel Rice. Well, the only Daniel Rice now."

Daniel's ears perked up. "The only?"

She bit her lip. "Sorry. They say you're here from the past. It must be so weird to know how it all ends."

Her eyes drooped slightly. "You were a hero to a lot of people. My mom was so sad to hear when you... I mean the older you... passed away." She perked up. "But now that you've arrived, maybe you can change that?"

A revelation coming from a salesperson who minutes ago hadn't known who he was. It made her statement all the more believable. Older Daniel was clearly dead. And apparently, it was common knowledge.

Why didn't they tell me? Christopher and Benjamin had both sidestepped the issue.

Daniel tried not to react. This young woman might be a better source of accurate information than any of the people upstairs. If they'd withheld his death, what else were they hiding? "Do you recall when the older version of me died?"

She bit her lip again. "April? I think so. Around April." She lowered her head. "I'm sorry. This is rude. I'm talking like it's somebody else. But in a way, it's you."

Daniel nodded, pondering his next move. He looked up at the young woman. "What's your name?"

"Rosie." She smiled.

"Thanks, Rosie. You've been very helpful. Take good care of yourself and your new baby."

Daniel grabbed the hangers and walked back into the shop. Brother Christopher stood up. "Found what you wanted?"

"And a bit more," Daniel said. "You and I need to talk."

23 Sanctum

Brother Christopher seemed embarrassed by his part in withholding information, but when confronted he admitted the deception. Daniel Rice, the older version, had indeed passed away in April. Of cancer. Christopher gave his condolences.

It was all bad timing, he said, and they weren't sure how to tell Daniel, so they'd kicked the responsibility up to the next level.

Given the bureaucracy Daniel had seen so far, the explanation rang true, but only partially. Christopher had certainly escorted Daniel for control purposes. There was probably more they didn't want him to know, and it was time to put a stop to it.

"Take me to your leader. Father, I believe you call him?"

Somewhat surprisingly, Brother Christopher agreed. He'd set it up immediately, he said.

While Christopher spoke with higher-ups via his olinwun, Daniel returned to the shop's dressing room and changed into the new suit. It fit perfectly, though the narrow lapels and skinny black tie—even a buttonhole for a flower stem—seemed a throwback to a distant past, a style he'd only seen in old movies and on television.

Fashions come and go. And then come around again.

He looked at himself in a full-length mirror. Despite being a suit that his grandfather might have worn, the look was beginning to grow on him. He imagined himself as a character from *The Man from U.N.C.L.E.*, an old television spy show from the 1960s that he'd seen online once or twice. The years might be jumbled, but playing the part of a futuristic-throwback Napoleon Solo was strangely appealing.

Just like any good secret agent, it's time to confront the guy at the top.

Now dressed for the part, Daniel rode the elevator with Brother Christopher in silence. They got out at floor ninety-seven and then walked a stairway three levels higher to Committee Directorate. Another reception area with another young woman at its desk. *Girls*, as they used to say in the 1960s, and she was dressed for her part in this historical throwback.

She scanned his olinwun, and he was handed off to Director Noah, who assured Daniel he could take him directly to Father. Passing through another security door, they started up a second spiral stairway.

"No elevators in these lofty realms?" Daniel asked his guide.

"The stairs represent attainment of a worthy goal," Director Noah replied. "The layout makes you think as you climb." He was a plump man in his fifties and wore the same retro suit as every other man but with a circular gold collar, wide enough that it folded down over his shoulders. It reminded Daniel of the collars worn by Egyptian kings, and it looked equally out of place.

Along the stairway wall, Daniel was surprised to find windows with a view over the city. Outside, an orange tinge, reflected from nearby buildings, revealed the coming sunset. From the ground, he hadn't noticed windows at the golden tip to this soaring building. Perhaps the exterior coloring formed a two-way mirror, hiding the people inside but allowing them to look out.

Noah opened a door at the top of the stairs into one more reception area, this one considerably more glamorous, with a floor that glowed in soft white light while overhead recessed lighting produced a subdued blue hue. There was no reception desk, but a young woman stood in the center, awaiting their entrance.

Her curly blond hair fell across a high lace collar on a white blouse with puffy sleeves. She wore a long skirt, as did many of the other women, and held a small tablet in her hand.

"Welcome, Dr. Rice," she said with a practiced voice. "Our blessed Father is so glad you could join us."

"Glad to be at the top. I am at the top, aren't I?"

She smiled and waved one hand forward. "Right this way."

Director Noah remained behind without comment while Daniel followed her around a tightly curving wall. The lighting become darker as they proceeded until the curving walkway opened to a large circular chamber, dimly lit by the sparkle of hundreds of points of light covering a domed ceiling. It reminded Daniel of a planetarium.

To the left side, a single door led to an exterior deck, the door's smoked glass partially obscuring a view of sunset and the city lights.

To the right stood a white oval ring, a shape Daniel immediately recognized as a portal to four-dimensional space. Its size and shape were no different than the portal Daniel recalled passing through at the Kennedy Space Center in Florida—an event that now seemed long ago.

In the center of the circular chamber, a raised portion of the floor with a brass railing around it looked like it might serve as an altar or a speaker's podium. A curving bench built into the wall served as seating for the audience.

"Beautiful room," Daniel said. "Is Father outside, or will he be arriving soon?" He motioned to the portal.

She stood at attention and consulted her tablet. "Soon."

They waited in silence for a minute until a band along the top of the portal oval began to glow in a violet light. There was a sound of crackling electricity, and a man dressed in a long black robe with purple stripes on both sleeves walked through the opening as if he'd passed through a pane of glass.

His head was partially covered by a white visor, which he removed and set on a tray next to the portal. His hair was nearly to his shoulders, gray and wavy. He wore a closely cropped beard, peppered with gray.

He lifted the robe's hood over his head and walked toward Daniel, his hand extended. "Dr. Rice, welcome."

Daniel noticed the young woman's head bowed, her eyes closed. He grasped the man's bony and weathered hand. "Nice entrance. Father?"

"Yes. In another time, you'll know me much better. These are very different circumstances." He spoke to the woman, her head still bowed. "Can you secure the portal please, Arabella?"

She nodded, still silently at attention.

"My apologies, Dr. Rice. These chambers are for instruction. Not suitable for our discussion. Would you care to join me outside? It's a glorious view." He held out a hand, and Daniel started toward the glass door.

"It won't take long. I really have only one question."

"But it will lead to others."

Daniel opened the door and stepped out to a deck that hung a hundred stories above the city and far above every other building. The tip of the spire reached another fifty feet over their heads. The building's asymmetric shape wrapped partly around the curving deck, giving its precarious perch at least some sense of security.

Beyond the railing, the city of Atlanta spread in every direction, with a mix of city lights and darkened hills to the north. The shadow of night was beginning to envelop the surroundings, punctuated by orange-tinted clouds hanging in the west to close out the day. Sounds of traffic far below reminded Daniel that the motionless city he'd traversed in empros time was very much alive.

"Stunning," Daniel said. The air was warm and humid, but at this height, a constant breeze kept it comfortable.

"The Lord reveals his handiwork each day."

Daniel soaked in the view and, when he turned around, found Father standing close behind. His long black robe fashioned an unsettling figure, and the hood framing his stern, heavily lined face seemed designed to intimidate.

175

Daniel stood tall and squared his shoulders. There was no reason to act like one of Father's minions. "I'll get right to the point. Apparently, I'm dead. I died very recently, and for some reason, your people kept this information hidden."

Father stood rigid, not blinking at the accusation. "You don't really think it was you who died, do you?"

"A version of me," Daniel said. "The same person at a different stage of life."

Father nodded, his eyes scanning the details of Daniel's younger self. "Yes. He is dead. A brain tumor that was diagnosed too late. It took him quickly."

Daniel leaned his hip against the railing, a daredevil move that surprisingly steadied his nerves. "Is there some reason that your organization didn't want me to know? Outside this building, my death is apparently widely known."

"Where did you hear of this?"

"Doesn't matter."

Father glanced at Daniel's new clothes and nodded. Perhaps he was making a note of their mistake, allowing Daniel to mingle briefly with the public.

"Everything has its place and time. There is a plan, whether you recognize it or not." He stepped back and began a slow walk, staring upward. "Now that your fate has been revealed, I believe your mission is more critical than ever."

"Why is that?" It was true that he'd no longer be able to validate the nuclear launch prevention plan with his future self, but that probably made little difference to the plan's execution.

Father circled around Daniel. "You've learned what most people never learn. How, when and where you will die. How will you react to this privileged information? Some people deny their fate. Even rebel against it. What kind of person are you?"

"I expect to fulfill this mission, if that's what you're asking. Return to my time and deliver the nuclear launch information."

His stroll ended at the rail. He leaned against it and looked out over the city. "That's good to hear. Yes, Dr. Rice, you *will* return to your own time. I will ensure that you do. You see, it was my fate to bring you here."

Daniel voiced a suspicion that had been building as he'd climbed the stairs to this pinnacle. "You gave the coin to Becton, didn't you?"

He smiled. "Not quite. You must understand that your jump to our time was well documented. The famous Dr. Daniel Rice, the world's first time traveler. Everyone knew you were coming, even if we didn't know how. But that changed a few months ago, last April. Elliott Becton's arrival was a complete surprise."

It made sense. Nothing was known about Becton's jump to the future, and he'd died before the police or the FBI could question him. With fewer historical records to work with, the people of the future could easily be caught unaware. Some, like Christopher, were still clueless. Father at least knew Becton's name.

Daniel listened intently as Father continued. "Becton's arrival changed everything. You see, Dr. Rice, when Becton arrived, I realized for the first time in my life that I was responsible for your historic jump. My fate was sealed by a force beyond my control. Three months ago, God sent Elliott Becton to me."

Daniel pondered his reasoning and figured he had the answer. "A pathway to the past. Backward time travel is impossible, but Becton opened that door for you."

Father nodded. "A conduit to reach you. It answered many questions for me, but it also sealed my fate."

"You gave him the coin."

Father suppressed a smile. "God's work is plainly in front of you, yet the scientist still cannot see it." He shook his head, his voice becoming serious. "No. I sent Becton home and asked him to return at a later date. He'll be arriving next week, in fact."

Daniel froze in thought. The idea was nonsensical. How does a dead man return next week? Daniel was still missing something. Father was clearly involved, confirming that Becton was the messenger who brought Daniel to the future. But if Father hadn't given the coin to Becton, who had?

The answer struck him like a brick in the face.

You're thinking linearly. Time isn't like that.

Daniel put a hand to his mouth. "The hair... inside the coin..."

Father nodded. "The hair is the key, isn't it?"

Father stood silently as Daniel reviewed the events of the past few hours in his mind: Brother Christopher providing an olinwun that hadn't initialized correctly, Security taking a few strands of his hair to reset that device. The pieces of the puzzle fit.

For the first time since he'd arrived, Daniel's logical mind became acutely aware of the bizarre reality of time travel and its profound implications. According to the FBI, the hair inside the coin wasn't gray. It couldn't have been taken from his older self.

"The hair inside Becton's coin was my own," Daniel whispered to himself. "Your people took the sample less than two hours ago. Soon, they'll combine those strands of hair with a special oil taken from a vial in a small church somewhere in Atlanta. Oil that is accurately dated to 2053."

"My plan, exactly."

Daniel faced Father. "You didn't give the coin to Becton. But you're *going* to give it to him next week."

Father nodded. "Odd, isn't it?"

Daniel let out a gasp. "Cause and effect reversed."

The surreal construction of a closed time loop was happening before his eyes. Daniel's arrival in 2053 had *preceded* its cause. The loop would be complete next week once Becton was given the coin. He would take it back to 2023 and provide Daniel with a reason to be here now. Completely illogical, but there it was.

Worse, time had revealed its seemingly impossible structure with disjointed events that were logically out of place. From the perspective of 2023, Becton was already dead. Yet, in the very near future, he would no doubt materialize, claim the coin and return to his starting point.

"Strange, yes," Father said. "But we each play a part in fate."

"Is that what you think this is?" Daniel looked him in the eye, attempting to determine what other revelations he might be withholding.

"Our fates are intertwined," Father said. "You were called here by evidence that was only collected today. But for you to be standing here at this moment, I must complete my part next week." He put a hand on Daniel's shoulder. "Dr. Rice, an intricate web surrounds us. We may not see it, but we cannot ignore it."

Daniel peered past Father's hood and into his dark eyes. "And you intend to complete the time loop?"

"The decision has already been made. When Elliott Becton first arrived three months ago, I knew it could not be a coincidence, not so close to your scheduled arrival date. Our historical records mention the coin you received, but not its source. Since this device was only invented in 2040, we knew it had time traveled. But how? Reaching to the past is impossible."

"Unless someone from the past comes to you," Daniel said with authority. "Becton was your path. Or will be."

"We think alike, Dr. Rice. I believe it is why God chose to intertwine us in this way. Even though we ascribe to different philosophies, my background is not so different than your own."

179

"You were once a scientist?" It hardly made sense, given the religious references that dominated his words.

"A computer scientist. Probably not the same as your field, but the logic is equivalent. In my youth, I was what they used to call a programmer." He held up his hands. "Yes, these fingers typed on an old-fashioned keyboard, writing code. Object-oriented code. Have you heard of it?"

"Yes, but I'm no coder myself."

"Object-oriented programming is quite fascinating—and surprisingly applicable to the manipulation of time. This discipline uses two concepts, a *class*, which is a detailed definition of complexity—for example, how a car's engine works—and an *object* that is a member of that class, the car itself."

"Interesting, but what does it have to do with time?"

Father put both hands on the rail and leaned out, breathing in the night air. "Few people know this, but I can tell you with some certainty that time is the same as object-oriented programming. I do not speak metaphorically, but realistically. Each of us is an instance of a class. You are Dr. Daniel Rice, but you are not the only one. You've already seen video from another version of you, another instance of the class of Dr. Daniel Rice. I've seen the same thing myself."

"You've been to your future?" Daniel had suspected it, but it was time to establish credentials and corroborate the evidence. Otherwise, Father and his organization might repeat half-truths all night.

"Yes, many times. I've had long conversations with myself. Several versions."

Daniel inhaled deeply. "That would be difficult."

"It's not. It's eye-opening. The true nature of our universe is revealed. I am one of many. One instance of a class. The same is true for you. There are countless Dr. Daniel Rices, each occupying a slice of time. A quantum bit of time, a chronon, as you scientists say."

"What's more," he continued, "each instance uniquely interacts with his world, just as objects within code do. Your instance asked to meet with me, and here we are. But another instance of you may have decided to speak with Brother Christopher instead."

"The many-worlds concept."

"As some call it. I prefer many instances. The world doesn't duplicate just because someone interacts with it, but paths through time branch regularly. I tell you this so that you'll understand our motivation. You will return to your time with information that will change our time. The instance of me that stands before you will know nothing of these changes. But other instances of my class will."

He hadn't provided any evidence, but his theory was possible. Altering the past might only affect the people of the past. Their future versions, if those versions could be thought of as separate people, might never know that a change had taken place.

"I have a duty to my class. We all do."

"Manipulate events in time, and your work will improve the lives of other versions of yourself. It's an interesting idea."

"It's more than interesting. Once you fully understand its power, the idea is compelling. It's why the Committee was formed. Our duty is to manage history not for ourselves, but for our classes." He took Daniel by the elbow and guided him back toward the door. "When your device is ready, return to your own time. Our people will give you an explicit procedure. Follow it. Do not deviate—your life depends on it. Once you are home, pass our instructions to the leaders of your day, and make sure they follow them precisely. Millions of lives are depending on it."

Daniel contemplated one piece of the puzzle that didn't seem to fit. Zin had examined a log file in the belt's controller and determined that Becton had made multiple jumps, presumably never flowing forward and therefore never testing the concept of snapback. And yet, on his final jump, snapback very likely killed him.

"If my safe return is guaranteed by this procedure, then why did Becton die?"

Father's face soured. "I'm sorry, I wasn't aware that Becton died."

Daniel shrugged. "I guess from your perspective, it hasn't happened yet. But unless something changes, when you send him home next week, he's going to die upon his return, possibly from an effect they call snapback."

Father shook his head. "Such an imbecilic idea, snapback. A fantasy perpetuated by elite alien machines who pass themselves off as one of God's creatures." Father's face was stern. "If Elliott Becton died, it was because he didn't follow the procedures given to him, the same procedures I give to you. There can be no deviation."

Daniel's head was spinning with the potential consequences of every interaction between the past and the future. According to Father, convincing Becton to follow the return procedure would save his life. He wouldn't die in an Orlando police station, as he had. The FBI might never learn about the mysterious coin. It might be delivered to Daniel in a completely different way. Or not at all.

Are we changing history even now? Or is something else going on?

24 Readiness

USS *Nevada*
North Pacific, 12 nautical miles southeast of Adak Island
October 9, 2023 16:07 Pacific Time

Lieutenant Commander Helen Tierney lowered her binoculars and stiffened as a cold gust of Alaskan wind blasted the bridge of the USS *Nevada*. Though well above the spray coming off ocean waves, the bridge on a ballistic missile submarine was no more than an indentation at the leading edge of the sail. Not much of a wind break.

"Visual is clear," she told Captain Cory Lundstrom, who stood by her side. The lack of nearby vessels confirmed what radar had already told them. They were alone, hidden below a thick cloud layer just south of the Aleutian Islands, exactly as planned.

Another blast of cold air raked across the bridge, and the submarine's executive officer grabbed her cap before it flew into the Pacific. "Nippy," she yelled in the wind.

"Let's get below," Lundstrom said. "Bring her down to launch depth."

"Aye, Captain."

Down several ladders and into warmer air, they entered the Command Center, where a dozen sailors manned multiple computer workstations surrounded by switches and glowing lights. Two of the sailors sat at control wheels like a pilot and copilot, ready to guide the eighteen-thousand-ton boat wherever the officers pointed.

"XO has command," the captain called as he walked in.

Tierney took over, barking out orders, and the room came alive with activity. A minute later, the deck tilted, forcing everyone standing to grab the nearest handrail. Launch depth was forty meters at the keel, enough to submerge the massive ship while leaving only the tip of a single antenna above the water.

Captain Lundstrom pulled a microphone from its hook on the bulkhead, his voice broadcasting from bow to stern. "All hands. Prepare for TRE, commencing in five minutes. This is a readiness exercise. Exercise only."

The TRE, or Tactical Readiness Examination, was standard procedure for the world's most deadly machine. A ballistic missile submarine was a weapon that no one expected to use, but to ensure that it *could* be used, regular drills were required. The TRE would bring every system online, walk through every step of launching their twenty-four Trident II D5 missiles, and ensure that every crewmember was ready to perform as required.

There were subtle differences between an exercise and the real thing. Targeting computers would use simulated authorizations, and the live fire control trigger would remain locked away in a safe, accessible only to the weapons control officer. Instead, they would use a simulation trigger whose signal to launch went only as far as the computer.

Weapons Control Officer Lieutenant Randall Kline tapped Tierney on the shoulder as he walked past. "Heading below. Let me know when you have the sim codes."

"Should be just a few minutes." She watched as Kline dropped through a hatch to the Fire Control Room, one deck below.

"Launch depth," a sailor called out.

"Steady as she goes," Tierney replied. "Compensate for ballast."

"Aye, ballast is nominal. Even keel."

"Very good." Tierney glanced toward the captain. "The boat is ready, sir."

Lundstrom nodded and spoke once more into his microphone. "All hands. Battle stations, missile. Spin up port and starboard tubes. Set condition to 1SQ."

The command was no different than he would have given if this were the real thing. Training wasn't useful unless it mimicked actual conditions. The condition code 1SQ was a signal to everyone on board that they were expected to be on high alert and treat every system as active. But like any training exercise, key safeguards would be included to ensure that no missiles ever left their tubes.

"Comm, give us some codes," Tierney called out. The communications officer was one of those safeguards. He would simulate the reception of a command that would come from Naval Operations if the president were to order a nuclear strike. The encrypted codes would provide randomly generated targets, many of them simply locations in the ocean.

A minute later, the communications officer had completed his task. "Ready, ma'am. Standing by."

"Ready, Captain," the XO said. She reached to a safe and dialed a combination that had been reset and memorized when they'd left port in Bangor, Washington. Inside was a ringed binder and a single key on a lanyard. The captain performed the same task at a safe on the far side of the room.

Tierney thumbed through the pages of the binder. "Got the authorization code?" The communications officer handed her a slip of paper with a lengthy sequence of letters and numbers printed on it, the decrypted first line of their simulated launch command. She compared to a page in the notebook.

"Launch command is authorized by the exec," she said and handed the slip of paper to the captain.

He examined it against his identical binder. "Launch command is authorized by the captain."

"Aye, Captain," she said. "Comm, send the codes to Fire Control."

The checks and double-checks would ensure that no single person gave the launch command or activated the systems. By design, it took the full complement of the submarine's crew to send a missile skyward.

The captain and exec stepped to opposite ends of the Control Room. Each lifted a cover and inserted their key into a switch.

"Ready, sir."

"Switch on," the captain commanded.

They both turned their keys simultaneously. A red light on one side of the control room started flashing. Tierney issued several more orders, and one by one, sailors confirmed the status of system readiness.

"All systems green. Standing by, sir," Tierney said.

The captain picked up his microphone. "Fire control, captain."

"Fire control, aye," came the response over a speaker. "Weapons Officer Kline. Codes received."

"Okay, Weps, you're authorized. Initialize the fire control system."

"Aye, Captain. Authorized on your orders."

****

One deck below in a small room on the starboard side of the submarine, two sailors stared intently at their computer screens. One of them, Fire Control Technician Second Class Joshua Swindell, had a single bead of sweat running down the side of his cheek.

186

Standing behind them, Weapons Officer Kline hung the microphone back in its cradle. "Let me know when you've got the targets loaded and confirmed."

He lifted an orange pistol grip from a slot on the desk. It looked like a cross between a video game controller and a handgun, complete with a trigger but without any gun barrel. The device was attached to the desk by a coiled wire and was labeled on both sides with the word SIM.

"Initialized," called out one sailor.

"Initialized," Joshua said.

Joshua had no idea what would happen next, and his lack of knowledge was just as terrifying as the task ahead. The Lord was testing him. If he was lucky, that was all it was, and he wouldn't have to carry the task to its completion.

He fingered the slip of paper in his pocket. It would only take a few seconds. Type the code into the computer and the simulated targets would be replaced. Impossible to accomplish with the weapons officer standing right behind him, but the Lord's vision had been explicit. Weps would be the first to die.

In Joshua's other pocket was a key normally kept in the safe on the wall, its combination known only by the weapons officer. How the Lord had extracted the key from the safe, Joshua would never know.

Joshua imagined the final task, his heart pounding. As the last person alive in Fire Control, he would unlock the trigger box. Inside would be a red-handled pistol grip, like the simulation version but with LIVE written on both sides. He would pull the trigger three times, and the floor beneath him would shudder as each missile exploded to the surface on a blast of flash-vaporized steam.

It would be the hardest thing he'd ever done.

25 Celebration

The mood was festive, the attendees numbered in the hundreds, and the musically synced light show that played out on the ceiling was extraordinary.

The "small party" that Brother Christopher had described required no less than the ballroom at a neighboring convention center. A moving sidewalk suspended over the city streets provided direct access from the Golden Spire.

Except for the glass of iced soda that he wished were bourbon, Daniel was surprised at how entertaining the grand event had turned out to be. A few of the partygoers wanted his autograph, usually scrawled across one body part or another. But for most of them, an autograph was hopelessly outdated. They wanted a *capture*.

The technique involved flipping an olinwun into the air, posing, twisting or jumping while the device collected 3-D images, surrounding sounds and even smells, and then catching the coin before it hit the ground. It was a form of entertainment, modeling and photography, all rolled into one.

Three elegantly dressed, highly energetic young women who couldn't be out of their teens had just finished a capture with Daniel at their center.

"Oh my God, it turned out great!" said one girl, pointing to the cone of light projecting upward from her olinwun. Within the cone was a fully three-dimensional video of the three girls posing like fashion models, laughing, jumping and screaming as they clung to Daniel's arms and shoulders. Daniel's part in the performance consisted of a stealthy smile with arms folded across his chest. His best Napoleon Solo impersonation.

The video clip could be rotated to any angle and even zoomed out to life-sized human figures when the olinwun was placed on the floor. On their encouragement, Daniel stepped through the elaborate projection, encountering the unmistakable scent of the girls' perfume as he did.

"A slice of reality, captured forever," he said. "I like it. What do you do with these captures?"

One girl shrugged. "Mmm, post them, exchange them. The guys usually upload them into games."

"Yeah, lots of games use them," her friend explained. "If you do a real-time interactive capture, you become part of the game."

"Like immersive virtual reality?" Daniel asked.

She rolled her eyes and smirked. "Way better than that."

Daniel laughed. "Sorry, I guess I've missed a lot."

The girls waved goodbye as another group approached, led by Brother Christopher, who had been popping in and out as Daniel's protective chaperone, though he claimed his role was no more than that of a helpful host. Daniel was unconvinced. At least Brother Benjamin had been upfront about hiding information. Christopher was all smiles. The kind designed to obscure.

The men in the group introduced their wives, who were the first older women Daniel had met since arriving in this very skewed future. They all seemed pleased to meet him, with several questions that boiled down to how the Stone Age man liked the modern world. Questions he answered as gracefully as he could.

Daniel recognized one of the men from Security, Brother Samuel, who had snipped the hair sample.

Time to push this investigation forward.

"Brother Samuel, it finally occurred to me the true purpose of that hair-clipping diversion," Daniel said to him.

"To sample your proteins," he answered. "To reset your olinwun."

"But there was more to it than that, wasn't there?"

189

Brother Samuel seemed unsure what to say next, stuttering without saying anything. It didn't appear to be an act.

Push a bit harder. "Some olinwuns have hidden compartments, I'm told."

Samuel still had the same questioning look. He clearly didn't know. Possibly due to their bureaucratic layers. One level didn't seem to know what the next-higher level was doing. But another answer might be time itself. Daniel had to keep reminding himself of the nonlinearity of events. Someone would prepare the coin that Father would give to Becton, but that might not have happened yet. Becton wouldn't even arrive until the following week.

"Sorry, my mistake," Daniel said. No reason to press the poor man any further. He simply wasn't the right target.

One of the women reached out. "Dr. Rice, now that you've seen how much more advanced things are now than they were years ago..." She hesitated, looking slightly embarrassed to ask her question. "Well... I just wondered if today might be the turning point for you personally."

"Turning point?"

"Yes, for your rejection of the old ways. You know... the reckless science of the past, before there was divine guidance."

"Sorry, I'm not really sure what you mean."

"Well, you're here to prevent the nuclear war. Isn't that right?"

"Yes, that's the mission." He didn't realize everyone else knew this fact, but it might have been part of the grade-school education that had made his name so well known.

"It just breaks our hearts to think that if the Committee had been around sooner to manage science, none of those people would have died."

No one had yet mentioned this role of the Committee. Father certainly hadn't. "Sorry, I don't really see science as something to be managed. It's a methodology for discovering what's real. But I hear your point. The nuclear weapons of the past may have been handled recklessly. I wish we'd found a way to eliminate them before they were used. But I see that as a political issue, not a scientific issue."

Her husband interjected, his Georgia drawl manifest. "She just means that in the past science was kind of every-man-for-himself, whereas today, things are much better controlled."

Another man added, "You're probably not aware of all the good things the Committee does. Government ministries, the guidance of our children through spiritual education, management of the historical archive and of contemporary journalism. Without their important work, our country would have been lost to the secularists a long time ago."

There seemed to be a slight separation of church and state issue among these people. The more he heard, the less he liked about the structure of this society. Still, he was the intruder, and his mission wasn't to correct their view of science, or guide their politics.

Impossible to ignore, though, once I'm home. There's no memory reset button on the belt.

Back in 2023, he still enjoyed a public platform, and sometimes when he spoke about the common misconceptions of science, people even listened.

"Changing the subject slightly, I'll be leaving in the morning, going back to the bad old days of reckless science. Any stock market tips you can give me?" Daniel said with a smile.

"CheerSoft," one man said, laughing.

"No, I'd go with Pink Toe," his wife said. "Every woman buys their products." She waved a hand at Daniel. "You'll make a fortune."

Daniel held up both hands and laughed. "No, really, I was joking. I'm sure there's some cosmic prohibition against inside information from the future."

As they laughed, Daniel looked beyond the group. An eye-catching figure of loveliness stood alone. Sister Jacquelyn, dressed to kill, her eyes locked on to Daniel like lasers.

His gape must have been obvious. One of the men in the group turned around to see what had caught his attention. "Time for us to go, ladies," the man said and ushered the group away. Even Brother Christopher left to get a refill of punch.

Never taking her eyes off Daniel, Sister Jacquelyn sauntered over. Her floor-length gown outlined the curves of her body and shimmered in iridescent colors. A single yellow flower decorated the dress at her collarbone.

She cozied up far too close for the average cocktail party conversation, brushed back a lock of hair from her forehead and unleashed large green eyes. Looking up at Daniel and then shyly to the floor, she purred, "Could I, uh... get an autograph?"

Daniel's heart beat a bit faster. "Why it's Sister Jacquelyn, from Committee Security." Formality might adjust the dynamic toward the mundane. "You look exquisite." Or, maybe not.

A splash of red at each cheekbone matched the highlights in her hair and accentuated her natural beauty without hiding it. Her dress, though modest, allowed a scant peek of the curve of her breasts.

Her eyes still locked on his, she pointed down with one finger. "I see your pen is ready."

Daniel nearly choked. "Uh... yeah, got it right here. What would you like me to sign?"

She pulled at the edge of her sleeveless dress, exposing one shoulder. "How about here?"

He'd already done it a few times. The shoulder seemed to be the preferred spot, except for one young man who had rolled up his shirtsleeve.

Daniel uncapped the pen and hovered its tip over her shoulder. "You sure you want that beautiful skin marked up?"

With lips tight and eyelids lowered, she cooed, "You won't hurt me, will you?"

Daniel couldn't help himself, playing along. "I'm always gentle."

A sultry smile appeared on her face, widening. "Then... I want everything you've got."

Daniel signed his name, put away his pen and did his best to clear the smirk from his face. He looked into her eyes.

"Shall we drop the game? Jacquelyn, you are one astonishing woman, and in any other circumstance, I'd follow you around like a puppy dog. But this day is different. For one, I'm not going to be here very long."

Her voice morphed from sultry to shy. "I don't mind. There's a lot we can do with one night." She ran a finger under the lapel of his jacket. "My apartment's really close."

"Yeah... about that." Daniel took a deep breath. "There's someone else. Back in my time. She's kind of special."

Jacquelyn looked down, her earnest voice returning. "She's very lucky." Shifting her dress exposed a bit more cleavage. "But she doesn't have to be the only one."

An image appeared in his mind of Nala curled up against his chest, napping in a hammock stretched between two palms. It brought back feelings of a rare kind of pleasure. A pleasure comfortable and warm, gentle and soft. Not how he'd normally describe their relationship, but jumping to a future where you were dead was a powerful reminder that life wasn't endless.

Daniel shook his head, surprised he was turning down such a beautiful woman. "I'm sorry. How about a dance instead?"

Jacquelyn reached around his neck and pulled him closer, whispering into his ear. "We need to talk. There's more going on than you know. I'll tell you everything, but only once we're in bed together. You don't have to fuck me if you don't want to, but please... come with me."

She stepped back and lifted her doe-like eyes. "Pretty please? It'll be fun."

In a varied and often stimulating life as a bachelor, Daniel had never had such a direct offer. Not from a sultry beauty like Jacquelyn. Not from anyone. It forced him to stop and think, not about taking her up on the offer, but why on Earth she'd made it. It wasn't just sexual enticement; this offer came with information.

"What's going on?" Daniel asked as plainly as he could. If she had information, he was listening, and there was no one else around.

Her words became hurried. "Just say yes. Take my hand and we'll walk out of here together. Really, it'll be okay." She touched the yellow flower on her dress. "No one will stop us. They might even encourage us."

She reached out, her eyes now pleading.

The earnest Jacquelyn was even more compelling than the sensuous version. Daniel was less than a millisecond away from taking her hand. But he hesitated. Spontaneous sex wasn't remotely within Daniel's mission guidelines, even if it did come with pillow talk.

"Jacquelyn, if there's something I need to know, tell me. Right here."

"I... I can't." She looked in both directions, her expression changing rapidly to one of fear. Daniel followed her gaze, at first noticing nothing but lots of people scattered across the ballroom, enjoying the party. But against one wall, a solo man stared into a tablet in his hands. He seemed out of place.

"Are you in trouble? What is it? Tell me."

194

"I'm sorry, I have to go. It was nice to see you again." She turned and hurried away, disappearing into the crowd. Daniel followed for a minute, but when the crowd parted, she was nowhere to be seen.

He looked in every direction. Gone.

He scanned along the walls. The man standing alone had disappeared too. This limited investigation had just skyrocketed to high alert, though he didn't have much to go on. A direct solicitation of sex along with promised information.

There's more going on than you know, she'd said. No doubt, but uncovering truth was highly dependent on who you talked to. He already regretted not taking Jacquelyn's hand as she'd asked, but it had all happened so quickly. Spontaneity wasn't one of Daniel's strengths.

He could continue to search the room for her or locate someone else and be blunt in his questions. Brother Christopher was the first choice, but direct confrontation had its limits as a method of interrogation. Like it or not, this wasn't going to be a get-in-get-out mission. To uncover whatever Jacquelyn was offering would require subtlety.

He stood alone, thinking about next steps. Nearby, a large fountain, the centerpiece of the party, sprayed streams of dark red punch into several large bowls with dipping ladles in each. Nothing alcoholic at this party.

His solitude didn't last more than a minute. A thin older woman with gray-and-black-striped hair smiled as she caught his eye.

Uninterested in any more captures or stock tips, Daniel turned toward the fountain of punch and drew a ladle into a cup. She didn't take the hint, walking up very close. Too close.

He turned and acknowledged her presence. "Nice party."

She looked Hispanic, with darker skin than most. Though her face was weathered and lined, it retained the intrinsic beauty of a youth concluded long ago.

"Not my kind of party," she said. The accent was strong, but she could have been from anywhere. Caribbean. Possibly South America. "My guess, Daniel, is that this party is not where you wish to be right now either."

Cutting through the small talk had always caught Daniel's attention. No one else in the room had called him Daniel, not even Sister Jacquelyn who was ready to jump into bed with him.

"And you are?"

She didn't answer, pouring herself a cup of punch from the fountain. "You should have followed Jacquelyn."

Now she really had his attention. Forget the subtlety. "That was a private conversation. Who are you?"

"Daniel, I will give you a second chance. This time, please make the right choice. It's not safe here for either of us."

"Why is it not safe? I'm getting tired of tip-offs that come with no information."

She set her cup down and wrapped her arms around him, pulling in close. "Do not move," she whispered. Her hand slid into his pants pocket, fumbling around like she was reaching for something.

Two direct women within minutes of each other was hard to manage. "Wait... wait... what are you doing?"

She pulled him even closer. "It's a lie, Daniel. Everything they told you. All lies." She withdrew her hand, now holding his olinwun. Before he could react, she reached over the fountain and dropped the coin into a punch bowl.

Daniel lunged for the device, which quickly sank to the bottom of the bowl. "What the hell are you doing?"

She jerked his arm back with more strength than he expected from a woman of her age. "You must come with me," she demanded. "This is your only chance."

"That coin contains vital information." He pushed against her hand, but she remained firm.

Her brow knit into an expression of determination. "The coin is worthless. There's no time to explain, they will spot me any minute. We go right now, or we will both be dead within the hour."

26 Unveiled

The older woman was wiry and strong but showed all the character lines that came from a life well-lived. But there was more—a burning passion from within. She was either one of those crazy old ladies who walk the streets yelling at passersby for no reason, or she was desperately trying to use her experience to change the game.

She'd claimed they were lying, and Daniel was ready to listen. He'd seen enough withholding of information to suspect the motives of quite a few of the people he'd met, but he'd also seen some genuine bewilderment at his questions. He'd need to sort it out, and a collaborator could help.

She glanced sideways to a hallway leading away from the ballroom. "The men's room is that way. Go there. Piss or fake it. When you leave, take the exit to the right. I will be waiting." He still hadn't placed her accent, a mix of Gypsy, German and Hispanic. She hadn't given a name, either.

She's working with Sister Jacquelyn. That much was clear. She knew about the olinwun that Committee Security had given him, and Jacquelyn was the receptionist on that floor. Two women in less than five minutes telling him that all was not well in futureland.

Don't make the same mistake twice. Go with her.

He glanced into the punch bowl. No sign of the olinwun, but it was down there somewhere. If the device was like any of the phones he'd owned, it was probably ruined by now.

"I'll be there." He looked toward the hallway she'd pointed to, and when he turned back, she was gone, disappearing into the crowded ballroom.

Daniel walked calmly but purposefully, found the men's room at the end of a well-lit hall and spent a few minutes inside. Several men came and went, but there was no indication he'd been followed.

He cracked the door and peered into the hall. Empty, for the moment. Taking the opportunity, he hurried down the hall and slipped through a double door with an exit sign overhead.

It led into a darkened stairwell, the only light coming from one floor below. When the door closed behind him, the weak light revealed two women flattened against the wall, one older, one younger.

"Jacquelyn," Daniel said. "Are you okay?"

Jacquelyn reached out and grabbed both of his hands. "Thank God you came. I was worried you wouldn't." She whispered. "The olinwun is gone?"

Daniel nodded. "Your friend here dropped it into a punch bowl."

Jacquelyn squeezed his hands. "Vitoria is trying to save you, Daniel. So am I. You're in grave danger." She lifted her eyebrows and sighed. "We all are now."

The sincerity in her face matched her words. "Sorry, I can be dense sometimes." He squeezed back on her hand. "It wasn't you. You were very compelling."

She seemed embarrassed now that her subterfuge had been exposed. She lowered her head. "Apparently not compelling enough."

The older woman, Vitoria, stepped away from the wall. She peered over the stairwell railing to the lighted landing below and whispered, "Jacquelyn's bedroom was the easiest path. Harder now, but we'll manage."

"Sorry, I think I, uh…"

"Yes, you did. Now we must wait. When it is safe to move, we'll receive a signal from below."

Jacquelyn's shrug seemed to confirm the plan. "Unfortunately, we have to go naked from here." She was still wearing her glittering ballgown and still just as stunning. But she wasn't making any moves to take it off.

"Excuse me?"

Vitoria rolled her eyes. "It's an expression. It means to go without digital guidance or communication of any kind. The olinwun does much more than clever projections. It's also a tracking device. They know where you are at all times, and they listen. They pry into your life. There are only two ways to get around their eyes and ears. To be literally naked while copulating, which Jacquelyn attempted but you rejected. Or to go figuratively naked, which is where we are now."

Her explanation was accompanied by the look of a teacher lecturing a dimwitted student. "By law, the olinwun automatically shuts off during sexual encounters, but we have found that its signal can also be disrupted by water."

"Ah, the punch bowl."

She nodded. "They will not find it for an hour. By then..."

"Who are they? The Committee?"

Vitoria's face hardened. "Committee enforcers. They discipline those who don't conform to their religious extremism with harassment, fines, job loss, even beatings. The punishments for those who support the resistance can be far worse."

Daniel shook his head in disbelief. He hadn't seen any evidence of violence, but he'd been escorted almost every minute. "I spoke with their leader, the man they call Father. Obsessed with fate, a little creepy, but he didn't seem violent."

"Father." Jacquelyn spat out the name like it was a foul taste. "Ask my friend how she broke her arm. It wasn't from a fall."

"What happened?"

Jacquelyn's lips tightened, and anger appeared in her eyes. "She dared to be herself. A short skirt worn in public. When the enforcers tried to shame her, she told them to fuck off. They hit her with a tire iron, shattering all the bones. The doctors say her arm might never heal."

Her story had the same feel of the Taliban, an extremist sect that, even in 2023, still bullied women in some parts of Afghanistan. "And you think these enforcers might kill too?"

Vitoria looked up with sad eyes. "They have before, and with no consequences. The government is weak, contained by these pious thugs. When Father has a prayer session with the president, expect something bad to follow."

They both seemed angry and bitter, but knowledgeable about a dysfunctional society that so far had been hidden behind friendly faces. Vitoria had declared the information on the olinwun to be worthless, which, if true, compromised his mission. There was little chance Daniel could return to his own time until he'd learned more, and these women were the starting point.

Vitoria was no doubt a resistance leader, but perhaps more than that. She'd seemed casual with Daniel from the start, as if she'd known him for many years.

Daniel gazed at her face, searching for recognition. "Who are you?"

"You keep asking." She looked up with a wistful smile with a faraway look. Her hard exterior seemed to soften, her eyes glistening. "And I will answer. But first, I must tell you a story."

She spoke quietly, carefully. "It's a story about a scientist with a strong voice and a young woman, passionate and political, who loved him. The world changed around them, and he spoke out against its abuses. When the powerful had finally suffocated the voices of reason, she watched her love beaten by brutes with strong arms but no education. She saw the cuts across his face, the blood on his shirt. She watched as they dragged him away from their home. She didn't know how long he would be in prison. Later, she didn't even know if he was still alive."

She was silent for a moment and then reached into a pocket and withdrew a ring. She held it out for Daniel's inspection and whispered, her head cast down. "Try it on, I'll bet it fits."

Daniel absorbed her story, doing the mental gymnastics to untangle its implications. He accepted the ring. Gold, with three small diamonds. A man's wedding ring. An inscription around the inside read:

Evidence of love. D & V.

The inscription sounded like something he might compose. Even in a marriage ceremony, science would be featured prominently. D for Daniel. He hardly needed to guess who belonged to the V.

He stepped closer, his throat tightening as he spoke. "I'm sorry, I wish I could remember you, but I don't."

She shrugged. "We meet now for the first time. Or the second. I don't know, it's too confusing." She looked up, her lined face still beautiful. "I am Vitoria Alvares. I am your wife. Or, will be."

27 Stealth

Somewhere below, a door opened in the stairwell. The light flickered and then went out, plunging Daniel, Vitoria and Jacquelyn into darkness.

Vitoria pushed a finger to Daniel's lips. They waited side by side in silence. The door below closed, and the stairwell was quiet once more.

"Our signal," Vitoria whispered. "Follow me."

Daniel could just make out the edges of the railing. It was enough. They crept down concrete steps, single file. Three floors down, they passed a sign too dark to read.

Vitoria pushed open a door. "Come, quickly."

It led outside to a walkway lined with shrubs. In the distance was a quiet side street where a streetlight illuminated parked cars and a deserted sidewalk. Vitoria waved them through a gap in the bushes and across grass landscaping. She ducked around the side of the building and paused in the shadows while Daniel and Jacquelyn caught up.

Vitoria scanned them both. "We had planned for a taxi at the main entrance to take you to Jacquelyn's apartment. That's not possible now. My car is on the other side of the park, about five blocks." Vitoria motioned to Jacquelyn's tight gown and high-heeled shoes. "Can you make it that far?"

Jacquelyn hiked up the dress and slipped both shoes off. "Sure, but maybe I should just go home?"

"No," Vitoria answered. "You're probably compromised." She paused in thought. "We'll get to a safe house and regroup there. Follow me."

Daniel held out an arm, and Jacquelyn took it, tiptoeing barefoot across the street. They followed an alley, keeping to the shadows where possible. Vitoria explained as they went. It wouldn't be long before

Committee Security figured out that Daniel was gone. They'd synchronize with Atlanta Police and determine his olinwun's last known location. That would lead them to the punch bowl, and from there, they'd call in the enforcers.

Daniel eyed his barefoot companion, who had wrapped both arms around his, an anxious expression on her face. Her explicit proposition still confused him. "If they're coming after us for leaving the party, how is it that you and I could have walked out the front door without being stopped?"

Jacquelyn's eyes darted. "It's complicated. I'll tell you later." She leaned her weight on his arm as she stepped on something sharp.

"Sorry, I just don't see…"

Vitoria turned her head, glaring at Daniel. "She said she'd tell you later. Start listening to her, it will do you good."

Daniel avoided any response. Vitoria was leading this escape, and she didn't seem ready to accommodate questions. He accepted that he was up against forces he didn't understand and was willing to abide by Vitoria's rules for now. But once the immediate danger had passed, he'd need some answers.

They crossed a well-lit street with a few cars passing and reached the edge of a city park on the other side. Daniel thought he recognized it as Centennial Park, but he didn't know Atlanta well. A large sculpture filled the center of a small circular amphitheater.

They were exposed here, and Jacquelyn's head pivoted in every direction, searching for danger, whether real or imagined. Her sparkling dress wasn't helping much in their attempt at stealth. She looked out of her element. Frightened, though it wasn't clear exactly what she feared might happen.

The walking was easier in the park, with soft grass for Jacquelyn's bare feet. Vitoria veered from the lighted area and into the shadows among a stand of trees where they intersected a dirt trail.

"Safer now," Vitoria announced. "No one uses this trail at night."

Daniel could sense the relief. Perhaps Vitoria would respond if his questions started with something simple. "You're Brazilian, aren't you?" He'd finally placed the accent.

"Originally," she said. "But I moved to Washington many years ago, working at the Brazilian embassy. It's where we met, my Daniel and I." She dropped back a step and walked alongside Daniel. "I'm sorry to have called you my husband earlier. I know you are not. My husband is in prison."

Daniel pulled Vitoria to a stop. "Wait. He's still in prison? My older self?"

"We think so. Did they tell you he was dead?"

"Yeah, of a brain tumor. Last April."

She nodded. "Another lie. It's the story they want the public to hear. But one of our informants saw him just last week in his prison cell."

The information was coming fast now. Real information, from an authentic source. The tears welling up in this woman's eyes were genuine. Daniel hooked his free arm with Vitoria's, and the three proceeded side by side with their walk.

"How long?" he asked delicately.

"More than three years now," she said. Her face was now shadowed, but her voice betrayed the grief.

"I'm sorry for him and for you," Daniel said, adhering to Vitoria's conviction that the two Daniels were different people. It was really the only way to make sense of this world. "How did it happen?"

"As it always does these days. They pass a law designed to subdue their opponents. Daniel was convicted of scientific intolerance."

"That one's new to me."

"It's new to us, too," she said. "Years ago, blasphemy laws were dismantled in every country of the world. But since the Committee took control, those wretched laws are back. At least, in America."

"And scientific intolerance is their euphemism for blasphemy?"

She was silent for a moment, perhaps deciding how to explain, perhaps deciding whether to explain at all. "It's very different now than it was thirty years ago. Doubting their god or pointing out flaws in their holy text is a crime. Science routinely does both, though usually indirectly. America has changed. I hardly recognize it." She patted his arm. "I'll tell you more when we get to our destination."

Daniel started to ask another question, but a tug from Jacquelyn cut him off. "She said she'll tell you later." The same admonishment, but at least Jacquelyn was smiling.

Women working as a team are impossible to defeat. Daniel acquiesced. "Okay, later."

They came to an opening in the trees where the trail ended at another street, this one well-lit. Vitoria looked both ways. Near one end, a man leaned against a car smoking a cigarette. She grimaced.

"Do you think?" Jacquelyn asked.

"Not sure," Vitoria answered. "My car is parked over there. Stay here. I'll go alone and pull up to this curb. Climb in quickly. If he follows, I can lose him."

Vitoria hurried across the street, her head down. The man continued his smoke as she climbed into a car not far from him. The car lights came on, and she made a quick U-turn, pulling up to the curb where Daniel and Jacquelyn waited. They piled into the small car, Jacquelyn in back, Daniel in front.

Vitoria sped away, making a sharp left turn on the next street. She studied the rearview mirror.

Jacquelyn faced the back window. "I don't see anyone following. No, wait… there is a car."

Daniel turned around too. A set of headlights loitered a few hundred yards behind.

"Hang on," Vitoria said, jamming the pedal to the floor. The electric engine screamed with more than enough power to push them into their seats. She swerved up an onramp that led to an elevated roadway and accelerated to an obscene speed. Just as quickly, she dropped down the next offramp only a few hundred yards further. The car plunged to the city street below and she made a hard right turn, sending everyone lurching to the left. Two more quick turns and she slammed on the brakes, bringing the car to a stop against a curb. She shut off the lights.

"Heads down!" she yelled.

They crouched and waited in silence. The surrounding buildings were old, possibly warehouses or abandoned properties. For several minutes, no cars approached or passed. The only sounds were small creaks from the cooling engine.

Vitoria lifted her head and looked around. "If they'd placed a tracking device on the car, they would have found us by now. I think we're safe." She started the car and pulled away. Jacquelyn resumed her position as lookout, surveying the scene out the back window.

Daniel fastened his seat belt, not having had a chance to do it until now. "Routine driving around here?"

Vitoria looked over and smiled. "Only when we have a guest in town."

"Well, you're very good at it. If this is a self-driving car, that's a hell of an override switch."

"I have no use for such technology." Her grin broadened. "I prefer naked in all things."

Daniel leered at the much older woman. "An expression?"

She laughed. "Don't worry, young man, only an expression."

"No, I didn't mean it—"

"Of course you did. You see an old woman. I understand." She drew a deep breath. "You are Daniel, but I am not your wife. Don't worry, there is no fate, nothing forcing your future. You are free to choose whomever you wish." She shrugged. "Assuming we can get you back to your time."

It was one of the many questions burning in his mind. If the Committee had lied about their role and about Daniel's death, what else had they lied about? For that matter, what had they done with Becton's belt? Getting home had just gotten a lot harder.

"Yeah, I was afraid you might say something like that."

They drove for another thirty minutes, down large boulevards and zigzagging through unfamiliar neighborhoods. Jacquelyn huddled in the backseat in her sparkling party dress, looking like a captured bird too beautiful to be in a cage.

I put her in this position. Compromised her cover.

Vitoria had said as much. Daniel's slow response was the only reason Jacquelyn wasn't safely back in her home, ready for whatever her next assignment might be. The thought made him ill. He was witnessing firsthand the damages that could be caused by meddling with a timeline. None of this should be happening. He could have locked himself in a room until the adjustments to the belt were completed.

Unless those adjustments are a lie too.

Eventually Vitoria pulled onto a tree-lined road with a cow pasture on one side. The pavement ended, and she followed a gravel driveway to a large two-story house surrounded by forest. Light shone from behind curtains in the front windows.

Daniel stepped out of the car to the sounds of chirping crickets and gravel crunching beneath his feet.

"I've heard about these places, but I've never been to one," Jacquelyn said, joining him.

Daniel held her hand as she tiptoed across the gravel. "I gather you're new at this cloak-and-dagger stuff?"

"You saw where I work," she answered. "Really, I'm a receptionist at Committee Security. But when Vitoria contacted me a few months ago, I didn't hesitate."

"For your friend with the broken arm?"

She nodded. "For her. And others. Me too. I'm tired of this bullshit."

"You got dragged in deeper than you expected. I should have gone with you when you'd asked."

Jacquelyn snickered. "Yes, you should have. We'd be in bed right now fucking ourselves silly."

Daniel paused, staring intently and catching a few glances of her large green eyes. There was no reason to perpetuate the sexual ruse. She'd flirted only to get him out of the ballroom.

"What?" she said, a smile breaking across her face. "You know, Daniel, not everything is a lie."

Huh. Maybe not a ruse.

There was something very odd going on with this woman. Either that, or he still didn't understand the female gender after forty-four years. Daniel just shook his head in wonder.

28 Refuge

Vitoria introduced Daniel and Jacquelyn to the safe house operator, Aiden, who showed them in and locked the door behind. He was young, probably late twenties, and skinny, with uncombed wavy hair and stubble across his face. A noticeable gap between his front teeth lent character to his otherwise youthful appearance.

Aiden offered water and a bathroom if they needed it. He even offered a change of clothes.

"That would be wonderful." Jacquelyn twisted in her tight gown. "Party's over, time to climb out of this thing." She tossed her shoes to a corner and unpinned the yellow flower from her dress. Aiden motioned to a hallway, and Jacquelyn followed him.

Vitoria sat in a chair by a fireplace, and Daniel strolled around the living room, checking out the books on a shelf. "A safe house would imply that the resistance is significant, even if you don't have the upper hand."

"We do our best. I think we are gaining. Just look at who we captured tonight." She gestured with an open hand toward Daniel, smiling at her victory.

"Glad I could help." He waved to the kitchen. "Aiden is one of many?"

"He's a hub coordinator," Vitoria explained, "but a special case since he's physically near the Golden Spire. Of course, the Committee would love to identify this house, so do your best to erase the location from your mind when you leave."

"The secret is safe with me. I really have no idea how you got here."

"Good. I did try."

Aiden returned with bottles of water and a bowl of pretzels. Daniel reached for a handful. "Thanks for the hospitality, Aiden, though I really don't know why I'm here."

Vitoria turned to Aiden. "I'm afraid our younger Daniel will need to learn from scratch."

"I can help with that," Aiden said. "I've been on the inside, and I know the history pretty well, too."

Jacquelyn returned, now wearing a t-shirt and cutoff shorts. The oversized shirt, emblazoned with a cowboy hat and the words *Hillbilly Pride*, was tied into a knot at the waist. With her long legs and midriff exposed, Daniel caught himself staring. Jacquelyn took a seat on the couch next to Daniel.

Vitoria, once she'd regained Daniel's attention, picked up the conversation. "Aiden used to work in Committee Information Systems. It's their privacy invasion network that ties into every olinwun in the country. His departure from that group was rather sudden."

"I was banging the director's daughter." Aiden grinned, the gap in his teeth the defining element of his smile.

Vitoria rolled her eyes. "But his quick exit provided cover. With the young lady's help, he literally walked out the door with an olinwun loaded with the access codes for their entire historical archive."

"Great teamwork. Loved that girl." Aiden grinned again. "The codes have been amazingly useful over the years. I learned a lot. It's a long and sordid tale, but as Vitoria says, best to start from scratch. Shall we talk about the nuclear war?"

Daniel settled in, eager to hear more.

"First, forget about what you've been told," Aiden started. "It's probably not accurate. Oh, the basics are legit. Three missiles. One obliterated San Francisco, another hit Vladivostok and a third took out a US ballistic missile submarine in the north Pacific, the USS *Nevada*.

Probably ten million killed in the Bay Area, another five around Vladivostok. At least those facts are undisputed."

Daniel listened intently, noting every detail. The name of the sub alone should be enough to prevent the launch. Unless the conspiracy went even higher in the military. Or, if Aiden was wrong.

"Everyone agrees on that much. But then it gets wacky. The leading theory is all three missiles were launched from the sub, though it's not clear why any submarine commander would destroy his own ship or his own country."

Did the Russians launch or not?

Brother Benjamin had claimed they had. There was a scientific way to test. Daniel let Aiden continue, listening for additional discrepancies with Benjamin's version of the story.

"Most people figured it was a rogue captain, something the military said couldn't happen. I've studied the personnel files, and I agree with the military. Captain Lundstrom was one of their best. So was his executive officer. There's no way either of them would have pulled the trigger. Unfortunately, with the sub destroyed, the military brass had no better explanation of what happened that day."

Daniel had spent eight years working as a scientific investigator for the Navy and could verify Aiden's assessment. Without exception, those who commanded such power were the Navy's best. Stable, rational and vigilant people. Labeling a submarine commander as a "rogue captain" was just a cop-out for those unwilling to search for the more complex reasons that human systems sometimes failed.

"Regardless of what really happened, the public's view was solidified. This unspeakable horror was not due to any international crisis, but to a careless system. Russia, of course, came very close to launching their weapons in retaliation, and for a few hours it looked like the world was going disappear in a giant mushroom cloud. Luckily, that didn't happen."

"Your description is already different than the version I heard earlier today," Daniel said. "Committee Security told me the Russians *did* launch. It was their missile that hit San Francisco."

"Not a chance," Aiden said. "You'll find quite a few books that claim the Russians fired, but recognize that the Committee dominates the information most Americans consume. As soon as you get outside this fucked-up country of ours, you'll hear a different story. The Russians are adamant they never fired, and the evidence backs them up."

"It wouldn't be hard to measure," Daniel said.

"It isn't. Nuclear fallout can be tracked as it circles the Earth. Measuring the levels of plutonium ions identifies the unique signature of the original fissile material, which tells you who manufactured the bomb."

"Secondary ion mass spectrometry," Daniel said. "I know something about it." Aiden's explanation of plutonium tracking was spot-on.

"Even our allies agreed that all three missiles came from the US. It was a defining moment for international relations. Virtually every country turned against us. An out-of-control warmonger, they called us. Inside the US, we became more isolationist, cut off from our former friends. They even started building another border wall—a razor-wire fence separating us from Canada."

Daniel lowered his head. The dystopian future was bad enough. That his own country was the cause was difficult to accept. But Aiden's scientific description rang true. It was the most reliable explanation Daniel had heard since he'd arrived.

"Disputed fact number two," Aiden continued. "You'd think we'd all agree on the date of this holocaust, but even that's not certain."

Daniel ventured a guess. "October nineteenth, 2023?" Only a few hours ago that date seemed certain. It gave him ten days to sort things out once he returned. He was beginning to doubt that he'd have that luxury now.

Aiden shook his head. "Probably propaganda, designed to mesh with the dates for other false narratives the government issued. Most people agree, including just about everyone who was an adult at the time that it wasn't the nineteenth. It was the ninth of October."

Monday, October 9, 2023. The date when I jumped.

"Holy hell." Daniel hung his head. "I might already be too late. The belt can't take me any further back than when I left. About eleven that morning. Eastern time."

"The missile hit San Francisco at five p.m. that evening. Rush hour. Something everyone remembers, so I know it's accurate."

Daniel did the math. "Nine hours to spare, including the time zone difference. Not much to work with." If he could get back—and even that much was now up in the air—he could relay the captain's name, the submarine name and time of launch to Griffith. The FBI coupled with the Navy would know what to do from there. They still had a chance, but the timing would be very tight.

Daniel shook his head. "First things first. I've got to get that belt back."

"Yeah." Aiden paused. "About that…"

"Start at the top," Vitoria advised. She obviously knew something about the belt she hadn't yet mentioned.

"All right. Backing up a little," Aiden said. "Ever heard of Christian reconstructionists?"

Daniel shook his head.

"A fundamentalist movement back in the twentieth century to bring America into compliance with the strictest interpretation of the Bible. It languished in the early 2000s but regained traction after the nuclear strike. Of course, you can find any passage you want in the Bible to support your predefined viewpoint, but some of their preachers were pretty effective in claiming that nuclear weapons were too dangerous to be managed by anyone who didn't have the direct blessing of God."

"I think I see where this is going," Daniel said. That oxymoron, *scientific intolerance*, was stuck in his thoughts.

"Yeah. They said the military, along with the corporations and scientists who created these weapons, couldn't be trusted. It became science versus the godly. Of course, we've seen this conflict before going all the way back to Galileo, but after the nuclear launch, it kept building. It just wouldn't go away."

"The propaganda didn't help much," Vitoria said.

"Yeah, America has always done a piss-poor job of defining what is news and what is misinformation. When you don't have any rules prohibiting it, misinformation always wins. It gives people exactly what they want to hear. Doesn't matter if it's true."

"Confirmation bias," Daniel said. "People accept what fits within their belief system and reject everything else."

Aiden stood up and paced the room, his body language becoming more agitated. "So, things got even worse. The Committee formed from the reconstructionist groups and started pressuring politicians. With a lot of money pouring in from TV evangelists, they had plenty to spread around in Washington. It wasn't long before allegiance to the principle that 'dangerous science must be controlled' became a litmus test for anyone holding public office."

"That's when scientific intolerance came into the picture," Vitoria said. "Researchers began to see consequences when they published ordinary scientific papers. It didn't matter the subject. Astronomy, biology, archeology. Anything that caused offense or that contradicted their beliefs was intolerant. Scientists were fined or lost their government jobs. A few were sent to prison."

Daniel shook his head in disbelief. "Attacking science isn't just intellectually senseless, it's counterproductive. Society doesn't make much progress without science. At least, that's what I'd be screaming to anyone who would listen."

215

Vitoria lowered her head but couldn't hide her smile. "Of course you would. My Daniel did too. He was a popular figure, at least within the opposition. Several bestselling books. Regular television appearances. They warned him, but he wouldn't keep quiet."

"So, they put him on trial?"

"Worse. They converted him."

Daniel gagged. "Converted? Not possible. Look, I know myself, and I'm not about to become a follower of any religion."

Vitoria rolled her eyes and motioned to Aiden. "You tell him, you know the technology better than me."

Aiden turned to Daniel. "Your time jump is well known. Today's date has been anticipated in books, movies, documentaries, you name it. But over the years, people became wary about messing with time, in part because your jump occurred just before the nuclear launch. Some people even say you caused the war, though there's plenty of evidence that you worked hard to stop it."

"But I failed?" It was a disturbing thought. He already knew the name of the submarine and the captain. Just keep the boat in port and the launch would never happen.

"Yes, you failed. But don't get me wrong, I'm in agreement with the Committee on this one. I think you can succeed."

"The second time around is different than the first?" Daniel asked.

"Or maybe this is the ten millionth time in an endless loop." Vitoria said. "Sorry, that's very depressing."

Aiden shrugged. "Look, all we know is that history says you made the jump, returned to 2023 and did your best. For whatever reason, you didn't prevent the launch, and this disaster is now recorded in our history books. Anyway, dial back to three years ago. Older Daniel, *our Daniel*, was a pain in their side, but the Committee knew they couldn't arrest him or put him on trial—he was too popular. So, they went for something just as devastating, maybe worse. They found a loophole, or created one, it doesn't really matter, and threw him in prison for scientific intolerance without a trial. No public announcement, he just disappeared. And then they used shard-motion technology to create 3-D videos of Daniel saying he'd converted."

"Shard-motion?"

"A new take on an old con. A method to produce a perfect fake. They record hours of video—a person speaking, for example—and then break the digital results down into small clips of a few pixels each, called shards. They can reassemble the shards into a new video that looks just as real as the original but is complete fantasy. They have software that automatically matches the shards to the facial motions required to say any word, so they can literally type out the words they want Daniel to say, press a button, and create an accurate 3-D video of him saying those exact words."

"You can't tell the difference between a shard-motion video and a live broadcast," Vitoria added.

"Well, you can," Aiden said, "but you need some pretty sophisticated analysis software, which we have. The Committee put out dozens of Daniel videos and they spread like wildfire across the olinwun network. Daniel meeting Father. Daniel giving thanks to the Committee for showing him the god he'd never understood. Daniel renouncing the unmanaged science of the past."

"Daniel telling me to come to the future," Daniel said.

Vitoria nodded. "I'm afraid so."

The depth of the deception was beginning to become clear. Daniel sighed. "They showed me a second video where he spoke directly into the camera and told me to trust them. Crafted on the spot, I suppose. Can they do that?"

Aiden nodded. "Just type the words and push a button. Once all the shards are in a database, they can generate a new video in seconds. Misinformation works, particularly when backed by good technology.

The net effect of their three-year campaign made their supporters joyous that a strong critic had converted to their side. Of course, the opposition was skeptical but remained supportive of the Daniel they knew. In the end, everyone came around to loving Daniel Rice."

"Explains a lot," Daniel said with a shake of his head. There hadn't been a single person he'd met that wasn't happy he was here.

"But it all changed last April," Jacquelyn said. She'd been listening quietly. Perhaps she'd heard these revelations before, or at least wasn't surprised by them.

"Yes, in April, they produced another video of Daniel in a hospital. He looked genuinely sick. I don't know how they managed that, but we confirmed it was a fake. At first, we thought they'd concocted the story of his death as cover for actually killing him. But if our informants are correct, he's still in prison. Or was, as of last week."

"We're worried, though," Vitoria said. "The enforcers could give the order to eliminate him at any time."

Aiden stood up and walked over to her. He squatted and held her hand. "Vitoria, we're not going to let that happen. We've got the plan worked out and plenty of help on the inside. It's risky, but I'm confident we can get him out."

"Yes, but can you keep him alive once he's out?" She looked bitter. "The enforcers will be everywhere."

"We'll get him. He'll be safe," Aiden assured.

Vitoria soured further and turned to Daniel. "You'd better hope Aiden is right. My Daniel is the only person who knows how to get you home alive."

29 Convolutions

The conversation had turned to the single most important topic—Daniel's return to 2023. An ominous turn, if Daniel had interpreted Vitoria's words correctly. Only older Daniel knew how to get home alive, and he was in prison.

"I hate to be the bearer of bad news." Aiden hung his head. "I'm no expert on time jumps, but my contacts in Europe describe something called snapback."

Zin had warned about it. Brother Christopher had said it could be managed. Father had scoffed at it. But if snapback was real, the human body wouldn't survive the return to uncompressed time. Damage to the atomic structure, disruption of the cardiovascular system resulting in a full-body hemorrhage. A nasty way to go. Becton had died from it, as far as anyone could tell.

"Their guy in Committee Reception, Christopher, said that temporal dislocation was the real issue but told me that adjustments to the belt would solve it. Was he lying?"

"He's lying," Aiden said.

"Just remember," Jacquelyn said. "Reception doesn't know half of what goes on in Security, my floor. And Security is probably just as clueless about the next level up. Brother Christopher is a good man, I can personally vouch for that. But he might not know."

A lie begun at the top and perpetuated by underlings who accepted it as truth was the hardest to detect. In hindsight, it had been probably a mistake to turn over the belt, even if Christopher was an honest man. If snapback was real, Daniel's fate had been sealed as soon as he'd flowed forward into the future.

"So there's no going back now?"

"I didn't say that," Aiden answered. "There's no question you can get back to your own time. It's just that..."

"I won't survive long."

Aiden nodded, unable to make eye contact. He reached into a pocket, pulled out a shiny coin with an eagle hologram and handed it to Daniel. "You already know about the submarine, but the same info is reproduced on the olinwun, in case... you know. Plus, there's intelligence on the early reconstructionists. Our main problem is that most of them are deceased today. But back in 2023, they wouldn't be hard to track down. Routine police work. All the details and contacts are there. Plus, I've hacked this olinwun's geolocation feature. The Committee can't track it."

The room became deathly quiet while Daniel absorbed a new reality. It was a different path than his predecessor had taken. Probably a good thing since the older version of himself had failed to prevent the launch. Aiden might be offering the only path to success.

If dying for a cause is considered success.

He examined both sides of the olinwun, not looking for anything in particular. Whatever data it contained wouldn't be visible, but the FBI had already figured out how to read the device. All Daniel had to do was hand the coin over to someone with authority, and his part in this mission was complete.

He pictured Becton stumbling into the Orlando police station, blood running from his nose and ears, doing very much the same thing. In Daniel's case, it might be Agent Griffith accepting the coin—if Daniel could find him before dying.

Staring at the coin, Daniel asked the question that had been on his mind since Aiden had provided the bad news. "Why do you think they want me dead?" The Committee had explicitly told him to flow forward. *It's your only path*, the note on the whiteboard had said. Now it was painfully clear that those instructions had ensured his death.

"Well, there's the political reason," Aiden answered. "You were trouble for them for many years. Bringing you to the future was one way to shut you up."

Daniel pondered the idea and shook his head. "No, that can't be it. Father was convinced of the multiverse theory of time—that there are many paths and many instances of each of us. Bringing me to the future doesn't erase the aggravation my older self already caused. For Father, that water is already under the bridge."

Jacquelyn shook her head. "My brain hurts just trying to follow this."

"Yeah, it's really convoluted," Daniel said. "But lay it out logically. If the information on the olinwun they gave me is bogus, that means they *want* me to return to my own time. They're certain to give the belt back to me because it's the only way that bogus information is going to get to 2023."

"True," Aiden said. "They want you to fail. They want the nuclear launch to happen."

"So, I return to my time, I die, and the coin does all the talking from there. But its message is a deception."

Exactly what happened to Becton.

"Sad, but that part makes sense," Aiden said. "What doesn't make sense is the multiple paths theory. Your failure would just create a new path. Here in 2053, we're unaffected. So why do it?"

Daniel thought about the question for a minute. The answer had been there all along. "We have to think like Father. He's preoccupied with his fate, almost obsessed. He talked about being an instance of a class and having a duty to his class. He talks about many versions of himself out there, and every version must help the others."

"So weird," Jacquelyn said.

"Yeah," Daniel continued. "But it explains his motivation. Sending me to my death, along with bogus information, ensures the launch takes place and eliminates me from that timeline. A two-for-one. If there's another version of Father who inhabits my timeline, he benefits."

221

Aiden nodded in agreement. "As bizarre as your interpretation sounds, I think I agree. But there's good news too. We already disrupted half of that plan when Vitoria dumped the bogus olinwun. This new coin is valid, and unless somebody examines it closely, they won't know the difference." He shrugged. "Of course, I still don't have a way to get you back home in one piece. Once they tricked you into flowing forward, it was game over."

"Not over," said Vitoria. She held her chin in her hands, elbows on knees. She looked deep in thought.

"Sure," said Aiden. "There's whatever Daniel in prison knows, if we can get him out."

She leaned back. "My Daniel told me about his jump. He returned safely. I don't know how, I never understood the details, but whatever he did, you must do the same."

"Maybe it really is a time loop," Daniel said. "I get hooked into the future by Committee treachery and then ask myself how to get back to my own time, so I can then grow old and repeat the same process every thirty years. Maybe it's happened a million times. Maybe it's been looping forever."

Aiden blew out a breath. "Whew, heavy stuff."

Vitoria stood up, pacing. "No, no, no." Her voice was angry, growing in intensity. "It's not the same! This, right now, the four of us in this room. It's not the same. When my Daniel jumped, there was no future Daniel in prison, there was no resistance group that kidnapped him from a party, no pretty girl with propositions, no safe house. For my Daniel, none of this ever happened. If it had, he would have told me about it. He would have known they would come to arrest him."

Daniel shrugged. "Yeah. He would have been me, listening to you say this."

She rubbed her temple with eyes closed. "That night when they broke down our door, beat him and dragged him away, I assure you the shock on his face was very real. He didn't know it was coming."

"So, it's not a loop," Daniel said, even though he still wasn't sure.

Vitoria stood over him. "No, it isn't a loop. We changed it. Jacquelyn and I prepared for weeks to take you from the party. Aiden recorded data on this olinwun." She spread her arms wide. "This day, this moment—right now—has never happened before. We changed our path." She pointed a finger at Daniel. "And you can too."

Daniel listened, doing his best to absorb her point of view. Events in time were malleable and layered, allowing for multiple paths even while permitting the bizarre implications that came with jumping to the future. It was a fair explanation, and so far, it matched the facts. He was even ready to accept her challenge to change his own path.

But he wasn't quite ready to accept his death as a consequence of that change. Vitoria herself had suggested the solution.

"I think we need one more Daniel in this room," Daniel said. "When can we break him out?"

Vitoria smiled. "Tomorrow."

****

Daniel stretched out on the couch. A small lamp on a table provided the only illumination, but thinking didn't require much light.

The others had retired for the night, with Aiden assigning Vitoria to a bedroom down the hall and Jacquelyn to a converted attic over the garage. He'd offered his own bedroom to Daniel, but the couch was comfortable enough.

It was a good time to absorb everything he'd learned. The breakdown of society, the deception from the Committee, Father's speech about the nature of time and Vitoria's contradiction. One believed firmly in fate, the other rejected it.

Then there was the small matter of returning to his own time. He had no belt to do it, and even if he could retrieve the belt and press the right buttons, death probably awaited. Zin had been right all along.

Daniel pushed thoughts of death away. Vitoria seemed to think they had connections inside the prison, and maybe she was right. Tomorrow would be a big day.

The floorboards behind him creaked and Daniel turned. Jacquelyn stood in the hallway wearing the same hillbilly t-shirt and shorts that she'd borrowed. She leaned against the wall and folded her arms.

"You're not really going to sleep on the couch, are you?"

Daniel tipped his head. "Probably won't sleep at all, I guess. Too much on my mind."

"Want some company? I'm wide awake too."

Daniel took his feet from the couch and Jacquelyn sat, snuggling close. "Sorry about all this, especially what Aiden was saying about your jump back. I'd hate to think you wouldn't make it, but then, I hate to think about you leaving at all."

Daniel didn't have a reply. There wasn't much to say.

Her shy persona kicked in. "I also wanted to apologize for... you know."

Daniel examined the pretty face framed by reddish-brown hair. Her nose turned up at the end, and her teeth weren't perfectly aligned, but the slight imperfections only added to her beauty. Flawless faces were for models.

"Don't worry about it." Daniel shrugged. "It's funny, really. You're sorry you propositioned me, and I'm sorry I didn't take you up on it. My mistake pulled you into a lot more than you expected. Vitoria said you might be compromised?"

"Yeah, maybe. Aiden's going to do some digging. I might still be able to go back to work, but I'll probably call in sick for tomorrow."

"You really are a receptionist, aren't you?"

She looked up. "Of course. What'd you think?"

"Well..."

"You thought I was a prostitute?"

"Maybe not that clear-cut, but..." The cutoff shorts and her long bare legs still reinforced the idea.

"No!" she whispered loudly and then paused. "Well, okay, I can see how you might think that. Some people would say I am." She hugged her knees to her chest and looked up. "I owe you an explanation."

Daniel could guess where it might start. "When we crossed the park tonight, I asked how we could have left the party without being stopped. That explanation?"

She reached over to the lamp table and picked up the yellow flower she'd removed from her dress earlier. Her eyes cast down, she handed it to Daniel.

"The flower says it all." She sighed. "I am a receptionist, but I'm also a satin sash."

Daniel examined the flower. "Not following."

"You didn't notice the women in the office wearing yellow satin sashes? Including me?"

He had, but he hadn't assigned any meaning to it. Their retro clothing seemed altogether odd. The sashes that some women wore just seemed to be part of their fashion.

"The sash is a signal. It means we're approachable. Ready and willing, so to speak. And that we have access to birth control pills."

Unexpected. Fascinating. But so explicit.

225

The sexual part wasn't surprising—she'd already shown that side of her. But the overt fashion implied that everyone knew and approved.

He twisted the yellow flower in his fingertips. "The flower is the same signal?"

"Sash for the office, a yellow rose worn at the collarbone for social events. That's the code."

"And the men all know this?"

She pushed his shoulder. "Of course, that's why we do it."

"The women too?"

She shifted, pulling up one leg and facing him. "Daniel, I didn't set up this system, and I don't like it either. But it does benefit me. I get access to birth control, which is illegal for everyone else. And I don't have to say yes. I can politely decline any offer. Usually we just say we have our period and they go away. When a guy hears that story enough, he gets the point."

"But when you say yes, you get something in return?"

She shrugged. "Yeah, usually. Job preference, higher pay, a better desk, whatever. Sometimes one guy can help fend off the other scumbags, so I give him special attention. But there are a few guys in the office that I fuck just for fun. I've told them I don't want anything. They're nice to me anyway."

"And what do the women think? The ones who don't wear the sash?"

"They understand. We're in this together. Nobody blames a woman for a rotten system that men set up. The sash is something any woman can put on or take off. Her choice, and one of the few choices we have left these days."

Daniel handed the flower back to her. "Thanks for telling me."

Jacquelyn focused her green eyes squarely on Daniel. "So, does that make me a prostitute?"

"No." Daniel shook his head resolutely. "Absolutely not. That makes you a survivor. Keeping your head above water, doing the best you can within a bad situation."

She laughed and tossed the flower across the room. "You know what? I'm done. Hell, I'm thirty-two years old. I can't keep doing this forever."

Another change in the timeline.

"Did I just screw up something else in your life? Jacquelyn, I'm not judging. The sash is entirely your call."

She laughed. "No, it's not you. I've been thinking about it for a while. Haven't accepted an offer for a couple of weeks now. I guess things changed when Vitoria asked me to join the resistance."

"And your first assignment was me?"

She smiled. "Yeah, that part I didn't mind at all. I was so excited when you walked into the office. I was ready to jump you right then."

"Yeah, I noticed."

They sat side by side in silence for a minute, their breathing becoming synchronized. "Well... with the sash gone, I guess that sets you free."

"I feel free," she whispered. "Like I can do what I want. It feels really good."

Pivoting on her knees, she threw one leg over and squatted on his lap, facing him. She wrapped her arms around his neck and pushed her nose up against his. Her breaths came strong, and he could feel her body shake with each powerful beat of her heart.

Daniel's pulse quickened as his lips brushed lightly against hers. His breathing became shaky. He wasn't sure how far this was going, but he didn't feel like stopping it either.

She grabbed his hand and pushed the knot at the midriff of her t-shirt into his palm. Between strong breaths, she whispered. "You don't have to... but if you want to... untie the knot."

Daniel's heart was suddenly pounding as hard as hers. His hand trembled, but the knot wasn't difficult to untie.

She reached down and slipped the shirt over her head, tossing it away. She lifted slightly on her knees and pushed her bare breasts to his face.

Daniel soaked in the moment, breathing in deeply. Her skin was velvety soft, with a slight scent of lavender. He ran his hands down her back, caressing each vertebra, her ribs just below smooth skin, and further down to the curves of her waist. She helped him slip her shorts off.

She lowered, allowing her lips to skim across his face, finally settling at his mouth. They kissed with intensity.

"My room in the attic over the garage," she whispered. "The bed is big enough for two."

"Yeah?" Daniel panted.

"Yeah. You don't want to sleep on the couch tonight. Do you?"

Daniel's lips wandered down her neck. "No, I really don't."

She hopped off his lap and held out a hand. "But I want to make this perfectly clear," she said in her serious, if breathy, persona. "You don't owe me anything. Okay?"

Daniel took her hand and stood up. "Okay."

She kissed him hard. "This fuck is just for fun."

****

Her deep breathing signaled sleep. He pulled the sheet over her bare skin and propped another pillow behind his head. There probably wouldn't be any sleep for him tonight as he pondered the deepest of thoughts. Mortality. And women.

Death might be close. He'd already accepted the high probability. Regardless, if he could find a way to return to his own time, it was the right thing to do. The only thing to do. He couldn't remain in the future, and it wasn't just about the nuclear launch. Nala was in the past, still waiting for him. Drawing him back like the strongest of magnets.

Shifting, he propped his head on an elbow and gazed upon the sleeping beauty next to him. Jacquelyn's hair cascaded across the pillow, the red highlights muted in the dark of the room. Her cute nose crinkled a little with each breath. Asleep, Jacquelyn was just as lovely. It wasn't hard to defend why he'd joined her in bed. She'd asked.

Well, more than asked. She stripped naked on my lap.

Daniel took a deep breath, acknowledging to himself that the story didn't end there. Yes, she'd asked, but he hadn't gone along just to be agreeable. He wanted her. He chose her, fully conscious of the complications.

But he had no regrets. He'd shared a delicious celebration of pleasure with a thoroughly delightful woman. He'd make the same choice again. Still, that didn't eliminate the complications.

Strangely, he wished Nala were here, so he could tell her everything.

"Wake up."

A hand pushed rhythmically on Daniel's shoulder. He opened his eyes. Vitoria leaned over the bed. He sat up, pulling the sheets away and exposing Jacquelyn's naked backside to bright light that streamed in from the hallway.

"What's up?" Daniel asked, his mind somewhat fuzzy. He hadn't expected to fall asleep, but sex had a way of relaxing the body and calming the mind.

"Get dressed. We are leaving," Vitoria said.

Jacquelyn stirred, noticed Vitoria and pulled the sheets up to cover herself. "Oh my God, sorry." She looked like she'd been caught by a parent.

"It doesn't matter," Vitoria said. "But playtime is over. It will be daylight soon, and we need to move while it's still dark."

Daniel jumped out of bed and pulled pants on. "Where are we going?"

"A transfer point that Aiden has arranged. I'll tell you more on the way." She left the room, leaving Daniel and Jacquelyn to get dressed.

Jacquelyn stood up, her eyes pleading. "I left my clothes downstairs." She clearly didn't want Vitoria to see her naked again.

"Just a sec." Daniel ran downstairs. Jacquelyn had thrown the t-shirt halfway across the living room. It draped across a lampshade. He grabbed her shorts along with a woman's jacket in a hall closet and returned to the bedroom.

"Thanks," she said as he handed the clothes to her. "Guess I got carried away last night."

"Me too." He kissed her on the cheek. "But no regrets. You were…" He watched her slide the t-shirt over her head. "You still are…"

"Playtime is over. So, says the boss." She slipped on the jacket and then rummaged through the closet until she came up with some casual sneakers that seemed to fit. "Wonder what the rush is about."

"We'll find out," Daniel said. They returned to the main level of the house and found Aiden and Vitoria in the kitchen, studying a map that had been projected into the air from a device lying on the counter.

"Things are happening fast, and we're probably not safe here," Aiden said. "My connection is secure, but that's always a relative thing. They can triangulate our position if they know what to look for."

"And they are looking," Vitoria said. "Enforcers everywhere, scouring Atlanta for you."

Aiden nodded. "The extra patrols on the street are a risk, but also an opportunity. My informants tell me the contingent of enforcers that are normally stationed at the prison have been called away. Only the regular staff is left, and most of them are sympathetic to the resistance. They say it's now or never, so we're pulling the trigger. Our Daniel should be out within the hour."

"No guns, no dynamite, no helicopters," Vitoria said, smiling. "Just lots of bribes and excellent connections." She patted Aiden on the shoulder.

"We've established a transfer point," Aiden said. "We'll take two cars. Vitoria will drive alone and you two come with me. They'll need satellite reconnaissance to spot us, and that's hard even when the sun is up. While it's still dark, we should be safe."

"Sounds good," Daniel said. "Let's go."

Aiden shut off the map, picked up a small bag and headed out the front door with the rest following. The night air was still and cool; even the crickets had calmed. No hint of any sunrise, though Vitoria said the drive to the arranged transfer location would take nearly an hour.

****

The main floor of the hundred-year-old building was longer than a football field, two levels high, with glass that ran down the centerline of the roof. The Atrium, as the prisoners affectionately called it. During the day, the glass let in the sun. In the early morning hours prior to dawn, the vast open space was equally bright, lit by two rows of spotlights down its length.

A single guard dressed in blue guided an older man down the center of the Atrium. A patch on the guard's shoulder read, *United States Federal Penitentiary, Atlanta*. The old man was dressed in orange with chains on his wrists. He walked slowly, his back hunched, his hair long and gray.

"June third, 2053," the old man said in a hoarse whisper. "He's here, isn't he?"

The guard made no reply. He glanced at the prisoner and his lips tightened into a careful smile. The guard gave a small nod.

"We're going for a stroll this morning?"

The guard nodded again.

"Thanks, Watson. You were always good to me."

At the far end of the atrium, they passed through a security door, and down a short hallway. Another guard dressed in the same uniform manned a desk in front of the next door. The guard grinned as they approached. He typed a few strokes on his computer keyboard, and a strip of plastic ejected from a printer. The guard assembled a security pass and handed it to his colleague.

"Be careful at the gate, Watson. Bennett is on duty this morning."

"Will do," Watson said. "That fuckhead better not give us any problems."

"Just keep your head low if he does. We'll get this done."

232

Another door marked *Release Prep* led to a small room with closets full of men's clothing. Watson pulled out a key and unlocked the chains from the old man's wrists. He eyed the stoop in the old man's stance, selected a hangar and handed a set of clothes to his prisoner. As he put them on, the old man seemed to marvel at his new clothes.

"Manny has the cameras offline. Maintenance issues. At least, that's the official statement. We've got about ten minutes. Should be smooth, but you never know."

"Will Vitoria be outside?"

"No. They're taking you to a transfer point. Even I don't know where it is."

The old man smiled. "Smart young lady."

Watson put a gentle hand on his shoulder. "You take care of yourself now. Your work is done. Let the next generation take over."

The old man looked better in a proper suit. He even stood a little taller, though his face showed the internal weariness that came naturally from years behind bars. Watson pulled a walking cane from a cabinet and handed it to him.

"It'll make you look distinguished."

"Thanks." He leaned on the cane and hopped a few inches into the air, almost managing to click his heels together before he came down. "Fit as an Olympian."

They passed through an exit to an outside courtyard. The sky was dark, but the ground was lit by spotlights mounted on the building and along a fence a hundred feet away. Rolls of razor wire decorated its top.

They started across a walkway toward a double gate but only made it halfway before another guard came running up.

"What the hell do you think you're doing, Watson!" he yelled, drawing a gun from a holster on his hip. He waved it wildly between the two of them.

"Just hold on, Bennett," Watson said. "This is not your business."

"The hell it isn't!" the frenzied guard yelled.

The old man held up a hand. "I'm so sorry, Officer Bennett. It's my fault. I meant no harm, but Officer Watson and I were talking about a rare conjunction of Venus and Mercury and since it was still dark, he very kindly offered to escort me out for a quick view."

He pointed the metal handle of his cane to the dark sky. "Do you see it? Right there. Very beautiful tonight."

The guard's eyes twitched left and right, and his head turned to the sky for a brief moment. The old man swung the cane, catching the guard at his left temple with a loud smack. The gun went clattering across the walkway, and the guard slumped to the ground.

The old man studied the cane, twirling it in his hands. "Doesn't have the same weighting as a good four-iron, but effective." He turned to Watson. "Sorry, this might cause some trouble for you."

Watson bent down, felt for a pulse at Bennett's neck and lifted one eyelid. Bennett's eye danced up and down, and he let out a groan.

"Nothing we can't explain. You escaped. I tried to stop you, but you managed to get Bennett's gun. I had no choice but to open the gate."

The old man extended a hand. "You're a good man, Watson. I won't forget." He turned to look over his shoulder as a pickup truck pulled into a parking lot just outside the gate.

****

Daniel and Jacquelyn climbed into the backseat of Aiden's car. The front passenger seat seemed to be crammed with electronics, a mobile command center. Daniel didn't fail to notice the semiautomatic pistol holstered just under the dashboard.

They sped away with Vitoria leading. "Relax. Sleep if you want," Aiden said, looking in the rearview mirror. "It'll be a while."

Sleep didn't seem likely, but at least the fireworks, if any, were an hour away. Daniel glanced at Jacquelyn, who had transformed once more in both her clothing and manner. A resistance fighter. Or so he imagined.

She reached out a hand, and he took it. "You ready for this?" she asked.

"What, the resistance?"

"No, meeting yourself. If all goes well, that's what's going to happen. Kind of weird, don't you think?"

"As long as it's a peaceful meeting, I won't complain." But she was right. Confronting yourself—not just a twin but a duplication of your own consciousness—would be every kind of weird.

They drove along dark roads of what seemed to be the outskirts of the city and then turned onto a country road with farm fields on either side.

Jacquelyn motioned to his jacket pocket. "Do you have a picture of her?"

Daniel pulled out his phone. "Who?" He suspected he knew but asked anyway.

"Your girlfriend. What's her name?"

"Nala. You want to see a photo of her?" It seemed an odd request.

"I'll bet she's pretty."

Daniel scrolled through some pictures until he found one of Nala walking on the beach in Haiti. He held the phone for Jacquelyn to see.

"Wow, she's gorgeous," Jacquelyn said. "Love the old bikini. We don't get to wear those anymore." Jacquelyn swiped her finger across the phone and looked at a few more pictures. A selfie of Daniel and Nala on the dance floor, a restaurant table by the sand. "Do you love her?"

Daniel held a tight smile in check. "Yeah, I think I do."

"That's nice," Jacquelyn said with sincerity. "I wish I had that. Just one guy, that's really all I want." She swiped through several more photos. Daniel's sister and niece. A hike in the Cascades.

Daniel handed the phone to her. "Go ahead, if you're interested."

"You don't mind? I really love looking at the old photos. The way things used to be. My mom has a device like this, and it still works too. She tells me stories. It makes me feel like... you know, like I'm there."

Daniel smiled. "I've got a few stories too."

She snuggled close. "I'd love to hear them."

For the next twenty minutes, they swiped through more photos. Daniel reminisced about the "old days," and Jacquelyn absorbed every word. She was particularly interested in the ordinary things. The furniture in people's houses, women's hairstyles, just the fact that people wore glasses, something no one did anymore.

She seemed less interested in the stories related to Fermilab or CERN, including the more fantastic events of his life, like walking through a 4-D portal into the heart of Core. Maybe those things just didn't register as being real. She explained that all that "alien stuff" happened in Europe or China. America was now very isolated.

The time passed quickly, and soon Aiden slowed as they approached a town. He pulled onto a small gravel road adjacent to a country grocery store and parked, turning off the car lights.

Vitoria parked her car in the front of the same store, but she didn't get out. A solitary light on a post lit the front of the darkened store.

Aiden checked the display of one of the electronics devices bolted haphazardly to his dashboard. "They're close," he said. He signaled an OK sign through the window to Vitoria, who nodded. "If anything goes wrong, we get out fast."

"And Vitoria?" Jacquelyn asked.

"She's on her own," Aiden said. "But we're not expecting any problems. The driver bringing Daniel here is a good man. Trustworthy."

Aiden reached for the gun under the dash and checked its magazine. Just being prepared, Daniel hoped.

Toward the east, an orange glow foretold the coming sunrise. A few minutes later, a pickup truck pulled into the grocery store parking lot. The driver stepped out and peered into Vitoria's car, then opened the passenger door and helped an old man climb out. He had long gray hair and walked slowly.

Vitoria jumped out and grabbed the old man around his waist, helping him into the passenger seat of her car. Once he was seated, she leaned in and kissed him. She flashed a huge smile and another OK sign back to Aiden.

"So far so good. We'll meet them at Cecille's."

"A safe place?" Daniel asked.

"Otherwise known as the resistance café," Aiden said with a smile. "Good people. They serve a great country breakfast too."

Thirty minutes later, with the rising sun just peeking over the treetops, they pulled up to a restaurant by the side of the road. There was only one other car in the lot, but the neon sign displaying *Cecille's* was lit.

A large black woman showed them to a table in a back room, giving Aiden a hug and whispering in his ear. She brought coffee and they waited.

It wasn't long. The café door opened, and Vitoria walked in with her husband. He looked ridiculously old. Gray, bloodless skin. Thin to the point of withered. He walked hunched over, one arm linked with his wife, the other hand holding a cane. This man was only in his seventies, but he looked older. Three years in prison might do that.

Daniel's intellect rebelled. His nerves tingled. *What's the protocol for meeting yourself?*

First things first. Daniel jumped up and supported the other side of the old man, helping him to a chair. Vitoria sat next to him, a broad smile across her face.

The two Daniels, young and old, eyed each other. Silent. Observing. The old man grinned, and Daniel grinned back. There was almost no reason to speak. Daniel knew exactly what his counterpart was thinking.

How does this guy differ from me?

The future was sitting right in from of him, connected in some strange way, yet unquestionably a separate consciousness. Like a clone, or maybe a father whose genes had somehow been transferred intact to his son. But it was more than that. Daniel couldn't quite wrap his mind around it. He simply felt it.

"You okay?" he finally asked.

The old man nodded. "Never better." He examined the handle of his cane. "Had a brief tussle with a guard this morning. My golf game's not as good as it used to be, and I might have twisted my back a bit. But I'm not complaining."

He looked around the restaurant and smiled. It probably didn't matter where he was. Anyplace was better than a prison cell. Daniel didn't probe further. There was no need. For that matter, there was no need to get acquainted. You already know yourself. Daniel felt it, and he knew the old man felt it too.

Vitoria poured a glass of water for him. She rubbed a hand on his shoulder and kissed his forehead.

Just a few feet away, but thirty years into the future, sat Daniel Rice and his Brazilian wife, Vitoria. The idea was mind-boggling, and Daniel could happily observe the bizarre dynamics all afternoon while his analytic mind came up with a hundred questions.

31 Infinite Regression

Daniel faced himself. Perhaps another version of himself who had made his own choices and lived a somewhat different life. But they were still the same person. His self-imposed limits on future knowledge now seemed as unworkable as keeping a kid away from Christmas presents until the adults had poured their morning coffee. It just wasn't going to happen.

Daniel paced the restaurant, unable to sit still with the rest of the group. The first of many questions popped into his head. "You didn't create that video that called me here, did you?"

The old man shook his head. "No. The same thing happened to me. A faked 3-D video brought me to the future. But you're one up on me. I never met myself. This is all new." His voice was scratchy and didn't really sound like Daniel's, but most people say they sound funny when they hear their own voice recorded.

"Which confirms this timeline has changed," Daniel said. "We're not in a perpetual loop."

Vitoria looked smug. "As I said."

Daniel nodded to Vitoria. "Not doubting your view, I'm just looking for evidence." He returned to the old man. "Your confirmation demonstrates a key element of time that we haven't talked about yet."

"Which is?" Vitoria asked.

"We're not the only Daniels. A third Daniel had to exist for the Committee to create that shard-motion video that called you to your future. And if there's a third, why not a fourth, and a fifth? You see where I'm going. There may be an infinite regression of Daniels, each jumping to the future at age forty-four and tangling with the Committee in his seventies. The exact circumstances may be different, but there's no telling how many times a similar scenario has occurred."

Old man Daniel seemed disturbed by this idea, probably because he recognized the pattern now that he was in contact with his younger self. Vitoria didn't look any better.

"What's more," Daniel said, "I'm the latest Daniel, but probably not the last."

"Only if you fail," Vitoria said. "But if you return to your time and prevent the nuclear launch, then the Committee might never form. In that altered timeline, there would be no one to call you to the future. It would break the cycle."

Daniel nodded, but he wasn't completely convinced of her argument. There was still something nonsensical about all of this. The evidence of multiple versions of himself sat before him—he couldn't deny that part. But the idea of multiple timelines meant that anything could happen and probably would. Every event on every timeline was independent. Changes on one timeline had no bearing on the others. Preventing a nuclear launch on his own timeline might save millions of lives, but that same launch would still occur on a thousand other timelines. In the grand scheme, would his actions have any real meaning?

He rubbed his chin and stared at the floor. "I don't know, I'm just not buying the multiple timelines idea. I guess I never did. It's the same concept as the multiverse, where every quantum fluctuation spawns an entirely new universe."

"But didn't we just prove that multiple timelines exist?" old man Daniel asked. "I jumped to this date, but I have an entirely different memory of it. This must be a different timeline."

"What if," Daniel asked, "there's only one timeline, but the universe allows changes? Time is not a static list of events like a history book; it's fluid, always changing, but there's only one flow, one path, one timeline. Your jump from thirty years ago no longer exists anywhere except in your mind. A new history has been written—I just wrote it—and I erased your version of events."

Old man Daniel nodded, grasping the idea easily. Daniel knew he would. "That means your jump will be replaced when another Daniel comes along behind you."

"Only if I fail. And that's not going to happen." Daniel glanced at Vitoria, who approved his optimism with a large smile. "With your help, I'm going to be the last in a long line of Daniels jumping to the future."

"But it's not just this jump," old Daniel said. "It's bigger. Think about it. Jumping to the future is not the *cause* of a succession of Daniels. Those different versions of us would be there anyway, even if we hadn't jumped."

Daniel nodded. The old man might be onto something. Of course, the old man was himself. That helped.

The older version continued with their shared theory. "What if there is just one timeline, but events along that line keep flowing repeatedly down that line like waves on a rope? Each wave replaces the wave in front of it. Each wave is a little different than the one before it."

"I see what you mean," Daniel said.

"I don't," said Jacquelyn. "You want to explain that so the rest of us simpletons can understand it?"

The longer Daniel thought about it, the more it made sense. "He's saying that we each exist in multiple versions, but on a single timeline. As we move along this line, events come at us, we interact with other people, we make decisions and the world around us changes. But our consciousness is just one wave on that timeline, and the actions we take replace whatever future was written by the previous wave. For better or worse."

He squatted in front of Jacquelyn. "So, it's not just me, it's you too. It's everyone. An infinite number of ourselves, each moving through time and making the best of the world around us at that instant. My only advantage is that I had the opportunity to peek into the future that I'm now changing."

She seemed to like the idea now that it had been generalized to include everyone. "So, there's a future Jacquelyn out there, forging her own path and making her own memories. I might not get to meet her, but I can change anything she did."

"Yeah, that's the idea. The future is real, and so is the past." He pointed to old Daniel and to himself. "But there's only one timeline, and the events in time are always changing as each wave passes through."

"A hopeful idea," older Daniel said, rubbing the same crick in his neck that younger Daniel sometimes got. "I don't mind being replaced by something better."

It wasn't far from the idea Father had brought up, even if the words were different. Instances of a class. One individual among many, all the same person and with a duty to improve their class. Perhaps Father was right.

Vitoria glanced back and forth as the two Daniels talked. A broad smile formed on her face. "I'm enjoying this. It's funny, I didn't think I would. But look at this. I have my husband back, and now we have a son who is just as smart." She rose from her chair and embraced Daniel. "I'm sorry, I must label you. Otherwise, I'll lose my mind. Or maybe I'm already crazy."

Daniel shook his head and hugged her tight. "I don't mind. I'm honored."

"Hey, youngster," the old man called out. "That's my wife you're fooling around with."

Daniel took a chair next to his very close relative. "She's pretty amazing. Determined, brave, resourceful. She got you out of prison. You picked a great wife."

The old man grinned, and not at Daniel but at Vitoria. "Pretty sure she picked me."

Vitoria snorted. "Nonsense, we picked each other. He was making eyes at me across a coffee shop and I told him he was being rude."

The old man reached out for her hand. "She walked right over, pushed my laptop closed and told me I'd better learn some manners or she wouldn't go out with me. I hadn't even asked her out."

They probably weren't doing it intentionally, but they were sharing a key moment in Daniel's future. Would the same event happen once more? How often had he sat in a coffee shop staring at his laptop? Perhaps one day he'd look up and notice a much younger Vitoria. He'd probably stare at her too, prompting her to chastise him for bad manners. What would he say to her?

It might be a moot point. He was currently locked in the future with no sure way of returning to his own time. Young Vitoria was just as far away as Nala.

"You two lovebirds should get some time alone," Daniel said. "But if you don't mind, we haven't talked about the single most burning question."

"Probably about empros time and Becton's belt," older Daniel replied.

"Wow. Connected minds."

"Not really. Vitoria told me about it on the drive over." He grinned.

Even though his need for information was deadly serious, Daniel didn't mind levity or the breezy conversation. The man had just been freed from prison; he had every right to be happy. But Daniel needed his input. "I seem to be stuck here. Snapback and all that. Maybe you can shed some light. How did you get back?"

Old man Daniel lowered his head and squeezed Vitoria's hand. "I wish I could help you, I really do. But my jump was different. Simpler." He looked up. "I never flowed forward. I never left empros time. I walked around a frozen world for most of two days. I gathered what I could and returned to 2023. For me, the dangers Zin mentioned weren't a factor." He kissed Vitoria's hand. "Don't blame Vitoria; she didn't know the details because I didn't tell her."

His revelation hit Daniel like a punch in the gut. It explained why his version of events was so different. The old man had never interacted with anyone, never met with the Committee or Father, never been given an olinwun. He'd probably pulled information from the whiteboard computer. He would have had access to whatever he might find in desk drawers, even Father's inner sanctum. But in the end, he returned safely to his own time—exactly as Zin and Chloe had advised.

It also explained why he'd failed to stop the nuclear launch. He'd never met Aiden or anyone else in the resistance. Whatever information he'd gathered was that same mix of real and fake that the Committee managed so well.

Daniel's decision to flow forward had changed everything, giving him a real chance at changing an ugly history. But it might also produce an early death.

The whole thing felt rotten. Unfair. Yet unavoidable. He could return to 2023. The Committee might even help him do it. The information on the new coin Aiden had provided might even stop the nuclear launch and prevent the Committee from ever forming. But he'd die in the process.

A sacrifice made for others, including other versions of myself.

If his theory of time was correct, another version of himself, following just behind on the timeline, would be unburdened by the history Daniel would erase. With the cycle broken, that even-younger version of himself would never be called to the future, would know nothing of a religious cult that turned into a dominant political force. That version would never meet Jacquelyn and would have no knowledge of Vitoria—unless he happened to meet her in a coffee shop.

But that version of himself would live out his life as it should be, making his own choices in a world without nuclear annihilation and without the grief suffered by millions.

My life is one instance of something much larger.

It was a comforting thought when facing death, making his decision a little easier.

32 Fugitives

Eggs, sausage, hash browns, even southern-style biscuits and gravy. The breakfast was large and appreciated, if the clean plates were any indication. The newly released convict pushed back from the table, his skin color and energy level noticeably improved.

While the surreal conversation with his older self continued, Daniel noticed that he spent more time looking at Vitoria than anyone else. Daniel took the hint and backed away from further questions.

Eventually, Vitoria asked if the others might excuse them for minute. "We need to talk about our options going forward."

Daniel and Jacquelyn took their cups of coffee to another table on the far side of the restaurant, and Aiden returned to his car to obtain the latest status from his sources.

"It's hard to believe," Jacquelyn said, sipping her coffee. "All that back-and-forth about time still has my head spinning. Do you really think there are versions of each of us?"

"Well, there's two of me right here in this restaurant. It's not a stretch to imagine more. But I still think it's just one person at different points in their life."

"You think you can go back and change things?"

"I don't know. But if I get the chance, I've decided that I'll make the jump."

"But you might die."

"Yeah. I might."

She stared into her coffee cup and sighed. "Could you take me with you?"

Their eyes connected, and he searched for the persona this actress might be portraying. The serious, earnest Jacquelyn stared back.

"Jacquelyn. Honestly, I don't know how to do that."

"That belt thing that brought you here. They'll give it back to you, I know they will. Just make it do whatever it does, and I'll hold on."

"And then you'll die too?"

"You won't let that happen. You're smart, you'll figure out a way."

"But why would you want to go back to 2023?"

"Oh, come on," she scoffed. "Look at my life. I'm already washed up at thirty-two. Sash is gone, and good riddance. But the job may be gone too."

"There's other work out there. I've seen it myself at the clothing shop."

"Age limit for women is thirty-six. If you're not on child leave by then, retirement is mandatory. They say it's to keep male unemployment rates under control, but really, they just don't want wrinkled old hags around the office."

"What is wrong with these people?" He'd seen male-dominated cultures before, mostly in the Middle East, but it was hard to believe this was the future of America.

She waved a hand. "You don't know the half of it. I could tell you stories... you know what it takes to get a satin sash?"

He could imagine, but he shook his head.

"Mine was easy. I only had to blow the VP of HR, but that was six years ago. These days, candidates do a full audition. Three guys. You have to do whatever they ask, and let me tell you, those guys in HR are the biggest pervs around. When you're done, they get together and rate you one to ten. You have to score at least a seven to get your sash and a birth control prescription."

Daniel sat ashen-faced, listening to her story of sanctioned sexual harassment and institutionalized exploitation. "They get away with this? No one sues them?"

She laughed. "Yeah, right. They stacked the courts years ago. You want a decent-paying job, this is what you have to put up with. It's everywhere." She pulled on his arm. "I like your time better. The rules for women weren't so messed up, and from what my mom told me, the men were pretty decent too."

With social struggles that never seemed to go away, Daniel had always thought of his own time as being in dire need of improvement. But, as his jump had proved, things could get worse.

He understood her reasons to return with him, but he didn't have a good answer. On the plus side, the belt and helmet were probably still in the possession of the Committee, probably still functional since the Committee clearly wanted him to return to his own time. With Aiden's help, he might even get it back.

But snapback was almost certainly real. He'd now heard the warning from multiple reliable sources who declared that death awaited his return. He could only speculate what the same jump might do to Jacquelyn, even if the belt and helmet could be rigged to send two people.

It was fantasy to believe any of it would work. "I'd take you back if I could, but I don't know how."

"But you'll try?" She perked up.

He sighed. "Yeah, sure. But I'm not pressing any buttons if I think it's going to kill you."

She reached across the table to hug him, apparently only hearing the good news, not the bad. "Thank you!" She pulled away. "Oh. Don't worry. Once we're there, I won't get between you and your girlfriend. Nala, right?"

Daniel nodded.

"Don't worry about me, I'll just blend into the crowd and you'll never see me again. Well, not unless you want to." Her shy persona returned. She pressed her lips together and looked like she might cry at any minute. "You do like me, don't you?"

He leaned in close. "How do you do that?"

"What?" She gave him a pout, complete with large, sad eyes.

"Switch between personalities like that. The shy girl is your best routine."

She wrapped both arms around his neck and pushed her lips close to his. Her voice lowered to a sultry whisper. "You bet your ass I can do shy, but my tiger act is a lot more fun."

"Ahem." It was Aiden, standing nearby.

Jacquelyn unwrapped herself from Daniel and returned her attention to her coffee.

"We need to leave," Aiden said. "Enforcers are in the area. We're splitting up. Vitoria and her Daniel in one car. You two will come with me to another safe house, and we'll work on next steps. I've just confirmed with an inside source that the belt was in Committee Engineering most of the day yesterday. They've apparently been tinkering with it, though what they changed I can't say."

"Matches what Brother Christopher told me they were going to do, so I guess that's good," Daniel said. "At least they didn't destroy it."

"And Jacquelyn, I've got a few options for you too."

"If it involves returning to the Committee, forget it. I don't want that job anymore."

Aiden tilted his head. "Well, then you won't be disappointed. The enforcers have got you pegged as being part of the resistance. At the very least, we'll need to get you out of Atlanta. I could put you into an admin job in New York. And get you a roommate. Or, we could sneak you across the border into Canada."

"Guess I'm on the run now too." Jacquelyn held her head high. "I made my choice and I'm proud of it. Thanks for the options. I might even have one more." She glanced to Daniel.

Aiden waved for them to go. Vitoria and her Daniel were already up. He still held her arm, but he looked stronger.

Vitoria hugged Jacquelyn. "We'll say goodbye here. Thank you for your help. Stay strong. It may take time, but we will win this fight for your generation and those who follow you."

"Doesn't sound like I'm going see you again," Jacquelyn said.

Vitoria shook her head. "Probably not. Aiden has arranged it. We leave tonight for a resistance command outpost in Bermuda. We will continue our work from there."

Daniel stood across from his older self, as if a buffer of empty space between them might prevent a matter-antimatter annihilation. "I have so much more I'd love to talk to you about, but I guess we've run out of time. Bermuda sounds like a good place to rest and recuperate. I know she'll take good care of you."

The two men embraced like father and son. The world didn't implode.

"Long life and happiness," Daniel said.

"Go fix this timeline," his counterpart answered. "For every version of us."

Vitoria wrapped her arms around both Daniels and kissed the younger version on his cheek. "I'm not good at long goodbyes, and this whole thing is going to send me into therapy anyway." She locked eyes with younger Daniel. "Your path may be the hardest of any of us. But I have great faith in you."

"Vitoria, it was amazing to meet you," Daniel said. They'd been in contact less than twenty-four hours, but he felt like he'd known her for much longer than that. "Uh... just on the off-chance that I end up in a coffee shop and bump into your younger self... any advice?"

She lowered her head and thought for a moment. "Tell her to be confident. She has already found her path—she just doesn't realize it. Then invite her to join you, or go your own way. Your choice."

Vitoria smiled and linked arms with her husband, and with less effort than it took to walk in, they left together.

Daniel expected their journey wouldn't be easy either, but his optimism in the future applied even to this dystopian society. Vitoria and her husband Daniel would make it to the airport. With help from an unseen web of supporters, they'd arrive in Bermuda. They'd continue their work as resistance leaders. He might write a book about his time in prison and the lies that had sent him there. Maybe he'd even write about meeting his younger self.

But mostly, they would be together, reunited with their life partner. There was no other way to think about the future. Cynicism and doubt just weren't a part of Daniel's nature.

"Let's go," Aiden said. Daniel and Jacquelyn followed him to his car.

They drove as before, with Daniel and Jacquelyn in the backseat and Aiden checking his array of electronics riding shotgun. The route returned to Atlanta, but he skirted the center of the city, staying mostly on major highways, where they blended with traffic.

Aiden seemed pleased with their unimpeded progress, but when he took an offramp from a freeway his disposition changed. Ahead, traffic slowed and came to a stop. Flashing red and blue lights on either side of the ramp provided a hint. Aiden gritted his teeth, looking right and left while slowing the car.

"An accident, maybe?" Jacquelyn said.

"Not sure," Aiden said, craning his neck for a better view.

Ahead, the cars were forming a single line, passing slowly between two police cars. Several policemen were checking each car as they passed.

"Shit," Aiden said. "This might be bad." He looked behind. Additional cars had already come off the freeway, blocking any escape route. A steep slope to the left and a fence to the right made it certain that going forward was the only path.

"Get down," Aiden said. "Be ready for anything." They ducked below the window line. The smoked windows already provided some cover, but it seemed unlikely that the police would simply glance in the front seat and let them pass. The other option of sitting up and playing it cool didn't seem so wise either. The chance that this roadblock was for some other purpose or that the police wouldn't recognize Daniel was slim.

A minute passed as the car crept forward. Daniel and Jacquelyn exchanged a nervous glance.

Aiden swiveled and spoke in a low voice. "Jacquelyn, sit up and lean against the door. Act like you're sick." Jacquelyn did as requested while Daniel remained crouched.

Aiden rolled down his window. "Sorry! Emergency! My wife is in labor!" He rolled the window up and sped off.

He made a hard right and accelerated down a busy street. Daniel emerged from the crouch and looked out the back window. Nothing following. Aiden swerved around some cars, slowing for the next traffic light and turned, the tires squealing as they flew around the corner.

"Don't see anything behind us," Daniel said.

"I'm not worried about those guys," Aiden yelled above the racing engine. "Atlanta police. They probably won't pursue, they'll just call us in. It's those things I'm worried about." He pointed as a pole with a camera mounted at its top passed by. "We're easy to track now. Citywide surveillance. Committee enforcers are tapped in to that feed."

"Options?" Daniel asked.

"Well, the CDC offices are nearby. Friendly faces there. We could ditch the car and hide out."

The Centers for Disease Control and Prevention was an Atlanta-based institution of science. It wasn't surprising that Aiden would have contacts there.

They sped down several tree-lined streets and into an area where medical facilities dominated. On a hill up ahead were two large office towers that formed a curving arc above the trees. Aiden turned past a sign for the CDC and skidded to a stop.

Ahead, a military vehicle painted in camouflage blocked the way. Four men in fatigues jumped out with military-style automatic weapons pointed at the car.

"Down!" yelled Aiden.

POP-POP-POP-POP.

Daniel ducked. Jacquelyn screamed. The windshield exploded, glass flying everywhere.

POP-POP-POP-POP.

More loud gunshots and bullets ripped through the front seat, just missing Daniel's head. Jacquelyn huddled on the floor, screaming with each explosion of leather and foam padding as the car seats were riddled with bullets.

Then it stopped.

A man yelled something. A radio voice answered. The front door of the car opened, followed by the back door on Jacquelyn's side. She shivered uncontrollably as a large brute shoved the muzzle of his gun toward her face. Another gun appeared over the seat, pointing at Daniel.

"Don't shoot," yelled Daniel. "We're unarmed." He held his hands up.

The soldier at the door yelled at Jacquelyn. "Get the fuck out of the car, bitch!" When she didn't move, he grabbed her hand and dragged her from the car.

"We're invited guests of Father," Daniel yelled, searching for the words that might calm these beasts or at least make them think twice.

"Out!" yelled another man. Daniel rose and climbed out, keeping his hands raised.

One man stood back, his weapon trained on Daniel while another grabbed Jacquelyn by the neck, lifting her feet off the ground. As she struggled to breathe, he snarled in her face. "Looks like we got the whore too. She's a pretty little thing."

"Leave her alone!" Daniel yelled. The bully in a soldier's uniform dropped Jacquelyn to the ground and lurched toward Daniel with unchecked anger burning in his eyes.

"Who's going to stop me? A fucking science faggot?" He lifted a boot and kicked Daniel squarely in the chest, knocking him against the car. Daniel dropped, gasping for air.

A boot pressed on the back of Daniel's neck, pushing his face into the pavement. He sucked in air that smelled of oil and blood. The man wrenched Daniel's arms behind his back and lashed his wrists together with a strap that dug into the skin.

The front door of the car stood open, revealing a grisly scene inside. Aiden's body slumped out, held up only by the seat belt. His shirt was soaked red, and a puddle of blood formed on the pavement in front of Daniel's face.

Daniel closed his eyes and thought of Vitoria's words.

Brutes with strong arms but no education.

33 Captives

Two of the thugs tossed Daniel into a compartment at the rear of the military transport vehicle. He landed on his shoulder, with pain shooting into his neck. A metal door slammed, enclosing him in darkness.

Daniel moaned, twisting his arms to relieve the pressure on his wrists from the tie straps. He tasted blood, feeling with his tongue to find the source, a split lower lip.

A hand touched his face, long fingernails lightly scratching against his ear.

"Jacquelyn?" He couldn't see a thing.

"I'm here," she answered. "Are you hurt?"

"Not bad. You?"

"My arm hurts, but I'll manage."

The engine started, and the vehicle turned a corner and accelerated. Daniel lifted his head to search for any signs of light. Nothing. They were probably inside a storage compartment. It smelled of rubber tires. He could hear the muffled sounds of the enforcers speaking. One man laughed.

"I'm scared," she said, tears in her voice. "I've seen what enforcers do to people."

"If they wanted us dead, they would have already done it."

"Nobody stops them. They're animals." She sobbed quietly.

She was likely worried about more than just death. Beatings, broken bones, rape. All possible. Wild animals out of control seemed to fit the description for these Neanderthals. While it was unlikely that the Committee wanted him dead, their captors had sprayed bullets haphazardly.

Reckless and dimwitted. But bullies are like that.

"Wherever they're taking us, there will be someone higher up in command. We'll do better there. I can use my conversation with Father to our advantage." It might not have been much comfort, but it was all he had.

Assess the situation. Take it from the top.

The Committee intended Daniel to take a carefully crafted but false narrative back to his own time and to die within minutes of arrival. That much probably hadn't changed even now that they'd captured him by force. But there were some loose ends to their plan.

Now that he'd been exposed to the resistance, he was no longer cooperative, but of course, they knew that. They probably already had a plan for how they'd ensure the bogus information still returned with him. Stuff a new olinwun in his pocket and force him back in time? Shoot him and press the button? Something along those lines.

But you can't return to an anchor in the past without first flowing empros, and he'd have to be alive at that point to select the next command on the belt. Once the world around him froze, he'd have a huge advantage.

It didn't make sense, though. Father wasn't stupid, having jumped through time himself. He certainly understood the power wielded by anyone in empros time. They'd probably have an answer.

Then there was the immediate situation. Hands tied and locked in a trunk by madmen who'd already killed and might kill again. Solutions weren't leaping out. He resolved to go down swinging if that was what it came to, but there might be small victories they could eke out.

One idea came to mind.

"Your hands are still bound?" he asked.

"Yeah. I can feel your face, that's about it." They were both lying on their right sides, with Jacquelyn in front.

The zippered compartment of his modern-throwback pants still contained the olinwun that Aiden had given him. He could feel the coin pressing against his thigh.

Protect your advantages, however limited.

"Can you move at all? Scoot along the floor?" The vehicle went over a bump in the road and their heads clunked in unison.

"Ow," she cried. "Yeah, uh, I think so. A little."

"Try to scoot toward your feet, and I'll scoot up. If you can get your hands to my right pocket, Aiden's olinwun is in there."

They shuffled, each bump in the road giving them momentary help as their bodies lifted from the floor. Her shoulder blades pressed against his face, and her hands fumbled around his waist.

"I'll roll on my back." He wiggled, positioning his pocket as close to her hands as he could. Her fingers searched and found the zipper.

"Got it," she said.

He slid down until he could feel her fingers against his face once more. "Put the coin in my mouth."

"What?"

"Just do it. I'll swallow it."

"How's that going to help?"

"According to Vitoria, olinwuns can't be tracked if they're in water."

"You've got to be kidding."

"Just do it. It might work. At least, they won't find it and take it away." He imagined he'd soon be in 2023, most likely dead, possibly with a phony olinwun in his hand, or pocket, or somewhere. But if he was lucky, the people of his own time would eventually extract the real one from his stomach. The FBI would figure it out from there.

She pushed the coin to his lips and he sucked it in, immediately wondering how this triple-sized horse pill was going to get down his throat.

He swallowed hard several times, gagging but trying to ignore the pain. At first, it lodged in the back of his throat, but with effort and patience, the lump descended, and the pain finally went away.

"You okay?"

"Sort of," he wheezed. "That was bad. Wish I had some water."

"Can we get some water back here?" Jacquelyn yelled. There were laughs up front and more muted, but incoherent words. The vehicle drove on without stopping.

"Thanks for trying."

"Now what?" she asked.

"Search this compartment for whatever might serve as a weapon. Anything, even a sliver of metal or a stick might help."

They slid across the floor, feeling in every recess. The space wasn't large and was mostly empty. "Found a rag," she said.

"A few scraps of paper over here," he said. He was hoping for a road flare or a crowbar, but no such luck.

They had no physical defense, but weapons came in different forms. Words were still a resource, and he had a few choice ones saved up for the soulless beasts that had murdered without hesitation. But no matter how eloquent or powerful, words launched at the uncaring, uneducated dregs of humanity simply dissolved into their idle gray matter like neutrinos passing unfettered through the Earth. He would need to speak with their leader, not these thugs.

At some point, this vehicle would stop and they'd be dragged out. They might be separated, they might be interrogated, she might become a hostage to force him to follow their orders. It wasn't hard to imagine the number of ways in which this could end badly.

Jacquelyn began trembling again, and he scooted closer until their bodies touched.

Daniel shoved the gloomy outcomes from his mind and focused only on what might give them an advantage. Success of any kind seemed remote, but he was convinced he'd find a path even if it hadn't yet formed. Throughout his life, he'd been showered by words of encouragement. *You're smart, you'll find a way.* Jacquelyn had said it herself.

Confidence in yourself is a power they can't take away.

Confidence provided a pathway for clear, rational thought. And clear thinking discovered alternatives that hadn't been considered before.

He lifted his head and whispered into her ear, his words never truer. "I promise you, I will get us out of this."

With some effort, she rolled over, and they touched noses in the darkness. She took a deep breath and the trembling stopped. Her voice wasn't shy or aggressive, but genuine. "I believe you. I don't know why, I just do."

She took another deep breath. "Maybe it's because you're so different than all the other guys. Maybe it's because I love you. Sorry, I shouldn't say that. I know you're already taken."

"It's okay, I understand."

If his arms had been free, he would have held her close. As it was, brushing his nose against hers was the best he could do.

****

The vehicle continued its route for another thirty minutes. Daniel's internal gyroscope had always done a good job of aligning with compass directions, enough to get a sense that they were moving west or north from their starting point.

The vehicle stopped briefly while their captors spoke with another voice coming from a speaker. They drove a few hundred yards further and stopped, turning off the engine. Doors slammed, and the compartment hatch opened. Rough hands grabbed him under the armpits and hoisted him out into the brightness of daylight.

Daniel filled his lungs with the fresh air of a country breeze while his eyes adapted. For the first time, he got a good look at the attackers. Four men in military camouflage fatigues, weapons slung over their shoulders. Clean-shaven faces. The guy issuing orders had a scar on his cheek.

Two other soldiers pulled Jacquelyn out. Her hair was mussed and her eyes showed fear, but she wasn't bleeding and seemed able to stand.

They were on a paved driveway. To one side was a large house with white columns in front. The surrounding estate of grass and trees seemed to stretch forever among rolling hills. The estate of someone important.

"Around the back," the man with the scar commanded, and he pushed Jacquelyn forward.

Roughly forty-five minutes west or north of Atlanta, Daniel judged. Location might be important, and he'd store as much information as he could to find a way out, or at least to stay alive. He would remain silent for now; these goons had no power to negotiate. They were only dumb muscle. The real power, no doubt, was inside this grand house.

They were pushed to an entrance at the back of one wing of the mansion, led down some steps and into a corridor. The group leader flipped on lights and stepped behind a desk. He pressed a button, and further down the corridor, a large metal door slowly swung open. They passed through a circular opening with a stainless-steel frame that was at least a couple of feet thick. It felt like stepping into a bank vault.

On the other side, the guard pressed a second button, and the massive door closed behind them. He shoved Daniel down the hall.

To one side was a narrow metal door with a small window at eye level. The goon slipped a key into a lock and pushed the door open, shoving Daniel and Jacquelyn inside. While another trained his weapon on them, the leader frisked them both, removing Daniel's phone from his jacket pocket. He brandished a knife and cut the tie straps from Jacquelyn and then Daniel, dropped a single water bottle on the floor and left, slamming the door shut. A heavy dead bolt clunked into place.

Daniel took a deep breath, allowing tension to release. No bullets, no beating and no rape. The worst possibilities hadn't materialized. He even had his arms free once more. He pulled Jacquelyn close and they embraced in silence.

It was a windowless room about twenty feet on each side. A single bulb inside a wire cage on the ceiling provided light. No place to sit other than the floor. A single bottle of water and no food. If it was a holding cell, he hoped they wouldn't be here long.

"You okay?" Daniel asked.

"Worried," she said. "They killed Aiden, didn't they?"

Daniel nodded. A smart young man had put his life on the line for strangers and lost.

"Goddamned storm troopers," she said.

Daniel shook his head. "Bullies with guns, dimwitted and cruel. History is filled with their kind. I thought the future might be better."

"Not this future."

Daniel released her and stepped to the metal door, peering through its window into the empty corridor. The glass was reinforced with a wire mesh. This place was designed to keep people in.

Satisfied they'd been left alone, he leaned against the wall and slumped to the floor, motioning to Jacquelyn to join him. "Let's figure this out together."

She curled up close, wrapping her arms around his elbow. Her fear and anger weren't going anywhere, and Daniel didn't blame her. Witnessing murder wasn't something that anyone could just let go. Daniel felt the same, but he'd need to ignore it for now and summon his intellect if they were going to survive this day.

"They want us alive, and not just me, you too," he said. "They're not police or we'd be in a station, so I presume they're enforcers."

"They are," she said. "The red-and-white patch on their arms."

"Okay, so who gives the orders to enforcers?"

"Any of the Committee Chamber members. The guys at the top."

"How many?"

"Five or six, including Father."

"Any rogue members that you know of? Any infighting among these top people?"

She shook her head. "If there is, we wouldn't hear about it down on my level."

"We should assume they know about the prison release by now, but let's not say anything about it, just in case. We want to give Vitoria and Daniel time to get out of the country."

She nodded.

"Since they didn't kill us, they must still want me to play the stooge in their plan. You must have a role in this too or they wouldn't have brought you here. I doubt they were being merciful."

She nodded once more, biting her lip. Her role as a hostage could mean almost anything.

"Okay. So, we need to find the holes in their plan. If they still have the belt, and if they haven't wiped it clean, its controller will still show time as compressed and should still have an anchor point in 2023."

"Lots of ifs."

Daniel nodded. "Yeah, but if they want me to return, they have no reason to destroy the belt or clear the anchor."

"So, where are the holes?"

He tipped his head. "Still thinking about that. The main hole is flowing empros. It's a different direction of time, and to compress or decompress, I have to flow empros first. When I do that, everything around me freezes—I mean literally freezes. Nobody moving, nobody thinking. Even a bullet in flight would freeze. Once I'm in empros time, they can't stop me."

She motioned to the small room. "Could you get out of here?"

"Unfortunately, I can't just walk through walls."

"Maybe they're going to take you somewhere else."

"Maybe."

They sat side by side for an hour, talking through the situation, looking for ways out. Most of it was guesswork, but Daniel was thankful to have someone who'd worked on the inside who could confirm his suspicions or answer his questions.

They eventually tired and dropped into silence. Jacquelyn rested her head on his shoulder. Daniel closed his eyes but remained deep in thought.

The sound of an electric motor told him the outer door was opening. Footsteps in the hallway were followed by the jangle of keys in the lock.

The door opened, and the muzzle of an automatic weapon poked through. The guard strode in and took a position on the opposite wall, keeping the weapon aimed at them.

Daniel stood up and helped Jacquelyn up beside him. They remained pressed against the wall, eyeing the guard but not saying a word.

The man with the scar stood at the doorway, keys in his hand. He stepped aside and lowered his head when another man in a skintight bodysuit passed by and into the room.

Daniel didn't recognize him at first. The long gray hair and beard were the same, but his spry movements were those of a man forty years younger. Father had changed since their meeting at the Golden Spire.

His face was still deeply lined, like an aging rock star who might have been wasted on drugs one too many times. But each step was agile, almost springy. The bodysuit he wore bore an exterior pattern of parallel lines that wrapped around his torso, legs and arms, mimicking muscle fibers. Daniel suspected the suit was the reason for his youthful mobility.

Father approached Daniel, glancing briefly at Jacquelyn with a sour look.

Jacquelyn bowed her head. "Blessed Father," she whispered.

Daniel understood her gambit to appease the man who held them captive, but he had no intention of playing an artificial game of reverence and awe. They'd speak as equals.

Father's voice was calm but creepy. "Dr. Rice. It's time for you to leave us."

34 Loops

Physically, Daniel was at every disadvantage. A gun pointed at his head, and another guard at the door. Father was clothed in technology that erased any of the physical limitations wrought by age. What other powers the bodysuit provided, he could only guess.

But Daniel wasn't helpless and began to form an engagement strategy. Father was clearly in charge, already an improvement over the chaos of brutes who only understood how to kill. He was talking, too. Better than the alternative.

The belt first.

Daniel held out both of his empty hands. "To leave, I'll need the devices that brought me here."

"The belt and helmet are safe," Father said. "I have no wish to keep you here. I never did."

"You call me here and then send me home. All part of your fate?"

"Yes, I believe it is."

"Including false information about the nuclear launch?"

Father's mouth turned up, exposing unusually white teeth for a man of his age. "On the contrary, you will return with information critical to the protection of your timeline. You're an important emissary, Dr. Rice. We each play a role, you and I."

Daniel's assessment of the Committee's plan had been correct, though Father wasn't admitting that a return to 2023 would be deadly. Once more, the man seemed to think he was a character in a stage play with no free will.

Step it up.

Though he seethed over Aiden's death, Daniel kept his voice as clinical as he could manage. "You've already murdered once today, and

I'm sure your goons will pull the trigger again if you command it. But can you really call that fate? Or do you just kill for the fun of it?"

Father lowered his brow. His eyes burned with intensity, yet his voice remained calm. "For a man in your position, you would be wise to learn some boundaries. Your mistress knows her place."

Jacquelyn maintained a bowed head, her eyes closed. Father put a gloved hand under her chin and lifted. She opened her eyes and tightened her lips but remained silent. "You seem to have lost your sash, my dear. Have you fallen in with the wrong company?" He tugged on the t-shirt, exposing more of her midriff.

She pushed his hand away. Her face stiffened, and her breathing became strong and rapid, but she remained silent.

"A pious woman knows when to show her skin and when to cover up. Unfortunately, this is a lesson you may need to learn the hard way." The guard behind him sneered, his weapon still trained on Daniel, but his lecherous eyes locked on to Jacquelyn.

Daniel stepped between Jacquelyn and Father. "She's not involved. This is between you and me. Let her go." Jacquelyn put a trembling hand on Daniel's shoulder and tucked herself close behind him.

Father stared eye to eye with Daniel, then turned and walked to the other side of the room. "That I cannot do. She's part of this story now. A useful part, I believe."

Keep him on defense.

"Rape is the ugliest of crimes," Daniel said. "An act of violence masquerading as intimacy."

Father sighed. "Rape? Dr. Rice, you've misunderstood me from the start. I'm a teacher. I guide lost souls. I am not your enemy, I'm your savior, and hers too. You must gain a wider view."

"Murder is justified in your wider view?"

"Your driver refused to stop on command. Police actions are hardly murder. In our work, we may hasten the judgment day for the depraved who stand in the way, but it is the Lord who will serve justice upon them, not me."

Father approached the guard and eyed the size of the brute's arms. His gaze moved to Jacquelyn who hugged even closer to Daniel. "Any child learns not to touch a hot stove when her finger is burned. Unless there are consequences, how will this yellow-sashed girl learn not to expose her skin to rough men?"

Daniel shook his head. "There's nothing righteous in murder and nothing instructional in rape."

Father sighed, a habit he seemed to display when confronted with reason. "Perhaps I've misjudged you too. I had thought you were a great scientist, but now I see that you're just another confused follower, easily led astray by the so-called resistance and unable to see the big picture."

"Educate me, then. I'll listen."

His voice calmed as if he'd become a patient father to a disobedient son. "Time manipulation is a tricky thing. Events out of order. Fate on full display. You fight with me, but I've already won this battle and you have already lost. I'm simply fulfilling my part in what has already happened."

"Evidence?"

Father shook his head. "Scientists. Instead of asking for evidence, you should seek out the full story. Don't ask for the dots, connect them. Our story has already ended, but your difficulty stems from having no understanding of its beginnings. You'll find that I'm not the monster you believe I am."

Daniel stood silent while Father stared at the floor.

"Many years ago, when I was a young man, devout but disengaged, I received a remarkable coin with markings that urged me to spin it upon a mirror. An odd circumstance, but I complied. The message hidden within the coin told me a great many things, about technology, about my future and my purpose in this world. The message burdened me with a mission, taught me how to gain access to fourth-dimensional technology and directed me to a sailor in the Navy who would become an accomplice."

"To my surprise, the prophecies in the message came true, including a devastating war that I had a hand in starting. In the early days, I had little understanding of my role beyond the initial mission, but as the years passed, I noticed the relationship between three seemingly unrelated events. The first event was the war itself and my role in it. The second was your documented jump to the future, well known even in the 2030s. But the third was a groundswell among the population for godly dominion over the triggers of such a devastating war."

Father paced, eyeing Daniel. Jacquelyn hung on Daniel's arm, a half step behind him. She listened but said nothing.

"I knew that the timing of these three events was no coincidence. These events foretold my fate. I had played, or would play, the central role in all three. It was a commandment from a divine power. The Lord wished for me to lead a new path for the righteous, even though the heinous act of war was a required first step. I had passed my earthly test and began to see my redemption, which continues to this day."

"As more years passed, I believed deeply in my heart that I would transform into the very person who would call you to the future. Even stranger, that I would be the one who would send the coin to my younger self."

A second closed loop.

"A clear example of the ontological paradox," Daniel said, still deep in thought. "You fulfilled a destiny that you created for yourself."

Daniel attempted to piece together the seemingly impossible parts of the story. A young preacher stirred to action by a coin from the future, but unaware of its source. Becton must have been the delivery mechanism for that coin too. Father's disclosures were filling important gaps. Keeping him talking could be helpful in finding a path out of this mess.

"Yes, destiny. It's very real. When the technology for the olinwun was finally invented in the 2040s, I was certain. Once I understood that it was my fate to bring you to the future and to advise my younger self, I set about to *do* those things. Fourth-dimensional technology was the starting point, and I began to research the incredible ability to reach into three-dimensional space from a fourth dimension. You may be aware that the keys required to launch a missile are locked away in a safe. But you must also know that reaching into a locked safe is child's play when you have access to alternate dimensions of space."

This much was true. Anyone pushed into a fourth dimension viewed the three-dimensional world as a flat drawing, where walls could be easily crossed, and locked doors were simply lines to jump over. Nala had done it herself while trapped in the void.

Father continued. "I sifted through records of evangelical ministries to find my accomplice in the Navy. I already knew his name because it was included in the coin I had received. Some things were easy, some were hard. But throughout those years of research I couldn't imagine how the coins would be transferred to the past."

"And then Becton arrived." Daniel eyed the guard with the gun and glanced at the guard at the door. There was little chance he could take them both out.

Father seemed pleased. "Yes, Elliott Becton arrived last April, a ready messenger for the Lord. He identified me as the keeper of time manipulation and made the first contact by leaving a note inside my private chamber. It certainly caught my attention. We passed more notes to each other over several weeks. He was there, unseen, never flowing forward, always remaining in that strange empros state that allowed him to see me, but not vice versa. He asked for advanced information about time travel. I fed him only what I wanted him to know and, in the end, I promised all that he'd asked for, but on one condition. That he would deliver two coins. One to a computer programmer and part-time preacher in Atlanta of long ago—myself—and the other to you. Even from empros time, he easily completed the first task which resolved the loop that had puzzled me for so many years. Very strange indeed; I gave the coin to myself. But when Becton returned and demanded further information about time manipulation, I knew I could not trust him to deliver the second coin."

"So, you tricked him?" Daniel could guess where this was going.

"*Convinced* him that I could provide the information he wanted, but only in person. He would need to flow forward, joining us in our time. I also convinced him that the information bestowed upon him would provide safe passage back to his own time."

"A lie."

"We must do whatever it takes to fulfill our fate."

"So, once Becton flowed forward into your time, you had him trapped. When he returned, he died from snapback."

"Dear Dr. Rice, your verb tenses are all wrong. You keep forgetting. That part of the story hasn't happened yet."

Father was right, he had forgotten. Daniel closed his eyes and sighed at the insanity of it all. "Becton arrives for the second time *next week.*"

"In just a few days," Father confirmed. "When he arrives—and he will—the second loop to the past will be complete. But in a very real sense, it is already over. You confirmed it yourself. As we stood on the balcony of the Golden Spire, you told me that Becton is already dead."

Daniel nodded. Becton was certainly dead, even if the cause of his death hadn't yet happened. Effect before cause, the ultimate in time paradoxes.

Father gloated at his victory in convoluted logic. "You see, Dr. Rice, Elliott Becton's fate is sealed. Just as yours is. I'll explain to Mr.

Becton that if anything goes wrong with his return, you'll fix it when you arrive in the future. I'm confident Becton will do everything in his power to deliver the coin to you. In fact, he already has. You cannot change these events. They've already happened."

It was like fighting an impossibly-nimble foe, swinging wildly with punches that never landed because he had already moved away. Daniel's hopes for a positive outcome were shrinking rapidly.

Have I already lost?

Daniel hesitated to say anything more, realizing that his words could still be used against him. But, if he could get the belt back, there might still be options. It was possible that Father saw them too. Staying silent wasn't going to help.

"If you've already won, why do you want me dead?"

"Dead in your own time, Dr. Rice. There's a distinction." He waited for a response, almost as if teasing the correct answer from Daniel.

A gun pointed at his head, but no one had pulled the trigger yet. Sending Daniel to die in his own time seemed to be a key element of Father's plan.

"You want to improve the odds for another instance of your class."

Father seemed relieved. "You can learn. Very good."

"If I die in my own time, another version of you benefits."

"I do my best to help my brethren. We're in this together. You will be much quieter when you're dead. Better still, your death from the mistakes of time travel will reinforce my argument that time travel cannot be trusted to the scientists."

Father's plan might even make sense—if the idea of a single person spread into nearly infinite versions of themselves could make sense. This madman seemed to embrace it wholeheartedly.

272

"But too much talk. Let's move on, shall we?" Father reached into a pocket at the side of his bodysuit and held up an olinwun. "I believe you lost this? My people discovered it at the bottom of a punch bowl of all places. Ordinarily I would have put it back in your pocket for your trip home, but now that you're uncooperative, I can't be sure you won't lose it again."

He held the edges of the metal coin between his gloved thumb and index finger and pinched. Astonishingly, the coin folded in half as if the hard metal was no sturdier than foil. He tossed the now half-moon-shaped piece of junk to the floor.

The bodysuit had given his fingers the leverage of a vise. It was a vivid demonstration of power, but a warning too. A grip like that could easily shatter a bone or close off a windpipe with a pinch.

"The coin is useless, so we've decided on another path for the nuclear launch information that people in your time will need."

He waved to the scar-faced guard at the door, who entered with a small towel in his hand. The man unwrapped the towel to reveal a stainless-steel tool that looked like a surgical instrument. A prong of steel protruded from a handle with a triangular razor at its tip. Tucked below the razor, a second prong held an electronics component on a clip.

While the armed guard provided cover, Scar Face advanced toward Daniel. "Roll up your sleeve," he commanded.

Jacquelyn gasped. Daniel hesitated.

Father grabbed Jacquelyn by her arm and pulled her away. "Step aside, my dear. The procedure is routine and it only hurts for a few minutes, but it's not pretty." His gloved hand wrapped around her upper arm and squeezed.

Jacquelyn doubled over, pushing against his arm to no avail. "You're hurting me!"

"Crushed bones are far more painful than a simple chip placed under the skin. I hope your man chooses to cooperate."

Daniel held up a hand. "Stop. I'll do it."

Father relinquished his pressure, and Jacquelyn stood up straight, pushing against Father's gloved hand which remained wrapped around her arm.

Daniel took a deep breath and rolled up his shirtsleeve.

Take what you can get, but concede when you must.

He'd managed to get information from Father. Now, he'd have to pay the price.

35 Loopholes

Daniel Rice had always hated needles, both the sharp sting as the needle pierced the skin and the whole idea of inserting something foreign into the body. This would be an entirely new level of discomfort.

The guard gripped Daniel's left forearm and laid the surgical tool flat against his skin. The blade at the end of its prong was a centimeter wide. It looked like it could do a lot of damage, though it wouldn't go deep if the tool remained parallel to his arm. He could only hope this beast wouldn't intentionally aim at a vein.

Father gripped Jacquelyn a few feet away. She looked near tears, grimacing either from the painful squeeze of Father's enhanced grip or the menacing device ready to stab Daniel.

With a push of his wrist, the guard jabbed the blade under Daniel's skin, allowing the full length of its prong to penetrate.

Daniel jerked, wincing.

Blood seeped out from a clean cut, and the prong continued further another two inches just below the skin. With another push, the electronics chip followed the blade, sending a jolt of pain up his arm. The guard withdrew the tool, leaving the chip as a lump under the skin.

A blue bruise quickly formed around a bulge, and blood trickled from the wound. Daniel gritted his teeth as the guard wrapped gauze around his arm, covering the cut and staunching the bleeding.

"More false data about the nuclear launch?" Daniel asked as calmly as he could through clenched teeth. The chip would be difficult to remove without another incision, and Daniel doubted he'd find any knives lying around once he entered empros time.

"Not false at all. Very real information, just somewhat misleading," Father said. "It will keep them busy long enough."

Aiden's olinwun was still in his stomach, and no one was brandishing any nasty tools to cut open his belly. If he made it back to his own time, even in death, there was still a chance of completing this mission.

The scar-faced guard who'd acted as a crude nurse left the room and returned carrying what was certainly Becton's belt and the helmet. The belt looked no different than it had when Daniel had given it to Brother Benjamin.

Father traded Jacquelyn for the time travel devices, and the guard pulled both of her arms behind her back. His sneer increased now that Jacquelyn was in his grip.

"I was fascinated to see this device in person," Father said. He ran a finger along one of the wires that connected the large battery pack to several electronics components. "I'd read the descriptions in the documentation of your jump. I'd seen the drawings. But I wasn't prepared for such crude construction. Honestly, what is this?" He pointed to Chloe's lip piercing, which still held a loose wire to the leather.

"Improvisation," Daniel replied. "Your security team maligned it too, but it got me here." Daniel rolled his shirtsleeve over the now-red bandage.

"And it will no doubt return you. We were careful not to disrupt the data stored in its controlling unit. The anchor point in time is still faithfully recorded and ready to whisk you back to 2023. But we did make a few adjustments to the software in the controller. Minor things, really. Any programmer could do it."

He handed the belt to Daniel. His command was sharp. "Put it on."

Daniel held the belt in his good hand, eyeing the guard with the automatic weapon. He might be just stupid enough to shoot, though Father would never command it. Of course, Jacquelyn was also in danger, but that was true whether Daniel jumped or not.

The belt provides an advantage. Use it.

Daniel wrapped the belt around his waist and buckled up as best he could with a bleeding arm. If there was any concern from Father now that Daniel had the belt, he didn't show it. Still, the armed guard flipped on a targeting laser, and a red dot appeared on Daniel's shirt.

He won't shoot. Father won't allow it. Just get to empros time.

Father studied the components glued to the inside of the helmet. "Being a time traveler myself, I'm well aware of the steps involved and of the unique ability to manipulate a frozen world once flowing empros. I can assure you, Dr. Rice, we're not going to permit that to happen."

He set the helmet on the floor just in front of Daniel. "We will now leave and lock the door. Your next steps are simple. Put on the helmet, flow empros, then select the decompress command. You'll find that this location was nothing but a peanut farm in your day. The walls of this cell will simply disappear."

The plan was simple, yes. But badly flawed for someone trying to deliver misinformation to the past. He must see his mistake. It was obvious.

Father smiled. "The gears are turning. You see the opening, don't you? Empros provides so many options, if not within this locked cell, then on the other end of the jump."

It was a glaring loophole. Once back in 2023, he'd have all the time in the world.

Simply remain in empros. Find Griffith and Chloe and leave them a note. Cut the chip out and destroy it. Then get to a hospital and flow forward.

"I'm glad we're thinking along the same lines, Dr. Rice. It confirms our partnership in these fateful steps that we take together. I am the manipulator of time, and you are the messenger."

Father pointed to the belt. "We've made a small adjustment to the decompress command by combining it with flow forward. The two

277

commands are now one. Returning to your anchor will automatically trigger the flow forward. Sorry, but once you're back, there won't be any lounging around in empros time, writing letters to your friends."

Of course. He's not stupid. Daniel sighed. "With one command, I jump back, flow into normal time, and quickly die from snapback."

Father shrugged. "I'm afraid so. We're located a good distance from Atlanta. By the time the local farmers find you and call for medical help, you'll be dead. Very tragic."

Daniel would still have all the empros time he wanted *before* jumping back, but he'd be inside a locked cell. There didn't seem to be much point in remaining in that state. He'd eventually die from natural causes long before a single minute had elapsed in forward time.

Loophole closed.

Daniel could only think of two remaining alternatives, and neither of them were very good. "What if I refuse to jump?"

Father shook his head. "Not an option."

"You'll do some bone crushing to convince me to go?"

Father wiggled the stretched fingers on one hand. "I could, of course, but I have something much better." Father reached to a sheath on his belt and withdrew a knife with a curved blade at least ten inches in length. "I find this tool works miracles to concentrate the mind."

He touched a recess on its handle, and the knife lit up with a white light that pulsated along the edge of the blade with an audible vibration. "It cuts like a razor but uses high voltage, much like a welder's arc. It cauterizes the wound as it slices, keeping things tidy. It also functions quite well while in empros time—handy when I'm traveling."

Daniel stared at the pulsating blade and contemplated a second not-so-great alternative. The helmet was only a few feet away. He'd have to flip on the power switch and press several buttons on the belt controller. Even if he was quick, it was certainly enough time for the guard to get off a shot. But if Father got closer, the guard might not pull the trigger.

Once flowing empros, this would all end. Everyone in the room would freeze instantly, rendering guns and knives harmless. He'd disarm all three, hoist Jacquelyn over his shoulder and walk out the open door. It was a long shot, but it was the last of his not-so-good alternatives.

Father stepped forward, the blade humming.

"You cut me, and they'll know I didn't die from the time jump." Last-resort logic was still worth a try.

Father shook his head. "Who said anything about cutting *you*?" He pivoted toward Jacquelyn. The guard at the door easily held her arms with one hand and wrapped another massive hand around her neck, pulling her head back.

As the blade approached, she struggled and screamed. "Quiet, dear child," Father said. "This may take some time. We'll start with the fingers."

She was in grave danger, but with all eyes focused on the vibrating blade, it was an opening he couldn't afford to pass up. Daniel grabbed the helmet and slapped it over his head. He triggered the power switch on the belt.

Father swiveled. "Stop him!"

Instead of firing, the second guard lurched forward, slamming Daniel to the wall. He pushed his rifle into Daniel's neck. Gasping for air, Daniel thrust a knee into the guard's hip, but the brute pushed harder. Daniel had his fingers on the controller. He could feel the keypad, but with his head pinned, couldn't see its display. He pressed what felt like the Enter key, but nothing happened.

"Stop or she dies!" Father held the electric blade over Jacquelyn's neck, ready to plunge it into her chest.

He hadn't been fast enough. Daniel held up both hands. "Okay, okay!"

Daniel could barely breathe with the guard's gun pressing into his neck. Father came close, his stale breath invading Daniel's space. He lifted the blade to Daniel's cheek, its white arc crackling with the heat of high voltage.

"I will kill both of you right now if I must," Father said, his voice angry, his words deliberate. "Not my first choice, but necessary if you leave me no alternative."

Daniel had been close to success, very close. But the clunky interface of the cobbled-together belt along with his limited experience made emergency use impossible.

Daniel nodded. "I'll do as you ask. I'll jump back. But if you hurt her, I'll force you to kill me."

Father paused, a growling coming from deep within his throat. "You have one minute." He lowered his blade. "If you're not gone, we will come back, and she loses more than just a finger. Keep your hands in the air until the door closes." He motioned to the guard by the door, who still gripped Jacquelyn. "If he goes for the belt again, shoot her."

Daniel kept his hands high and his back against the wall as the guard loosened the pressure on Daniel's neck and stepped away. They left, the door slammed, and the dead bolt clunked into place, leaving Daniel alone with Jacquelyn once more.

One guard peered through the window. He held up a single finger. One minute.

Daniel lowered his hands and Jacquelyn ran to him. "Oh, my God, I thought that was the end." Her head fell against his chest, her body shaking with sobs.

Daniel hugged her, caressing her hair. "This will have to be a quick goodbye. When I'm gone, they'll come for you, but you have leverage. Tell them that I—"

Both of his arms snapped to his waist like he'd been hit with a bolt of lightning. In the same instant, Jacquelyn vanished.

280

It happened so fast his brain hardly registered the sudden change. There was no outline of where she'd stood just a moment before, no puff of smoke, nothing. Jacquelyn was simply gone.

People disappear. It happens, especially in this wacked-out world of quantum space and time. His mind raced.

There were two possibilities. One, she'd moved into a fourth dimension of space, though that required a neutrino beam or a portal. Two, she'd transitioned into empros time. Far more likely, but he couldn't fathom how she'd done it. He still wore the belt and helmet, the only means of getting there. The yellow light on the helmet hadn't flashed.

His shoulders ached. The wound on his left arm seeped bright red through his shirtsleeve. But the reason for his pain was clear. Both arms had been pushed down in a millionth of a second. He'd done the same thing to Chloe.

Less clear was where Jacquelyn had gone. If her disappearance had involved empros time, she would still have no way to leave the locked cell. Hundreds of years would have passed in empros time by now, and she'd be nothing more than a withered skeleton leaning against the wall.

If she wasn't in empros time, then something else was going on. Daniel had run out of guesses.

He looked to the door. The guard had seen Jacquelyn vanish too, and his keys jangled in the lock.

Daniel's heart raced. One more chance. One more loophole. He glanced down to the controller, initializing its function. An LED lit up on the belt.

He heard the dead bolt slide open.

They'd made their fatal mistake, but only if he could finish before a gun was at his head. Daniel selected the command from the controller display.

tcs_flow_empros

The guard's hand appeared around the opening door just as Daniel hit the Enter key.

36 Future

A brilliant yellow light flashed.

Daniel opened his eyes, removed the helmet and looked around the empros-darkened room, the only light coming from the LEDs on the belt. No sign of Jacquelyn, but he didn't really expect to see her—or her body.

The door stood open six inches, the guard's hand frozen on its edge. The brute's dimwitted brain was now running even slower; one synapse tick per hour. He'd never know how big a mistake he'd just made.

Daniel pried the heavy metal door from his hand and swung it open. The guard stood immobile with a stupid expression on his face.

With all the strength he could muster, Daniel slammed the heavy door against its frame, crushing the man's hand in between. Snaps and cracks verified the punishment of broken bones. "That's for Aiden, you fucking bastard."

He pulled the man's forearm closer to the door frame and slammed the door once more. "And that's for me." The guard's expression remained the same even though his forearm was now bent at an angle. Nerves would need a few milliseconds to react.

The guard's other, unbroken hand carried a pistol. Daniel pried it from his fingers and held the gun to the man's head. He hesitated, and then lowered the weapon. "Your lucky day. Unlike you, I'm not a murderer." Daniel tucked the gun under his belt, wondering if the weapon could even be fired in empros time.

Daniel lifted a foot and kicked the frozen man's chest, slamming him against the corridor wall, the body tumbling to the floor like a poorly balanced mannequin.

Daniel peered into the darkened corridor, empty. In one direction was the vault-like door that they'd passed through on their way in, unfortunately now closed. Daniel walked to the door's control panel and pressed the button marked Open. The heavy metal door remained motionless. To get electricity, he'd need to flow forward once more. It was something he could do, but returning to forward time would take away his advantage.

He noticed a small peephole in the center of the massive door. Difficult to see through given the darkness, but he could just make out the figures of Father and a second guard on the other side, their backs turned toward him. If he flowed forward, he'd only have a few seconds before the guard turned his automatic weapon on him. Not a great escape plan, but an option.

At least I have options.

He found his phone lying on a desk next to the vault door and returned it to his jacket pocket. A useful resource if he managed to get back to his time.

What I really need is an exit.

He headed down the corridor, past the cell and the guard slumped on the floor. The corridor ended at a second door. Turning the handle, he peered inside. On one wall, a bed. On the other wall, a standing closet with a few clothes on hangers. No windows and no door to the outside. It was probably a guard's sleeping post, but it didn't come with any weapons—or ideas.

Returning to the open cell door, Daniel squatted next to the guard. "Just you and me, it appears, and only one way out. What do you have that might be helpful?"

He frisked the guard, finding a pack of cigarettes, a lighter and an olinwun. No hand grenades or dynamite—either of those would have been handy.

Are explosions possible in empros time?

Daniel sat on the floor against the wall and examined the guard's pistol. A single-shot handgun, maybe ten rounds in the magazine. Hardly a match against an automatic weapon, but it was all he had.

Daniel sighed. "A one-sided gun battle is no exit plan. You've got to think your way out."

Jacquelyn came to mind first. Her disappearance without a trace was disturbing, but at the same time, comforting. She would have been raped, possibly killed by these goons not long after he'd jumped. Where she'd gone was anybody's guess, but he could at least rule out the corridor. How she'd disappeared in both time and space might remain a mystery forever.

Getting out was next on his mind. The options were limited, but they were a whole lot better now that he was free from the locked cell.

Option one. Flow forward, press the button to open the vault door, and a gunfight would ensue. He might get lucky, but he'd already witnessed how slowly the vault door opened. He wouldn't have the advantage of surprise.

Then there was option two. Flow forward, partially open the vault door, then flow empros again to freeze the opponents. Better, but the guard would have plenty of time to shove his weapon through the opening door. Timing would have to be perfect.

Option three was still available: Father's plan. Simply return to 2023. He had the equipment to do it. He even had an olinwun somewhere down in his stomach that would ultimately lead to a successful mission. The coroner would find it.

But was snapback reality? And to what degree? There'd been so many lies, it was getting hard to sort through every aspect of time jumping. He'd only need a single command: decompress. He'd be back in his own time in a flash—and flowing forward, now that they'd fused those commands into one.

Even if he ended up hemorrhaging from his eyes, ears, nose, and everywhere else inside, he might still have a chance. He had a phone. He could call for help, and they might get there in time with life-saving medical procedures.

Daniel took a deep breath. *Not likely. Becton didn't make it.*

Still, even in death, his mission would be a success. He could stop the nuclear launch. Maybe it was the right choice. He already knew too much about his own future, and that couldn't be a good thing.

Daniel sat in silence for several minutes, thinking.

It's still Monday back home.

Whatever "back home" meant. The anchor point was still set. Monday morning, October 9, just three days after Griffith had walked into Daniel's office and dragged him into this mess.

Four and a half days if you count time spent in the future.

In this jumble of time frames, he could sit in the corridor for days more of empros time, and not a single second would pass in either 2023 or 2053. Elapsed time was becoming meaningless.

He chuckled. "Maybe none of this is real. In some alternate timeline, I'm hiking the Appalachian Trail right now with Nala."

Thoughts of Nala were the hardest to ignore. If he performed his duty but died, she'd be collateral damage. She'd never said she loved him, at least not in those words, but she'd shown it in countless other ways. Her joyful voice picking up the phone. Her buoyant smile when they met after time apart. Her playfulness that showed up only for him, no one else. Her soft embrace as they settled into sleep at night.

There'd been far too many nights apart, her home in Illinois, his in Virginia. Long-distance relations were handicapped from the start.

No more time apart, he resolved. *I'm coming home.*

He could start a gun battle and he might even manage to fight his way out of this building. But he'd still be in 2053 with no safe way to return. It would just delay the inevitable. Jumping backward to his anchor risked instant death, but as Aiden had confirmed, it was really all he had.

He tucked the gun back under his belt, grabbed the helmet and put it on. The belt was already powered up, a flashing prompt on the controller display awaiting his command. He scrolled to Decompress Forward.

Decompress. The opposite of compress.

The high-frequency compressed standing wave of time would relax, drawing him backward to his anchor point. His mind spun with thoughts of how time worked, or at least, how it had been described by Zin. As he thought, an idea deep in the recesses of his mind rose to consciousness.

Compress. The opposite of decompress.

A chill ran up his body. It was the answer he'd been looking for. Better information, deeper expertise. Access to scientists and knowledge and higher technology. The distant future would be full of unknowns, but it lay wide open, accessible with just a touch of the keypad.

A smile crept across his face as he set a new node, dialing in a date selected almost at random. The next command was off the scale for risk, but it just might be the most brilliant choice he'd ever made.

tcs_compress_forward

Without hesitation, Daniel pressed the Enter key. The astonishingly bright yellow light flashed once more, carrying him not toward home but much further away.

* * * * * * * * * * * * * * * * * * *

Centuries flew by in an instant. Or had they really passed at all? The standing wave of time had merely compressed further, maintaining the same anchor point but using a new destination node far into the future.

He hadn't even been sure of the year he'd typed in. It didn't matter. Twenty-four something. Four hundred years would probably be enough, but not too much.

Of course, there was no telling how far science and technology had come in the twenty-fifth century, or what the people of this future were like. For that matter, there was no guarantee there would be people at all.

But he could take his time to find out. Flowing empros was like stepping out of time, providing the freedom to study at leisure. He could jump forward as often as needed, and the anchor point of the past would still be waiting when he was ready to rejoin it.

Daniel removed the helmet and the flash faded from his eyes. He stood in the same corridor, but no longer dark, and better still, no longer closed at the end.

Only a few paces past the guard's room, the corridor opened to a stone-lined walkway, with a stone wall along the right side and a trellis of grapevines overhead. A row of columns defined the left side of the walkway, thankfully open to the outside.

Daniel took a deep breath of fresh air and stared at the serene view beyond the columns. Rolling green hills, with clumps of trees, and in the distance, a city of tall spires. Even in the dim light of empros time, with its muted colors, still air and utter lack of the ordinary sounds of outdoors, the view was a simple pleasure that represented freedom.

The exit I needed, precisely aligned with a corridor from a now four-hundred-year-old structure. Almost like it was planned.

He walked a few steps along the stone breezeway and stepped through the columns and into a gravel courtyard decorated with potted plants. Behind him, the mansion still stood, looking not much different than it had in 2053.

To one side of the courtyard, a fountain sprayed streams of water that hung in midair. The sound of gravel crunching under his feet reassured him that this world was very real, just suspended in time.

A voice, not far away, called out. "This way."

Daniel's head reflexively jerked toward the breezeway. A woman's voice, not threatening, but very unexpected. Hair prickled across his neck, serving as an anxious reminder that a twenty-first-century human had been thrown hundreds of years into an unfamiliar future.

"This way," the pleasant monotone voice sounded again. Curiosity got the better of anxiety. Daniel stepped between columns to the stone walkway and peered down its length.

Thirty yards further, the columns ended at a small circular building with a dome on top. A rotunda, in architectural terms, like a miniature version of the Jefferson Memorial back in D.C.

"This way," the woman's voice called out once more. A pulsating pink-lavender light emanated from an arched entryway leading into the rotunda.

He'd made the jump to find answers. Nerves or not, contact would be required. Like a schoolboy called to the teacher, he walked toward the light.

Stopping at the archway, he peered inside to a darkened enclosure. In the center of an oval-shaped room, a brightly glowing woman stood on a raised pedestal above the stone floor. One arm bent at the elbow as if in a greeting. A mix of bright colors—pink, lavender, rose and others—radiated from her skin, piercing the dark shadows of empros time. The colorful light throbbed in a rhythmic pulse.

It was almost as if he'd stumbled upon a futuristic museum. A dark alcove with a glowing statue on a pedestal. But she was more than a statue. The pulsating psychedelic colors disclosed life.

She moved, gently lowering her arm and clasping her hands together at the waist. Bright pink lips formed a placid smile.

Daniel stepped inside the alcove. "Hello?"

Long braids of hair spilled over her shoulders. She wore a floor-length veil with folds that gently waved in the wind, though there was no wind. Thousands of glowing speckles of pink, lavender, indigo and crimson dotted one side of her face as if someone had flicked a wet paintbrush just above her skin. Swirls of the same colors cascaded down her neck to complete a magical effect of phosphorescent body paint. The speckles and swirls glowed beneath her veil following a curving path that wrapped around her body and finished with a flourish down one leg.

She embodied the exquisite artwork of a glowing galaxy.

Her eyes sparkled bright blue, displaying a kindness beyond their bold color. "Welcome," she said, though her mouth barely moved.

An apparition appeared above her head. An oval image. A view of the same scene through the columns outside. Rolling green hills, blue sky with puffs of white clouds. It wasn't a window, more likely a projection of the countryside as seen in the daylight of forward time.

"Where am I?" Daniel asked.

Her body was fully three-dimensional, with an appearance of flesh and blood, even if the body art glowed.

"Georgia," she said. "More specific?" Her head tilted to one side with the question.

"That's close enough," Daniel replied, his nerves calming. He'd jumped in time, but his location was still the same. Still named the same too. Perhaps not surprising; place names sometimes lasted thousands of years.

"Who are you?" he asked.

The colors of her face included long pink lashes to match her lips. Gentle hand motions accompanied unhurried words, almost mesmerizing in combination with her soothing and softly spoken tone.

"A guide... waiting for you... and one other."

"You knew I was coming?" It seemed inconceivable that his second jump forward could have been recorded in history. He'd made the decision on the spur of the moment, with no one else around to watch him go. Of course, he might still tell the tale upon return to his own time, a positive thought that made him smile.

She smiled back. Gentle and limited, matching her words.

"You wait for one other, besides me?" Daniel asked.

"Yes."

"Who?"

She remained silent, her soft smile speaking for her.

"Have you been waiting long?" Daniel asked.

"Less than one year. More specific?" Her head tilted again.

Her mannerisms were fascinating; the head tilt, the long lashes blinking with intention, the slow-motion smile. Like her dress, her hair moved in the nonexistent breeze. He could happily watch her for hours. "Are you human? Or machine?"

"Neither. More specific?"

"No, that's fine, I probably don't need to know." He would have loved to go deeper, but it would only be out of curiosity. He'd made it to the distant future, even more reason to avoid gathering too much knowledge. "Can you help me return to my time?"

"Yes."

"Um... more specific, if you don't mind."

"You are Daniel Rice?"

"Yes, I am."

Expected. Certainly, a good thing.

She reached out with her right hand, palm up. A swirl of deep blue with pink speckles glowed across the skin. She curled her index finger, leaving the other fingers straight. "Please verify."

A handshake? The gesture was slightly odd but not threatening. Daniel set the helmet down and formed his right hand in a complementary manner, palm down, index finger curled. He placed his hand on hers, their index fingers forming a bridge at the knuckle and their thumbs touching at the side.

Her skin was cool, soft and moist. Very humanlike, except for the colors. If she was sampling DNA or proteins, she'd make an excellent nurse. No skin prick, no swab. Nothing but a gentle touch.

"Thank you," she said, her pleasant but otherwise blank expression remaining unchanged. Daniel withdrew his hand.

Her eyes closed momentarily, then reopened. "For you, Daniel Rice. Information from Sagittarius Novus. Impart?"

"Yes, please. I'd love to see it." The galactic alliance of civilizations was somehow involved, perhaps even prepared for Daniel's visit.

Need to learn how time travel works? Ask the experts.

He imagined Earth would be a full-fledged member of Sagittarius Novus by now. Either that or reduced to a cinder, which apparently hadn't happened. She did say this was Georgia. Maybe the city of spires in the distance was still named Atlanta.

Her eyes closed once more, and the tone of her voice changed, becoming deeper and more resonant, with a quicker clip to her words. "Welcome, Daniel Rice. The time jump you have made is unique in human history. One of the first jumps, and one of the last uncontrolled. In this year, while time jumps are still undertaken, they are rare, researched in advance and coordinated."

Behind her, the scene of the countryside changed, replaced by a bird's-eye view above the city of spires. The view swooped down, flying between buildings and passing just above a surface of crisscrossing walkways, roadways and tracks. A sleek glass-and-metal train of sorts slid across the foreground, and the view dropped into one of the buildings, passing through rooms filled with people and then out the other side. It seemed to be a virtual tour and like any good promotional video, the city appeared vibrant and energetic.

"We have studied your mission, even though it is not yet complete. There is much to be gained by its success, and much to be lost by failure. While we can assess the probabilities of your actions, we have no power to affect the past. Only you can do that."

An image of an extended family, including babies and elderly, appeared behind her. Though clothing, hair and grooming styles were unfamiliar, the faces of humans hadn't changed.

"As it has been for thousands of generations, those who live in the present craft the future. Changes in your present will create a new future, but use your power judiciously. Always remember that wisdom is a balance between action and restraint." Multiple images of warfare blended together, including a mushroom cloud.

She opened her eyes, and a ring of glass appeared in her hands. At first, Daniel thought it was another projection, but unlike the images, the ring was fully three-dimensional. About two feet in diameter, it looked like a fluorescent lightbulb formed into a circle and just as fragile.

"To complete your journey, we have prepared a device that may help. The ring is as unique as your jump and is not suitable for general use. Its design is sufficient to create a pathway between this time and your anchor."

Her voice returned to a more feminine, gentle tone. Her words came slower. "For you." She held the glass ring out.

Her hand had been real enough, but the clear ring seemed too ghostly to grasp. Daniel reached out with both arms and she placed the ring in his hands.

"Thank you," he said. No more than a half inch thick, the glass ring weighed almost nothing. A thin film, almost like a soap bubble, spanned its interior, transparent but also somewhat reflective. The entire setup seemed absurdly fragile. Squeeze too hard and it might break. "How do I use it?"

Rolling green hills and the city of spires formed the glowing woman's backdrop once more. She raised both hands. "Hold above your head. Then drop. More specific?"

"That's it?" He held it up to his chest, measuring. The ring was wide enough to drop without hitting his shoulders. "What do I do with the belt?"

"Nothing."

"And by dropping this ring over me, I'll return to my anchor point?"

"Yes."

"Safe from snapback?"

"Yes." She gently waved a hand toward the breezeway behind Daniel. "A safe jump point. Do it there."

No dialing in a date, no scrolling through commands, no Enter key. Drop the ring over his head and he'd return to his anchor. Or so she said.

Daniel looked into her sparkling eyes, searching for the humanity that might reside within this enigmatic intelligence. "Thank you. You've been very helpful, and I appreciate your kindness. Do you understand what I mean by that?"

"Yes. I am aware."

Daniel held out his hand, palm up, his index finger curled. She smiled and put her hand out, palm down, index finger curled. Whether it was a new style of handshake or a medical procedure that he'd misunderstood probably didn't matter. They touched, human to artificial being. Or whatever she was.

Daniel backed away. Though he might not need it, he reached down and retrieved his helmet. When he looked up, the woman's figure was gone, replaced by a thin column of pulsating pink-lavender light that reached from the pedestal to the dome of the rotunda.

Thank you again, Lady Pink. Only one step away from home.

Footsteps echoed on the stones behind him, and Daniel spun around. At the entryway to the rotunda stood a dark figure, bearded and wearing a skintight bodysuit.

"Very tender," Father murmured.

Blocking the only exit from the alcove, he reached to a sheath on his belt and withdrew a curving blade that lit with an electric arc that crackled and snapped.

37 Ring

With surprising agility, Father lunged forward. The humming blade narrowly missed as Daniel leaped backward to the opposite side of the pedestal, passing through the pulsating beam of pink-lavender light shooting straight up from its center.

A referee for this fight would have been useful, but Lady Pink failed to materialize.

Daniel lifted the glass ring, hesitated and then lowered it. The lady had indicated the safe jump point was just outside the alcove. No telling what might happen if he tried it here.

Father remained on the other side of the pedestal, still blocking the only entrance to the alcove. Daniel pulled the guard's gun from his belt and aimed. The bodysuit certainly imparted strength and agility far beyond Father's age, and it might also act as body armor, but the old man wore nothing on his head.

Ignoring the gun, Father's voice was matter-of-fact. "It took some time to find you. More than a year. I recognized my mistake the next day after you and the girl disappeared from our holding cell."

Four hundred years into the future with a date selected almost at random. Yet he still found me, even hidden in empros time.

No mention of finding Jacquelyn. Daniel hadn't either, and he wasn't sure if that was good or bad.

Daniel held the gun in one hand, keeping the ring behind his back with the other. He could get several shots off, even one-handed, and likely hit his target, but this was empros time. *Would it even fire?*

Father eyed the beam of pink-lavender light directly between them, glancing up to the ceiling of the alcove. He seemed more concerned with the light than the gun Daniel held.

"One of the funny things about time jumping, it gives you a second chance to correct your errors. Once I realized you could have jumped further into the future, I began a systematic search. It really didn't matter how many jumps were required or how long it took. If you had gone to the future, you'd be waiting for me at a specific date. When jumping across time, catching up really has no meaning."

Father was clearly here to finish the job. There was no point in waiting. Daniel aimed at his head and pulled the trigger. The hammer clicked metal to metal, but the gun didn't fire. He pulled again. The result was somewhat expected. A forward-facing gun in empros-facing time.

Father shook his head. "Oh, it's firing. Right now, the oxidizer molecules in the primer are waking up to a small spark. In another hour or two—empros time, of course—the primer will expand into the gunpowder. Possibly by tomorrow or the next day, the bullet might even separate from the cartridge and begin its trip down the barrel."

He waved his electric blade, buzzing through the air. "Much more effective."

Daniel tossed the gun to the floor and reached for the motorcycle helmet. It wasn't much of a shield, but it might deflect a blow. He was more concerned about protecting the glass ring. He'd need to get outside the alcove to use it.

Father slowly circled the pedestal, keeping the blade in front. He wasn't far away, and a quick jump across would put the weapon within reach. But he seemed unwilling to cross the beam of light coming from the pedestal.

"How did you find me?" Daniel asked.

Let him talk. Maybe Lady Pink will return. She did say she was expecting one other.

"At first I jumped only a few months. Then a few years. But there was no record of your presence in the timeline. So, I jumped a thousand years, but still no trace of you. Going beyond that is pointless because languages change, and the technology for record-keeping becomes difficult to recognize. I knew it would be difficult for you too, so I refocused on less than five hundred years."

If Daniel could keep Father circling, he might have a shot at sprinting out the opening, holding the ring over his head and dropping it before Father could reach him. Of course, the fair lady hadn't given the specifics on how the ring worked, or how long it might take to initiate. Father's blade could do a lot of damage in a short amount of empros time.

"A few more jumps and I finally found a record for the construction of this extension to my home. Another jump and I discovered the colorful apparition standing on this pedestal. She wasn't nearly as cooperative for me."

Father stepped up to the pedestal. Now would be a good time for the gentle guide to return. At the very least, her appearance could create a distraction and a chance for Daniel to reach the exit.

Father passed his blade through the beam of light. It sparkled and hissed as it interrupted the pulsating light, but no glowing woman reappeared. Perhaps Lady Pink wasn't waiting for Father after all.

He seemed satisfied with his test. "Once I discovered this alcove, I simply narrowed your arrival time with a few jumps back and forth until I located this day, November third, 2441."

He sidestepped the beam and moved directly toward Daniel, a determined look in his eye. "But this is where it ends. I'm tired of hunting you down, tired of forcing you to play your part in our shared fate. The belt will take you back, not this interloping ring—even if I have to kill you first."

It was an obscure disadvantage Daniel hadn't considered until now. With a second person flowing empros, he needn't be alive to jump back. Father could select the command on the controller even after Daniel's death.

The lines on Father's bodysuit compressed, making it clear the time for talk was over. He leaped forward, propelled by a spring-like force. Daniel ducked, and the knife narrowly missing his shoulder. Like an agile cat, Father bounced off the far wall and back to Daniel.

The blade slashed. The air vibrated. Using the helmet as a shield, Daniel deflected its path. The helmet split cleanly in two pieces, each portion clattering across the stones in different directions.

With the alcove entrance no longer blocked, Daniel lunged across the pedestal toward the breezeway, but the vibrating blade slashed once again. With a loud buzz, it sliced an arc across his right side, cutting through clothes, skin and bone as if they were tissue paper.

Searing pain pierced Daniel's body. He slammed to the ground. The ring dislodged from his hand and skittered across the stones through the alcove entrance, bouncing like a flat rock skipping on water. Light flashed at each contact with the stone floor, but the ring didn't shatter. It skidded to a stop in the breezeway, unbroken, glowing—and hovering an inch above the stones.

Daniel rolled to his left side, groaning. His shirt was splashed with blood. He sensed Father's approach from behind and kicked upward, catching him off guard and dropping him to the ground. The electric blade clattered to the far side of the alcove.

Choices. Go for the ring, the knife or hand-to-hand against a bodysuit that gave its wearer extraordinary strength and agility.

Daniel glanced at the mysteriously hovering ring.

Electromagnetic. The only force capable of offsetting gravity beyond atomic distances. A possible defense mechanism.

He opted for the ring.

Wincing with pain, he rose to his knees and crawled through the alcove opening. Father sprang back into the alcove to retrieve the blade.

On his knees, Daniel grasped the glowing ring still hovering above the stones, feeling a tingle in his fingers. His hair stood on end, like touching a Van de Graaff sphere.

High voltage, even if low current.

With a single leap, Father jumped from the alcove and raised his crackling blade. Ignoring the pain across his side, Daniel swiveled and raised the ring just as Father's blade came down. The blade's edge contacted the ring with a loud pop, and electric sparks spewed in every direction.

Father screamed, his head jerking backward. He dropped to his knees, eyes wide with his mouth open and gasping. He teetered and then slumped to the stone floor.

Quiet returned, the only sound coming from the slightly vibrating ring, still in Daniel's hand and still intact.

Daniel's heart raced, his fingers tingled, but the high-voltage current had taken a different path to ground. He rolled over on his back, groaned and dabbed a finger to the slice across his ribs.

He breathed in place for a full minute, then rose to his knees and surveyed his opponent.

Smoke curled from several points on the bodysuit. The charred remains of his beard and the black lines crisscrossing his face told the story of death by electrocution. It had been a guess on Daniel's part, but the ring had provided some clues. It had repelled the blade's current with even higher voltage.

The knife lay a few feet away, now inert.

Getting to his feet was harder, the pain across his ribs intense. Daniel's shirt had been sliced open and beneath it was a red line about ten inches long. The bleeding had already stopped, the result of the searing hot blade, but the cut was to the bone, and probably even deeper. He buttoned his undamaged jacket over the wound, which provided enough pressure to push the skin together, even if it did nothing for the pain.

Daniel stepped over Father's body, giving it a nudge with his foot. No movement. He retrieved the blade and its scabbard and tucked the weapon under his belt. Even with Father dead, Daniel wasn't convinced there were no more time tricks that might come into play, and his mind was in no condition to think through the possibilities.

Get home. Now.

He examined the ring. It had stopped glowing, returning to an ordinary glass surface with a thin soap-bubble film spanning the circle. There wasn't a mark on it.

The columns walkway is a safe jump point. Do it there, the glowing guide had told him. She had pointed to a spot just outside the alcove, roughly where he stood now. By safe, she'd probably meant he wouldn't materialize inside of a hill or barn or tree once back in 2023. He could only hope they'd done their research.

Here goes.

He lifted the ring, the pain in his ribs spiking as he did. He paused and thought for a moment, like he was forgetting something.

Even though it was now unneeded, he still wore the belt around his waist, but the helmet lay in the alcove, shattered into two pieces. Maybe not technology he should leave behind. He returned to the alcove and recovered the pieces.

The lower chin guard had been separated from the rest of the helmet, but it was nothing more than protective plastic. The upper portion appeared to be undamaged, including the electronics chip and the yellow light pasted to the inside of its visor. It might still work, giving him a backup plan.

He fit the damaged helmet on his head, completing the time jumper's outfit and clearing the feeling that he might be neglecting something. He returned to the jump spot in the columned breezeway.

Gritting his teeth against the pain, he lifted the ring once more, held it parallel to the ground and looked up. The soapy film spanning its interior provided a reflection, but surprisingly, it wasn't a reflection of the stone floor at his feet. It looked more like red dirt.

301

Fascinating.

He tipped the ring, studying its reflection of furrows and the remains of plowed-under plants jutting from the dirt.

My destination? Father had said this area was farmland in 2023. The ring seemed to provide not just a passage to his anchor point, but a view to it.

Daniel took a deep breath, released the ring and watched with amazement as it floated down in slow motion, moving past his head and shoulders and surrounding him in a thin translucent veil as it dropped.

38 Fate

Dizzy with a vague sense of not being fully conscious, like waking in the middle of the night. Dreamlike.

His head hung down, his view a pair of shoes partially dug into rust-colored dirt. Were they his feet? Surrounding the shoes, a glass ring. It seemed familiar, but he couldn't quite recall its purpose.

Daniel lifted his head. He stood in a field, but with somewhat blurred vision it was impossible to distinguish much more than dirt and a few trees in the distance. His ribs hurt. A headache was starting.

Better than dead.

Memory slowly returned. The ring had performed its function, drifting down as if it were made of tissue paper and leaving behind a soapy film that had enveloped him. The ring had met the stone floor of the breezeway, and then nothing.

Is this 2023? Am I flowing forward?

He looked up to a bright sun with puffy clouds drifting by. The leaves on the trees rustled, and a breeze cooled his skin. Empros time wasn't like this.

His vision sharpened, though the ache across his side didn't abate. Nausea swelled in his stomach and then passed, possibly from the metal coin that was still down there somewhere.

Flowing forward. Injured but alive. I'll take it.

He retrieved the phone from his jacket pocket. Three bars of service, but not much battery life left. He dialed, smiling when a familiar gruff voice responded. "Daniel, where the hell are you?" Griffith had never sounded so wonderful.

"A farm somewhere outside Atlanta. We don't have much time, so here's what you need to know. USS *Nevada*, a ballistic missile sub on patrol in the north Pacific. They will launch later today, with one missile hitting Vladivostok and a second hitting San Francisco at five p.m. Pacific time. Captain's name is Lundstrom. Stop them. Whatever they're doing, stop it. Shut every system down on that sub. Hell, tell the Navy to blow the ship out of the water if they have to."

"Got it. This is cutting it close, but I know who to call."

"I'll have a lot more information for you on a religious cult that's involved, but right now that evidence is in my stomach. I'll be checking into a hospital next."

"Huh?"

"Long story. Work the Navy angle. Hurry."

"I'm on it. Good job, Daniel."

Daniel hung up. Griffith would be busy. So would the Navy, but the ball was rolling. Daniel had worked with the Navy and knew their procedures well. They could instantly communicate with any submarine, even when submerged. If that didn't solve the problem, a guided missile destroyer could launch a hypersonic missile that could hit any target in the Pacific within thirty minutes. The only catch was they'd need to know where to strike. If the sub had gone dark, not even the US Navy would know where they were.

Daniel's phone had already gone into power-saving mode. Probably just enough juice for one more call. He dialed.

"Nine-one-one. What's your emergency?"

"I'm not sure where I am, but I need medical attention. Can you help?"

After a pause, "We have your location." She collected his name and vitals and suggested he find a shady place to sit. Given his remote location, it might be twenty minutes before an ambulance could arrive.

Twenty minutes. It would do. Thanks to instant cauterization, blood loss was minimal. The chip stuck in his forearm wasn't bad. The pain in his ribs was manageable. He could use some water, but the only farmhouse within sight looked at least a mile away.

The upper portion of the helmet lay in the dirt nearby. He put it back on his head, the best shade he'd likely find in this treeless field. He retrieved the glass ring from the dirt. The shimmering film in its center still reflected, but with different colors. He held it up, expecting once more to see the reflected red dirt, but the image was now of stones.

He tilted the ring, locating breezeway columns within its reflection.

Wow. Back to the future.

The amazing device provided an accurate view of his surroundings, but from the opposite end of a time tunnel. The stone walkway fronted by columns and with a rotunda at one end would someday be built right here in this farm field.

He searched the ring view for a body and found a crumpled shape to one side. The image from empros time was too dark to make out any detail.

He's dead. Permanently dead, he tried to assure himself. The nagging feeling of multiple versions of Father bouncing around in time wouldn't go away, but at least none of them could reach into the past.

Daniel took a few steps forward and held the ring up once more. Its reflection displayed a fountain in a gravel courtyard. Another tilt and he could make out the corridor leading into the mansion. All he'd need to do is walk across this dirt field and he'd be standing precisely where the holding cell would be someday.

On the morning of June 3, 2053, he and Jacquelyn would be standing in that cell. Father and his goons would enter, threaten Jacquelyn and force Daniel to jump. These future events were as real as any. He'd just lived through them, every detail fresh in his mind.

An idea formed. A powerful urge, almost a destiny. There was no ignoring its message. Before any ambulance arrived at this 2023 farm field, he had one more task to complete. Jacquelyn's life depended on it.

Daniel stepped further to his left, walking through red dirt but along an imagined stone breezeway. He checked his position repeatedly by holding up the ring. Satisfied he'd found the right location, he stopped and powered up the belt.

I'll stay in empros. It won't consume even a single second of forward time.

Typing on the belt's controller, he reinitialized the anchor point and set a new destination node: June 3, 2053 10:00 AM. The exact time was a guess, but just as Father had done, he could easily jump again if he missed.

His final mission to the future might be fate or it might be personal, but it wasn't optional. Moreover, he was one hundred percent certain it would succeed. It already had.

Daniel held the glass ring under one arm and pressed the Enter key.

The bright flash was followed by near darkness.

He hadn't materialized inside a wall, that much was clear. It took a minute for his eyes to adjust to empros darkness, but the LEDs on the belt helped. He stood in a small room with a bed on one wall and a closet on the other. The guard's sleeping quarters in 2053. Exactly on target. More importantly, the glass ring, still in his hands, had made the jump too.

The room and corridor outside were still and quiet. No sign of any empros-flowing intruders with electric blades.

Good so far, but did I get the time right?

Further down the corridor, the cell door was wide open. The scar-faced guard stood just inside with Jacquelyn in his grip. One of the brute's arms was wrapped around Jacquelyn's neck, pulling her head back. The fear on her face was like a snapshot from a recurring nightmare.

306

A few feet away, Father threatened with his blade, a smirk of contempt on his face.

No one moved. The blade made no vibration.

Perfect.

Daniel slipped past the smug guard and into the cell. "Be careful where you put that hand. Somebody might slam a door on it very soon."

Inside the cell, the other guard pointed his automatic rifle at frozen Daniel, backed against the wall.

Inside the cell. Now just fast-forward a few minutes.

He adjusted the time on the belt's controller, stepped to the far corner of the room and compressed time once more. The yellow light flashed again, washing out the darkened scene before him. When his eyes readjusted, the tableau had changed.

Father and both guards were gone, and the cell door was now closed. In the center of the room, frozen Daniel and Jacquelyn embraced.

"Spot-on!" Daniel set the ring down and circled the frozen figures in their goodbye embrace.

"Both of you are about to be very confused, you especially, Daniel. But never fear, it'll all work out." He pushed frozen Daniel's arms to his side, taking care with the arm wrapped in gauze. "You're going to be sore. Sorry about that. Unfortunately, it gets worse." He patted his counterpart on the ribs.

Frozen Daniel wore his own version of the belt. Odd that two copies of the same item could exist in the same moment, but then there were two copies of himself too. His frozen version would need that belt and Daniel didn't touch it.

He studied their positions, her arms still wrapped around his neck, her head against his chest. "Yeah, I need to separate you two."

Unclasping her hands, he lowered her arms, hugged her from behind, and dragged her back a few feet as best he could, given the pain in his side. As if she were a mannequin, he repositioned her legs and arms until she looked balanced.

Daniel removed his own belt and wrapped it around Jacquelyn's waist, buckling it securely, then positioned the damaged helmet over her hair. He stepped back to review his preparation.

Would it work? The helmet was missing a large chunk, exposing Jacquelyn's chin, but the visor with its electronics and light still covered her face. He would only need a single command, flow empros. It wouldn't disrupt the anchor point set in the controller's memory. He was already flowing empros, so if part of the flash caught him it shouldn't change anything.

All guesses. It would be nice to have an expert like Chloe around to weigh in.

He looked into Jacquelyn's frozen eyes. "This is going to be weird for you, but if all goes well, I'll explain in just a second."

From Daniel's viewpoint, the controller was upside-down, making it harder to select the command. His nervous tension didn't make it any easier. He shaded his eyes with a hand, reached out and pressed the Enter key. The room lit up with the flash.

He uncovered his eyes. The room was still dark, no change there.

She moved her arm, rubbing her shoulder. Her head pivoted.

He let out a deep breath. "Holy hell, it actually worked."

Jacquelyn blinked and squinted. "Daniel? It's dark."

He grabbed her hands. "I'm here, don't worry. Let your eyes adjust."

She looked dazed, studying his face. "What happened?" She put a hand to the helmet on her head, and Daniel helped her take it off.

He pointed to the other Daniel, still frozen in place. Her mouth dropped open and she circled the frozen figure, even touching him. "How is this possible? What did you do?"

Daniel joined her, studying himself. "I'm him, just an hour or two later. I managed to get out of here with some special help from a friend in the distant future." He motioned to the ring lying on the floor. "It might not look like much, but they've got some pretty amazing technology in 2441."

Her eyes flitted between the two nearly identical copies of Daniel. "You jumped further into the future?"

"Four hundred years, then all the way back to 2023. Sorry, it's confusing. But I knew I had to return for you."

Her lips tightened, and that look of fear that had marked her face just moments before returned. "Father?" she whispered.

Daniel nodded. "I'm not sure you would have survived." He motioned to frozen Daniel. "I was thankful when you disappeared. At the time, I didn't understand how it happened. Turns out, I did it. Just now."

She held a hand to her forehead. "This is too weird."

"Very weird. Remember when I told you about empros time? We're in it, right now." He pointed to frozen Daniel. "He's in forward time, so he can't see us. Neither can the guard." He pointed to the guard's face peering through the window.

Her lips turned up at the corners. It was the first time she'd smiled since they'd been dragged from Aiden's car. She wrapped her arms around Daniel and took a deep breath. "So, what do we do now?"

He took a deep breath. "It's a little complicated, but I do have an escape plan."

He picked the ring up from the floor, held it high and studied its reflection. No stones or columns; it was just a reflection of the floor they stood on, which made sense since this cell would still exist in 2441. He tilted the ring toward the closed and locked cell door. The reflection in the ring's center showed the door standing wide open to a corridor.

Better still, the corridor was lit by a pink-lavender light.

Daniel smiled. "This just might work."

"You can take me with you? To your time?" Jacquelyn asked. Her plea was as earnest as he'd ever heard from her.

Daniel shook his head. There was no sugarcoating it. "I can't. I'm sorry, there's just no way to take you backward. I wish I could, but I don't think you'd survive. You're not from my time, and you've been flowing forward your whole life. The snapback would kill you."

He placed the ring in her hands. "But you can get away to a better place. I've seen it. It's a time when people have not only mastered science and technology, but they've overcome our own bad instincts. It's a better time than yours, better than mine too. I'm confident this ring can take you there."

Her eyes filled with tears. "I can't go with you?"

Daniel shook his head. "I still have a mission to complete, and it's back in 2023. I didn't flow forward with this jump, so the belt should take me home safely." He put his hand on hers. "But only me."

If Chloe were there to advise, she would almost certainly agree. The belt was never designed for two, and no explanation of time jumping had ever covered taking a person backward from their own time. It seemed like certain death.

But the ring was different. It appeared to be a reversible tunnel and it was now pointing the way—back to the future.

Jacquelyn nodded, head down. "I get it. You have a world to save." She unbuckled the belt and handed it to him. When she looked up, tears streamed down her cheeks.

Daniel wrapped the belt around his waist and buckled up. "You'll meet a friend when you get there. A woman, of sorts. She's very colorful, and really remarkable. She told me she was waiting for 'one other,' and now I know who she meant. She's waiting for you."

"She'll help me in this future?" Jacquelyn brushed the tears from her cheeks.

Daniel nodded. "I think she will. She was my guide, and she'll be yours too." He could picture Jacquelyn stepping into the alcove, almost like a video playing in his mind. The glowing figure would be waiting. No doubt.

"When you get there, she'll call out for you. Walk to her voice. If you see a body lying in the corridor, don't look. Hurry past it, straight to an alcove at the end." There were potential dangers, but any phantoms of Father that might be roaming through time would be searching for another version of Daniel, not Jacquelyn.

She may have to pass through a battlefield, but she'll be safe. The speckled pink lady will ensure it.

Confident in his assessment, Daniel held out his hand, palm up, index finger curled. "When you meet her, try this as an icebreaker."

Jacquelyn looked confused and he helped shape her hand in the same way, lying on top of his. Jacquelyn smiled. Lady Pink would too, Daniel was sure.

"Thanks for the tips." Jacquelyn bowed her head and whispered. "I'm really going to miss you."

Daniel pulled her close. Her path would be different than his. With the glowing woman's help, Jacquelyn would join a new world and start a new life, free from the cruelty and abuse of her own time. Much would be unfamiliar, but Jacquelyn would adapt. Anyone who could conjure up a different personality at will would find her place among the people of the future.

"I'll miss you too," Daniel said. "But you'll do great. Maybe you'll even be a celebrity."

"Just like you." She grinned. "A new me. I think I could do famous." She threw her head high, posing as if on the cover of a magazine.

Daniel laughed. "You'll be a star."

They separated, and Jacquelyn held the ring in both hands, unsure what to do next. "Just hold it over your head and drop it. The ring will take care of the rest."

She lifted it over her head, more tears flooding her eyes. "Goodbye, Daniel, thanks for everything."

Daniel wiped his own eyes. "Goodbye, Jacquelyn. It was wonderful to get to know you."

She flashed her beautiful toothy smile and dropped the ring. It fell slowly, erasing her body from existence as it dropped. When it touched the floor, the ring disappeared altogether, and Jacquelyn was gone.

Daniel stood quietly for several seconds, absorbing the magic of advanced technology as well as his own complex feelings. A feeling of loss, but a satisfaction that he'd helped her move on to a better place. Most of all, he was curious how her life might unfold in the distant future.

A new life in the twenty-fifth century. She's the real time traveler in this story.

Daniel sighed. He'd never see her again. Probably a good thing. "Time to get home. I've got an ambulance to catch."

Daniel donned the partial helmet, tipped his head to his frozen self, and pressed the buttons on the belt controller. The yellow light flashed for the last time.

With it came instant pain and nausea.

He stood in the farm field, sun beating down, head woozy and an overwhelming feeling of flu-like sickness wracking his body. Pressure in his ears. His head throbbed. He felt a trickle run over his lips and down his chin. He rubbed a hand across his face and his fingers came back right red.

He took a feeble step. Dizzy and weak. Stepped once more. In the distance, the sound of a siren. His legs wobbled uncontrollably. The world began spinning, and Daniel dropped face-first to the rust-colored dirt.

39 Inflection Point

Agent Griffith stuffed his phone into a pocket. Messages from various contacts throughout the FBI had been coming in fast and furious. Was Rice sure? Why that particular submarine? He answered each as best he could, but he didn't have much to go on.

His first call had been to the Washington, D.C. office of the Chief Master-at-Arms, United States Navy. The military police unit provided base security but also employed specialists trained in counterterrorism and internal security breaches. The conversation was brief and concise. They were already on high alert. A senior officer assured Griffith they would handle it.

The next call was to the national security advisor at the White House. Griffith provided the same limited information, along with Daniel's recommendation to kill the submarine if that's what it came to. The NSA agreed.

From there it was every senior director within the FBI. They all had similar questions, none of which Griffith could yet answer. The FBI's job would be to uncover the culprits.

For inexplicable reasons, the evidence was somewhere in Daniel's stomach. He'd said so himself, though, at the time, Griffith had thought he must be joking. Now he wasn't so sure.

Griffith stood in the mostly empty waiting room at Piedmont Atlanta Hospital. Daniel had been brought in unconscious, found in a farmer's field more than forty miles from where he'd started his jump at Freedom Plaza.

A doctor dressed in light blue scrubs held a black-and-white MRI image. He pointed to an abnormally bright object.

"He's got a second chip in his body?" Griffith asked incredulously. The doctors had run the MRI after a relatively simple surgery to remove an electronics chip from Daniel's left arm. The chip was already in the hands of the Atlanta FBI office.

The doctor shrugged. "It's probably not a chip. It's circular. It might be a coin. But if it is, it's a big one."

"Like a silver dollar?"

"Could be. I can't imagine how he swallowed it."

Griffith couldn't imagine it either, but if the object was anything like a coin, the FBI would need it. Probably even more than the chip. "Get it out. Soon as you can. This is a national emergency."

"We're prepping him. But with all the internal hemorrhaging, we have to be careful."

"Right now. I mean it," Griffith commanded. "I want him to survive too, but I need that coin just as fast as you can cut it out."

The doctor's eyes widened, but he nodded and left.

Daniel's life might be on the line, but so were the lives of millions. The Navy already had the key bits of information, but based on Daniel's phone call, the coin would lead them to the people involved.

A half hour later, the same doctor placed a silver-and-gold coin in Griffith's hand. It was almost identical to the coin that had started all this business, including instructions written around its outside.

Ten minutes later and one mirror ripped off a bathroom wall, Griffith had the answers he needed. The message from the future echoed the same information Daniel had called in. USS *Nevada*. Captain Cory Lundstrom. The time and places of attack, confirming what Griffith had already passed along to the Navy.

But it contained more. The names, positions, backgrounds and the last known contact points for key individuals who were long dead in 2053 but were still alive today. Some were right here in Atlanta.

* * * * * * * * * * * * * * * * * * *

315

USS *Nevada*
North Pacific, 12 nautical miles southeast of Adak Island
October 9, 2023 16:20 Pacific Time

Lieutenant Commander Helen Tierney sat in the executive officer's watch chair, a seat positioned physically higher than everyone else in the Command Center of the USS *Nevada*. She surveyed the activity at each station and ran through a mental checklist of the progress of their readiness drill.

The submarine was holding steady at their launch depth of forty meters. Simulated targets had been generated by the communications officer and passed to Fire Control. Two launch keys, her own and the captain's, were inserted and activated. All twenty-four missile tubes showed green ready-to-launch lights. The only thing left was the captain's verbal authorization to launch. A simulated launch, of course. All of them were.

Smooth as silk, she thought. *Well, almost.*

The live video feed of the activity down in Fire Control, one level below, wasn't perfect. The monitor was small, and the picture quality wasn't great. It was easy enough to see the trigger in the weapons officer's hand, but harder to tell that it was colored orange and labeled SIM. The other trigger, the red one marked LIVE, would still be locked away with a key accessible only to the weapons officer.

Tierney made a mental note to suggest a change when they got back to port. Replace the tiny monitor with something bigger. A small improvement, but the low-quality monitor felt like a weak link in the chain.

Things like that had been on her mind ever since they'd received a top secret communication from COMSUBPAC. An unusual message, and one only she and the captain were privy to read. Be on high alert, it warned, for signs of a possible security breach. No further details. No intelligence. No background check revisions.

It made every sailor on board a suspect.

Oh yeah... and keep doing your job.

Sometimes it was hard to tell if the higher-ups even knew what her job was. At this very moment, she was overseeing a readiness exercise that brought enough firepower online capable of destroying half the planet. Every electronic and mechanical system had been powered up. If it weren't for the computer safeguards and the good people aboard this vessel, in less than five minutes, those deadly missiles would actually launch. With that kind of responsibility, she couldn't afford to have doubts about a single person.

"Command, Fire Control," the weapons officer's voice boomed over the intercom. "Targets loaded. Confirm?"

Tierney looked over the shoulder of one of the sailors in the Command Center. His finger scrolled through a list of the five simulated targets loaded into the fire control computer. The sailor gave a thumbs-up.

Tierney grabbed a microphone from its perch over the station. "XO confirms. Targets are good."

"Very good. Fire Control is standing by."

"Final check for launch," Tierney called out to the dozen sailors staring at their displays. "Systems?"

"Systems, aye. We're go for launch."

"Navigation?"

"Navigation, aye."

"Comm?"

The communications officer held up a hand. He pushed a headset tight against his ear and studied text scrolling across his display.

"Comm?" she repeated.

"Uh, we've got a problem, ma'am."

She stepped over to the station. The captain held his position at the opposite side of the room as prescribed by procedure.

"Whatcha got?" She looked over the comm officer's shoulder. His VLF communications display only provided a message header. From COMSUBPAC, Naval headquarters for submarine operations in Pearl Harbor, Hawaii.

PRIORITY. Clearance: Top Secret. Eyes: Captain or Exec only.

If this were an actual launch, a priority message might be a change in targets, or, potentially, an abort command. Even in a tactical readiness drill, she'd need to play it that way. The comm officer pushed away from the station, and she squatted in his place, touching the screen and quickly skimming the message that came up.

Disturbing. The worst possible news. The security breach they'd been warned about had been traced to their crew.

"Stand down," Tierney called out. "Captain, you're going to need to see this."

Captain Cory Lundstrom picked up a microphone and broadcast across the submarine. "All hands. Stand down from the TRE. Repeat, stand down." He switched off his launch key, slipped the lanyard over his neck and joined Tierney at the comm station.

Together they read the alarming message. A specific crewmember had been identified as compromised. Fire Control Technician Joshua Swindell. He was to be arrested for questioning immediately.

"What the fu...?" the captain said, shaking his head. He looked Tierney in the eye, thinking.

"Lockdown?" she whispered.

He nodded silently in agreement.

Tierney took a deep breath. She'd never thought she'd have to issue the commands, but she'd been trained for every contingency. The lockdown procedure would turn this vessel into a crime scene. But with a compromised sailor on board and no reason to believe there might not be accomplices, a crime scene might be exactly what it was.

"Chief!" she called out. A chief petty officer wearing a security badge stood up at the far side of the room. "Come with me."

She stepped through a door and dropped down a ladder, hands on the rails and feet never touching a step. When the chief reached the bottom, she noted his holstered firearm and gave him a quick summary. "We're making an arrest. This is not a drill. Swindell in Fire Control. No one else, at least for now. Got cuffs with you?"

"Yes, ma'am."

"Let's go, then."

Fire Control was the next door down, and when they entered, Swindell seemed ready for them. He jumped from his chair and lunged for the door, but the chief caught him, wrestled an arm behind his back and slapped handcuffs on him. The sailor looked confused and frightened, but he stopped struggling.

"What the hell is going on?" shouted the weapons officer. It was a good sign that he hadn't been compromised too.

"Stand back," Tierney announced. "This is a lockdown."

The chief propped Swindell up. His eyes darted left and right. Tierney stepped to within inches of his face. "What have you been up to, sailor?"

He didn't answer, but the guilt was written on his face. She patted him down, then reached into his pants pockets and drew out a slip of paper and a key.

"Well, look at this. A Fire Control lockbox key?" She motioned to the weapons officer, who dialed a combination on a safe on the wall. Empty inside.

"How the hell did you get that out?"

319

"I didn't," Swindell answered, his eyes filling with tears. "The Lord did." He started to shake.

Tierney examined the slip of paper, immediately recognizing the format of a launch code. "Oh God." A sick feeling twisted in her gut. Swindell was one of the few on board with login access to change a target. Inexplicably, he also had a key that would put the live launch trigger in his hand.

A live launch to a real target. They'd come very close.

There would be a lot of questions, and not just for Swindell. Everyone would be interviewed, officers and enlisted alike. Every locker and personal space would be searched. The crew would understand. It was the price they paid to preserve the trust placed in their hands. The guilty, Swindell and anyone else, would be handed over to authorities once they were safely back in port.

****

At 7:30 that evening, Griffith stepped out of the passenger side of the FBI squad car and surveyed the primary target of their investigation. A church. A simple one-story building. Aging brickwork, a white wooden steeple that needed paint, and weeds in the front lawn.

It didn't seem to match the ambitious sign out front: Lord's Covenant First Temple of Blessed Reconstruction. A small banner was tacked on one side: Worship with us, Sunday 10 a.m.

At least they were advertising.

Information deciphered from the coin had led them to this place, as unlikely as it seemed. Home to a radical preacher with ties to organized crime figures in Colombia and Russia. Apparently, this guy would become a key figure in the future.

Bank records weren't hard to get, and the flow of money confirmed the coin's message. Foreign money, coming to this small organization over several years. There was clearly more to this building than its weathered exterior.

Two other FBI agents, Kenney and Williams, climbed out of the car. Normally, they would have been enough for this portion of the investigation, but since the church was in Atlanta, Griffith had decided to tag along.

The porch was lit by a bare bulb. Kenney kicked the double front doors, and they swung open. In the foyer, a single folding table was covered with printed brochures promoting the church. A bulletin board listed upcoming church activities.

All three agents drew their firearms before heading down the main church aisle. Dark. Empty.

A door on one side led into a hallway with the light on. They passed an empty office and a desk covered with papers. Agent Kenney peeled off to search for evidence.

Griffith silently motioned to another door at the end of the hallway, with a sign indicating *Bible Study*. Light streamed out from under the door. Agent Williams followed, his gun pointing up.

The door was unlocked, and Griffith peered inside. No one there. The room was filled with boxes and tables stacked with electronics. A metal-framed shelf held computer equipment connected by cables. Lights flashed across the front panels.

To one side of the room, a white oval frame stood by itself. About six feet high, it looked like an airport metal detector. Lights blinked on and off around its interior edge.

Griffith entered first, pointing his gun as he surveyed each corner of the room. No one in this room either. It seemed to be an equipment room of some sort, though it was hard to imagine what a church would be doing that would require such a setup.

"What do you make of it?" Griffith asked.

"He's probably not communicating with God," Williams answered.

Griffith chuckled and examined the electronics rack. Possibly communications equipment, but it could be almost anything. They'd need a technology expert to figure it out.

A sharp cracking sound interrupted the silence, and Griffith jerked his head toward the white oval. A violet light erupted around its edge, and the space within its interior wavered like hot air over a sunbaked desert highway.

From nowhere, a young man wearing a white visor over long stringy hair stepped through the oval and into the room. His head pivoted, and his jaw dropped. He quickly turned back to the oval, but Williams grabbed one arm and dragged him away.

"FBI! Freeze!" Griffith yelled, pointing his gun.

The man struggled in Williams's grip. "No! You must not stop me. You don't know what you're doing!"

With a single twist, Williams dropped him to the floor, wrenched his arms behind his back and cuffed him. Griffith holstered his gun and squatted down closer to the man's face compressed against the hard floor. His eyes were wild with rage. He matched the description of their target.

Griffith shook his head in disbelief. "Pretty fancy setup you have here, especially for a preacher. Why don't you tell us about it?"

****

Griffith loved it when all the loose ends of an investigation were wrapped up. It was comfortable. Secure. Almost heart-warming.

Atlanta police had hauled away the preacher for booking. The Navy was still reporting the all-clear hours after the predicted launch time. They'd arrested a sailor on board the USS *Nevada*, and the submarine was now on a lockdown protocol, every missile secure in its silo.

One of the many messages on Griffith's phone was from the president's national security advisor, congratulating Griffith on their success. That one felt pretty good. It allowed his mind to focus on different things.

Griffith hopped into the front passenger seat of the unmarked FBI car. "Thanks, guys. I appreciate the unplanned stop."

Agent Williams gave him a blank stare, put the car in gear and pulled out of the parking lot of an all-night tattoo and piercing shop. The car headed toward a significantly more upscale part of Atlanta, where they'd booked a hotel for the night.

Some of the messages on Griffith's phone were from a contact recently added, Chloe Demers. She was already at the hotel, using the time to complete her research into something she was tentatively calling "anchor drift". Griffith didn't fully understand the time physics, but Chloe thought it might explain why Daniel hadn't returned from his jump and why he'd reappeared forty miles from where he'd started, and more than three hours later.

According to Chloe, Daniel should have reappeared almost instantaneously, just as she'd done in her test of the belt back in Geneva. They'd waited at Freedom Plaza for more than an hour. No Daniel. Further searches in the area around the Ebenezer Church hadn't turned up anything either. The church's reverend had seen Daniel prior to the jump, but not after. No one had.

As the car pulled onto a freeway, Griffith checked his phone once more. Another message from Chloe.

Je suis au bar. Bonne connexion internet, excellent vin.

Prior to this assignment, Griffith would have struggled to string more than three French words together. But when Chloe spoke, the language didn't seem difficult at all. She was apparently sipping wine at the hotel bar, waiting for him.

Griffith examined the small box in his hand, gift-wrapped. He didn't care what the other FBI guys thought about their inexplicable stop at a peculiar shop in a seedy neighborhood. Chloe would love it.

40 Home

A regular electronic beep tugged Daniel into consciousness. He lifted heavy eyelids.

An inclined bed with rails on both sides. An IV drip feeding into his left arm. A clip pinching the end of his index finger with a wire running to a monitor that signaled each heartbeat.

Alive is good.

The nausea was gone, the pain subdued. The haziness in his head was probably drug induced.

Drugs are good too. Thank you, modern medicine.

He was alone in a small room, with a curtain drawn across the door. No call button in sight, but summoning a nurse wouldn't be hard. He pulled the clip from his finger, allowing the regular beeping to be replaced by a continuous tone.

A minute later, a stout woman pulled the curtain back and put a hand on her chest. "Don't do that!" she commanded, placing the monitor back on his finger.

"Sorry, didn't see any other way to get your attention." The words came out slightly slurred as his tongue struggled to function.

She frowned and pointed to a plastic square at the bedside, a red button in its center.

"Huh. Guess I missed that. Any drugs in my system, perchance?" His lips felt thick and sluggish.

"Light sedation," she said. "We've been dialing it down all morning. I figured you'd wake up sometime."

"How long have I been out?"

"Mmm. Just about twenty-four hours now. That's not unusual with internal hemorrhaging. What'd you do? Swan-dive off a tall building?" She smiled.

"Something like that."

Snapback, though apparently not significant enough to kill him. Maybe one too many jumps. Or else he'd pushed his luck with the combination ring-belt technology. He'd exceeded every operational limit suggested by Mathieu, Chloe; even Lady Pink on the Pedestal.

He'd been unconscious for twenty-four hours.

Forward time. Not empros time. Not future time. Twenty-four hours of now time.

Daniel's analytic mind finally subdued the pharmaceutical cocktail still lingering in his system. Startling the nurse, he grabbed her hand. "I'm going to need emergency surgery. There's a coin in my stomach and the FBI—"

She laughed. "Oh, honey, we took that out yesterday!"

Good news, perhaps. "Where's the coin now?"

"Heck if I know. That pushy FBI guy took it."

Even better news. "Agent Griffith?"

"Yeah, that's him. He was all over the docs, bugging the admins. I was worried he was going to pull a knife and cut that coin out all by himself. Lucky for you, the docs pulled it out the right way—through your esophagus. No sir, the only surgery you had was to get that electronic thing out of your arm. Plus, about twenty stiches in that wound across your ribs."

A white bandage covered his left forearm just above the IV. He felt another bandage across his chest. "The coin is important. I need to get in touch with Griffith right away. Can you get my phone?"

His futuristic-old-fashioned clothes hung in an open closet on the far side of the room. She patted his hand. "Don't worry, honey, we've got everything under control. Mr. Griffith said he'd be back, but only when you're healthy enough for a visitor."

Griffith has it figured out. The coin, not the chip.

326

"Have any wars broken out recently?" Daniel asked.

Her brow knitted, and she gave Daniel a peculiar look. "None that I know of." She adjusted the flow on the IV drip, hopefully dialing the drugs down, not up.

No launch. His phone call from the farm field had been enough, and the coin was in good hands. Griffith would know what to do. He'd probably done it already. Still, they needed to talk.

"I'm fine. I could have a visitor now." It wasn't the complete truth. His ribs ached, but with good drugs, it was a pain level easily ignored.

She examined one of the machines by the bed. "Well, we got the hemorrhaging under control, but you're still anemic. I'll talk with the doctor and maybe you can have a visitor or two. There's a woman out in the lobby. I think she might have slept there last night. Nadine? Something like that."

"Nala?"

"That's her. Poor dear was really upset."

A lump appeared in Daniel's throat. "Can you bring her in?"

She patted his hand. "Maybe. I'll check." She fluffed up a pillow behind Daniel's head.

"Thanks for saving my life."

"You're the most famous patient we've had all year, Dr. Rice. We couldn't just let you die, now could we?"

"Famous or not, thanks just the same."

She offered a gentle smile and left. Daniel relaxed into the soft pillow. Just as the nurse had said, things were under control.

Nala was here. He could imagine what she must be thinking. He hadn't told her much and she hadn't asked. *Do your job,* she'd said before he'd jetted off to Florida with Griffith. It seemed like months ago.

He badly wanted to see her, to tell her everything. He had no idea how she'd react to the insanity of the time jump or to the personal parts of the story. He wouldn't hide anything, but anxiety built. It was exactly why doctors put limits on visitors for recovering patients.

A few minutes later, the door opened, and she peeked around the curtain. Her hair was out of place, bags under watery eyes, but to Daniel, Nala had never looked more radiant. Her cheek-to-cheek smile spoke volumes.

She burst across the room to his bedside, wrapping arms around sheets, tubes, wires and Daniel. "You're back! You're really here!"

He put his only good arm around her shoulders and kissed the top of her head. "I can hardly believe it myself."

She looked up, tears in her eyes. "I thought I'd lost you."

He hugged her tight even though his ribs ached doing it. "I wish I'd told you more. Things got out of control in a hurry."

She buried her face in his chest. "A jump into the future. Yeah, I heard. Not your everyday government assignment."

"Griffith told you?"

"Mostly Chloe Demers. Remember, we're colleagues. She called and I flew down yesterday. Had to practically beat the story out of Griffith this morning. They're both still here, in Atlanta."

Daniel adjusted his position, groaning. Nala released her hug. "Sorry, did I hurt you?"

"Ribs, mainly. A few other issues, but they say I'm on the road to recovery."

She stood and leaned over the bed rail, her hair falling around his face. She whispered, "Your lips aren't hurt, are they?"

He smiled and shook his head. An awkward sideways position, but she kissed him with passion, withdrew and came back for another. He could kiss this woman ten thousand times and still want more.

328

She pulled away. "Hang on, I've got to earn the FBI briefing Griffith gave me." She dialed and held her phone to her ear. "He's awake. Yeah… you bet… see you in a few." She disconnected. "Griffith is just around the corner. He says you shouldn't say anything about your mission until he gets here."

"A lot to tell," Daniel said. "But not everything is for the FBI. There's a few parts just between you and me."

"Your future? Or mine?" She waved both hands. "Maybe I don't want to know."

"A woman I met. Two, actually." Daniel started to explain, but Nala held up a hand, frowning.

"Shhh." She paused, thinking—possibly about what Daniel might have done with women from the future, though with Nala it could be almost anything. "Don't go there. FBI orders, and as you might recall, I don't have a good history with these guys."

The nurse opened the door and poked her head through. "Dr. Rice, you've got two more visitors, but I'm warning them, and you too, miss, I'm clearing everyone out in twenty minutes."

Nala beckoned with a wave. "Bring them in. I think we're done with all the kissy stuff." Daniel hoped she didn't mean that literally. Like, forever.

The door opened once more, revealing two more familiar faces. Griffith offered a hand. "Great job, Daniel. Welcome back."

Chloe's tight-lipped smile and caring eyes were ample greeting, but she leaned in and kissed him on the cheek. She had a new lip piercing. "Feeling better?"

"A bit of damage here and there, but with a few more kisses, I'll pull through." Daniel glanced at Nala. She rolled her eyes.

Chloe hugged Nala and they exchanged bonjour greetings with a quick back-and-forth in French that Daniel didn't understand.

Griffith gave a thumbs-up. "Mission accomplished."

"You got the coin?" Daniel asked.

"You didn't make it easy, but we got it. The information confirmed the submarine's security breach plus a lot more. The Navy made an arrest yesterday. Found one of those futuristic coins in the guy's locker. Apparently, the crew was deep into a launch drill and very nearly pulled the trigger."

"Wow. Another prediction confirmed. The launch really would have happened."

"Yup. The Navy might want to adjust a few procedures, but we're safe for now. Plus, we bagged a preacher last night who was probably involved. Off-the-charts crazy guy running a religious cult right here in Atlanta. Fire and brimstone stuff. Christian reconstructionism, I think they call it."

"I know all about him," Daniel said, holding his ribs. "He did some of the damage I'm recovering from."

"The preacher had a coin too," Griffith said.

"Wow, olinwuns everywhere. They do more than project 3-D videos, which are faked, by the way."

"Hmm." Griffith nodded. "The first video was a lure, then?"

"I'm afraid so." Daniel explained the shard-motion technology and warned against using any information that might be on the chip they'd pulled from his arm. Griffith said they'd already pursued its leads but found nothing but dead ends.

"Father wanted it that way. Your preacher," Daniel said. "He pretty much runs the show in 2053. Or did."

"Is the old future gone?" Chloe asked.

"I sure hope so," Daniel replied. "It wasn't a place you'd want to live."

"Yup, it's gone," Griffith said with confidence. "No launch. No destruction, plus we've uncovered some shady overseas connections that we'll shut down." He explained how the preacher had gained access to 4-D technology and how he'd reached into a locked safe aboard the submarine.

"I think we have it all covered," Griffith said. "But you saw the future. Anything else we should follow up on?"

With the stimulus of conversation, Daniel felt the effect of the drugs disappearing. His ribs hurt a bit more, but it was worth it for a clearer head.

"Their plan was to lure me to the future under false pretenses and ensure that I returned with bogus information. The launch happens, the preacher and his followers claim science can't be trusted, and with some choice misinformation, the public goes along. I return and suffer the same death that killed Elliott Becton, which eliminates me from the public discussion for the next thirty years. At least, that's the way Father saw it. But if he's out of the picture, I think the whole scheme collapses."

"You couldn't have learned all of this from empros time. You flowed forward?" Chloe's French accent was still thick, but her English seemed less halting than before. A couple of days immersed in America might do that.

Daniel explained the message on the whiteboard, and his decision to flow forward after returning to his jump point in the plaza. "You and Griffith weren't there. I figured the warning on the whiteboard was right. The past had already changed."

"Ahh. This time the universe played a trick on you." She seemed almost delighted.

Griffith nodded. "We waited for you. You never showed up, but Chloe figured it out yesterday."

"You remember when I used the belt?" Chloe asked.

Daniel nodded. She'd tested it in Geneva, grabbing a croissant from one day in the future.

Chloe continued. "My phone has an app that keeps time independently from the phone service. Upon my return, its time was off by seven seconds. Do you see?"

"You lost seven seconds of forward time in your jump?"

She nodded. "The anchor point drifted forward by seven seconds. Since your jump was much bigger, your anchor drifted further. You left the plaza at eleven o'clock. I recorded the time. But your call to Griffith was just past two that afternoon. More than three hours later."

Daniel nodded. "The times should have been the same."

"Exactly. When you returned to the plaza still flowing empros, three hours had passed in forward time, and Griffith and I were already gone."

A mystery solved, but it also meant that they'd come three hours closer to the launch. The trick of time had nearly cost millions of lives. It was a scientific topic they'd need to learn more about. "You think anchor drift is natural?"

"Yes!" Chloe's smile spread across her face, stretching the various piercings to their limits. "It is evidence for a very strange theory. Time itself is slowing down."

"Wow!" Nala was suddenly very interested in what Chloe had to say. "Dark energy goes poof!"

"You know the theory, too." The two physicists were all smiles. "You explain it. Your English is better."

Nala gazed at her colleague. "Holy shit, Chloe. Nobel Prize coming your way." She turned to Daniel. "The universe is not only expanding, but that expansion is *accelerating*. Those of us in particle physics have been searching for the force particle that might cause the acceleration—dark energy, we call it—but no one has ever found it. An off-the-wall alternative is that time has been slowing down ever since the Big Bang, skewing the astronomers' measurements of velocity. If true, the acceleration doesn't even exist, and neither does dark energy."

"Sounds big," Daniel said, impressed with the impromptu physics discoveries happening in a hospital room. "Nice work, Chloe."

"Just the tip of the iceberg," Chloe said. "Time physics is a new field, wide open."

Daniel couldn't agree more. And Chloe, with her colored hair, piercings and avant-garde dress that ignored convention, was just the person to investigate.

"I can give you one more thing to research. Cause and effect. In the big picture, it might not exist either." Daniel explained how he had escaped from a locked cell, only to return to that cell later and create the distraction that became the catalyst for his escape. There didn't seem to be any rule of the universe that prevented an effect prior to its cause.

"Very freaky," Chloe said.

"Brain damaging," Nala said. "You're going to need more than just physical recovery; you'll need some mental rehab." She reached out and grabbed Daniel's hand.

The nurse poked her head in the door and glared. Griffith took the hint. "This is all way over my head, but we're going to want every detail of your jump in a full report. For now, get some rest and heal up."

He reached out and shook Daniel's hand one more time. "Thanks for your service. You made a profound difference, and at great personal risk. We're briefing the president tomorrow."

"*Très courageux.*" Chloe kissed him once more, then hooked her hand in Griffith's arm. Together, they turned toward the door.

"Wait," Daniel said. Griffith and Chloe paused, turning their heads. Daniel waved a finger between them. "Um… are you two…?"

Chloe smiled and pulled Griffith close. "My protector. So dependable. So honest. He's taking me to New York and learning French too!" She lifted her tattoo-decorated eyes to the older man and beamed.

The grizzled FBI veteran smiled too, a rarity for him. "I bought her a new lip piercing." He shrugged. "You know... one thing led to another. *C'est la vie.*"

Daniel chuckled under his breath. *Never saw that coming.* "Well, then, congratulations. When I'm back in D.C., maybe we can get together sometime and do... whatever it is that you two do."

A rave dance party followed by target practice at the shooting range?

He admonished himself for even considering the jest. The world would be a pretty boring place if it weren't for the bewildering variety of its human inhabitants. Once in a while, people from opposite corners managed to find each other.

They left, leaving only Nala and a glaring nurse. Nala held up five fingers. "Can we get five more minutes? I promise I won't kiss him again." The nurse smiled and closed the door.

Nala walked around to the other side of the bed, hopping on and forcing Daniel to scoot over. "You've done some pretty mind-bending things, Mr. Scientist. Cause and effect mixed up, time slowing down? Pretty fucking deep."

Daniel made room for her, the pain in his ribs happily ignored now that she'd chosen to get close, even if she planned to withhold more kisses. "Really, it all happened."

"Oh, I believe you. I've seen some weird shit myself." She kicked off her shoes and slid under the covers, turning on her side to face Daniel. She seemed to be planning on staying a while.

Daniel looked into her eyes and reached out for her hand. "There's a bit more. I owe you an explanation."

"Sounds like you do. Something about two women from the future."

"I'll need to start from the beginning."

"Best place to start. And you better get going before the nurse comes back."

He took a deep breath. Nala was open-minded and their relationship had always been somewhat hazy, but this was a talk that would bother anyone. "Her name was Jacquelyn."

Daniel explained it all. Jacquelyn's role in the Committee, her come-on at the celebration and their tryst at the safe house. He didn't sugarcoat it; shading the truth never worked.

Nala absorbed it all, adding only a few "uh-huhs" and "yeahs" as he talked. His words were heartfelt. He hoped she felt it too, especially when he stopped, looked into her eyes and said, "I'm sorry".

She nodded, not saying anything.

The story got darker once he got to the enforcers and his escape after Jacquelyn disappeared. As the story reached its bizarre conclusion in the far future, her interest became stronger, and not just about Jacquelyn.

"This ring could send people both ways? Four hundred years into the future and back to your anchor point?"

"I think so, but I can't be sure she made it to 2441."

"Well, I sure hope she did. Sounds like she risked it all to help you."

"I'm glad you see it that way. You're not jealous?"

"Jealous? Not really. Jesus, she's a fucking freedom fighter. Hard to knock that even if she did start out as a call girl."

Nala paused in thought. "Look, Daniel... I don't own you. I can't stop you from jumping into bed with alluring women, and I wouldn't want to try. But you'll need to figure out how to deal with assertive women. I'm one of them. We go after what we want, and we don't apologize for it."

She was right. He'd been with plenty of assertive women in his life. A pattern? Was he just a docile participant, swept up in relationships with strong women? It almost seemed like another manifestation of fate versus free will. There were some lessons to be learned from the future. If he rejected fate, he'd need to fully embrace free will.

Nala had remained silent while he thought. She was good at that. She was also pretty good at knowing when it was time to move on. "It seems to me you mentioned a second woman in this story?"

He looked up. "Vitoria."

"Vitoria jumped you too? Busy social schedule."

Daniel shook his head, a gentle smile on his lips. "No. Totally different."

He went back to the celebration and explained Vitoria's role in their escape to the safe house. He told her about meeting his older self in the restaurant. But he hesitated before revealing the true nature of Vitoria's relationship. The sexual contact wasn't there, but the implications were even larger.

"Um... Vitoria told me that she's my wife, or his wife. You know what I mean."

Nala sat up straight. "Vitoria is married to your future self?"

"Yeah."

"Do you know her now?"

"Never met her."

"Okay, that's just too weird." Nala pulled out her phone. "We need to figure this out. Last name? Occupation? City of residence?"

Daniel gave her what he knew. In today's world, Vitoria might still be in Brazil, though she'd moved to Washington just before they'd met.

After some searching, Nala turned the phone toward Daniel. "Is this her?"

A young woman stood at a podium with the flag of Brazil on the front. She was probably thirty-five and very attractive. Definitely Vitoria, but vibrant and young. It seemed odd that she was somewhere out there in the world, right now. Almost like she was waiting for him.

"Wow." He wasn't hiding his interest in the photo very well.

"Yeah, she's stunning." Nala stared at the photo too. "So... is she going to be your wife?"

Daniel pushed the phone away. "I don't believe in fate."

Nala sighed. "I don't either, but you experienced your future. Even if you don't know her now, you know she's out there. How bad is that going to screw up your mind?"

"It really wasn't my future. Just one possibility."

They didn't speak for a minute. Nala didn't seem to have any more questions, and Daniel had nothing left to explain.

She looked up and tapped a finger on her chin, talking to the ceiling. "Okay, so he's admitted it all... not bad. The girl he slept with in the future is *literally* a little girl today... wow, not going there! But she's also an adult who's cruising around in her Jetsons flying car four hundred years from now... weird, but kind of fun to think about. And he's got a wife, but he hasn't met her yet... cause and effect mixed up, but..." She tilted her head left and right. "Acceptable, I guess. Too bizarre to really process that one."

She looked back at Daniel and spoke with an upbeat voice. "Okay, I'm good."

337

She was impulsive, the kind of person who made snap decisions and didn't look back. But this was new territory for their relationship.

Perhaps he hadn't interpreted her instant assessment correctly. "You're good with everything?"

"Yeah, I'm good. Everything." She put away her phone. "Just do me one favor. Don't follow Vitoria on Twitter, okay? Stuff like that would hurt."

"I wouldn't do that. I never meant to hurt you."

Nala shrugged. "I know you didn't. But knowledge of the future could seriously scramble your brain if you let it."

Her concern was justified, but her acceptance of the events from the future had already provided therapy. There was no fate. No being swept up as a passive player. Daniel was quickly coming to the same conclusion that Nala had.

I'm good too. Everything. I love that Nala is assertive. I wouldn't want her any other way.

His body would heal. His relationship with Nala might too.

"Can we switch topics?" Daniel asked.

"To what?"

"Our next beach trip."

"What did you have in mind?"

Daniel thought. "How about Tahiti? They speak French there."

She snuggled down into the covers and wrapped one arm around him. *"J'adore la langue française.* Tell me about Tahiti."

41 Bora Bora

The dance floor was crowded with people of all ages and nationalities, moving their bodies to the fast rhythm of the Tahitian drumbeat produced by four bare-chested men pounding enthusiastically on traditional wooden instruments. With cheers and claps from the dancing crowd, the noise level was high and getting higher. The throng gave room in the center of the dance floor for the impromptu star of the night.

Nala looked spectacular, dancing barefoot and wearing a grass skirt, bright yellow poms on each hip, a bikini top and a feather headdress. Her legs pushed up and down, hips thrusting left and right in rapid motion with the rhythm. Her Tahitian instructor danced nearby.

"Lift your feet and throw your hips," the instructor encouraged. "A little quicker on the ami. Good thrust! You've got it!"

Daniel encouraged from the sidelines, clapping along with the crowd. Nala was a natural, maybe from her years of ballet training, maybe from her spontaneous enthusiasm for anything new. Her face glowed, her eyes sparkled, and her smile was irresistible. Daniel wasn't the only man staring at the superstar tourist who'd mastered the Tahitian ote'a in one evening.

Nala held her arms out gracefully, her torso barely moving even as her feet lifted and hips thrust wildly in directions that seemed impossible.

"Let's try the fa'arapu," the instructor yelled over the drumbeat, shifting her own hips in rapid pulses. Nala watched and mimicked, shaking wildly and laughing as the poms accentuated each jerk.

The drumbeat increased its pace, and her hips shook faster still. She looked to the sky and howled a joyous scream. A shirtless young man jumped out from the crowd and danced opposite Nala, closing in as he twisted back and forth. He seemed ready to kiss her, but she sent him away with a gentle push on the chin, not missing a beat with her shaking hips.

Daniel watched in amazement at her natural grace and style. He was equally amazed at his good luck. This irresistible beauty could attract any man in the world.

She's captivating without even trying, just by being herself.

With her hips swinging, she stepped forward, the crowd parting as she approached Daniel with a beckoning look. She pointed a finger at him. Daniel feigned a "who, me?" and the onlookers roared with laughter. Her poms flapping right and left to the drumbeat, she cozied up close, grabbed his shirt and pulled him to her waiting lips. Applause erupted across the dance floor.

She tugged him with each beat out to the center of the floor, where the instructor joined them, showing Daniel how to move his hips. Daniel was hopelessly inept at the more naturally feminine moves, but he gave it his best shot, and the men in the crowd cheered him on.

The drumbeat crescendoed, and the drummers gave one last coordinated slam to their instruments and then stopped cold. Everyone cheered.

Nala dropped from her toes and threw her arms around Daniel's neck. Through panting breaths and a pounding heart, she yelled to be heard above the crowd noise. "Oh my God, that was so much fun!"

He held her face in his hands. "You are truly amazing."

Several people passed by with congratulations and praise, including the instructor, who jokingly asked if Nala wanted to teach her next class.

Nala beamed, hanging on Daniel's shoulder. "I'd dance all night if I could manage it." She removed the feather headdress and grass skirt, returning them to the instructor. "But right now, I need some water and a rest!"

Daniel took her hand. "Come on." He picked up a bottle of water from the bar and stepped off the open-air dance floor and onto soft white sand.

They strolled across a never-ending beach hand in hand. The waning moon rose above a darkened volcanic peak, casting a long reflection across the calm lagoon. Nala leaned against Daniel as they walked.

The noise of the crowd was soon far behind, with nothing left but the rustling of palm trees and the rhythm of small waves lapping at the shore. They found a spot where the sand sloped to the water and plopped down to enjoy the tranquil nighttime view.

She took a gulp of water and caught her breath. "That's a hell of an exercise. No wonder Tahitian women look so good."

"There's not a woman on this island who could compete with you," Daniel said. "Tell me again how I got so lucky?"

"Let's see." Nala put a finger to her upper lip. "Um, first, you saved my ass from being arrested by the FBI. Then you helped me get my Fermilab job back. After that, when I'd launched myself and Thomas into the void, you rescued us—no, actually, Marie Kendrick did most of the rescuing, but you were at the smokestack in Texas when we climbed down." She took on a quizzical look. "But, now that you mention it... what have you done for me lately?"

"Took you on a trip to Bora Bora?"

"There's that. You did buy the tickets and pay for the resort. But on a more personal level..." She leaned in close with sensuous eyes.

He kissed her neck, soaking up a fragrance of perfume mixed with her own natural scent from the effort of her dance. "Personal attention coming up as soon as we get back to the room."

"I think I'm the lucky one." She waved a hand to the lagoon, bounded by a coral reef that formed an arc across water that glittered in the moonlight. "Just look at that. It's so beautiful here."

"It really is. I could do this forever."

"Forever." Her voice trailed off. "We don't do forever very well."

It was a reference to their on-again, off-again relationship, a sore point for both of them. Daniel had known the topic would come up. He'd even rehearsed what he was going to say.

"The long-distance thing doesn't work, does it? Seeing you on three-day weekends is like a tease. I want more."

"Me too."

He was hoping she'd say that. He'd been worried this talk might go in the opposite direction. "Nala, I've been thinking... I might leave D.C. I never really liked it there anyway, and I'm sure I could find a job in Chicago."

"Something that doesn't require jumping into the future?"

Daniel laughed. "Right. How about a policy job? Or a strategy and planning job. You know, the job I was *supposed* to have at OSTP."

She ran a finger through the sand, forming an infinity sign, tracing it repeatedly. "Funny, I was thinking the same thing, but not Chicago. There's a new physics team forming down at the Los Alamos national lab. The director gave me a call. He's got a job waiting for me if I want it. New Mexico. Ever been there?"

Daniel couldn't have been more enthusiastic in his response. "I adore Santa Fe! Historic. Lots of art. Great restaurants. Fun people too."

"I've only seen pictures, but it seems really nice with all the mountains and trees. I'm pretty sure everyone who works at Los Alamos lives in Santa Fe."

"Government jobs there, too," Daniel said. "I even know some people."

She paused for a minute, her head down and still drawing infinities in the sand. "So, what do you think? Should we?"

"No complaints from me."

She grinned. "Really? You'd move there?"

"I would, no hesitation."

A thousand obstacles faded. She was reaching out too. A complex issue that had kept them apart simply evaporated. In place of a chasm, a new bridge formed between them—a shared dream full of possibilities. The feeling was exhilarating.

His mind raced ahead into unexplored territory. "Um… Nala?" He hadn't rehearsed this part, but he couldn't repress it just because the words might come out mangled. "Something else I've been thinking about." His nerves skyrocketed. He had no idea how she might react.

"You've changed my life in ways I never imagined. It's… like I just woke up and hadn't realized I'd been asleep. I love being with you. I love our adventures together, and our quiet times, too. And I love you. When we get to Santa Fe… would you marry me?"

Her mouth opened, half in smile and half in surprise. She turned away, staring into the distance. "Whoa. Pretty traditional. I wasn't expecting that." She looked back with a quizzical expression, not saying a word while she studied his face.

Daniel waited, his heart pounding and concern rising over what she might say or do. Laugh? Run in the lagoon? Find that younger guy back at the dance floor? Nala was spontaneous. Anything was possible.

She lowered her head and spoke quietly. "I have to tell you, you're not the first person to ask."

He squinted, not sure he wanted to know. "How many?"

She shrugged. "Three. I said no every time." She looked up. "I didn't feel any guilt either… it was the right choice for me."

The last thing he wanted was to force her into something she'd regret. "Forget I mentioned it. I understand."

A crooked smile formed on her lips. "I don't think you do. Those guys were different. I was different too." She leaned in, put her arms around his neck and kissed him. "I'm ready for something new. I'd love to marry you, Daniel Rice."

His mouth opened but the words weren't there. A feeling of comfort spread throughout his body, even as a chill ran up his neck. They stared at each other with incredulous smiles mirroring the other for what must have been hours or days, though no one was counting.

She finally blinked. "Wait a second. Did we just create a new timeline? A new branch in the universe? None of this was supposed to happen, right?"

"Does it matter?"

"Yes, it matters. The future isn't just fantasy. You saw it. Are we erasing something we shouldn't be?"

Daniel cleared his throat and mimicked. "Knowledge of the future can seriously scramble your brain if you let it."

She smiled. "I said that, didn't I?"

"You did."

"So, just let it go? Full speed ahead on our new path? No Vitoria? No Jackie Jetson?"

Daniel gazed up at the starry sky. "Some of the future that I witnessed has already been erased. Millions of people in San Francisco and Vladivostok now have lives to lead. Our country won't fall prey to a madman armed with misinformation. There's nothing wrong with erasing one future and replacing it with something better."

"Hell yeah." She snuggled close. "But if you and I move to Santa Fe and get married, is that better than what it would have been?"

He put an arm around her. "Who knows? The only thing I learned about your future is that it didn't involve me. So yeah, we're both creating something new. But that's exactly as it should be. The future is wide open, just waiting to be written. Waiting for you, me— everyone. We can mold it into anything we want."

"Daniel?"

"What?"

"Do me one more big favor."

"Anything."

She looked up, the starlight reflected in her eyes. "Kiss me. And press whatever button you press to suspend time. I don't want it to end."

He smiled. "Very syrupy. I didn't know you had it in you."

She laughed, pushed up onto his lap, and pressed her face to his. They kissed, a lingering kiss, perhaps even an infinite kiss while time simply suspended its flow.

THE END

Afterword

I hope you enjoyed the story. Maybe I should linger a while longer at the tranquil beach... waves lapping at the shore and a moon over the mountains... a Tahitian drumbeat in the background and someone special in your arms. Ahh...

All very nice. But time to wake up. The story may be over, but our time together isn't. Notice how often I use the word "time" in this book? (By my count, 576. I have a writing tool plugin that checks for overused words. It's screaming at me.)

I really enjoyed writing this story, though I must admit that keeping track of all the jumping around was challenging. To help, I made a timeline diagram complete with jump arrows and event markers. It looks like one of those airline route maps. Complicated.

Books are an odd form of communication. On one side is the author who has a story in mind and on the other are readers who interpret that story in a thousand ways. I suspect some readers will take this particular story for what it is: fictional, part science, part entertainment. But some readers may look deeper—as they do with any time travel story—questioning the method of time manipulation or searching for holes in the logic ("wait... if Daniel pushed his own frozen arms down, wouldn't that mean...?")

If you're that type, have at it! Post whatever you find on my Facebook or Twitter pages and I'll be happy to participate. But I'm not going to dive into time travel logic quirks here. Instead, let's talk science and how it relates to the story you just finished.

We've all been entertained by time travel stories. Is there anyone in the world who hasn't seen *Back to the Future*? (At least ten times, for me. Fun stuff.) Even *A Christmas Carol* is a time travel story in its own quaint, nineteenth-century way.

But is there any reality to jumping through time? Or is it all just fantasy?

Time Jumping

In Chapter 4, Isotope, Daniel points out to the FBI that travel to the future is possible if you have the right technology. The easiest way to get there is to hang out near any large gravitational field where, as Einstein's general theory of relativity tells us, time slows down.

The effects of gravitational time dilation are very real and measurable. Put an ordinary wrist watch in a strong enough field, wait a week, and it will have slowed by hours when you retrieve it. From the watch's perspective, it has jumped to the future.

It works for people too. You don't even need to find a black hole (see the movie, *Interstellar*). A neutron star would do just as well. There are millions more of them and they're easier to find. At least one neutron star is within 400 light-years from Earth. (Piece of cake to get there with quantum space compression, right?)

If you spent a few months orbiting a neutron star, when you got back to Earth everyone you know would be old or dead. People would say you didn't age (time slowed down for you). But you'd say that time must have gone faster for them. From your perspective, you've jumped to the future.

In 2014, a mistake that launched two European global positioning satellites into an elliptical orbit gave ESA the opportunity to measure time dilation precisely. As it turns out, the atomic clocks onboard those satellites slow down by 200 nanoseconds as they get closer to Earth and speed up as they move away. Time dilation is weird, but very real.

So, just lasso a neutron star and drag it somewhere near Earth (but not too near) and you'll have a time machine capable of sending you to any year desired. Five orbits and you jump to 2050. Ten orbits and you're in 2080. Simple.

Of course, it's a one-way trip. But it's a trip some people would not hesitate to take. If you were offered a seat onboard a one-way flight to say, 2441, would you take it? Jacquelyn did. A bold move. Nala seemed to think so; she dubbed her Jackie Jetson.

Forward time travel just requires a good spaceship and lots of gravity. But is it possible to move backward in time? Physicists aren't sure. But unless backward time travel is prohibited by some universal parameter that we don't yet understand, the most likely mechanism is the same as forward time travel: a strong gravitational field. Among astrophysicists, *timelike curves* in gravitational fields are an intense area of current study.

A timelike curve is a path through spacetime that never strays beyond the cone of space accessible at the speed of light. In other words, it's a path that a spacecraft could follow (an ordinary, non-Star-Trek-warp-drive kind of spacecraft).

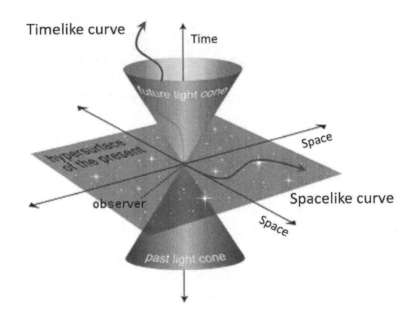

When influenced by an intense gravitational field, the light cone tips toward warped space (a.k.a., gravity). Enough tipping and the timelike curve twists back on itself, eventually into a complete circle. It's what astrophysicists call a *closed timelike curve*, or CTC.

Closed timelike curves come in several forms but they all have one startling characteristic in common: a portion of the path points backward in time. Any spacecraft following that portion of the CTC path would end up in the past. Crazy, but theoretically true and mathematically proven.

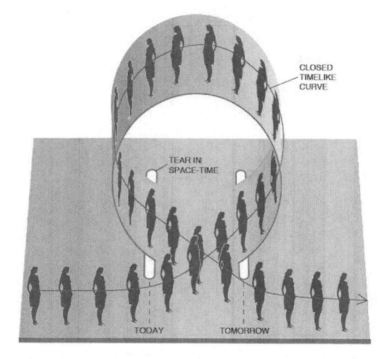

CTC's are not hard to imagine and can be derived from Einstein's field equations (I can't, but people smarter than me can). But that's math, not reality. Physicist Stephen Hawking believed that, in practice, a CTC could not be constructed no matter how hard an advanced civilization might try. He coined the term, *chronology protection*, a sort-of cosmic prohibition against time travel to the past, though he never identified how the universe might erect barriers along the CTC path.

Other physicists are not so sure those barriers exist. Kip Thorne, an astrophysicist at Caltech (and scientific advisor for the movie, *Interstellar*), wrote an advanced paper on closed timelike curves, identifying multiple ways in which a CTC could be constructed and then searched for mechanisms that might provide chronology protection. He didn't find any.

Responding to Hawking's theorized limitation, Thorne wrote, "The laws of general relativity by themselves do not enforce chronology protection." Thorne agreed that future advances in our understanding of quantum gravity might ultimately find the cosmic prohibition that Hawking imagined. But based on our current scientific knowledge, the universe appears to allow time travel to the past.

This fact alone makes my head hurt. If travel to the past is allowed, then every paradox that springs up in my story is possible. For example:

An effect that precedes its cause: Becton died in 2023 but his death was caused by a lie from 2053.

An idea with no beginning: A young preacher is told of his future by his older self who then must fulfill his destiny to contact his younger self.

A name plucked out of the air: Father only knew Joshua Swindell's name because he gave this name to his younger self.

The potential for an infinitely repeating loop: Daniel is called to the future only to meet himself where he learns how to return to the past so that he can grow old and explain it to himself.

Fun stuff? Or brain damaging? You decide.

Additional Dimensions of Time

In Chapter 7, Florida, we first learn about empros time from Marie Kendrick. "Facing *empros*," she says. "I'm not sure what it means, but I overheard Zin and Becton speaking about it a few weeks ago." When Daniel arrives in Geneva to unravel its meaning, a second dimension of time is not only described, but demonstrated. Daniel examines a frozen world. Chloe even visits tomorrow while flowing in this alternate dimension of time.

I'm with Chloe. I'd love to flow empros. Maybe I'd head to London and take a few of the crown jewels out of their cases. Give a diamond tiara to my wife to wear to her book group and then remake the royal scepter into a really snazzy putter for my next round of golf. Those frozen guards would never catch me. How would they even know?

Or maybe I'd get scientific like Daniel thought he might do. Walking through rain while in empros time would be fun. Each droplet hung in the air. Would you still be able to see a rainbow in empros time? Dimmer, but still there? A stroke of lightning would slowly creep from sky to ground. (Or is it ground to sky?)

Theoretical physicists have long suggested that an additional dimension of time might exist. It's a component of M-theory, which is an attempt to unite relativistic physics with quantum physics and explain the surprising symmetry between position and momentum that has long puzzled quantum physicists. I'll explain.

In classical physics (you know, the Isaac-Newton-apple-falling-on-the-head type of physics) two key properties are position and momentum. A baseball arriving over the plate has a three-dimensional position that can be easily measured and even drawn as an arc across the television screen as the pitcher throws the ball. Likewise, the momentum of the ball (its velocity times its mass) can also be measured by a radar gun. We can know both position and momentum at the same time.

But it doesn't work this way in quantum physics. A tiny particle like an electron orbits the nucleus of an atom, but we cannot know both the electron's position and momentum. It's not possible. The universe just doesn't allow it. It's called the Heisenberg uncertainty principle, and it basically says you can know the position accurately or you can know the momentum accurately, but never both. No one really understands why this is true.

If you've ever listened to a press conference from CERN or Fermilab, you might have heard one of the physicists mention gauge symmetry or symmetry breaking. They use the word symmetry when they're talking about properties like position and momentum. Symmetry just means that these properties are interchangeable within the mathematics of quantum physics. Nothing about the mathematics is different regardless of whether you're talking about position or momentum.

But why should these properties be symmetric? Mathematically, they're quite different. Position is derived only from space—x, y, z. But momentum is derived from time because

momentum = velocity times mass

and

velocity = distance divided by time

Momentum has a time component, but position does not. That doesn't seem very symmetrical. Something else must be going on.

One physicist, Itzhak Bars, a professor at the University of Southern California, thinks he has the answer. Bars has developed what he calls 2T-physics to explain the surprising symmetry among these properties. He postulates that position *does* have a dependency on time, except it's a brand new kind of time. A second dimension of time.

"If I make position and momentum indistinguishable from one another, then something is changing about the notion of time," says Bars. "If I demand a symmetry like that, I must have an extra time dimension."

But where is that other dimension of time? It certainly exists within the 2T-physics mathematics and it solves the symmetry question. But is this dimension real? Will we find it someday, curled up down at the subatomic level of quantum particles? I honestly don't know, but it's not beyond the realm of possibility.

CERN

At a sprawling facility on the Swiss-French border, an international team of physicists and engineers are currently exploring the nature of reality by examining the smallest components of our cosmos: quarks, leptons, and bosons. In my previous books, I placed several scenes at Fermilab, in Illinois, where similar particle physics experiments are carried out (mostly related to neutrinos). But CERN is special. They have the world's most powerful accelerator, the Large Hadron Collider, and that opens the door to some amazing discoveries.

In Chapter 9, Alpha Prime, Daniel and Griffith meet Mathieu and Chloe and are led to a mysterious secret lab (in novels, labs are always mysterious and always secret). Mathieu explains that by studying antimatter, they have discovered an astonishing fact: an antihydrogen ion decays more rapidly than its ordinary matter counterpart, hydrogen. Voilà, they identified a second dimension of time!

Is this science real? Well, there really is a laboratory called Alpha (Building 193 in Meyrin) and the scientists there really do create and study antimatter. They produce antihydrogen atoms and can confine these volatile particles inside a Penning trap for up to sixteen minutes before they annihilate by coming in contact with ordinary matter. (Technical note: there's no explosion! Just a tiny burst of energy that requires a very sensitive instrument to detect.)

Amazing stuff, given our limited understanding of antimatter and why it's so rare in the natural world. Alas, as far as I know, the CERN scientists have not measured differences in antihydrogen ion decay rates. But, as they continue to explore the properties of antimatter, maybe they will discover something exotic. It would certainly make for an exciting announcement. Stay tuned.

The Flow of Time

I read a lot of books about time, both fiction and non-fiction. Some are great fun, some are deathly boring. You'd think that any physicist who works in such a fascinating field could tell a good story.

Alas, that's not always true. (I so miss Carl Sagan, the best scientific storyteller we've ever had.)

So, let's focus on the fun stuff.

We all say that time flows, but as Zin points out in Chapter 11, flow has no meaning unless there's something fixed and unmoving to measure against. If you were floating in a foggy river and couldn't see the shoreline, you'd have no sense of movement.

So, how do we know time is flowing at all? It may be all in our minds. We see motion—leaves rustling on a tree, cars going by—and we put a mental frame around that motion. A before and after. Ticks of the clock.

Our memories of the past are a powerful psychological influence. We *know* time is flowing because the *now* is constantly changing. We remember what happened a second ago. But now it has changed. And changed again.

I sometimes wonder how we would think of time if our brains had evolved without any mechanism to retain memories. Suppose we were perfectly capable of reacting to events, but a nanosecond later that event was completely forgotten. (Clearly an evolutionary disadvantage!) Without any recognition of the past, would we also have no concept of the future? Would we live only in the now and perhaps never have invented clocks?

A significant portion of physicists say that the flow of time is a creation of our mind. It doesn't really happen, we just interpret physical motion and our memories as movement through a dimension that is, in reality, fixed.

Brian Greene is one of those physicists. In his book, The Fabric of the Cosmos, he expertly demolishes our sense of linear time by exploring the concept of simultaneity. Einstein demonstrated (way back in 1905) that two people moving at high velocity relative to each other will not agree on the timing of an event they both observe. As velocity approaches the speed of light, the rate of time changes significantly making it impossible for multiple observers to agree that a flash of light, for example, happened exactly at 12:04:00 even if their watches were synchronized in advance. Once relativity is considered, there is no such thing as "now". It depends on your frame of reference.

An intelligent species living in a galaxy far, far away would not agree with us that the universe is 13.8 billion years old. Their now would be different and there'd be no way for us to compare notes (our light-speed communication might take a billion years). Greene takes this notion a step further by pointing out that you can always find a reference point somewhere in the universe that considers now to be any one of those 13.8 billion years or any year in the future. Since there's no reason to prefer our reference point over any other, it implies that every now since the Big Bang is just as real as the one we experience. Past, present, and future are just an illusion. Every moment in time exists, all at once, equally valid.

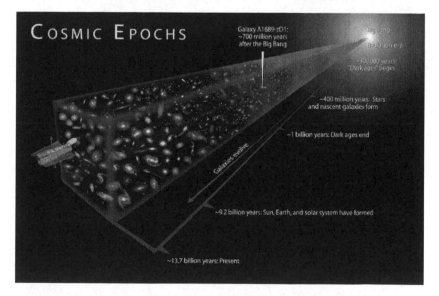

Image credit: NASA, ESA, and A. Feild (STScI)

Physicists call this the block universe concept. Every event, past and future, across the immensity of time exists simultaneously as if embedded in a cosmic block of ice. Any notion we have of time passing in our tiny path through this ice is simply a fantasy that plays in our minds.

I'm not fond of the block universe idea even if it is a valid description of the universe. Like most of us, I prefer to think of future events as undetermined, though I realize those events may just be hidden from my current consciousness.

Does the Flow of Time Change?

Let your mind wander back in time to the 1920's. Southern California. The roaring twenties. Prohibition. Hollywood was producing the first talkies and much of the Los Angeles region was still covered by orange groves. In that setting, American astronomer Edwin Hubble spent many lonely nights at the top of nearby Mt. Wilson observing Cepheid variable stars whose brightness curiously pulsates in a regular rhythm.

The astronomers of Hubble's day had already figured out that the rate at which these stars pulsate was directly related to their intrinsic luminosity. Stars with a slower beat were naturally brighter. Hubble realized he could use these stars to determine their distance from Earth, a feat that was previously calculated by the far-less-accurate parallax method. By comparing the observed luminosity to the star's intrinsic luminosity, Hubble could calculate the star's distance accurately. He found many Cepheids scattered across the sky and plotted their distances on a single chart.

Then Hubble compared the distances with the red-shift of each star's light which he knew gave a good measure of motion relative to Earth. There was a surprising correlation. Virtually all of the Cepheids were moving away from the Earth and those stars furthest away were moving the fastest. Hubble's exciting conclusion: the universe was expanding.

It was an astonishing discovery and very unexpected. It changed everything about our understanding of the cosmos. It was the first evidence that the universe was "born" from an initial point (the Big Bang) and the first indication of the age of the universe (now known to be 13.77 billion years – and yes, the number is that precise).

Much later, and after many more measurements, astronomers discovered that not only is the universe expanding, but that the expansion is accelerating. Something, it seemed, was pushing space apart faster and faster every year. To this day, no one knows what that *something* is. It's been given a name: dark energy. There are theories that say dark energy is an intrinsic property of space and that its force has varied with time.

But there's only circumstantial evidence for the existence of dark energy. No one at Fermilab or CERN or any other lab has found it, though they're trying. But without dark energy, there's no explanation for the acceleration of the universe's expansion. Or is there?

It's not just the dark energy force that varies with time. Astronomers also claim that the cosmological constant (the energy density of space itself) varies with time (it's not quite a constant). The same with the Hubble parameter (the rate of expansion)—it also varies with time.

Lots of values that all seem to be variable for some unknown reason. But there's another explanation. What if time itself is changing? What if time is slowing down? A group of Spanish physicists from the University of Salamanca have proposed exactly that.

According to this radical theory, time is like a spinning coin. Its rate slows as it spins. Ultimately, it will stop altogether. By shifting the change to time, all the other variable parameters become constants. The universe is still expanding, but that expansion is at a constant rate. The cosmological constant really is a constant. So is the Hubble parameter.

This view of the universe is simpler. It even makes a certain amount of sense in a weird way. But no one knows if this conjecture is true. We'll need more evidence one way or another.

In *Quantum Time*, Chloe is the scientist who finds some of that evidence. In Chapter 40, Home, she says that her discovery of anchor drift is "just the tip of the iceberg." Chloe won't get the Nobel Prize until her work is complete but if time really is slowing down, I'd like to think that someone like her will figure it out.

Reconstructionists

Every novel has an antagonist—a bad guy. I prefer stories that more closely resemble reality and, frankly, I've never encountered the evil mastermind who wants to take over the world from his perch on top of a Swiss mountain (even though I love the old James Bond movies).

Until this book, my bad guys blundered into their role as the opposition or let their greed get the better of them. This story is a slight departure. The evil-doers in *Quantum Time* are somewhat evil, even if a good portion of their malevolence is due to their extremist worldview.

Christian reconstructionism is a real thing. It was a movement, started in the 1980's, by a preacher named RJ Rushdoony who intended to place a strict reading of the Bible into everyday American life. Reconstructionists, along with their more modern offshoot, the dominionists, believe that God's law should supplant civil law. Many believe (wrongly) that the United States was founded as a Christian nation and that we "strayed" over time. The reality is quite the opposite.

The founders of the United States debated long and hard over the idea of separation of church and state and most of them came firmly down on the side of a secular government free from any state-sponsored religion. The US constitution makes no mention of anyone's god, nor any religious covenant or commandment. The words "In God We Trust" first appeared on the dollar bill in 1957. The Pledge of Allegiance was first used in 1892 but the words "under God" were inserted in 1954. For a country founded 243 years ago, this lurch toward theism is a relatively new thing.

Ron Paul ran for president in 2012 and received 190 delegates at the Republican convention that year. Most people think of him as a libertarian, but he was one of the original adherents to Christian reconstructionism and he heavily promoted Christian home schooling as way to subvert public (non-religious) education.

In America, every branch of science is currently under attack from people who haven't even learned nineteenth century biology—namely evolution. It feels like we're on the edge of plunging backward into another dark age of ignorance. I shudder to think of what would happen to the US public education system, or to our scientific leadership in the world, if these people get their way.

While conducting research for *Quantum Time*, I discovered a fascinating aspect of fundamentalism that I'd never known before. Numerology is a big thing.

Numerology is the belief that specific numbers have a divine or mystical connection to events in our lives. But Christian numerology is a bit weirder than your average horoscope. Angel numbers, as they call them, are direct communications from guardian angels. Who knew?

For example, the number 97 is a prompting from those angels that "the time is ripe for becoming a spiritual guide and take up spirituality as a vocation to enlighten others with spiritual understanding and practices." All that from a single number!

With insight into the universe this deep, I decided I had to use angel numbers in the story, thus Committee Reception shines an empros light across darkened Atlanta from the 97th floor of the Golden Spire. Sorry, angel number people. I couldn't help myself.

Submarines

I'm no expert on ballistic missile submarines, but from what I've read, you and I are safe from an accidental missile launch. Fortunately, this portion of the story probably couldn't happen. (I am thankful for the professionalism of our military and I hope my awe for what they do came through as you read the military scenes throughout this book).

If there's the slightest chance of a screwup, I think it would happen during a readiness exercise. Military experts will probably tell me that even in a readiness exercise, there's still very little chance of an accidental launch. In my defense, this story *is* fiction.

There are approximately 3,700 deployed nuclear warheads in the world today. A big number, but much lower than the 70,000 that were active as of 1986. We've made progress! United States and Russia each maintain about 1,700 warheads and most of them sit atop missiles on board submarines. No single person can initiate a launch. But once commanded, there is no question that the military will do their jobs. It seems to me then, that the weakest link in the chain is the person at the very top; the president, premier, prime minister, chairman or dictator. We've seen belligerent, angry and impulsive people occupy these top spots in every country that maintains a nuclear arsenal. They make me nervous.

The Ultimate Paradox

The ontological, or bootstrap, paradox is one of the most illogical of paradoxes that crops up in time travel stories. It's the situation where an object or event has no beginning, no cause or no origin. Someone from the future places it in the past where it transitions to the future so that it can be placed into the past.

Quantum Time includes some subtle cases but let me leave you with the whopper of all ontological paradoxes. Nothing beats this paradox. Nothing could.

It's the idea that the beginning of our universe was caused by an event in our distant future. Something that hasn't happened yet. Possibly an intervention by an incredibly advanced technology or civilization. They will do something. We don't know what.

But whatever it is (or will be), this technological intervention reached into the deep past all the way back to the nothingness just before the Big Bang and provided the spark that ignited everything.

Very literally, the universe created itself from an event in its own future.

When you think about it, it's as good an explanation as any other for how this universe came to be. We already know the components of the universe—the quarks, leptons and bosons. I don't doubt for a second that in some distant future we'll find ways to cause those components to spring into existence from the vacuum energy of space. It's not too great a leap to think that some advanced civilization would be able to manufacture a planet, or a star, or perhaps a whole galaxy.

And if jumping to the past is possible, why shouldn't we believe that at the very limits of technology there might be a mechanism to reach to the furthest point in the past and trigger everything. Every bit of matter and energy, every event, every living creature that occupied a trillion planets across a trillion years of time might owe their existence to the ultimate ontological paradox—a creation mechanism that sprung from the very universe it created.

Augh! My brain hurts!

****

If you'd like more details plus a lot of pictures and diagrams related to the story, please go to my web page: http://douglasphillipsbooks.com. While you're there, add your name to my email list and I'll keep you informed about additional books I'm writing and upcoming events.

I hoped you enjoyed this third book in the Quantum Series. If you did, please consider writing a short review. It takes only a minute, and your review helps future readers as well as the author (books and book series really do live or die on reviews). For more information on how to leave a review, go to http://douglasphillipsbooks.com/contact.

Thanks for reading!

Douglas Phillips

Acknowledgments

Thanks to all the authors at Critique Circle, but especially Kathryn Hoff and Travis Leavitt. You read a very early version of this story and saw each one of its flaws. Your advice was spot-on, and our back and forth conversations produced a cleaner more coherent story. I learn so much when I get the chance to talk with other authors. I can't wait for your books to come out. I'll tell everyone I know.

Thanks to Rena Hoberman for another fantastic cover. The coin was a fairly simple concept, one that we worked out more than a year ago. But as additional elements were added (the writing around the edge, the eagle popping out) the integration turned out to be more complex than I had anticipated. I think it turned out great!

I think of the editing process as my opportunity to peer into someone else's head and find out how the story I wrote played in their mind. Did my scene descriptions create the visual image I intended? Did the characters flub any lines? Was the science clear? How many commas did I misplace? (Answer: all of them.)

My editor, Eliza Dee, kicked off the editing process. She really wrapped her head around this complex story, analyzing the details I'd almost forgotten about, and finding fascinating meaning I hardly knew was there.

Thanks also to six special people who jumped in at the just the right time to help shape the final story and the characters. We had some intense back and forth and you provided outstanding feedback. Thank you Lili, Michael, Jeff, Kim, Nancy, and Bill for your time and help.

Much appreciation to Christine Lane, who *will find* all the miscellaneous mistakes. Like this story, I'm reaching into the future because Christine's part of the editing process comes last—after I've already written this section.

Thanks once more to my wife, Marlene. Daily, I retreated to my man-cave to work on "the book" for hours on end. But you never once complained, you always encouraged me and picked up the slack elsewhere in our lives when I was locked away in thought. No writer could ask for more.

Writing a novel is fun. But this time around was harder. Just a few days after I'd finished the first draft, a dear friend died unexpectedly. Phil Hamre was my biggest fan, always providing encouragement, giving honest (yet ego-soothing) feedback, and letting me know exactly what he thought of my characters—especially Nala. I wish I could reach back in time. I'd tell myself to write just a little faster and get an early copy into Phil's hands. He never got the chance to read this story, but I know he would have liked it. None of us knows when our life might take a sudden turn. Don't waste a single chronon. Many thanks, Phil, for your timeless support.

About the Author

Douglas Phillips is the best-selling author of the Quantum Series, a trilogy of science fiction thrillers set in the fascinating world of particle physics where bizarre is an everyday thing. In each story, the pace is quick and the protagonists—along with the reader—are drawn deeper into mysteries that require intellect, not bullets, to resolve.

Douglas has two science degrees, has designed and written predictive computer models, reads physics books for fun and peers into deep space through the eyepiece of his backyard telescope.

The Quantum Series

<u>Quantum Incident</u> (Prologue)

The long sought Higgs boson has been discovered at the Large Hadron Collider in Geneva. Scientists rejoice in the confirmation of quantum theory, but a reporter attending the press conference believes they may be hiding something.

Nala Pasquier is a particle physicist at Fermi National Laboratory in Illinois. Building on the 2012 discovery, she has produced a working prototype with capabilities that are nothing less than astonishing.

Daniel Rice is a government science investigator with a knack for uncovering the details that others miss. But when he's assigned to investigate a UFO over Nevada, he'll need more than scientific skills. He'll need every bit of patience he can muster.

<u>Quantum Space</u> (Book 1)

High above the windswept plains of Kazakhstan, three astronauts on board a Russian Soyuz capsule begin their reentry. A strange shimmer in the atmosphere, a blinding flash of light, and the capsule vanishes in a blink as though it never existed.

On the ground, evidence points to a catastrophic failure, but a communications facility halfway around the world picks up a transmission that could be one of the astronauts. Tragedy averted, or merely delayed? A classified government project on the cutting edge of particle physics holds the clues, and with lives on the line, there is little time to waste.

Daniel Rice is a government science investigator. Marie Kendrick is a NASA operations analyst. Together, they must track down the cause of the most bizarre event in the history of human spaceflight. They draw on scientific strengths as they plunge into the strange world of quantum physics, with impacts not only to the missing astronauts, but to the entire human race.

Quantum Void (Book 2)

Particle physics was always an unlikely path to the stars, but with the discovery that space could be compressed, the entire galaxy had come within reach. The technology was astonishing, yet nothing compared to what humans encountered four thousand light years from home. Now, with an invitation from a mysterious gatekeeper, the people of Earth must decide if they're ready to participate in the galactic conversation.

The world anxiously watches as a team of four katanauts, suit up to visit an alien civilization. What they learn on a watery planet hundreds of light years away could catapult human comprehension of the natural world to new heights. But one team member must overcome crippling fear to cope with an alien gift she barely understands.

Back at Fermilab, strange instabilities are beginning to show up in experiments, leading physicists to wonder if they ever really had control over the quantum dimensions of space.

Quantum Time (Book 3)

A dying man stumbles into a police station and collapses. In his fist is a mysterious coin with strange markings. He tells the police he's from the future, and when they uncover the coin's hidden message, they're inclined to believe him.

Daniel Rice never asked for fame but his key role in Earth's first contact with an alien civilization thrust him into a social arena where any crackpot might take aim. When the FBI arrives at his door and predictions of the future start coming true, Daniel is dragged into a mission to save the world from nuclear holocaust. To succeed, he'll need to exploit cobbled-together alien technology to peer into a world thirty years beyond his own.

For these and other works by Douglas Phillips, please visit http://douglasphillipsbooks.com. While you're there, sign up to the mailing list to stay informed on new books in the works and upcoming events.